# DEBBIE MACOMBER

## Yours and Mine

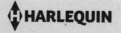

ISBN-13: 978-1-335-66248-4

Recycling programs
for this product may
not exist in your area.

Yours and Mine
First published in 1989.
This edition published in 2023.
Copyright © 1989 by Debbie Macomber

Hers for the Summer
First published in 2021.
This edition published in 2023.
Copyright © 2021 by Ripple Effect Press, LLC

For questions and comments about the quality of this book,
please contact us at CustomerService@Harlequin.com.

Harlequin Enterprises ULC
22 Adelaide St. West, 41st Floor
Toronto, Ontario M5H 4E3, Canada
www.Harlequin.com

Printed in U.S.A.

# CONTENTS

YOURS AND MINE                                          7
Debbie Macomber

HERS FOR THE SUMMER                                   201
Jill Kemerer

**Debbie Macomber** is a #1 *New York Times* bestselling author and a leading voice in women's fiction worldwide. Her work has appeared on every major bestseller list, with more than a hundred and seventy million copies in print, and she is a multiple award-winner. The Hallmark Channel based a television series on Debbie's popular Cedar Cove books. For more information, visit her website, debbiemacomber.com.

### Books by Debbie Macomber

### MIRA

### *Blossom Street*

*The Shop on Blossom Street*
*A Good Yarn*
*Susannah's Garden*
*Back on Blossom Street*
*Twenty Wishes*
*Summer on Blossom Street*

### *Cedar Cove*

*16 Lighthouse Road*
*204 Rosewood Lane*
*311 Pelican Court*
*44 Cranberry Point*
*50 Harbor Street*
*6 Rainier Drive*

Visit the Author Profile page
at Harlequin.com for more titles.

# YOURS AND MINE

Debbie Macomber

For Simone Hartman,
the sixteen-year-old German girl who came to
live with us to learn about America. Instead,
she taught us about love, friendship, Wiener schnitzel
and fun, German-style. We love you, Simone!

# Chapter One

"Mom, I forgot to tell you, I need two dozen cupcakes for tomorrow morning."

Joanna Parsons reluctantly opened her eyes and lifted her head from the soft feather pillow, squinting at the illuminated dial of her clock radio. "Kristen, it's after eleven."

"I know, Mom, I'm sorry. But I've *got* to bring cupcakes."

"No, you don't," Joanna said hopefully. "There's a package of Oreos on the top shelf of the cupboard. You can take those."

"Oreos! You've been hiding Oreos from me again! Just what kind of mother are you?"

"I was saving them for an emergency—like this."

"It won't work." Crossing her arms over her still-flat

chest, eleven-year-old Kristen sat on the edge of the mattress and heaved a loud, discouraged sigh.

"Why not?"

"It's got to be cupcakes, home-baked chocolate ones."

"That's unfortunate, since you seem to have forgotten to mention the fact earlier. And now it's about four hours too late for baking anything. Including chocolate cupcakes." Joanna tried to be fair with Kristen, but being a single parent wasn't easy.

"Mom, I know I forgot," Kristen cried, her young voice rising in panic, "but I've got to bring cupcakes to class tomorrow. It's important! Really important!"

"Convince me." Joanna used the phrase often. She didn't want to seem unyielding and hard-nosed. After all, she'd probably forgotten a few important things in her thirty-odd years, too.

"It's Mrs. Eagleton's last day as our teacher—remember I told you her husband got transferred and she's moving to Denver? Everyone in the whole class hates to see her go, so we're throwing a party."

"Who's *we*?"

"Nicole and me," Kristen answered quickly. "Nicole's bringing the napkins, cups and punch, and I'm supposed to bring homemade cupcakes. Chocolate cupcakes. Mom, I've just got to. Nicole would never forgive me if I did something stupid like bring store-bought cookies for a teacher as wonderful as Mrs. Eagleton."

Kristen had met Nicole almost five months before at the beginning of the school year, and the two girls had been as thick as gnats in August from that time on. "Shouldn't the room mother be organizing this party?"

That made sense to Joanna; surely there was an adult who would be willing to help.

"We don't have one this year. Everyone's mother is either too busy or working."

Joanna sighed. Oh, great, she was going to end up baking cupcakes until the wee hours of the morning. "All right," she muttered, giving in to her daughter's pleading. Mrs. Eagleton *was* a wonderful teacher, and Joanna was as sorry as Kristen to see her leave.

"We just couldn't let Mrs. Eagleton move to Denver without doing something really nice for her," Kristen pressed.

Although Joanna agreed, she felt that Oreos or Fig Newtons should be considered special enough, since it was already after eleven. But Kristen obviously had her heart set on home-baked cupcakes.

"Mom?"

Even in the muted light, Joanna recognized the plea in her daughter's dark brown eyes. She looked so much like Davey that a twinge of anguish worked its way through Joanna's heart. They'd been divorced six years now, but the pain of that failure had yet to fade. Sometimes, at odd moments like these, she still recalled how good it had felt to be in his arms and how much she'd once loved him. Mostly, though, Joanna remembered how naive she'd been to trust him so completely. But she'd come a long way in the six years since her divorce. She'd gained a new measure of independence and self-respect, forging a career for herself at Columbia Basin Savings and Loan. And now she was close to achieving her goal of becoming the first female senior loan officer.

"All right, honey." Joanna sighed, dragging her thoughts back to her daughter. "I'll bake the cupcakes.

Only next time, please let me know before we go to bed, okay?"

Kristen's shoulders slumped in relief. "I owe you one, Mom."

Joanna resisted the urge to remind her daughter that the score was a lot higher than one. Tossing aside the thick warm blankets, she climbed out of bed and reached for her long robe.

Kristen, flannel housecoat flying behind her like a flag unfurling, raced toward the kitchen, eager to do what she could to help. "I'll turn on the oven and get everything ready," she called.

"All right," Joanna said with a yawn as she sent her foot searching under the bed for her slippers. She was mentally scanning the contents of her cupboards, wondering if she had a chocolate cake mix. Somehow she doubted it.

"Trouble, Mom," Kristen announced when Joanna entered the well-lighted kitchen. The eleven-year-old stood on a chair in front of the open cupboards above the refrigerator, an Oreo between her teeth. Looking only mildly guilty, she ate the cookie whole, then shook her head. "We don't have cake mix."

"I was afraid of that."

"I guess we'll have to bake them from scratch," Kristen suggested, reaching for another Oreo.

"Not this late, we won't. I'll drive to the store." There was an Albertson's that stayed open twenty-four hours less than a mile away.

Kristen jumped down from the chair. The pockets of her bathrobe were stuffed full of cookies, but her attempt to conceal them failed. Joanna pointed toward the cookie jar, and dutifully Kristen emptied her pockets.

When Kristen had finished, Joanna yawned again and ambled back into her bedroom.

"Mom, if you're going to the store, I suppose I should go with you."

"No, honey, I'm just going to run in and out. You stay here."

"Okay," Kristen agreed quickly.

The kid wasn't stupid, Joanna thought wryly. Winters in eastern Washington were often merciless, and temperatures in Spokane had been well below freezing all week. To be honest, she wasn't exactly thrilled about braving the elements herself. She pulled on her calf-high boots over two pairs of heavy woolen socks. Because the socks were so thick, Joanna could only zip the boots up to her ankles.

"Mom," Kristen said, following her mother into the bedroom, a thoughtful expression on her face. "Have you ever thought of getting married again?"

Surprised, Joanna looked up and studied her daughter. The question had come from out of nowhere, but her answer was ready. "Never." The first time around had been enough. Not that she was one of the walking wounded, at least she didn't think of herself that way. Instead, her divorce had made her smart, had matured her. Never again would she look to a man for happiness; Joanna was determined to build her own. But the unexpectedness of Kristen's question caught her off guard. Was Kristen telling her something? Perhaps her daughter felt she was missing out because there were only the two of them. "What makes you ask?"

The mattress dipped as she sat beside Joanna. "I'm not exactly sure," she confessed. "But you could remarry, you know. You've still got a halfway decent figure."

Joanna grinned. "Thanks… I think."

"I mean, it's not like you're really old and ugly."

"Coming from you, that's high praise indeed, considering that I'm over thirty."

"I'm sure if you wanted to, you could find another man. Not like Daddy, but someone better."

It hurt Joanna to hear her daughter say things like that about Davey, but she couldn't disguise from Kristen how selfish and hollow her father was. Nor could she hide Davey's roving eye when it came to the opposite sex. Kristen spent one month every summer with him in Seattle and saw for herself the type of man Davey was.

After she'd finished struggling with her boots, Joanna clumped into the entryway and opened the hall cupboard.

"Mom!" Kristen cried, her eyes round with dismay.

"What?"

"You can't go out looking like that!" Her daughter was pointing at her, as though aghast at the sight.

"Like what?" Innocently Joanna glanced down at the dress-length blue wool coat she'd slipped on over her rose-patterned flannel pajamas. Okay, so the bottoms showed, but only a little. And she was willing to admit that the boots would look better zipped up, but she was more concerned with comfort than fashion. If the way she looked didn't bother her, then it certainly shouldn't bother Kristen. Her daughter had obviously forgotten why Joanna was venturing outside in the first place.

"Someone might see you."

"Don't worry, I have no intention of taking off my coat." She'd park close to the front door of the store, run inside, head for aisle three, grab a cake mix and be back at the car in four minutes flat. Joanna didn't exactly feel like donning tights for the event.

"You might meet someone," Kristen persisted.

"So?" Joanna stifled a yawn.

"But your hair… Don't you think you should curl it?"

"Kristen, listen. The only people who are going to be in the grocery store are insomniacs and winos and maybe a couple of pregnant women." It was highly unlikely she'd run into anyone from the bank.

"But what if you got in an accident? The policeman would think you're some kind of weirdo."

Joanna yawned a second time. "Honey, anyone who would consider making cupcakes in the middle of the night has a mental problem as it is. I'll fit right in with everyone else, so quit worrying."

"Oh, all right," Kristen finally agreed.

Draping her bag strap over her shoulder, Joanna opened the front door and shivered as the arctic wind of late January wrapped itself around her. Damn, it was cold. The grass was so white with frost that she wondered, at first, if it had snowed. To ward off the chill, she wound Kristen's purple striped scarf around her neck to cover her ears and mouth and tied it loosely under her chin.

The heater in her ten-year-old Ford didn't have a chance to do anything but spew out frigid air as she huddled over the steering wheel for the few minutes it took to drive to the grocery store. According to her plan, she parked as close to the store as possible, turned off the engine and dashed inside.

Just as she'd predicted, the place was nearly deserted, except for a couple of clerks working near the front, arranging displays. Joanna didn't give them more than a fleeting glance as she headed toward the aisle where baking goods were shelved.

She was reaching for the first chocolate cake mix to come into sight when she heard footsteps behind her.

"Mrs. Parsons! Hello!" The shrill excited voice seemed to ring like a Chinese gong throughout the store.

Joanna hunched down as far as she could and cast a furtive glance over her shoulder. Dear Lord, Kristen had been right. She was actually going to bump into someone who knew her.

"It's me—Nicole. You remember me, don't you?"

Joanna attempted a smile as she turned to face her daughter's best friend. "Hi, there," she said weakly, and raised her right hand to wave, her wrist limp. "It's good to see you again." So she was lying. Anyone with a sense of decency would have pretended not to recognize her and casually looked the other way. Not Nicole. It seemed as though all the world's eleven-year-olds were plotting against her tonight. One chocolate cake mix; that was all she wanted. That and maybe a small tub of ready-made frosting. Then she could return home, get those cupcakes baked and climb back into bed where most sane people were at this very moment.

"You look different," Nicole murmured thoughtfully, her eyes widening as she studied Joanna.

Well, that was one way of putting it.

"When I first saw you, I thought you were a bag lady."

Loosening the scarf that obscured the lower half of her face, Joanna managed a grin.

"What are you doing here this late?" the girl wanted

to know next, following Joanna as she edged her way to the checkout stand.

"Kristen forgot to tell me about the cupcakes."

Nicole's cheerful laugh resounded through the store like a yell echoing in an empty sports stadium. "I was watching 60 Minutes with my dad when I remembered I hadn't bought the juice and stuff for the party. Dad's waiting for me in the car right now."

Nicole's father allowed her to stay up that late on a school night? Joanna did her utmost to hide her disdain. From what Kristen had told her, she knew Nicole's parents were also divorced and her father had custody of Nicole. The poor kid probably didn't know what the word *discipline* meant. No doubt her father was one of those weak-willed liberal parents so involved in their own careers that they didn't have any time left for their children. Imagine a parent letting an eleven-year-old wander around a grocery store at this time of night! The mere thought was enough to send chills of parental outrage racing up and down Joanna's backbone. She placed her arm around Nicole's shoulders as if to protect her from life's harsher realities. The poor sweet kid.

The abrupt whoosh of the automatic door was followed by the sound of someone striding impatiently into the store. Joanna glanced up to discover a tall man, wearing a well-cut dark coat, glaring in their direction.

"Nicole, what's taking so long?"

"Dad," the girl said happily, "this is Mrs. Parsons—Kristen's mom."

Nicole's father approached, obviously reluctant to acknowledge the introduction, his face remote and unsmiling.

Automatically Joanna straightened, her shoulders

stiffening with the action. Nicole's father was exactly as she'd pictured him just a few moments earlier. Polished, worldly, and too darn handsome for his own good. Just like Davey. This was exactly the type of man she went out of her way to avoid. She'd been burned once, and no relationship was worth what she'd endured. This brief encounter with Nicole's father told Joanna all she needed to know.

"Tanner Lund," he announced crisply, holding out his hand.

"Joanna Parsons," Joanna said, and gave him hers for a brisk cold shake. She couldn't take her hand away fast enough.

His eyes narrowed as they studied her, and the look he gave her was as disapproving as the one she offered him. Slowly his gaze dropped to the unzipped boots flapping at her ankles and the worn edges of the pajamas visible below her wool coat.

"I think it's time we met, don't you?" Joanna didn't bother to disguise her disapproval of the man's attitude toward child-rearing. She'd had Nicole over after school several times, but on the one occasion Kristen had visited her friend, the child was staying with a babysitter.

A hint of a smile appeared on his face, but it didn't reach his eyes. "Our meeting is long overdue, I agree."

He seemed to be suggesting that he'd made a mistake in allowing his daughter to have anything to do with someone who dressed the way she did.

Joanna's gaze shifted to Nicole. "Isn't it late for you to be up on a school night?"

"Where's Kristen?" he countered, glancing around the store.

"At home," Joanna answered, swallowing the words

that said home was exactly where an eleven-year-old child belonged on a school night—or any other night for that matter.

"Isn't she a bit young to be left alone while you run to a store?"

"N-not in the least."

Tanner frowned and his eyes narrowed even more. His disapproving gaze demanded to know what kind of mother left a child alone in the house at this time of night.

Joanna answered him with a scornful look of her own.

"It's a pleasure to meet you, Mr. Lund," she said coolly, knowing her eyes relayed a conflicting message.

"The pleasure's mine."

Joanna was all the more aware of her disheveled appearance. Uncombed and uncurled, her auburn hair hung limply to her shoulders. Her dark eyes were nice enough, she knew, fringed in long curling lashes. She considered them her best asset, and purposely glared at Tanner, hoping her eyes were as cold as the blast from her car heater had been.

Tanner placed his hands on his daughter's shoulders and drew her protectively to his side. Joanna was infuriated by the action. If Nicole needed shielding, it was from an irresponsible father!

Okay, she reasoned, so her attire was a bit outlandish. But that couldn't be helped; she was on a mission that by rights should win her a nomination for the mother-of-the-year award. The way Tanner Lund had implied that *she* was the irresponsible parent was something Joanna found downright insulting.

"Well," Joanna said brightly, "I have to go. Nice to

see you again, Nicole." She swept two boxes of cake mix into her arms and grabbed what she hoped was some frosting.

"You, too, Mrs. Parsons," the girl answered, smiling up at her.

"Mr. Lund."

"Mrs. Parsons."

The two nodded politely at each other, and, clutching her packages, Joanna walked regally to the checkout stand. She made her purchase and started back toward the car. The next time Kristen invited Nicole over, Joanna mused on the short drive home, she intended to spend lots of extra time with the girls. Now she knew how badly Nicole needed someone to nurture her, to give her the firm but loving guidance every child deserved.

The poor darling.

# Chapter Two

Joanna expertly lowered the pressure foot of her sewing machine over the bunched red material, then used both hands to push the fabric slowly under the bobbing needle. Straight pins, tightly clenched between her lips, protruded from her mouth. Her concentration was intense.

"Mom." A breathless Kristen bounded into the room.

Joanna intercepted her daughter with one upraised hand until she finished stitching the seam.

Kristen stalked around the kitchen table several times, like a shark circling its kill. "Mom, hurry, this is really important."

"Wlutt?" Joanna asked, her teeth still clamped on the pins.

"Can Nicole spend the night?"

Joanna blinked. This wasn't the weekend, and Kristen knew the rules; she had permission to invite friends over only on Friday and Saturday nights. Joanna removed the pins from her mouth before she answered. "It's Wednesday."

"I know what day it is." Kristen rolled her eyes towards the ceiling and slapped the heel of her hand against her forehead.

Allowing his daughter to stay over at a friend's house on a school night was exactly the kind of irresponsible parenting Joanna expected from Tanner Lund. Her estimation of the man was dropping steadily, though that hardly seemed possible. Earlier in the afternoon, Joanna had learned that Nicole didn't even plan to tell her father she and Kristen were going to be performing in the school talent show. The man revealed absolutely no interest in his daughter's activities. Joanna felt so bad about Tanner Lund's attitude that she'd volunteered to sew a second costume so Nicole would have something special to wear for this important event. And now it seemed that Tanner was in the habit of farming out his daughter on school nights, as well.

"Mom, hurry and decide. Nicole's on the phone."

"Honey, there's school tomorrow."

Kristen gave her another scornful look.

"The two of you will stay up until midnight chattering, and then in the morning class will be a disaster. The answer is no!"

Kristen's eager face fell. "I promise we won't talk. Just this once, Mom. Oh, please!" She folded her hands prayerfully, and her big brown eyes pleaded with Joanna. "How many times do I ask you for something?"

Joanna stared incredulously at her daughter. The list was endless.

"All right, forget I asked that. But this is important, Mom, real important—for Nicole's sake."

Every request was argued as urgent. But knowing what she did about the other little girl's home life made refusing all the more difficult. "I'm sorry, Kristen, but not on a school night."

Head drooping, Kristen shuffled toward the phone. "Now Nicole will have to spend the night with Mrs. Wagner, and she hates that."

"Who's Mrs. Wagner?"

Kristen turned to face her mother and released a sigh intended to evoke sympathy. "Her babysitter."

"Her father makes her spend the night at a babysitter's?"

"Yes. He has a business meeting with Becky."

Joanna stiffened and felt a sudden chill. "Becky?"

"His business partner."

*I'll just bet!* Joanna's eyes narrowed with outrage. Tanner Lund was a lowlife, kicking his own daughter out into the cold so he could bring a woman over. The man disgusted her.

"Mrs. Wagner is real old and she makes Nicole eat health food. She has a black-and-white TV, and the only programs she'll let Nicole watch are nature shows. Wouldn't you hate that?"

Joanna's mind was spinning. Any child would detest being cast from her own bed and thrust upon the not always tender mercies of a babysitter. "How often does Nicole have to spend the night with Mrs. Wagner?"

"Lots."

Joanna could well believe it. "How often is 'lots'?"

"At least twice a month. Sometimes even more often than that."

That poor neglected child. Joanna's heart constricted at the thought of sweet Nicole being ruthlessly handed over to a woman who served soybean burgers.

"Can she, Mom? Oh, please?" Again Kristen folded her hands, pleading with her mother to reconsider.

"All right," Joanna conceded, "but just this once."

Kristen ran across the room and hurled her arms around Joanna's neck, squeezing for all she was worth. "You're the greatest mother in the whole world."

Joanna snorted softly. "I've got to be in the top ten percent, anyway," she said, remembering the cupcakes.

"Absolutely not," Tanner said forcefully as he laid a neatly pressed shirt in his open suitcase. "Nicole, I won't hear of it."

"But, Dad, Kristen is my very best friend."

"Believe me, sweetheart, I'm pleased you've found a soulmate, but when I'm gone on these business trips I need to know you're being well taken care of." And supervised, he added mentally. What he knew about Kristen's mother wasn't encouraging. The woman was a scatterbrain who left her young daughter unattended while she raided the supermarket for nighttime goodies—and then had the nerve to chastise him because Nicole was up a little late. In addition to being a busybody, Joanna Parsons dressed like a fruitcake.

"Dad, you don't understand what it's like for me at Mrs. Wagner's."

Undaunted, Tanner continued packing his suitcase. He wasn't any happier about leaving Nicole than she was, but he didn't have any choice. As a relatively new half owner of Spokane Aluminum, he was required to do a certain amount of traveling. More these first few months than would be necessary later. His business trips were essential, since they familiarized him with the clients and their needs. He would have to absorb this information as quickly as possible in order to determine if the plant was going to achieve his and John Becky's five-year goal. In a few weeks, he expected to hire an assistant who would assume some of this responsibility, but for now the task fell into his hands.

Nicole slumped onto the edge of the bed. "The last time I spent the night at Mrs. Wagner's she served baked beef heart for dinner."

Involuntarily Tanner cringed.

"And, Dad, she made me watch a special on television that was all about fungus."

Tanner gritted his teeth. So the old lady was a bit eccentric, but she looked after Nicole competently, and that was all that mattered.

"Do you know what Kristen's having for dinner?"

Tanner didn't care to guess. It was probably something like strawberry ice cream and caramel-flavored popcorn. "No, and I don't want to know."

"It isn't sweet-and-sour calf liver, I can tell you that."

Tanner's stomach turned at the thought of liver in any kind of sauce. "Nicole, the subject is closed. You're spending the night with Mrs. Wagner."

"It's spaghetti and meatballs and three-bean salad and milk and French bread, that's what. And Mrs. Parsons said I could help Kristen roll the meatballs—but that's all right, I'll call and tell her that you don't want me to spend the night at a home where I won't be properly looked after."

"Nicole—"

"Dad, don't worry about it, I understand."

Tanner sincerely doubted that. He placed the last of his clothes inside the suitcase and closed the lid.

"At least I'm *trying* to understand why you'd send me to someplace like Mrs. Wagner's when my very best friend *invited* me to spend the night with her."

Tanner could feel himself weakening. It was only one night and Kristen's weird mother wasn't likely to be a dangerous influence on Nicole in that short a time.

"Spaghetti and meatballs," Nicole muttered under her breath. "My all-time favorite food."

Now that was news to Tanner. He'd thought pizza held that honor. He'd never known his daughter to turn down pizza at any time of the day or night.

"And they have a twenty-inch color television set."

Tanner hesitated.

"With remote control."

Would wonders never cease? "Will Kristen's mother be there the entire night?" he asked.

"Of course."

His daughter was looking at him as though he'd asked if Mrs. Parsons were related to ET. "Where will you sleep?"

"Kristen has a double bed." Nicole's eyes brightened. "And we've already promised Mrs. Parsons that we'll go straight to bed at nine o'clock and hardly talk."

It was during times such as this that Tanner felt the full weight of parenting descend upon his shoulders. Common sense told him Nicole would be better off with Mrs. Wagner, but he understood her complaints about the older woman as well. "All right, Nicole, you can stay at Kristen's."

His daughter let out a whoop of sheer delight.

"But just this once."

"Oh, Dad, you're the greatest." Her arms locked around his waist, and she squeezed with all her might, her nose pressed against his flat stomach.

"Okay, okay, I get the idea you're pleased with my decision," Tanner said with a short laugh.

"Can we leave now?"

"Now?" Usually Nicole wanted to linger at the apartment until the last possible minute.

"Yes. Mrs. Parsons really did say I could help roll the meatballs, and you know what else?"

"What?"

"She's sewing me and Kristen identical costumes for the talent show."

Tanner paused—he hadn't known anything about his daughter needing a costume. "What talent show?"

"Oops." Nicole slapped her hand over her mouth. "I wasn't going to tell you because it's on Valentine's Day and I know you won't be able to come. I didn't want you to feel bad."

"Nicole, it's more important that you don't hide things from me."

"But you have to be in Seattle."

She was right. He'd hate missing the show, but he was scheduled to meet with the Foreign Trade Commission on the fourteenth regarding a large shipment of aluminum to Japan. "What talent do you and Kristen have?" he asked, diverting his disappointment for the moment.

"We're lip-synching a song from Heart. You know, the rock group?"

"That sounds cute. A fitting choice, too, for a Valentine's Day show. Perhaps you two can be persuaded to give me a preview before the grand performance."

Her blue eyes became even brighter in her excitement. "That's a great idea! Kristen and I can practice while you're away, and we'll show you when you come back."

It was an acceptable compromise.

Nicole dashed out of his bedroom and returned a couple of minutes later with her backpack. "I'm ready anytime you are," she announced.

Tanner couldn't help but notice that his daughter looked downright cheerful. More cheerful than any of the other times he'd been forced to leave her. Normally she put on a long face and moped around, making him feel guilty about abandoning her to the dreaded Mrs. Wagner.

By the time he picked up his briefcase and luggage, Nicole was waiting at the front door.

"Are you going to come in and say hello to Mrs. Parsons?" Nicole asked when Tanner eased his Mercedes into Kristen's driveway fifteen minutes later. Even in the fading late-afternoon light, he could see that the house was newly painted, white with green shutters at the windows. The lawn and flower beds seemed well maintained. He could almost picture rose bushes in full bloom. It certainly wasn't the type of place he'd associated with Kristen's loony mother.

"Are you coming in or not?" Nicole asked a second time, her voice impatient.

Tanner had to mull over the decision. He wasn't eager to meet that unfriendly woman who wore unzipped boots and flannel pajamas again.

"Dad!"

Before Tanner could answer, the door opened and Kristen came bowling out of the house at top speed. A gorgeous redhead followed sedately behind her. Tanner felt his jaw sag and his mouth drop open. No, it couldn't be! Tall, cool, sophisticated, this woman looked as though she'd walked out of the pages of a fashion magazine. It couldn't be Joanna Parsons—no way. A relative perhaps, but certainly not the woman he'd met in the grocery store that night.

Nicole had already climbed out of the car. She paused as though she'd forgotten something, then ran around to his side of the car. When Tanner rolled down his window, she leaned over and gave him one of her famous bear hugs, hurling her arms around his neck and squeezing enthusiastically. "Bye, Dad."

"Bye, sweetheart. You've got the phone number of my hotel to give Mrs. Parsons?"

Nicole patted her jeans pocket. "It's right here."

"Be good."

"I will."

When Tanner looked up, he noted that Joanna was standing behind her daughter, her hands resting on Kristen's shoulders. Cool, disapproving eyes surveyed him. Yup, it was the same woman all right. Joanna Parsons's gaze could freeze watermelon at a Fourth of July picnic.

# Chapter Three

"Would you like more spaghetti, Nicole?" Joanna asked for the second time.

"No, thanks, Mrs. Parsons."

"You asked her that already," Kristen commented, giving her mother a puzzled look. "After we've done the dishes, Nicole and I are going to practice our song."

Joanna nodded. "Good idea, but do your homework first."

Kristen exchanged a knowing look with her friend, and the two grinned at each other.

"I'm really glad you're letting me stay the night, Mrs. Parsons," Nicole said, as she carried her empty plate to the kitchen sink. "Dinner was great. Dad tries, but he isn't much of a cook. We get take-out food a lot." She wandered back to the table and fingered the blue-quilted place mat. "Kristen told me you sewed these, too. They're pretty."

"Thank you. The pattern is really very simple."

"They have to be," Kristen added, stuffing the last slice of toasted French bread into her mouth. "'Cause Mom let me do a couple of them."

"You made two of these?"

"Yeah," Kristen said, after she'd finished chewing. Pride beamed from her dark brown eyes. "We've made lots of things together since we bought the house. Do you have any idea how expensive curtains can be? Mom made the entire set in my room—that's why everything matches."

"The bedspread, too?"

"Naturally." Kristen made it sound like they'd whipped up the entire set over a weekend, when the project had actually taken the better part of two weeks.

"Wow."

From the way Nicole was staring at her, Joanna half expected the girl to fall to her knees in homage. She felt a stab of pity for Nicole, who seemed to crave a mother's presence. But she had to admit she was thrilled by her own daughter's pride in their joint accomplishments.

"Mom sews a lot of my clothes," Kristen added, licking the butter from her fingertips. "I thought you knew that."

"I… No, I didn't."

"She's teaching me, too. That's the best part. So I'll be able to make costumes for our next talent show." Kristen's gaze flew from Nicole to her mother then back to Nicole. "I bet my mom would teach you how to sew. Wouldn't you, Mom?"

"Ah…"

"Would you really, Mrs. Parsons?"

Not knowing what else to say, Joanna agreed with a quick nod of her head. "Why not? We'll have fun learning together." She gave an encouraging smile, but she wondered a bit anxiously if she was ready for a project like this.

"That would be great." Nicole slipped her arm around Kristen's shoulders. Her gaze dropped as she hesitated. "Dinner was really good, too," she said again.

"I told you what a great cook my mom is," Kristen boasted.

Nicole nodded, but kept her eyes trained to the floor. "Could I ask you something, Mrs. Parsons?"

"Of course."

"Like I said, Dad tries real hard, but he just isn't a very good cook. Would it be rude to ask you for the recipe for your spaghetti sauce?"

"Not at all. I'll write it out for you tonight."

"Gee, thanks. It's so nice over here. I wish Dad would let me stay here all the time. You and Kristen do such neat things, and you eat real good, too."

Joanna could well imagine the kind of meals Tanner Lund served his daughter. She already knew that he frequently ordered out, and the rest probably came from the frozen-food section of the local grocery. That was if he didn't have an array of willing females who did his cooking for him. Someone like this Becky person, the woman he was with now.

"Dad makes great tacos, though," Nicole was saying. "They're his specialty. He said I might be able to have a slumber party for my birthday in March, and I want him to serve tacos then. But I might ask him to make spaghetti instead—if he gets the recipe right."

"You get to have a slumber party?" Kristen cried, her eyes widening. "That's great! My mom said I could have two friends over for the night on my birthday, but only two, because that's all she can mentally handle."

Joanna pretended an interest in her leftover salad, stirring her fork through the dressing that sat in the bottom of the bowl. It was true; there were limits to her mothering abilities. A house full of screaming eleven- and twelve-year-olds was more than she dared contemplate on a full stomach.

While Nicole finished clearing off the table, Kristen loaded the dishwasher. Working together, the two completed their tasks in only a few minutes.

"We're going to my room now. Okay, Mom?"

"Sure, honey, that's fine," Joanna said, placing the leftovers in the refrigerator. She paused, then decided to remind the pair a second time. "Homework before anything else."

"Of course," answered Kristen.

"Naturally," added Nicole.

Both vanished down the hallway that led to Kristen's bedroom. Watching them, Joanna grinned. The friendship with Nicole had been good for Kristen, and Joanna intended to shower love and attention on Nicole in the hope of compensating her for her unsettled home life.

Once Joanna had finished wiping down the kitchen counters, she made her way to Kristen's bedroom. Dutifully knocking—since her daughter made emphatic comments about privacy these days—she let herself in. Both girls were sitting cross-legged on the bed, spelling books open on their laps.

"Need any help?"

"No, thanks, Mom."

Still Joanna lingered, looking for an excuse to stay and chat. "I was placed third in the school spelling bee when I was your age."

Kristen glanced speculatively toward her friend. "That's great, Mom."

Warming to her subject, Joanna hurried to add, "I could outspell every boy in the class."

Kristen closed her textbook. "Mrs. Andrews, our new teacher, said the school wasn't going to have a spelling bee this year."

Joanna walked into the room and sat on the edge of the bed. "That's too bad, because I know you'd do well."

"I only got a B in spelling, Mom. I'm okay, but it's not my best subject."

A short uneasy silence followed while both girls studied Joanna, as though waiting for her to either leave or make a formal announcement.

"I thought we'd pop popcorn later," Joanna said, flashing a cheerful smile.

"Good." Kristen nodded and her gaze fell pointedly to her textbook. This was followed by another long moment of silence.

"Mom, I thought you said you wanted us to do our homework."

"I do."

"Well, we can't very well do it with you sitting here watching us."

"Oh." Joanna leapt off the bed. "Sorry."

"That's all right."

"Let me know when you're done."

"Why?" Kristen asked, looking perplexed.

Joanna shrugged. "I... I thought we might all sit around and chat. Girl talk, that sort of thing." Without being obvious about it, she'd hoped to offer Nicole maternal advice and some much needed affection. The thought of the little girl's father and what he was doing that very evening was so distasteful that Joanna had to force herself not to frown.

"Mom, Nicole and I are going to practice our song once we've finished our homework. Remember?"

"Oh, right. I forgot." Sheepishly, she started to walk away.

"I really appreciate your sewing my costume, Mrs. Parsons," Nicole added.

"It's no trouble, Nicole. I'm happy to do it."

"Speaking of the costumes," Kristen muttered, "didn't you say something about wanting to finish them before the weekend?"

"I did?" The look Kristen gave her suggested she must have. "Oh, right, now I remember."

The girls, especially her daughter, seemed relieved when Joanna left the bedroom. This wasn't going well. She'd planned on spending extra time with them, but it was clear they weren't keen on having her around. Taking a deep breath, Joanna headed for the living room, feeling a little piqued. Her ego should be strong enough to handle rejection from two eleven-year-old girls.

She settled in the kitchen and brought out her sewing machine again. The red costumes for the talent show were nearly finished. She ran her hand over the polished cotton and let her thoughts wander. She and Kristen had lived in the house only since September. For the six years following the divorce, Joanna had been forced to raise her daughter in a small apartment. Becoming a home owner had been a major step for her and she was proud of the time and care that had gone into choosing their small one-story house. It had required some repairs, but nothing major, and the sense of accomplishment she'd experienced when she signed her name to the mortgage papers had been well worth the years of scrimping. The house had only two bedrooms, but there was plenty of space in the backyard for a garden, something Joanna had insisted on. She thought that anyone studying her might be amused. On the one hand, she was a woman with basic traditional values, and on the other, a goal-setting businesswoman struggling to succeed in a male-dominated field. Her boss would have found it difficult to understand that the woman who'd set her sights on the position of senior loan officer liked the feel of wet dirt under her fingernails. And he would have been surprised to learn that she could take a simple piece of bright red cotton and turn it into a dazzling costume for a talent show.

An hour later, when Joanna was watching television and finishing up the hand stitching on the costumes, Kristen and Nicole rushed into the living room, looking pleased about something.

"You girls ready for popcorn?"

"Not me," Nicole said, placing her hands over her stomach. "I'm still full from dinner."

Joanna nodded. The girl obviously wasn't accustomed to eating nutritionally balanced meals.

"We want to do our song for you."

"Great." Joanna scooted close to the edge of the sofa, eagerly awaiting their performance. Kristen plugged in her MP3 player, then hurried to her friend's side, striking a pose until the music started.

"I can tell already that you're going to be great," Joanna said, clapping her hands to the lively beat.

She was right. The two did astonishingly well, and when they'd finished Joanna applauded loudly.

"We did okay?"

"You were fabulous."

Kristen and Nicole positively glowed.

When they returned to Kristen's bedroom, Joanna followed them. Kristen turned around and seemed surprised to find her mother there.

"Mom," she hissed between clenched teeth, "what's with you tonight? You haven't been yourself since Nicole arrived."

"I haven't?"

"You keep following us around."

"I do?"

"Really, Mom, we like you and everything, but Nicole and I want to talk about boys and stuff, and we can't very well do that with you here."

"Oh, Mrs. Parsons, I forgot to tell you," Nicole inserted, obviously unaware of the whispered conversation going on between Kristen and her mother. "I told my dad about you making my costume for the talent show, and he said he wants to pay you for your time and expenses."

"You told your dad?" Kristen asked, and whirled around to face her friend. "I thought you weren't going to because he'd feel guilty. Oh, I get it! That's how you got him to let you spend the night. Great idea!"

Joanna frowned. "What exactly does that mean?"

The two girls exchanged meaningful glances and Nicole looked distinctly uncomfortable.

"What does what mean?" Kristen repeated the question in a slightly elevated voice Joanna recognized immediately. Her daughter was up to one of her schemes again.

Nicole stepped in front of her friend. "It's my fault, Mrs. Parsons. I wanted to spend the night here instead of with Mrs. Wagner, so I told Dad that Kristen had invited me."

"Mom, you've got to understand. Mrs. Wagner won't let Nicole watch anything but educational television, and you know there are special shows we like to watch."

"That's not the part I mean," Joanna said, dismissing their rushed explanation. "I want to know what you meant by not telling Mr. Lund about the talent show because he'd feel guilty."

"Oh...that part." The two girls glanced at each other, as though silently deciding which one would do the explaining.

Nicole raised her gaze to Joanna and sighed, her thin shoulders moving up and down expressively. "My dad won't be able to attend the talent show because he's got a business meeting in Seattle, and I knew he'd feel terrible about it. He really likes it when I do things like the show. It gives him something to tell my grandparents about, like I was going to be the next Madonna or something."

"He has to travel a lot to business meetings," Kristen added quickly.

"Business meetings?"

"Like tonight," Kristen went on to explain.

"Dad has to fly someplace with Mr. Becky. He owns half the company and Dad owns the other half. He said it had to do with getting a big order, but I never listen to stuff like that, although Dad likes to explain every little detail so I'll know where he's at and what he's doing."

Joanna felt a numbing sensation creeping slowly up her spine. "Your dad owns half a company?"

"Spokane Aluminum is the reason we moved here from West Virginia."

"Spokane Aluminum?" Joanna's voice rose half an octave. "Your dad owns half of Spokane Aluminum?" The company was one of the largest employers in the Northwest. A shockingly large percentage of their state's economy was directly or indirectly tied to this company. A sick feeling settled in Joanna's stomach. Not only was Nicole's father wealthy, he was socially prominent, and all the while she'd been thinking... Oh, dear heavens. "So your father's out of town tonight?" she asked, feeling the warmth invade her face.

"You knew that, Mom." Kristen gave her mother another one of those searching gazes that suggested Joanna might be losing her memory—due to advanced age, no doubt.

"I... I thought—" Abruptly she bit off what she'd been about to say. When Kristen had said something about Tanner being with Becky, she'd assumed it was a woman. But of course it was *John* Becky, whose name was familiar to everyone in that part of the country. Joanna remembered reading in the *Review* that Becky had taken on a partner, but she hadn't made the connection. Perhaps she'd misjudged Tanner Lund, she reluctantly conceded. Perhaps she'd been a bit too eager to view him in a bad light.

"Before we came to Spokane," Nicole was saying now, "Dad and I had a long talk about the changes the move would make in our lives. We made a list of the good things and a list of the bad things, and then we talked about them. One bad thing was that Dad would be gone a lot, until he can hire another manager. He doesn't feel good about leaving me with strangers, and we didn't know a single person in Spokane other than Mr. Becky and his wife, but they're real old—over forty, anyway. He even went and interviewed Mrs. Wagner before I spent the night there the first time."

The opinion Joanna had formed of Tanner Lund was crumbling at her feet. Evidently he wasn't the irresponsible parent she'd assumed.

"Nicole told me you met her dad in the grocery store when you bought the mix for the cupcakes." Kristen shook her head as if to say she was thoroughly disgusted with her mother for not taking her advice that night and curling her hair before she showed her face in public.

"I told my dad you don't dress that way all the time," Nicole added, then shifted her gaze to the other side of the room. "But I don't think he believed me until he dropped me off tonight."

Joanna began to edge her way toward the bedroom door. "Your father and I seem to have started off on the wrong foot," she said weakly.

Nicole bit her lower lip. "I know. He wasn't real keen on me spending the night here, but I talked him into it."

"Mom?" Kristen asked, frowning. "What did you say to Mr. Lund when you met him at the store?"

"Nothing," she answered, taking a few more retreating steps.

"She asked my dad what I was doing up so late on a school night, and he told me later that he didn't like her attitude," Nicole explained. "I didn't get a chance to tell you that I'm normally in bed by nine thirty, but that night was special because Dad had just come home from one of his trips. His plane was late and I didn't remember to tell him about the party stuff until after we got home from Mrs. Wagner's."

"I see," Joanna murmured, and swallowed uncomfortably.

"You'll get a chance to settle things with Mr. Lund when he picks up Nicole tomorrow night," Kristen stated, and it was obvious that she wanted her mother to make an effort to get along with her best friend's father.

"Right," Joanna muttered, dreading the confrontation. She never had been particularly fond of eating crow.

# Chapter Four

Joanna was breading pork chops the following evening when Kristen barreled into the kitchen, leaving the door swinging in her wake. "Mr. Lund's here to pick up Nicole. I think you should invite him and Nicole to stay for dinner...and explain about, you know, the other night."

Oh, sure, Joanna mused. She often invited company owners and acting presidents over for an evening meal. Pork chops and mashed potatoes weren't likely to impress someone like Tanner Lund.

Before Kristen could launch into an argument, Joanna shook her head and offered the first excuse that came to mind. "There aren't enough pork chops to ask him tonight. Besides, Mr. Lund is probably tired from his trip and anxious to get home."

"I bet he's hungry, too," Kristen pressed. "And Nicole thinks you're a fabulous cook, and—"

A sharp look from her mother cut her off. "Another night, Kristen!"

Joanna brushed the bread crumbs off her fingertips and untied her apron. Inhaling deeply, she paused long enough to run a hand through her hair and check her reflection in the window above the sink. No one was going to mistake her for Miss America, but her appearance was passable. Okay, it was time to hold her head high, spit the feathers out of her mouth and get ready to down some crow.

Joanna forced a welcoming smile onto her lips as she stepped into the living room. Tanner stood awkwardly just inside the front door, as though prepared to beat a hasty retreat if necessary. "How was your trip?" she ventured, straining to make the question sound cheerful.

"Fine. Thank you." His expression didn't change.

"Do you have time for a cup of coffee?" she asked next, doing her best to disguise her unease. She wondered quickly if she'd unpacked her china cups yet. After their shaky beginning, Joanna wasn't quite sure if she could undo the damage. But standing in the entryway wouldn't work. She needed to sit down for this.

He eyed her suspiciously. Joanna wasn't sure she should even try to explain things. In time he'd learn she wasn't a candidate for the loony bin—just as she'd stumbled over the fact that he wasn't a terrible father. Trying to tell him that she was an upstanding member of the community after he'd seen her dressed in a wool coat draped over pajamas, giving him looks that suggested he be reported to Children's Protective Services, wasn't exactly a task she relished.

Tanner glanced at his wristwatch and shook his head.

"I haven't got time to visit tonight. Thanks for the invitation, though."

Joanna almost sighed aloud with relief.

"Did Nicole behave herself?"

Joanna nodded. "She wasn't the least bit of trouble. Nicole's a great kid."

A smile cracked the tight edges of his mouth. "Good."

Kristen and Nicole burst into the room. "Is Mr. Lund going to stay, Mom?"

"He can't tonight…"

"Another time…"

They spoke simultaneously, with an equal lack of enthusiasm.

"Oh." The girls looked at each other and frowned, their disappointment noticeable.

"Have you packed everything, Nicole?" Tanner asked, not hiding his eagerness to leave.

The eleven-year-old nodded reluctantly. "I think so."

"Don't you think you should check my room one more time?" Kristen suggested, grabbing her friend's hand and leading her back toward the hallway.

"Oh, right. I suppose I should." The two disappeared before either Joanna or Tanner could call them back.

The silence between them hummed so loudly Joanna swore she could have waltzed to it. But since the opportunity had presented itself, she decided to get the unpleasant task of explaining her behavior out of the way while she still had her nerve.

"I think I owe you an apology," she murmured, her face flushing.

"An apology?"

"I thought…you know… The night we met, I assumed you were an irresponsible parent because Nicole was up so late. She's now told me that you'd just returned from a trip."

"Yes, well, I admit I did feel the sting of your disapproval."

This wasn't easy. Joanna swallowed uncomfortably and laced her fingers together forcing herself to meet his eyes. "Nicole explained that your flight was delayed and she forgot to mention the party supplies when you picked her up at the babysitter's. She said she didn't remember until you got all the way home."

Tanner's mouth relaxed a bit more. "Since we're both being truthful here, I'll admit that I wasn't overly impressed with you that night, either."

Joanna dropped her gaze. "I can imagine. I hope you realise I don't usually dress like that."

"I gathered as much when I dropped Nicole off yesterday afternoon."

They both paused to share a brief smile and Joanna instantly felt better. It hadn't been easy to blurt all this out, but she was relieved that they'd finally cleared the air.

"Since Kristen and Nicole are such good friends, I thought, well, that I should set things right between us. From everything Nicole's said, you're doing an excellent job of parenting."

"From everything she's told me, the same must be true of you."

"Believe me, it isn't easy raising a preteen daughter," Joanna announced. She rubbed her palms together a couple of times, searching for something brilliant to add.

Tanner shook his head. "Isn't that the truth?"

They laughed then, and because they were still awkward with each other the sound was rusty.

"Now that you mention it, maybe I could spare a few minutes for a cup of coffee."

"Sure." Joanna led the way into the kitchen. While Tanner sat down at the table, she filled a mug from the pot keeping warm on the plate of the automatic coffee-maker and placed it carefully in front of him. Now that she knew him a bit better, she realized he'd prefer that to a dainty china cup. "How do you take it?"

"Just black, thanks."

She pulled out the chair across the table from him, still feeling a little ill at ease. Her mind was whirling. She didn't want to give Tanner a second wrong impression now that she'd managed to correct the first one. Her worry was that he might interpret her friendliness as a sign of romantic interest, which it wasn't. Building a new relationship was low on her priority list. Besides, they simply weren't on the same economic level. She worked for a savings-and-loan institution and he was half owner of the largest employer in the area. The last thing she wanted was for Tanner to think of her as a gold digger.

Joanna's thoughts were tumbling over themselves as she struggled to find a diplomatic way of telling him all this without sounding like some kind of man hater. And without sounding presumptuous.

"I'd like to pay you," Tanner said, cutting into her reflections. His chequebook was resting on the table, Cross pen poised above it.

Joanna blinked, not understanding. "For the coffee?"

He gave her an odd look. "For looking after Nicole."

"No, please." Joanna shook her head dismissively. "It wasn't the least bit of trouble for her to stay the night. Really."

"What about the costume for the talent show? Surely I owe you something for that."

"No." Once more she shook her head for emphasis. "I've had that material tucked away in a drawer for ages. If I hadn't used it for Nicole's costume, I'd probably have ended up giving it away later."

"But your time must be worth something."

"It was just as easy to sew up two as one. I was happy to do it. Anyway, there'll probably be a time in the future when I need a favor. I'm worthless when it comes to electrical outlets and even worse with plumbing."

Joanna couldn't believe she'd said that. Tanner Lund wasn't the type of man to do his own electrical repairs.

"Don't be afraid to ask," he told her. "If I can't fix it, I'll find someone who can."

"Thank you," she said, relaxing. Now that she was talking to Tanner, she decided he was both pleasant and forthright, not at all the coldly remote or self-important man his wealth might have led her to expect.

"Mom," Kristen cried as she charged into the kitchen, "did you ask Mr. Lund yet?"

"About what?"

"About coming over for dinner some time."

Joanna felt the heat shoot up her neck and face until it reached her hairline. Kristen had made the invitation sound like a romantic tryst the three of them had been planning the entire time Tanner was away.

Nicole, entering the room behind her friend, provided a timely interruption.

"Dad, Kristen and I want to do our song for you now."

"I'd like to see it. Do you mind, Joanna?"

"Of course not."

"Mom finished the costumes last night. We'll change and be back in a minute," Kristen said, her voice high with excitement. The two scurried off. The minute they were out of sight, Joanna stood up abruptly and refilled her cup. Actually she was looking for a way to speak frankly to Tanner, without embarrassing herself—or him. She thought ironically that anyone looking at her now would be hard put to believe she was a competent loan officer with a promising future.

"I think I should explain something," she began, her voice unsteady.

"Yes?" Tanner asked, his gaze following her movements around the kitchen.

Joanna couldn't seem to stand in one place for long. She moved from the coffeepot to the refrigerator, finally stopping in front of the stove. She linked her fingers behind her back and took a deep breath before she trusted herself to speak. "I thought it was important to clear up any misunderstanding between us, because the girls are such good friends. When Nicole's with Kristen and me, I want you to know she's in good hands."

Tanner gave her a polite nod. "I appreciate that."

"But I have a feeling that Kristen—and maybe Nicole, too—would like for us to get to know each other, er, better, if you know what I mean." Oh Lord, that sounded so stupid. Joanna felt herself grasping at straws. "I'm not interested in a romantic relationship, Tanner. I've got too much going on in my life to get involved, and I don't want you to feel threatened by the girls and their schemes. Forgive me for being so blunt, but I'd prefer to have this out in the open." She'd blurted it out so fast, she wondered if he'd understood. "This dinner invitation was Kristen's idea, not mine. I don't want you to think I had anything to do with it."

"An invitation to dinner isn't exactly a marriage proposal."

"True," Joanna threw back quickly. "But you might

think… I don't know. I guess I don't want you to assume I'm interested in you—romantically, that is." She slumped back into the chair, pushed her hair away from her forehead and released a long sigh. "I'm only making matters worse, aren't I?"

"No. If I understand you correctly, you're saying you'd like to be friends and nothing more."

"Right." Pleased with his perceptiveness, Joanna straightened. Glad he could say in a few simple words what had left her breathless.

"The truth of the matter is, I feel much the same way," Tanner went on to explain. "I was married once and it was more than enough."

Joanna found herself nodding enthusiastically. "Exactly. I like my life the way it is. Kristen and I are very close. We just moved into this house and we've lots of plans for re-decorating. My career is going nicely."

"Likewise. I'm too busy with this company to get involved in a relationship, either. The last thing I need right now is a woman to complicate my life."

"A man would only come between Kristen and me at this stage."

"How long have you been divorced?" Tanner asked, folding his hands around his coffee mug.

"Six years."

The information appeared to satisfy him, and he nodded slowly, as though to say he trusted what she was telling him. "It's been five for me."

She nodded, too. Like her, he hadn't immediately jumped into another relationship, nor was he looking for one. No doubt he had his reasons; Joanna knew she had hers.

"Friends?" Tanner asked, and extended his hand for her to shake.

"And nothing more," Joanna added, placing her hand in his.

They exchanged a smile.

"Since Mr. Lund can't be here for the talent show on Wednesday, he wants to take Nicole and me out for dinner next Saturday night," Kristen announced. "Nicole said to ask you if it was all right."

"That's fine," Joanna returned absently, scanning the front page of the Saturday evening newspaper. It had been more than a week since she'd spoken to Tanner. She felt good about the way things had gone that afternoon; they understood each other now, despite their rather uncertain start.

Kristen darted back into the kitchen, returning a minute later. "I think it would be best if you spoke to Mr. Lund yourself, Mom."

"Okay, honey." She'd finished reading Dear Abby and had just turned to the comics section, looking for Garfield, her favourite cat.

"Mom!" Kristen cried impatiently. "Mr. Lund's on the phone now. You can't keep him waiting like this. It's impolite."

Hurriedly Joanna set the paper aside. "For heaven's sake, why didn't you say so earlier?"

"I did. Honestly, Mom, I think you're losing it."

Whatever *it* was sounded serious. The minute Joanna was inside the kitchen, Kristen thrust the telephone receiver into her hand.

"This is Joanna," she said.

"This is Tanner," he answered right away. "Don't feel bad. Nicole claims I'm losing *it*, too."

"I'd take her more seriously if I knew what *it* was."

"Yeah, me, too," Tanner said, and she could hear the laughter in his voice. "Listen, is dinner next Saturday evening all right with you?"

"I can't see a problem at this end."

"Great. The girls suggested that ice-cream parlor they're always talking about."

"The Pink Palace," Joanna said, and managed to swallow a chuckle. Tanner was really letting himself in for a crazy night with those two. Last year Kristen had talked Joanna into dinner there for her birthday. The hamburgers had been as expensive as T-bone steaks, and tough as rawhide. The music was so loud it had impaired Joanna's hearing for an entire week afterward. And the place was packed with teenagers. On the bright side, though, the ice cream was pretty good.

"By the way," Joanna said, "Nicole's welcome to stay here when you're away next week."

"Joanna, that's great. I didn't want to ask, but the kid's been at me ever since the last time. She was worried I was going to send her back to Mrs. Wagner."

"It'll work best for her to stay here, since that's the night of the talent show."

"Are you absolutely sure?"

"Absolutely. It's no trouble at all. Just drop her off— and don't worry."

"Right." He sounded relieved. "And don't wear anything fancy next Saturday night."

"Saturday night?" Joanna asked, lost for a moment.

"Yeah. Didn't you just tell me it was all right for the four of us to go to dinner?"

# Chapter Five

"I really appreciate this, Joanna," Tanner said. Nicole stood at his side, overnight bag clenched in her hand, her eyes round and sad.

"It's no problem, Tanner. Really."

Tanner hugged his daughter tightly. He briefly closed his eyes and Joanna could feel his regret. He was as upset about missing his daughter's talent-show performance as Nicole was not to have him there.

"Be good, sweetheart."

"I will."

"And I want to hear all the details about tonight when I get back, okay?"

Nicole nodded and attempted a smile.

"I'd be there if I could."

"I know, Dad. Don't worry about it. There'll be plenty of other talent shows. Kristen and I were thinking that if we do really good, we might take our act on the road, the way Daisy Gilbert does."

"Daisy who?" Tanner asked, and raised questioning eyes to Joanna, as if he expected her to supply the answer.

"A singer," was the best Joanna could do. Kristen had as many albums as Joanna had runs in her tights. She found it impossible to keep her daughter's favorite rock stars straight. Apparently Tanner wasn't any more knowledgeable than she was.

"Not just *any* singer, Mom," Kristen corrected impatiently. "Daisy's special. She's only a little older than Nicole and me, and if she can be a rock star at fifteen, then so can we."

Although Joanna hated to squelch such optimism, she suspected that the girls might be missing one minor skill if they hoped to find fame and fortune as professional singers. "But you don't sing."

"Yeah, but we lip-synch real good."

"Come on, Nicole," Kristen said, reaching for her friend's overnight bag. "We've got to practice."

The two disappeared down the hallway and Joanna was left alone with Tanner.

"You have the telephone number for the hotel and the meeting place?" he asked.

"I'll call if there's a problem. Don't worry, Tanner, I'm sure everything's going to be fine."

He nodded, but a tight scowl darkened his face.

"For heaven's sake, stop looking so guilty."

His eyes widened in surprise. "It shows?"

"It might as well be flashing from a marquee."

Tanner grinned and rubbed the side of his jaw with his left hand. "There are only two meetings left that

I'll have to deal with personally. Becky's promised to handle the others. You know, when I bought into the company and committed myself to these trips, I didn't think leaving Nicole would be this traumatic. We both hate it—at least, she did until she spent the night here with you and Kristen the last time."

"She's a special little girl."

"Thanks," Tanner said, looking suitably proud. It was obvious that he worked hard at being a good father, and Joanna felt a twinge of conscience for the assumptions she'd made about him earlier.

"Listen," she murmured, then took a deep breath, wondering how best to approach the subject of dinner. "About Saturday night…"

"What about it?"

"I thought, well, it would be best if it were just you and the girls."

Already he was shaking his head, his mouth set in firm lines of resolve. "It wouldn't be the same without you. I owe you, Joanna, and since you won't accept payment for keeping Nicole, then the least you can do is agree to dinner."

"But—"

"If you're worried about this seeming too much like a date—don't. We understand each other."

Her responding smile was decidedly weak. "Okay, if that's the way you want it. Kristen and I'll be ready Saturday at six."

"Good."

Joanna was putting the finishing touches to her makeup before the talent show when the telephone rang.

"I'll get it," Kristen yelled, racing down the hallway

as if answering the phone before the second ring was a matter of life and death.

Joanna rolled her eyes toward the ceiling at the importance telephone conversations had recently assumed for Kristen. She half expected the call to be from Tanner, but then she heard Kristen exclaim, "Hi, Grandma!" Joanna smiled softly, pleased that her mother had remembered the talent show. Her parents were retired and lived in Colville, a town about sixty miles north of Spokane. She knew they would have attended the talent show themselves had road conditions been better. In winter, the families tended to keep in touch by phone because driving could be hazardous. No doubt her mother was calling now to wish Kristen luck.

Bits and pieces of the conversation drifted down the hallway as Kristen chatted excitedly about the show, Nicole's visit and their song.

"Mom, it's Grandma!" Kristen yelled. "She wants to talk to you."

Joanna finished blotting her lipstick and hurried to the phone. "Hi, Mom," she said cheerfully. "It's nice of you to call."

"What's this about you going out on a date Saturday night?"

"Who told you that?" Joanna demanded, groaning silently. Her mother had been telling her for years that she ought to remarry. Joanna felt like throttling Kristen for even mentioning Tanner's name. The last thing she needed was for her parents to start pressuring her about this relationship.

"Why, Kristen told me all about it, and sweetie, if you don't mind my saying so, this man sounds just perfect for you. You're both single parents. He has a daughter, you have a daughter, and the girls are best friends. The arrangement is ideal."

"Mother, please, I don't know what Kristen told you, but Tanner only wants to thank me for watching Nicole while he's away on business. Dinner on Saturday night is not a date!"

"He's taking you to dinner?"

"Me and Kristen and his daughter."

"What was his name again?"

"Tanner Lund," Joanna answered, desperate to change the subject. "Hasn't the weather been nasty this week? I'm really looking forward to spring. I was thinking about planting some annuals along the back fence."

"Tanner Lund," her mother repeated, slowly drawling out his name. "Now that has a nice solid feel to it. What's he like, sweetie?"

"Oh, honestly, Mother, I don't know. He's a man. What more do you want me to say?"

Her mother seemed to approve that piece of information. "I find it interesting that that's the way you view him. I think he could be the one, Joanna."

"Mother, please, how many times do I have to tell you? I'm not going to remarry. Ever!"

A short pause followed her announcement. "We'll see, sweetie, we'll see."


"Aren't you going to wear a dress, Mom?" Kristen gave her another of those scathing glances intended to melt a mother's confidence into puddles of doubt. Joanna had deliberated for hours on what to wear for this evening out with Tanner and the girls. If she chose a dress, something simple and classic like the ones she wore to the office, she might look too formal for a casual outing. The only other dresses she owned were party dresses, and those were so outdated they were almost back in style.

Dark wool pants and a wheat-colored Irish cable-knit sweater had seemed the perfect solution. Or so Joanna had thought until Kristen looked at her and frowned.

"Mom, tonight is important."

"We're going to the Pink Palace, not the Spokane House."

"I know, but Mr. Lund is so nice." Her daughter's gaze fell on the bouquet of pink roses on the dining-room table, and she reverently stroked a bloom. Tanner had arranged for the flowers to be delivered to Nicole and Kristen the night of the talent show. "You can't wear slacks to dinner with the man who sent me my first real flowers," she announced in tones of finality.

Joanna hesitated. "I'm sure this is what Mr. Lund expects," she said with far more confidence than she felt.

"You think so?"

She hoped so! She smiled, praying that her air of certainty would be enough to appease her sceptical daughter. Still, she had to agree with Kristen: Tanner *was* nice. More than nice—that was such a weak word. With every meeting, Joanna's estimation of the man grew. He'd called on Friday to thank her for minding Nicole, who'd gone straight home from school on Thursday afternoon since her father was back, and mentioned he was looking forward to Saturday. He was thoughtful, sensitive, personable and a wonderful father. Not to mention one of the best-looking men she'd ever met. It was unfortunate, really, that she wasn't looking for a husband, because Tanner Lund could easily be a prime candidate.

The word *husband* bounced in Joanna's mind like a ricocheting bullet. She blamed her mother for that. What she'd told her was true—Joanna was finished with marriage, finished with love. Davey had taught her how difficult it was for most men to remain faithful, and Joanna had no intention of repeating those painful lessons. Besides, if a man ever did become part of her life again, it would be someone on her own social and economic level. Not like Tanner Lund. But that didn't mean she was completely blind to male charms. On the contrary, she saw handsome men every day, worked with several, and had even dated a few. However, it was Tanner Lund she found herself thinking about lately, and that bothered Joanna. It bothered her a lot.

The best thing to do was nip this near relationship in the bud. She'd go to dinner with him this once, but only this once, and that would be the end of it.

"They're here!" The drape swished back into place as Kristen bolted away from the large picture window.

Calmly Joanna opened the hall closet and retrieved their winter coats. She might appear outwardly composed, but her fingers were shaking. The prospect of seeing Tanner left her trembling, and that fact drained away what little confidence she'd managed to accumulate over the past couple of days.

Both Tanner and Nicole came to the front door. Kristen held out her hands, and Nicole gripped them eagerly. Soon the two were jumping up and down like pogo sticks gone berserk.

"I can tell we're in for a fun evening," Tanner muttered under his breath.

He looked wonderful, Joanna admitted grudgingly. The kind of man every woman dreams about—well, almost every woman. Joanna longed to think of herself as immune to the handsome Mr. Lund. Unfortunately she wasn't.

Since their last meeting, she'd tried to figure out when her feelings for Tanner had changed. The roses had done it, she decided. Ordering them for Kristen and Nicole had been so thoughtful, and the girls had been ecstatic at the gesture.

When they'd finished lip-synching their song, they'd bowed before the auditorium full of appreciative parents. Then the school principal, Mr. Holliday, had stood at their side and presented them each with a beautiful bouquet of long-stemmed pink roses. Flowers Tanner had wired because he couldn't be there to watch their act.

"Are you ready?" Tanner asked, holding open the door for Joanna.

She nodded. "I think so."

Although it was early, a line had already begun to form outside the Pink Palace when they arrived. The minute they pulled into the parking lot, they were accosted by a loud, vibrating rock-and-roll song that might have been an old Jerry Lee Lewis number.

"It looks like we'll have to wait," Joanna commented. "That lineup's getting longer by the minute."

"I had my secretary make reservations," Tanner told her. "I heard this place really grooves on a Saturday night."

"Grooves!" Nicole repeated, smothering her giggles behind her cupped palm. Kristen laughed with her.

Turner leaned his head close to Joanna's. "It's difficult to reason with a generation that grew up without Janis and Jimi!"

Janis Joplin and Jimi Hendrix were a bit before Joanna's time, too, but she knew what he meant.

The Pink Palace was exactly as Joanna remembered. The popular ice-cream parlor was decorated in a fifties theme, with old-fashioned circular booths and outdated jukeboxes. The waitresses wore billowing pink skirts with a French poodle design and roller-skated between tables, taking and delivering orders. Once inside, Joanna, Tanner and the girls were seated almost immediately and handed huge menus. Neither girl bothered to read through the selections, having made their choices in the car. They'd both decided on cheeseburgers and banana splits.

By the time the waitress, chewing on a thick wad of bubble gum, skated to a stop at their table, Joanna had made her selection, too.

"A cheeseburger and a banana split," she said, grinning at the girls.

"Same here," Tanner said, "and coffee, please."

"I'll have a cup, too," Joanna added.

The teenager wrote down their order and glided toward the kitchen.

Joanna opened her purse and brought out a small wad of cotton wool.

"What's that for?" Tanner wanted to know when she pulled it apart into four fluffy balls and handed two of them to him, keeping the other pair for herself.

She pointed to her ears. "The last time I was here, I was haunted for days by a ringing in my ears that sounded suspiciously like an old Elvis tune."

Tanner chuckled and leaned across the table to shout, "It does get a bit loud, doesn't it?"

Kristen and Nicole looked from one parent to the

other then shouted together, "If it's too loud, you're too old!"

Joanna raised her hand. "Guilty as charged."

Tanner nodded and shared a smile with Joanna. The smile did funny things to her stomach, and Joanna pressed her hands over her abdomen in a futile effort to quell her growing awareness of Tanner. A warning light flashed in her mind, spelling out danger.

Joanna wasn't sure what had come over her, but whatever it was, she didn't like it.

Their meal arrived, and for a while, at least, Joanna could direct her attention to that. The food was better than she remembered. The cheeseburgers were juicy and tender and the banana splits divine. She promised herself she'd eat cottage cheese and fruit every day at lunch for the next week to balance all the extra calories from this one meal.

While Joanna and Tanner exchanged only the occasional remark, the girls chattered happily throughout dinner. When the waitress skated away with the last of their empty plates, Tanner suggested a movie.

"Great idea!" Nicole cried, enthusiastically seconded by Kristen.

"What do you think, Joanna?" asked Tanner.

She started to say that the evening had been full enough—until she found two eager young faces looking hopefully at her. She couldn't finish her sentence; it just wasn't in her to dash their good time.

"Sure," she managed instead, trying to insert a bit of excitement into her voice.

"*Teen Massacre* is showing at the mall," Nicole said, shooting a glance in her father's direction. "Donny

Rosenburg saw it and claims it scared him out of his wits, but then Donny doesn't have many."

Kristen laughed and nodded, apparently well-acquainted with the witless Donny.

Without the least bit of hesitation, Tanner shook his head. "No way, Nicole."

"Come on, Dad, everyone's seen it. The only reason it got an adult rating is because of the blood and gore, and I've seen that lots of times."

"Discussion is closed." He spoke without raising his voice, but the authority behind his words was enough to convince Joanna she'd turn up the loser if she ever crossed Tanner Lund. Still, she knew she wouldn't hesitate if she felt he was wrong, but in this case she agreed with him completely.

Nicole's lower lip jutted out rebelliously, and for a minute Joanna thought the girl might try to argue her case. But she wasn't surprised when Nicole yielded without further argument.

Deciding which movie to see involved some real negotiating. The girls had definite ideas of what was acceptable, as did Tanner and Joanna. Like Tanner, Joanna wasn't about to allow her daughter to see a movie with an adult rating, even if it was "only because of the blood and gore."

They finally compromised on a comedy that starred a popular teen idol. The girls thought that would be "all right," but they made it clear that *Teen Massacre* was their first choice.

Half an hour later they were inside the theater, and Tanner asked, "Anyone for popcorn?"

"Me," Kristen said.

"Me, too, and could we both have a Coke and chocolate-covered raisins, too?" Nicole asked.

Tanner rolled his eyes and, grinning, glanced toward Joanna. "What about you?"

"Nothing." She didn't know where the girls were going to put all this food, but she knew where it would end up if she were to consume it. Her hips! She sometimes suspected that junk food didn't even pass through her stomach, but attached itself directly to her hip bones.

"You're sure?"

"Positive."

Tanner returned a moment later with three large boxes of popcorn and other assorted treats.

As soon as they'd emptied Tanner's arms of all but one box of popcorn, the girls started into the auditorium.

"Hey, you two, wait for us," Joanna called after them, bewildered by the way they'd hurried off without waiting for her and Tanner.

Kristen and Nicole stopped abruptly and turned around, a look of pure horror on their young faces.

"You're not going to sit with us, are you, Mom?" Kristen wailed. "You just can't!"

"Why not?" This was news to Joanna. Sure, it had been a while since she'd gone to a movie with her daughter, but Kristen had always sat with her in the past.

"Someone might see us," her daughter went on to explain, in tones of exaggerated patience. "No one sits with their parents anymore. Not even woosies."

"Woosies?"

"Sort of like nerds, only worse!" Kristen said.

"Sitting with us is obviously a social embarrassment to be avoided at all costs," Tanner muttered.

"Can we go now, Mom?" Kristen pleaded. "I don't want to miss the previews."

Joanna nodded, still a little stunned. She enjoyed going out to a movie now and again, usually accompanied by her daughter and often several of Kristen's friends. Until tonight, no one had openly objected to sitting in the same row with her. However, now that Joanna thought about it, Kristen hadn't been interested in going to the movies for the past couple of months.

"I guess this is what happens when they hit sixth grade," Tanner said, holding the auditorium door for Joanna.

She walked down the center aisle and paused by an empty row near the back, checking with Tanner before she entered. Neither of them sat down, though, until they'd located the girls. Kristen and Nicole were three rows from the front and had slid down so far that their eyes were level with the seats ahead of them.

"Ah, the joys of fatherhood," Tanner commented, after they'd taken their places. "Not to mention motherhood."

Joanna still felt a little taken aback by what had happened. She thought she had a close relationship with Kristen, and yet her daughter had never said a word about not wanting to be anywhere near her in a movie theater. She knew this might sound like a trivial concern to some, but she couldn't help worrying that the solid foundation she'd spent a decade reinforcing had started to crumble.

"Joanna?"

She turned to Tanner and tried to smile, but the attempt was unconvincing.

"What's wrong?"

Joanna fluttered her hand weakly, unable to find her voice. "Nothing." That came out sounding as though she might burst into tears any second.

"Is it Kristen?"

She nodded wildly.

"Because she didn't want to sit with us?"

Her hair bounced against her shoulders as she nodded again.

"The girls wanting to be by themselves bothers you?"

"No... Yes. I don't know what I'm feeling. She's growing up, Tanner, and I guess it just hit me right between the eyes."

"It happened to me last week," Tanner said thoughtfully. "I found Nicole wearing a pair of tights. Hell, I didn't even know they made them for girls her age."

"They do, believe it or not," Joanna informed him. "Kristen did the same thing."

He shook his head as though he couldn't quite grasp the concept. "But they're only eleven."

"Going on sixteen."

"Has Kristen tried pasting on those fake fingernails yet?" Tanner shuddered in exaggerated disgust.

Joanna covered her mouth with one hand to hold back an attack of giggles. "Those press-on things turned up every place imaginable for weeks afterward."

Tanner turned sideways in his seat. "What about makeup?" he asked urgently.

"I caught her trying to sneak out of the house one morning last month. She was wearing the brightest eye shadow I've ever seen in my life. Tanner, I swear if she'd been standing on a shore, she could have guided lost ships into port."

He smiled, then dropped his gaze, looking uncomfortable. "So you do let her wear makeup?"

"I'm holding off as long as I can," Joanna admitted. "At the very least, she'll have to wait until seventh grade. That was when my mother let me. I don't think it's so unreasonable to expect Kristen to wait until junior high."

Tanner relaxed against the back of his seat and nodded a couple of times. "I'm glad to hear that. Nicole's been after me to 'wake up and smell the coffee,' as she puts it, for the past six months. Hell, I didn't know who to ask about these things. It really isn't something I'm comfortable discussing with my secretary."

"What about her mother?"

His eyes hardened. "She only sees Nicole when it's convenient, and it hasn't been for the past three years."

"I... I didn't mean to pry."

"You weren't. Carmen and I didn't exactly part on the best of terms. She's got a new life now and apparently doesn't want any reminders of the past—not that I totally blame her. We made each other miserable. Frankly, Joanna, my feelings about getting married again are the same as yours. One failed marriage was enough for me."

The theater lights dimmed then, and the sound track started. Tanner leaned back and crossed his long legs, balancing one ankle on the opposite knee.

Joanna settled back, too, grateful that the movie they'd selected was a comedy. Her emotions were riding too close to the surface this evening. She could see herself bursting into tears at the slightest hint of sadness—for that matter, joy. Bambi traipsing through the woods would have done her in just then.

Joanna was so caught up in her thoughts that when Tanner and the others around her let out a boisterous laugh, she'd completely missed whatever had been so hilarious.

Without thinking, she reached over and grabbed a handful of Tanner's popcorn. She discovered that the crunchiness and the buttery, salty flavor suited her mood. Tanner held the box on the arm between them to make sharing easier.

The next time Joanna sent her fingers digging, they encountered Tanner's. "Sorry," she murmured, pulling her hand free.

"No problem," he answered, tilting the box her way.

Joanna munched steadily. Before she knew it, the popcorn was gone and her fingers were laced with Tanner's, her hand firmly clasped in his.

The minute he reached for her hand, Joanna lost track of what was happening on the screen. Holding hands seemed such an innocent gesture, something teenagers did. He certainly didn't mean anything by it, Joanna told herself. It was just that her emotions were so confused lately, and she wasn't even sure why.

She liked Tanner, Joanna realised anew, liked him very much. And she thoroughly enjoyed Nicole. For the first time since her divorce, she could imagine getting involved with another man, and the thought frightened her. All right, it terrified her. This man belonged to a different world. Besides, she wasn't ready. Good grief, six years should have given her ample time to heal, but she'd been too afraid to lift the bandage.

When the movie was over, Tanner drove them home.

The girls were tired, but managed to carry on a lively backseat conversation. The front seat was a different story. Neither Tanner nor Joanna had much to say.

"Would you like to come in for coffee?" Joanna asked when Tanner pulled into her driveway, although she was silently wishing he'd decline. Her nerves continued to clamor from the hand holding, and she wanted some time alone to organise her thoughts.

"Can we, Dad? Please?" Nicole begged. "Kristen and I want to watch the Saturday night videos together."

"You're sure?" Tanner looked at Joanna, his brow creased with concern.

She couldn't answer. She wasn't sure of anything just then. "Of course," she forced herself to say. "It'll only take a minute or two to brew a pot."

"All right, then," Tanner said, and the girls let out whoops of delight.

Occasionally Joanna wondered if their daughters would ever get tired of one another's company. Probably, although they hadn't shown any signs of it yet. As far as she knew, the two girls had never had a serious disagreement.

Kristen and Nicole disappeared as soon as they got into the house. Within seconds, the television could be heard blaring rock music, which had recently become a familiar sound in the small one-storey house.

Tanner followed Joanna into the kitchen and stood leaning against the counter while she filled the automatic coffeemaker with water. Her movements were jerky and abrupt. She felt awkward, ungraceful—as though this was the first time she'd ever been alone with a man. And that was a ridiculous way to feel, especially since the girls were practically within sight.

"I enjoyed tonight," Tanner commented, as she removed two cups from the cupboard.

"I did, too." She tossed him a lazy smile over her shoulder. But Tanner's eyes held hers, and it was as if she was seeing him for the first time. She half turned toward him, suddenly aware of how tall and lean he was, how thick and soft his dark hair. With an effort, Joanna looked from those mesmerising blue eyes and returned to the task of making coffee, although her fingers didn't seem willing to cooperate.

She stood waiting for the dark liquid to filter its way into the glass pot. Never had it seemed to take so long.

"Joanna."

Judging by the loudness of his voice, Tanner was standing directly behind her. A beat of silence followed before she turned around to face him.

Tanner's hands grasped her shoulders. "It's been a long time since I've sat in a movie and held a girl's hand."

She lowered her eyes and nodded. "Me, too."

"I felt like a kid again."

She'd been thinking much the same thing herself.

"I want to kiss you, Joanna."

She didn't need an analyst to inform her that kissing Tanner was something best avoided. She was about to tell him so when his hands gripped her waist and pulled her away from the support of the kitchen counter. A little taken aback, Joanna threw up her hands, as if to ward him off. But the minute they came into contact with the muscled hardness of his chest, they lost their purpose.

The moment Tanner's warm mouth claimed her lips, she felt an excitement that was almost shocking in its intensity. Her hands clutched the collar of his shirt as she eagerly gave herself up to the forgotten sensations. It had been so long since a man had kissed her like this.

The kiss was over much too soon. Far sooner than Joanna would have liked. The fire of his mouth had ignited a response in her she'd believed long dead. She was amazed at how readily it had sprung back to life. When Tanner dropped his arms and released her, Joanna felt suddenly weak, barely able to remain upright.

Her hand found her chest and she heaved a giant breath. "I...don't think that was a good idea."

Tanner's brows drew together, forming a ledge over his narrowed eyes. "I'm not sure I do, either, but it seemed right. I don't know what's happening between us, Joanna, and it's confusing the hell out of me."

"You? I'm the one who made it abundantly clear from the outset that I wasn't looking for a romantic involvement."

"I know, and I agree, but—"

"I'm more than pleased Kristen and Nicole are good friends, but I happen to like my life the way it is, thank you."

Tanner's frown grew darker, his expression both baffled and annoyed. "I feel the same way. It was a kiss, not a suggestion we live in sin."

"I...really wish you hadn't done that, Tanner."

"I apologize. Trust me, it won't happen again," he muttered, and buried his hands deep inside his pockets. "In fact it would probably be best if we forgot the entire incident."

"I agree totally."

"Fine then." He stalked out of the kitchen, but not before Joanna found herself wondering if she *could* forget it.

# Chapter Six

A kiss was really such a minor thing, Joanna mused, slowly rotating her pencil between her palms. She'd made a criminal case out of nothing, and embarrassed both Tanner and herself.

"Joanna, have you had time to read over the Osborne loan application yet?" her boss, Robin Simpson asked, strolling up to her desk.

"Ah, no, not yet," Joanna said, her face flushing with guilt.

Robin frowned as he studied her. "What's been with you today? Every time I see you, you're gazing at the wall with a faraway look in your eye."

"Nothing's wrong." Blindly she reached toward her In basket and grabbed a file, although she hadn't a clue which one it was.

"If I didn't know better, I'd say you were daydreaming about a man."

Joanna managed a short, sarcastic laugh meant to deny everything. "Men are the last thing on my mind," she said flippantly. It was a half-truth. Men in the plural didn't interest her, but *man*, as in Tanner Lund, well, that was another matter.

Over the years Joanna had gone out of her way to avoid men she was attracted to—it was safer. She dated occasionally, but usually men who might be classified as pleasant, men for whom she could never feel anything beyond a mild friendship. Magnetism, charm and sex appeal were lost on her, thanks to a husband who'd possessed all three and systematically destroyed her faith in the possibility of a lasting relationship. At least, those qualities hadn't piqued her interest again, until she met Tanner. Okay, so her dating habits for the past few years had been a bit premeditated, but everyone deserved a night out now and again. It didn't seem fair to be denied the pleasure of a fun evening simply because she wasn't in the market for another husband. So she'd dated, not a lot, but some and nothing in the past six years had affected her as much as those few short hours with Nicole's father.

"Joanna!"

She jerked her head up to discover her boss still standing beside her desk. "Yes?"

"The Osborne file."

She briefly closed her eyes in a futile effort to clear her thoughts. "What about it?"

Robin glared at the ceiling and paused, as though pleading with the light fixture for patience. "Read it and get back to me before the end of the day—if that isn't too much to ask?"

"Sure," she grumbled, wondering what had put Robin in such a foul mood. She picked up the loan application and was halfway through it before she realized the name on it wasn't Osborne. Great! If her day continued like this, she could blame Tanner Lund for getting her fired.

When Joanna arrived home three hours later she was exhausted and short-tempered. She hadn't been herself all day, mainly because she'd been so preoccupied with thoughts of Tanner Lund and the way he'd kissed her. She was overreacting—she'd certainly been kissed before, so it shouldn't be such a big deal. But it was. Her behaviour demonstrated all the maturity of someone Kristen's age, she chided herself. She'd simply forgotten how to act with men; it was too long since she'd been involved with one. The day wasn't a complete waste, however. She'd made a couple of important decisions in the last few hours, and she wanted to clear the air with her daughter before matters got completely out of hand.

"Hi, honey."

"Hi."

Kristen's gaze didn't waver from the television screen where a talk-show host was interviewing a man whose brilliant red hair was so short on top it stuck straight up and so messy in front it fell over his face, almost reaching his left eye and part of his nose.

"Who's that?"

Kristen gave a deep sigh of wonder and adolescent love. "You mean you don't know? I've been in love with Ed Sheeran for a whole year and you don't even know him when you see him?"

"No, I can't say that I do."

"Oh, Mom, honestly, get with it."

There *it* was again. First she was losing *it* and now she was supposed to get with *it*. Joanna wished her daughter would decide which she wanted.

"We need to talk."

Kristen reluctantly dragged her eyes away from her idol. "Mom, this is important. Can't it wait?"

Frustrated, Joanna sighed and muttered, "I suppose."

"Good."

Kristen had already tuned her out. Joanna strolled into the kitchen and realised she hadn't taken the hamburger out of the freezer to thaw. Great. So much for the tacos she'd planned to make for dinner. She opened and closed cupboard doors, rummaging around for something interesting. A can of tuna fish wasn't likely to meet with Kristen's approval. One thing about her daughter that the approach of the teen years hadn't disrupted was her healthy appetite.

Joanna stuck her head around the corner. "How does tuna casserole sound for dinner?"

Kristen didn't even look in her direction, just held out her arm and jerked her thumb toward the carpet.

"Soup and sandwiches?"

Once more Kristen's thumb headed downward, and Joanna groaned.

"Bacon, lettuce and tomato on toast with chicken noodle soup," she tried. "And that's the best I can do. Take it or leave it."

Kristen sighed. "If that's the final offer, I'll take it. But I thought we were having tacos."

"We were. I forgot to take out the hamburger."

"All right, BLTs," Kristen muttered, reversing the direction of her thumb.

Joanna was frying the bacon when Kristen joined her, sitting on a stool while her mother worked. "You wanted to talk to me about something?"

"Yes." Joanna concentrated on spreading mayonnaise over slices of whole-wheat toast, as she made an effort to gather her scattered thoughts. She cast about for several moments, trying to come up with a way of saying what needed to be said without making more of it than necessary.

"It must be something big," Kristen commented. "Did my teacher phone you at work or something?"

"No, should she have?" She raised her eyes and scrutinised Kristen's face closely.

Kristen gave a quick denial with a shake of her head. "No way. I'm a star pupil this year. Nicole and I are both doing great. Just wait until report-card time, then you'll see."

"I believe you." Kristen had been getting top marks all year, and Joanna was proud of how well her daughter was doing. "What I have to say concerns Nicole and—" she hesitated, swallowing tightly "—her father."

"Mr. Lund sure is good-looking, isn't he?" Kristen said enthusiastically, watching for Joanna's reaction.

Reluctantly Joanna nodded, hoping to sound casual. "I suppose."

"Oh, come on, Mom, he's a hunk."

"All right," Joanna admitted slowly. "I'll grant you that Tanner has a certain amount of…appeal."

Kristen grinned, looking pleased with herself.

"Actually it was Mr. Lund I wanted to talk to you

about," Joanna continued, placing a layer of tomato slices on the toast.

"Really?" The brown eyes opened even wider.

"Yes, well, I wanted to tell you that I... I don't think it would be a good idea for the four of us to go on doing things together."

Abruptly Kristen's face fell with surprise and disappointment. "Why not?"

"Well...because he and I are both really busy." Even to her own ears, the statement sounded illogical, but it was difficult to tell her own daughter that she was frightened of her attraction to the man. Difficult to explain why nothing could come of it.

"Because you're both busy? Come on, Mom, that doesn't make any sense."

"All right, I'll be honest." She wondered whether an eleven-year-old could grasp the complexities of adult relationships. "I don't want to give Nicole's dad the wrong idea," she said carefully.

Kristen leaned forward, setting her elbows on the kitchen counter and resting her face in both hands. Her gaze looked sharp enough to shatter diamonds. "The wrong idea about what?" she asked.

"Me," Joanna said, swallowing uncomfortably.

"You?" Kristen repeated thoughtfully, a frown creasing her smooth brow. She relaxed then and released a huge sigh. "Oh, I see. You think Mr. Lund might think you're in the marriage market."

Joanna pointed a fork at her daughter. "Bingo!"

"But, Mom, I think it would be great if you and Nicole's dad got together. In fact, Nicole and I were talking about it just today. Think about all the advantages. We could all be a real family, and you could have more babies… I don't know if I ever told you this, but I'd really like a baby brother, and so would Nicole. And if you married Mr. Lund we could take family vacations together. You wouldn't have to work, because… I don't know if you realize this, but Mr. Lund is pretty rich. You could stay home and bake cookies and sew and stuff."

Joanna was so surprised that it took her a minute to find her voice. Openmouthed, she waved the fork jerkily around. "No way, Kristen." Joanna's knees felt rubbery, and before she could slip to the floor, she slumped into a chair. All this time she'd assumed she was a good mother, giving her daughter everything she needed physically and emotionally, making up to Kristen as much as she could for her father's absence. But she apparently hadn't done enough. And Kristen and Nicole were scheming to get Joanna and Tanner together. As in married!

Something had to be done.

She decided to talk to Tanner, but an opportunity didn't present itself until much later that evening when Kristen was in bed, asleep. At least Joanna hoped her daughter was asleep. She dialled his number and prayed Nicole wouldn't answer.

Thankfully she didn't.

"Tanner, it's Joanna," she whispered, cupping her hand over the mouthpiece, taking no chance that Kristen could overhear their conversation.

"What's the matter? Have you got laryngitis?"

"No," she returned hoarsely, straining her voice. "I don't want Kristen to hear me talking to you."

"I see. Should I pretend you're someone else so Nicole won't tell on you?" he whispered back.

"Please." She didn't appreciate the humor in his

voice. Obviously he had yet to realize the seriousness of the situation. "We need to talk."

"We do?"

"Trust me, Tanner. You have no idea what I just learned. The girls are planning on us getting married."

"Married?" he shouted.

That, Joanna had known, would get a reaction out of him.

"When do you want to meet?"

"As soon as possible." He still seemed to think she was joking, but she couldn't blame him. If the situation were reversed, no doubt she would react the same way. "Kristen said something about the two of them swimming Wednesday night at the community pool. What if we meet at Denny's for coffee after you drop Nicole off?"

"What time?" He said it as though they were planning a reconnaissance mission deep into enemy territory.

"Seven ten." That would give them both a few extra minutes to make it to the restaurant.

"Shall we synchronise our watches?"

"This isn't funny, Tanner."

"I'm not laughing."

But he was, and Joanna was furious with him. "I'll see you then."

"Seven-ten, Wednesday night at Denny's," he repeated. "I'll be there."

On the evening of their scheduled meeting, Joanna arrived at the restaurant before Tanner. She already regretted suggesting they meet at Denny's, but it was too late to change that now. There were bound to be other customers who would recognise either Tanner or her, and Joanna feared that word of their meeting could somehow filter back to the girls. She'd been guilty of underestimating them before; she wouldn't make the same mistake a second time. If Kristen and Nicole did hear about this private meeting, they'd consider it justification for further interference.

Tanner strolled into the restaurant and glanced around. He didn't seem to recognise Joanna, and she moved her sunglasses down her nose and gave him an abrupt wave.

He took one look at her, and even from the other side of the room she could see he was struggling to hold in his laughter.

"What's with the scarf and sunglasses?"

"I'm afraid someone might recognize us and tell the girls." It made perfect sense to her, but obviously not to him. Joanna forgave him since he didn't know the extent of the difficulties facing them.

But all he said was, "I see." He inserted his hands in the pockets of his overcoat and walked lazily past her, whistling. "Should I sit here or would you prefer the next booth?"

"Don't be silly."

"I'm not going to comment on that."

"For heaven's sake," Joanna hissed, "sit down before someone notices you."

"Someone notices me? Lady, you're wearing sunglasses at night, in the dead of winter, and with that scarf tied around your chin you look like an old woman."

"Tanner," she said, "this is not the time to crack jokes."

A smile lifted his features as he slid into the booth opposite her. He reached for a menu. "Are you hungry?"

"No." His attitude was beginning to annoy her. "I'm just having coffee."

"Nicole cooked dinner tonight, and frankly I'm starving."

When the waitress appeared he ordered a complete dinner. Joanna asked for coffee.

"Okay, what's up, Sherlock?" he asked, once the coffee had been poured.

"To begin with I... I think Kristen and Nicole saw you kiss me the other night."

He made no comment, but his brow puckered slightly.

"It seems the two of them have been talking, and from what I gather they're interested in getting us, er, together."

"I see."

To Joanna's dismay, Tanner didn't seem to be the slightest bit concerned by her revelation.

"That troubles you?"

"Tanner," she said, leaning toward him, "to quote my daughter, 'Nicole and I have been talking and we thought it would be great if you and Mr. Lund got together. You could have more babies and we could go on vacations and be a real family and you could stay home and bake cookies and stuff.'" She waited for his reaction, but his face remained completely impassive.

"What kind of cookies?" he asked finally.

"Tanner, if you're going to turn this into a joke, I'm leaving." As far as Joanna was concerned, he deserved to be tormented by two dedicated eleven-year-old matchmakers! She started to slide out of the booth, but he stopped her with an upraised hand.

"All right, I'm sorry."

He didn't sound too contrite, and she gave a weak sigh of disgust. "You may consider this a joking matter, but I don't."

"Joanna, we're both mature adults," he stated calmly. "We aren't going to let a couple of eleven-year-old girls manipulate us!"

"Yes, but—"

"From the first, we've been honest with each other. That isn't going to change. You have no interest in remarriage—to me or anyone else—and I feel the same way. As long as we continue as we are now, the girls don't have a prayer."

"It's more than that," Joanna said vehemently. "We need to look past their schemes to the root of the problem."

"Which is?"

"Tanner, obviously we're doing something wrong as single parents."

He frowned. "What makes you say that?"

"Isn't it obvious? Kristen, and it seems equally true for Nicole, wants a complete family. What Kristen is really saying is that she longs for a father. Nicole is telling you she'd like a mother."

The humour drained out of Tanner's eyes, replaced with a look of real concern. "I see. And you think this all started because Kristen and Nicole saw us kissing?"

"I don't know," she murmured, shaking her head. "But I do know my daughter, and when she wants something, she goes after it with the force of a bulldog and won't let up. Once she's got it in her head that you and I are destined for each other, it's going to be pretty difficult for her to accept that all we'll ever be is friends."

"Nicole can get that way about certain things," he said thoughtfully.

The waitress delivered his roast beef sandwich and refilled Joanna's coffee cup.

Maybe she'd overreacted to the situation, but she couldn't help being worried. "I suppose you think I'm making more of a fuss about this than necessary," she said, flustered and a little embarrassed.

"About the girls manipulating us?"

"No, about the fact that we've both tried so hard to be good single parents, and obviously we're doing something wrong."

"I will admit that part concerns me."

"I don't mind telling you, Tanner, I've been in a panic all week, wondering where I've failed. We've got to come to terms with this. Make some important decisions."

"What do you suggest?"

"To start with, we've got to squelch any hint of personal involvement. I realize a certain amount of contact will be unavoidable with the girls being such close friends." She paused and chewed on her bottom lip. "I don't want to disrupt their relationship."

"I agree with you there. Being friends with Kristen has meant a good deal to Nicole."

"You and I went months without talking to each other," Joanna said, recalling that they'd only recently met. "There's no need for us to see each other now, is there?"

"That won't work."

"Why not?"

"Nicole will be spending the night with you again next Thursday—that is, unless you'd rather she didn't."

"Of course she can stay."

Tanner nodded, looking relieved. "To be honest, I don't think she'd go back to Mrs. Wagner's anymore without raising a big fuss."

"Taking care of Nicole is one thing, but the four of us doing anything together is out of the question."

Once more he nodded, but he didn't look pleased with the suggestion. "I think that would be best, too."

"We can't give them any encouragement."

Pushing his plate aside, Tanner reached for his water glass, cupping it with both hands. "You know, Joanna, I think a lot of you." He paused, then gave her a teasing smile. "You have a habit of dressing a little oddly every now and then, but other than that I respect your judgment. I'd like to consider you a friend."

She decided to let his comment about her choice of clothing slide. "I'd like to be your friend, too," she told him softly.

He grinned, and his gaze held hers for a long uninterrupted moment before they both looked away. "I know you think that kiss the other night was a big mistake, and I suppose you're right, but I'm not sorry it happened." He hesitated, as though waiting for her to argue with him, and when she didn't, he continued. "It's been a lot of years since I held a woman's hand at a movie or kissed her the way I did you. It was good to feel that young and innocent again."

Joanna dropped her gaze to her half-filled cup. It had felt right for her, too. So right that she'd been frightened out of her wits ever since. She could easily fall in love with Tanner, and that would be the worst possible thing for her. She just wasn't ready to take those risks again. They came from different worlds, too, and she'd never fit comfortably in his. Yet every time she thought about that kiss, she started to shake from the inside out.

"In a strange sort of way we need each other," Tanner went on, his look thoughtful. "Nicole needs a strong loving woman to identify with, to fill a mother's role, and she thinks you're wonderful."

"And Kristen needs to see a man who can be a father, putting the needs of his family before his own."

"I think it's only natural for the two of them to try to get us together," Tanner added. "It's something we should be prepared to deal with in the future."

"You're right," Joanna agreed, understanding exactly what he meant. "We need each other to help provide what's lacking in our daughters' lives. But we can't get involved with each other." She didn't know any other way to say it but bluntly.

"I agree," he said, with enough conviction to lay aside any doubt Joanna might still hold.

They were silent for a long moment.

"Why?"

Strangely, Joanna knew immediately what he was asking. She had the same questions about what had happened between him and Nicole's mother.

"Davey was—is—the most charming personable man I've ever met. I was fresh out of college and so in love with him I didn't stop to think." She paused and glanced away, not daring to look at Tanner. Her voice had fallen so low it was almost a whisper. "We were engaged when my best friend, Carol, told me Davey had made a pass at her. Fool that I was, I didn't believe her. I thought she was jealous that Davey had chosen me to love and marry. I was sick that my friend would stoop to anything so underhand. I always knew Carol found him attractive—most women did—and I was devastated that she would lie that way. I trusted Davey so completely that I didn't even ask him about the incident. Later, after we were married, there were a lot of times when he said he was working late, a lot of unexplained absences, but I didn't question those, either. He was building his career in real estate, and if he had to put in extra hours, well, that was understandable. All those nights I sat alone, trusting him when he claimed he was working, believing with all my heart that he was doing his utmost to build a life for us...and then learning he'd been with some other woman."

"How'd you find out?"

"The first time?"

"You mean there was more than once?"

She nodded, hating to let Tanner know how many times she'd forgiven Davey, how many times she'd taken him back after he'd pleaded and begged and promised it would never happen again.

"I was blind to his wandering eye for the first couple of years. What they say about ignorance being bliss is true. When I found out, I was physically sick. When I realised how I'd fallen for his lies, it was even worse, and yet I stuck it out with him, trusting that everything would be better, everything would change...someday. I wanted so badly to believe him, to trust him, that I accepted anything he told me, no matter how implausible it sounded.

"The problem was that the more I forgave him, the lower my self-esteem dropped. I became convinced it was all my fault. I obviously lacked something, since he...felt a need to seek out other women."

"You know now that's not true, don't you?" His voice

was so gentle, so caring, that Joanna battled down a rush of emotion.

"There'd never been a divorce in my family," she told him quietly. "My parents have been married nearly forty years, and my brothers all have happy marriages. I think that was one of the reasons I held on so long. I just didn't know how to let go. I'd be devastated and crushed when I learned about his latest affair, yet I kept coming back for more. I suppose I believed Davey would change. Something magical would happen and all our problems would disappear. Only it never did. One afternoon—I don't even know what prompted it... All I knew was that I couldn't stay in the marriage any longer. I packed Kristen's and my things and walked out. I've never been back, never wanted to go back."

Tanner reached for her hand, and his fingers wrapped warmly around hers. A moment passed before he spoke, and when he did, his voice was tight with remembered pain. "I thought Carmen was the sweetest, gentlest woman in the world. As nonsensical as it sounds, I think I was in love with her before I even knew her name. She was a college cheerleader and a homecoming queen, and I felt like a nobody. By chance, we met several years after graduation when I'd just begun making a name for myself. I'd bought my first company, a small aluminum window manufacturer back in West Virginia. And I was working night and day to see it through those first rough weeks of transition.

"I was high on status," Tanner admitted, his voice filled with regret. "Small-town boy makes good—that kind of stuff. She'd been the most popular girl in my college year, and dating her was the fulfilment of a fantasy. She'd recently broken up with a guy she'd been involved with for two years and had something to prove herself, I suppose." He focused his gaze away from Joanna. "Things got out of hand and a couple of months later Carmen announced she was pregnant. To be honest, I was happy about it, thrilled. There was never any question whether I'd marry her. By then I was so in love with her I couldn't see straight. Eight months after the wedding, Nicole was born…" He hesitated, as though gathering his thoughts. "Some women are meant to be mothers, but not Carmen. She didn't even like to hold Nicole, didn't want anything to do with her. I'd come home at night and find that Carmen had neglected Nicole most of the day. But I made excuses for her, reasoned everything out in my own mind—the unexplained bruises on the baby, the fear I saw in Nicole's eyes whenever her mother was around. It got so bad that I started dropping Nicole off at my parents', just so I could be sure she was being looked after properly."

Joanna bit the corner of her lip at the raw pain she witnessed in Tanner's eyes. She was convinced he didn't speak of his marriage often, just as she rarely talked about Davey, but this was necessary if they were to understand each other.

"To be fair to Carmen, I wasn't much of a husband in those early months. Hell, I didn't have time to be. I was feeling like a big success when we met, but that didn't last long. Things started going wrong at work and I damn near lost my shirt.

"Later," he continued slowly, "I learned that the entire time I was struggling to hold the company together, Carmen was seeing her old boyfriend, Sam Dailey."

"Oh, Tanner."

"Nicole's my daughter, there was no doubting that.

But Carmen had never really wanted children, and she felt trapped in the marriage. We separated when Nicole was less than three years old."

"I thought you said you'd only been divorced five years?"

"We have. It took Carmen a few years to get around to the legal aspect of things. I wasn't in any rush, since I had no intention of ever marrying again."

"What's happened to Carmen since? Did she re-marry?"

"Eventually. She lived with Sam for several years, and the last thing I heard was they'd split up and she married a professional baseball player."

"Does Nicole ever see her mother?" Joanna remembered that he'd said his ex-wife saw Nicole only when it was convenient.

"She hasn't in the past three years. The thing I worry about most is having Carmen show up someday, demanding that Nicole come to live with her. Nicole doesn't remember anything about those early years—thank God—and she seems to have formed a rosy image of her mother. She keeps Carmen's picture in her bedroom and every once in a while I'll see her staring at it wistfully." He paused and glanced at his watch. "What time were we supposed to pick up the kids?"

"Eight."

"It's five after now."

"Oh, good grief." Joanna slung her bag over her shoulder as they slid out of the booth and hurried toward the cash register. Tanner insisted on paying for her coffee, and Joanna didn't want to waste time arguing.

They walked briskly toward their cars, parked beside each other in the lot. "Joanna," he called, as she fumbled with her keys. "I'll wait a couple of minutes so we don't both arrive at the same time. Otherwise the girls will probably guess we've been together."

She flashed him a grateful smile. "Good thinking."

"Joanna." She looked at him questioningly as he shortened the distance between them. "Don't misunderstand this," he said softly. He pulled her gently into the circle of his arms, holding her close for a lingering moment. "I'm sorry for what Davey did to you. The man's a fool." Tenderly he brushed his lips over her forehead, then turned and abruptly left her.

It took Joanna a full minute to recover enough to get into her car and drive away.

# Chapter Seven

"Mom," Kristen screeched, "the phone's for you."

Joanna was surprised. A call for her on a school night was rare enough, but one that actually got through with Kristen and Nicole continually on the line was a special occasion.

"Who is it, honey?" No doubt someone interested in cleaning her carpets or selling her a cemetery plot.

"I don't know," Kristen said, holding the phone to her shoulder. She lowered her voice to whisper, "But whoever it is sounds weird."

"Hello." Joanna spoke into the receiver as Kristen wandered toward her bedroom.

"Can you talk?" The husky male voice was unmistakably Tanner's.

"Y-yes." Joanna looked toward Kristen's bedroom to be certain her daughter was out of earshot.

"Can you meet me tomorrow for lunch?"

"What time?"

"Noon at the Sea Galley."

"Should we synchronize our watches?" Joanna couldn't resist asking. It had been a week since she'd last talked to Tanner. In the meantime she hadn't heard a word from Kristen about getting their two families together again. That in itself was suspicious, but Joanna had been too busy at work to think about it.

"Don't be cute, Joanna. I need help."

"Buy me lunch and I'm yours." She hadn't meant that quite the way it sounded and was grateful Tanner didn't comment on her slip of the tongue.

"I'll see you tomorrow then."

"Right."

A smile tugged at the edges of her mouth as she replaced the telephone receiver. Her hand lingered there for a moment as an unexpected tide of happiness washed over her.

"Who was that, Mom?" Kristen asked, poking her head around her bedroom door.

"A…friend, calling to ask if I could meet…her for lunch."

"Oh." Kristen's young face was a study in scepticism. "For a minute there I thought it sounded like Mr. Lund trying to fake a woman's voice."

"Mr. Lund? That's silly," Joanna said with a forced little laugh, then deftly changed the subject. "Kristen, it's nine thirty. Hit the hay, kiddo."

"Right, Mom. 'Night."

"'Night, sweetheart."

"Enjoy your lunch tomorrow."

"I will."

Joanna hadn't had a chance to walk away from the phone before it pealed a second time. She gave a guilty start and reached for it.

"Hello," she said hesitantly, half expecting to hear Tanner's voice again.

But it was her mother's crisp clear voice that rang over the wire. "Joanna, I hope this isn't too late to call."

"Of course not, Mom," Joanna answered quickly. "Is everything all right?"

Her mother ignored the question and asked one of her own instead. "What was the name of that young man you're dating again?"

"Mother," Joanna said with an exasperated sigh, "I'm not seeing anyone. I told you that."

"Tanner Lund, wasn't it?"

"We went out to dinner *once* with both our daughters, and that's the extent of our relationship. If Kristen let you assume anything else, it was just wishful thinking on her part. One dinner, I swear."

"But, Joanna, he sounds like such a nice young man. He's the same Tanner Lund who recently bought half of Spokane Aluminum, isn't he? I saw his name in the paper this morning and recognised it right away. Sweetie, your dad and I are so pleased you're dating such a famous successful man."

"Mother, please!" Joanna cried. "Tanner and I are friends. How many times do I have to tell you, we're not dating? Kristen and Tanner's daughter, Nicole, are best friends. I swear that's all there is to—"

"Joanna," her mother interrupted. "The first time you mentioned his name, I heard something in your voice that's been missing for a good long while. You may be

able to fool yourself, but not me. You like this Tanner."
Her voice softened perceptively.

"Mother, nothing could possibly come of it even if I
was attracted to him—which I'm not." Okay, so that last
part wasn't entirely true. But the rest of it certainly was.

"And why couldn't it?" her mother insisted.

"You said it yourself. He's famous, in addition to
being wealthy. I'm out of his league."

"Nonsense," her mother responded in a huff.

Joanna knew better than to get into a war of words
with her stubborn parent.

"Now don't be silly. You like Tanner Lund, and I say
it's about time you let down those walls you've built
around yourself. Joanna, sweetie, you've been hiding
behind them for six years now. Don't let what happened
with Davey ruin your whole life."

"I'm not going to," Joanna promised.

There was a long pause before her mother sighed
and answered, "Good. You deserve some happiness."

At precisely noon the following day, Joanna drove
into the Sea Galley parking lot. Tanner was already
there, waiting for her by the entrance.

"Hi," she said with a friendly grin, as he walked toward her.

"What, no disguises?"

Joanna laughed, embarrassed now by that silly scarf
and sunglasses she'd worn when they met at Denny's.
"Kristen doesn't know anyone who eats here."

"I'm grateful for that."

His smile was warm enough to tunnel through snow
drifts, and as much as Joanna had warned herself not
to be affected by it, she was.

"It's good to see you," Tanner added, taking her arm to escort her into the restaurant.

"You, too." Although she hadn't seen him in almost a week, Tanner was never far from her thoughts. Nicole had stayed with her and Kristen when Tanner flew to New York for two days in the middle of the previous week. The Spokane area had been hit by a fierce snowstorm the evening he left. Joanna had felt nervous the entire time about his traveling in such inclement weather, yet she hadn't so much as asked him about his flight when he arrived to pick up Nicole. Their conversation had been brief and pleasantly casual, but her relief that he'd got home safely had kept her awake for hours. Later, she'd been furious with herself for caring so much.

The Sea Galley hostess seated them right away and handed them thick menus. Joanna ordered a shrimp salad and coffee. Tanner echoed her choice.

"Nicole's birthday is next week," he announced, studying her face carefully. "She's handing out the party invitations today at school."

Joanna smiled and nodded. But Tanner's eyes held hers, and she saw something unidentifiable flicker there.

"In a moment of weakness, I told her she could have a slumber party."

Joanna's smile faded. "As I recall, Nicole did mention something about this party," she said, trying to sound cheerful. The poor guy didn't know what he was in for. "You're obviously braver than I am."

"You think it was a bad move?"

Joanna made a show of closing her eyes and nodding vigorously.

"I was afraid of that," Tanner muttered, and he rearranged the silverware around his place setting a couple of times. "I know we agreed it probably wouldn't be a good idea for us to do things together. But I need some advice—from a friend."

"What can I do?"

"Joanna, I haven't the foggiest idea about entertaining a whole troop of girls. I can handle contract negotiations and make split-second business decisions, but I panic at the thought of all those squealing little girls sequestered in my apartment for all those hours."

"How do you want me to help?"

"Would you consider..." He gave her a hopeful look, then shook his head regretfully. "No. I can't ask that of you. Besides, we don't want to give the girls any more ideas about the two of us. What I really need is some suggestions for keeping all these kids occupied. What do other parents do?"

"Other parents know better."

Tanner wiped a lock of dark brown hair from his brow and frowned. "I was afraid of that."

"What time are the girls supposed to arrive?"

"Six."

"Tanner, that's too early."

"I know, but Nicole insists I serve my special tacos, and she has some screwy idea about all the girls crowding into the kitchen to watch me."

Now it was Joanna's turn to frown. "That won't work. You'll end up with ten different pairs of hands trying to help. There'll be hamburger and cheese from one end of the place to the other."

"I thought as much. Good Lord, Joanna, how did I get myself into this mess?"

"Order pizza," she tossed out, tapping her index finger against her bottom lip. "Everyone loves that."

"Pizza. Okay. What about games?"

"A scavenger hunt always comes in handy when things get out of hand. Release the troops on your unsuspecting neighbours."

"So far we've got thirty minutes of the first fourteen hours filled."

"Movies," Joanna suggested next. "Lots of movies. You can go on Netflix and browse for something, maybe pick an old favourite like *Pretty in Pink*, and the girls will be in seventh heaven."

His eyes brightened. "Good idea."

"And if you really feel adventurous, take them roller-skating."

"Roller-skating? You think they'd like that?"

"They'd love it, especially if word leaked out that they were going to be at the rink Friday night. That way, several of the boys from the sixth-grade class can just happen to be there, too."

Tanner nodded, and a smile quirked the corners of his mouth. "And you think that'll keep everyone happy?"

"I'm sure of it. Wear 'em out first, show a movie or two second, with the lights out, of course, and I guarantee you by midnight everyone will be sound asleep."

Their salads arrived and Tanner stuck his fork into a fat succulent shrimp, then paused. "Now what was it you said last night about buying you lunch and making you mine?"

"It was a slip of the tongue," she muttered, dropping her gaze to her salad.

"Just my luck."

They laughed, and it felt good. Joanna had never had a relationship like this with a man. She wasn't on her guard the way she normally was, fearing that her date would put too much stock in an evening or two out. Because their daughters were the same age, they had a lot in common. They were both single parents doing their damnedest to raise their daughters right. The normal dating rituals and practised moves were unnecessary with him. Tanner was her friend, and it renewed Joanna's faith in the opposite sex to know there were still men like him left. Their friendship reassured her—but the undeniable attraction between them still frightened her.

"I really appreciate your suggestions," he said, after they'd both concentrated on their meals for several moments. "I've had this panicky feeling for the past three days. I suppose it wasn't a brilliant move on my part to call you at home, but I was getting desperate."

"You'll do fine. Just remember, it's important to keep the upper hand."

"I'll try."

"By the way, when *is* Hell Night?" She couldn't resist teasing him.

He gave a heartfelt sigh. "Next Friday."

Joanna slowly ate a shrimp. "I think Kristen figured out it was you on the phone last night."

"She did?"

"Yeah. She started asking questions the minute I hung up. She claimed my 'friend' sounded suspiciously like Mr. Lund faking a woman's voice."

Tanner cleared his throat and answered in a high falsetto. "That should tell you how desperate I was."

Joanna laughed and speared another shrimp. "That's what friends are for."

# Chapter Eight

"Mom, hurry or we're going to be late." Kristen paced the hallway outside her mother's bedroom door while Joanna finished dressing.

"Have you got Nicole's gift?"

"Oh." Kristen dashed into her bedroom and returned with a gaily wrapped oblong box. They'd bought the birthday gift the night before, a popular board game, which Kristen happened to know Nicole really wanted.

"I think Mr. Lund is really nice to let Nicole have a slumber party, don't you?"

"Really brave is a more apt description. How many girls are coming?"

"Fifteen."

"Fifteen!" Joanna echoed in a shocked voice.

"Nicole originally invited twenty, but only fifteen could make it."

Joanna slowly shook her head. He'd had good reason to feel panicky. With all these squealing, giddy preadolescent girls, the poor man would be certifiable by the end of the night. Either that or a prime candidate for extensive counseling.

When they arrived, the parking area outside Tanner's apartment building looked like the scene of a rock concert. There were enough parents dropping off kids to cause a minor traffic jam.

"I can walk across the street if you want to let me out here," Kristen suggested, anxiously eyeing the group of girls gathering outside the building.

"I'm going to find a parking place," Joanna said, scanning the side streets for two adjacent spaces—so that she wouldn't need to struggle to parallel park.

"You're going to find a place to leave the car? Why?" Kristen wanted to know, her voice higher pitched and more excited than usual. "You don't have to come in, if you don't want. I thought you said you were going to refinish that old chair Grandpa gave us last summer."

"I was," Joanna murmured with a short sigh, "but I have the distinct impression that Nicole's father is going to need a helping hand."

"I'm sure he doesn't, Mom. Mr. Lund is a really organized person. I'm sure he's got everything under control."

Kristen's reaction surprised Joanna. She would have expected her daughter to encourage the idea of getting the two of them together.

She finally found a place to park and they hurried across the street, Kristen apparently deep in thought.

"Actually, Mom, I think helping Mr. Lund might be a good idea," she said after a long pause. "He'll probably be grateful."

Joanna wasn't nearly as confident by this time. "I have a feeling I'm going to regret this later."

"No, you won't." Joanna could tell Kristen was about to launch into another one of her little speeches about babies, vacations and homemade cookies. Thankfully she didn't get the chance, since they'd entered the building and encountered a group of Kristen's other friends.

Tanner was standing in the doorway of his apartment, already looking frazzled when Joanna arrived. Surprise flashed through his eyes when he saw her.

"I've come to help," she announced, peeling off her jacket and pushing up the sleeves of her thin sweater. "This group is more than one parent can reasonably be expected to control."

He looked for a moment as though he wanted to fall to the ground and kiss her feet. "Bless you."

"Believe me, Tanner, you owe me for this." She glanced around at the chaos that dominated the large apartment. The girls had already formed small groups and were arguing loudly with each other over some subject of earth-shattering importance—like Adam Levine's age, or the real color of Niall Horan's hair.

"Is the pizza ready?" Joanna asked him, raising her voice in order to be heard over the din of squeals, shouts and rock music.

Tanner nodded. "It's in the kitchen. I ordered eight large ones. Do you think that'll be enough?"

Joanna rolled her eyes. "I suspect you're going to be eating leftover pizza for the next two weeks."

The girls proved her wrong. Never had Joanna seen a hungrier group. They were like school of piranha attacking a hapless victim, and within fifteen minutes everyone had eaten her fill. There were one or two slices left of four of the pizzas, but the others had vanished completely.

"It's time for a movie," Joanna decided, and while the girls voted on which film to see first Tanner started dumping dirty paper plates and pop cans into a plastic garbage sack. When the movie was finished, Joanna calculated, it would be time to go skating.

Peace reigned once Tom Cruise appeared on the television screen and Joanna joined Tanner in the bright cheery kitchen.

He was sitting dejectedly at the round table, rubbing a hand across his forehead. "I feel a headache coming on."

"It's too late for that," she said with a soft smile. "Actually I think everything is going very well. Everyone seems to be having a good time, and Nicole is a wonderful hostess."

"You do? She is?" He gave her an astonished look. "I keep having nightmares about pillow fights and lost dental appliances."

"Hey, it isn't going to happen." Not while they maintained control. "Tanner, I meant what I said about the party going well. In fact, I'm surprised at how smoothly everything is falling into place. The kids really are having a good time, and as long as we keep them busy there shouldn't be any problems."

He grinned, looking relieved. "I don't know about you, but I could use a cup of coffee."

"I'll second that."

He poured coffee into two pottery mugs and carried them to the table. Joanna sat across from him, propping her feet on the opposite chair. Sighing, she leaned back and cradled the steaming mug.

"The pizza was a good idea." He reached for a piece and shoved the box in her direction.

Now that she had a chance to think about it, Joanna realized she'd been so busy earlier, serving the girls, she hadn't managed to eat any of the pizza herself. She straightened enough to reach for a napkin and a thick slice dotted with pepperoni and spicy Italian sausage.

"What made you decide to give up your evening to help me out?" Tanner asked, watching her closely. "Kristen told Nicole that you had a hot date tonight. You were the last person I expected to see."

Joanna wasn't sure what had changed her mind about tonight and staying to help Tanner. Pity, she suspected. "If the situation were reversed, you'd lend me a hand," she replied, more interested in eating than conversation at the moment.

Tanner frowned at his pizza. "You missed what I was really asking."

"I did?"

"I was trying to be subtle about asking if you had a date tonight."

Joanna found that question odd. "Obviously I didn't."

"It isn't so obvious to me. You're a single parent, so there aren't that many evenings you can count on being free of responsibility. I would have thought you'd use this time to go out with someone special, flap your wings and that sort of thing." His frown grew darker.

"I'm too old to flap my wings," she said with a soft chuckle. "Good grief, I'm over thirty."

"So you aren't dating anyone special?"

"Tanner, you know I'm not."

"I don't know anything of the sort." Although he didn't raise his voice, Joanna could sense his disquiet.

"All right, what's up?" She didn't like the looks he was giving her. Not one bit.

"Nicole."

"Nicole?" she repeated.

"She was telling me that other day that you'd met someone recently. 'A real prince' is the phrase she used. Someone rich and handsome who was crazy about you—she claimed you were seeing a lot of this guy. Said you were falling madly in love."

Joanna dropped her feet to the floor with a loud thud and bolted upright so fast she nearly tumbled out of the chair. She was furiously chewing her pepperoni-and-sausage pizza, trying to swallow it as quickly as she could. All the while, her finger was pointing, first toward the living room where the girls were innocently watching *Top Gun* and then at Tanner who was staring at her in fascination.

"Hey, don't get angry with me," he said. "I'm only repeating what Kristen supposedly told Nicole and what Nicole told me."

She swallowed the piece of pizza in one huge lump. "They're plotting again, don't you see? I should have known something was up. It's been much too quiet lately. Kristen and Nicole are getting devious now, because the direct approach didn't work." Flustered, she started pacing the kitchen floor.

"Settle down, Joanna. We're smarter than a couple of school kids."

"That's easy for you to say." She pushed her hair away from her forehead and continued to pace. Little wonder Kristen hadn't been keen on the idea of her helping Tanner tonight. Joanna whirled around to face him. "Well, aren't you going to say something?" To her dismay, she discovered he was doing his best not to chuckle. "This isn't a laughing matter, Tanner Lund. I wish you'd take this seriously!"

"I am."

Joanna snorted softly. "You are not!"

"We're mature adults, Joanna. We aren't going to allow two children to dictate our actions."

"Is that a fact?" She braced both hands against her hips and glared at him. "I'm pleased to hear you're such a tower of strength, but I'll bet a week's pay that it wasn't your idea to have this slumber party. You probably rejected the whole thing the first time Nicole suggested it, but after having the subject of a birthday slumber party brought up thirty times in about thirty minutes you weakened, and that was when Nicole struck the fatal blow. If your daughter is anything like mine, she probably used every trick in the book to talk you into this party idea. Knowing how guilty you felt about all those business trips, I suppose Nicole brought them up ten or twelve times. And before you knew what hit you, there were fifteen little girls spending the night at your apartment."

Tanner paled.

"Am I right?" she insisted.

He shrugged and muttered disparagingly, "Close enough."

Slumping into the chair, Joanna pushed the pizza box aside and forcefully expelled her breath. "I don't mind telling you, I'm concerned about this. If Kristen and Nicole are plotting against us, then we've got to form some kind of plan of our own before they drive us out of our minds. We can't allow them to manipulate us like this."

"I think you may be right."

She eyed him hopefully. "Any suggestions?" If he was smart enough to manage a couple of thousand employees, surely he could figure out a way to keep two eleven-year-olds under control.

Slouched in his chair, his shoulders sagging, Tanner shook his head. "None. What about you?"

"Communication is the key."

"Right."

"We've got to keep in touch with each other and keep tabs on what's going on with these two. Don't believe a thing they say until we check it out with the other."

"We've got another problem, Joanna," Tanner said, looking in every direction but hers.

"What?"

"It worked."

"What worked?" she asked irritably. Why was he speaking in riddles?

"Nicole's telling me that you'd been swept off your feet by this rich guy."

"Yes?" He still wasn't making any sense.

"The purpose of that whole fabrication was to make me jealous—and it worked."

"It worked?" An icy numb feeling swept through her. Swallowing became difficult.

Tanner nodded. "I kept thinking about how much I liked you. How much I enjoyed talking to you. And then I decided that when this slumber party business was over, I was going to risk asking you out to dinner."

"But I've already told you I'm not interested in a romantic relationship. One marriage was more than enough for me."

"I don't think that's what bothered me."

"Then what did?"

It was obvious from the way his eyes darted around the room that he felt uncomfortable. "I kept thinking about another man kissing you, and frankly, Joanna, that's what bothered me most."

The kitchen suddenly went so quiet that Joanna was almost afraid to breathe. The only noise was the faint sound of the movie playing in the other room.

Joanna tried to put herself in Tanner's place, wondering how she'd feel if Kristen announced that he'd met a gorgeous blonde and was dating her. Instantly she felt her stomach muscles tighten. There wasn't the slightest doubt in Joanna's mind that the girls' trick would have worked on her, too. Just the thought of Tanner's kissing another woman produced a curious ache, a pain that couldn't be described—or denied.

"Kissing you that night was the worst thing I could have done," Tanner conceded reluctantly. "I know you don't want to talk about it. I don't blame you—"

"Tanner," she interjected in a low hesitant voice, which hardly resembled her own. "It would have worked with me, too."

His eyes were dark and piercing. "Are you certain?"

She nodded, feeling utterly defeated yet strangely excited. "I'm afraid so. What are we going to do now?"

The silence returned as they stared at one another.

"The first thing I think we should do is experiment a little," he suggested in a flat emotionless voice. Then he released a long sigh. "Almost three weeks have passed since the night we took the girls out, and we've both had plenty of time to let that kiss build in our minds. Right?"

"Right," Joanna agreed. She'd attempted to put that kiss completely out of her mind, but it hadn't worked, and there was no point in telling him otherwise.

"It seems to me," Tanner continued thoughtfully, "that we should kiss again, for the sake of research, and find out what we're dealing with here."

She didn't need him to kiss her again to know she was going to like it. The first time had been ample opportunity for her to recognise how strongly she was attracted to Tanner Lund, and she didn't need another kiss to remind her.

"Once we know, we can decide where to go from there. Agreed?"

"Okay," she said impulsively, ignoring the small voice that warned of danger.

He stood up and held out his hand. She stared at it for a moment, uncertain. "You want to kiss right now?"

"Do you know of a better time?"

She shook her head. Good grief, she couldn't believe she was doing this. Tanner stretched out his arms and she walked into them with all the finesse of tumbleweed. The way she fit so snugly, so comfortably into his embrace worried her already. And he hadn't even kissed her yet.

Tanner held her lightly, his eyes wide and curious as he stared down at her. First he cocked his head to the right, then abruptly changed his mind and moved it to the left.

Joanna's movements countered his until she was certain they looked like a pair of ostriches who couldn't make up their minds.

"Are you comfortable?" he asked, and his voice was slightly hoarse.

Joanna nodded. She wished he'd hurry up and do it before one of the girls came crashing into the kitchen and found them. With their luck, it would be either Kristen or Nicole. Or both.

"You ready?" he asked.

Joanna nodded again. He was looking at her almost anxiously as though they were waiting for an imminent explosion. And that was exactly the way it felt when Tanner's mouth settled on her, even though the kiss was infinitely gentle, his lips sliding over hers like a soft summer rain, barely touching.

They broke apart, momentarily stunned. Neither spoke, and then Tanner kissed her again, moving his mouth over her parted lips in undisguised hunger. His hand clutched the thick hair at her nape as she raised her arms and tightened them around his neck, leaning into him, absorbing his strength.

Tanner groaned softly and deepened the kiss until it threatened to consume Joanna. She met his fierce urgency with her own, arching closer to him, holding onto him with everything that was in her.

An unabating desire flared to life between them as he kissed her again and again, until they were both breathless and shaking.

"Joanna," he groaned, and dragged in several deep breaths. After taking a long moment to compose himself, he asked, "What do you think?" The question was murmured into her hair.

Joanna's chest was heaving, as though she'd been running and was desperate for oxygen. "I… I don't know," she lied, silently calling herself a coward.

"I do."

"You do?"

"Good Lord, Joanna, you taste like heaven. We're in trouble here. Deep trouble."

# Chapter Nine

The pop music at the roller-skating rink blared from huge speakers and vibrated around the room. A disc jockey announced the tunes from a glass-fronted booth and joked with the skaters as they circled the polished hardwood floor.

"I can't believe I let you talk me into this," Joanna muttered, sitting beside Tanner as she laced up her rented high-top white skates.

"I refuse to be the only one over thirty out there," he replied, but he was smiling, obviously pleased with his persuasive talents. No doubt he'd take equal pleasure in watching her fall flat on her face. It had been years since Joanna had worn a pair of roller skates. *Years*.

"It's like riding a bicycle," Tanner assured her with that maddening grin of his. "Once you know how, you never forget."

Joanna grumbled under her breath, but she was actually beginning to look forward to this. She'd always loved roller-skating as a kid, and there was something about being with Tanner that brought out the little girl in her. *And the woman*, she thought, remembering their kiss.

Nicole's friends were already skating with an ease that made Joanna envious. Slowly, cautiously, she joined the crowd circling the rink.

"Hi, Mom." Kristen zoomed past at the speed of light.

"Hi, Mrs. Parsons," Nicole shouted, following her friend.

Staying safely near the side, within easy reach of the handrail, Joanna concentrated on making her feet work properly, wheeling them back and forth as smoothly as possible. But instead of the gliding motion achieved by the others, her movements were short and jerky. She didn't acknowledge the girls' greetings with anything more than a raised hand and was slightly disconcerted to see the other skaters giving her a wide berth. They obviously recognized danger when they saw it.

Tanner glided past her, whirled around and deftly skated backward, facing Joanna. She looked up and threw him a weak smile. She should have known Tanner would be as confident on skates as he seemed to be at everything else—except slumber parties for eleven-year-old girls. Looking at him, one would think he'd been skating every day for years, although he claimed it was twenty years since he'd been inside a rink. It was clear from the expert way he soared across the floor that he didn't need to relearn anything—unlike Joanna, who felt as awkward as a newborn foal attempting to stand for the first time.

"How's it going?" he asked, with a cocky grin.

"Great. Can't you tell?" Just then, her right foot jerked out from under her and she groped desperately for the rail, managing to get a grip on it seconds before she went crashing to the floor.

Tanner was by her side at once. "You okay?"

"About as okay as anyone who has stood on the edge and looked into the deep abyss," she muttered.

"Come on, what you need is a strong hand to guide you."

Joanna snorted. "Forget it, fellow. I'll be fine in a few minutes, once I get my sea legs."

"You're sure?"

"Tanner, for heaven's sake, at least leave me with my pride intact!" Keeping anything intact at the moment was difficult, with her feet flaying wildly as she tried to pull herself back into an upright position.

"Okay, if that's what you want," he said shrugging, and sailed away from her with annoying ease.

Fifteen minutes later, Joanna felt steady enough to join the main part of the crowd circling the rink. Her movements looked a little less clumsy, a little less shaky, though she certainly wasn't in complete control.

"Hey, you're doing great," Tanner said, slowing down enough to skate beside her.

"Thanks," she said breathlessly, studying her feet in an effort to maintain her balance.

"You've got a gift for this," he teased.

She looked up at him and laughed outright. "Isn't that the truth! I wonder if I should consider a new career as a roller-skating waitress at the Pink Palace."

Amusement lifted the edge of his sensuous mouth. "Has anyone ever told you that you have an odd sense of humor?"

Looking at Tanner distracted Joanna, and her feet floundered for an instant. "Kristen does at least once a day."

Tanner chuckled. "I shouldn't laugh. Nicole tells me the same thing."

The disc jockey announced that the next song was for couples only. Joanna gave a sigh of relief and aimed her body toward the nearest exit. She could use the break; her calf muscles were already protesting the unaccustomed exercise. She didn't need roller-skating to remind her she wasn't a kid.

"How about it, Joanna?" Tanner asked, skating around her.

"How about what?"

"Skating together for the couples' dance. You and me and fifty thousand preteens sharing center stage." He offered her his hand. The lights had dimmed and a mirrored ball hanging in the middle of the ceiling cast speckled shadows over the floor.

"No way, Tanner," she muttered, ignoring his hand.

"I thought not. Oh well, I'll see if I can get Nicole to skate with her dear old dad." Effortlessly he glided toward the group of girls who stood against the wall flirtatiously challenging the boys on the other side with their eyes.

Once Joanna was safely off the rink, she found a place to sit and rest her weary bones. Within a couple of minutes, Tanner lowered himself into the chair beside her, looking chagrined.

"I got beat out by Tommy Spenser," he muttered.

Joanna couldn't help it—she was delighted. Now Tanner would understand how she'd felt when Kristen announced she didn't want her mother sitting with her at the movies. Tanner looked just as dejected as Joanna had felt then.

"It's hell when they insist on growing up, isn't it?" she said, doing her best not to smile, knowing he wouldn't appreciate it.

He heaved an expressive sigh and gave her a hopeful look before glancing out at the skating couples. "I don't suppose you'd reconsider?"

The floor was filled with kids, and Joanna knew the minute she moved onto the hardwood surface with Tanner, every eye in the place would be on them.

He seemed to read her mind, because he added, "Come on, Joanna. My ego has just suffered a near-mortal wound. I've been rejected by my own flesh and blood."

She swallowed down a comment and awkwardly rose to her feet, struggling to remain upright. "When my ego got shot to bits at the movie theatre, all you did was share your popcorn with me."

He chuckled and reached for her hand. "Don't complain. This gives me an excuse to put my arm around you again." His right arm slipped around her waist, and she tucked her left hand in his as they moved side by side. She had to admit it felt incredibly good to be this close to him. Almost as good as it had felt being in his arms for those few moments in his kitchen.

Tanner must have been thinking the same thing, because he was unusually quiet as he directed her smoothly across the floor to the strains of a romantic ballad. They'd circled the rink a couple of times when

Tanner abruptly switched position, skating backward and holding onto her as though they were dancing.

"Tanner," she said, surprise widening her eyes as he swept her into his arms. "The girls will start thinking… things if we skate like this."

"Let them."

His hands locked at the base of her spine and he pulled her close. Very close. Joanna drew a slow breath, savoring the feel of Tanner's body pressed so intimately against her own.

"Joanna, listen," he whispered. "I've been thinking."

So had she. Hard to do when she was around Tanner.

"Would it really be such a terrible thing if we were to start seeing more of each other? On a casual basis— it doesn't have to be anything serious. We're both mature adults. Neither of us is going to allow the girls to manipulate us into anything we don't want. And as far as the past is concerned, I'm not Davey and you're not Carmen."

Why, Joanna wondered, was the most important discussion she'd had in years taking place in a roller-skating rink with a top-forty hit blaring in one ear and Tanner whispering in the other? Deciding to ignore the thought, she said, "But the girls might start making assumptions, and I'm afraid we'd only end up disappointing them."

Tanner disagreed. "I feel our seeing each other might help more than it would hinder."

"How do you mean?" Joanna couldn't believe she was actually entertaining this suggestion. Entertaining was putting it mildly; her heart was doing somersaults at the prospect of seeing Tanner more often. She was thrilled, excited…and yet hesitant. The wounds Davey had inflicted went very deep.

"If we see each other more often we could include the girls, and that should lay to rest some of the fears we've had over their matchmaking efforts. And spending time with you will help satisfy Nicole's need for a strong mother figure. At the same time, I can help Kristen, by being a father figure."

"Yes, but—"

"The four of us together will give the girls a sense of belonging to a whole family," Tanner added confidently.

His arguments sounded so reasonable, so logical. Still, Joanna remained uncertain. "But I'm afraid the girls will think we're serious."

Tanner lifted his head enough to look into her eyes, and Joanna couldn't remember a time they'd ever been bluer or more intense. "I am serious."

She pressed her forehead against his collarbone and willed her body to stop trembling. Their little kissing experiment had affected her far more than she dared let him know. Until tonight, they'd both tried to disguise or deny their attraction for each other, but the kiss had exposed everything.

"I haven't stopped thinking about you from the minute we first met," he whispered, and touched his lips to her temple. "If we were anyplace else right now, I'd show you how crazy I am about you."

If they'd been anyplace else, Joanna would have let him. She wanted him to kiss her, needed him to, but she was more frightened by her reaction to this one man than she'd been by anything else in a very long while. "Tanner, I'm afraid."

"Joanna, so am I, but I can't allow fear to rule my

life." Gently he brushed the loose wisps of curls from the side of her face. His eyes studied her intently. "I didn't expect to feel this way again. I've guarded against letting this happen, but here we are, and Joanna, I don't mind telling you, I wouldn't change a thing."

Joanna closed her eyes and listened to the battle raging inside her head. She wanted so badly to give this feeling between them a chance to grow. But logic told her that if she agreed to his suggestion, she'd be making herself vulnerable again. Even worse, Tanner Lund wasn't just any man—he was wealthy and successful, the half owner of an important company. And she was just a loan officer at a small local bank.

"Joanna, at least tell me what you're feeling."

"I… I don't know," she hedged, still uncertain.

He gripped her hand and pressed it over his heart, holding it there. "Just feel what you do to me."

Her own heart seemed about to hammer its way out of her chest. "You do the same thing to me."

He smiled ever so gently. "I know."

The music came to an end and the lights brightened. Reluctantly Tanner and Joanna broke apart, but he still kept her close to his side, tucking his arm around her waist.

"You haven't answered me, Joanna. I'm not going to hurt you, you know. We'll take it nice and easy at first and see how things develop."

Joanna's throat felt constricted, and she couldn't answer him one way or the other, although it was clear that he was waiting for her to make a decision.

"We've got something good between us," he continued, "and I don't want to just throw it away. I think we should find out whether this can last."

He wouldn't hurt her intentionally, Joanna realised, but the probability of her walking away unscathed from a relationship with this man was remote.

"What do you think?" he pressed.

She couldn't refuse him. "Maybe we should give it a try," she said after a long pause.

Tanner gazed down on her, bathing her in the warmth of his smile. "Neither of us is going to be sorry."

Joanna wasn't nearly as confident. She glanced away and happened to notice Kristen and Nicole. "Uh-oh," she murmured.

"What's wrong?"

"I just saw Kristen zoom over to Nicole and whisper into her ear. Then they hugged each other like long-lost sisters."

"I can deal with it if you can," he said, squeezing her hand.

Tanner's certainty lent her courage. "Then so can I."

# *Chapter Ten*

Joanna didn't sleep well that night, or the following two. Tanner had suggested they meet for dinner the next weekend. It seemed an eternity, but there were several problems at work that demanded his attention. She felt as disappointed as he sounded that their first real date wouldn't take place for a week.

Joanna wished he hadn't given her so much time to think about it. If they'd been able to casually go to a movie the afternoon following the slumber party, she wouldn't have been so nervous about it.

When she arrived at work Monday morning, her brain was so muddled she felt as though she were walking in a fog. Twice during the weekend she'd almost called Tanner to suggest they call the whole thing off.

"Morning," her boss murmured absently, hardly

looking up from the newspaper. "How was your week-end?"

"Exciting," Joanna told Robin, tucking her purse into the bottom drawer of her desk. "I went roller-skating with fifteen eleven-year-old girls."

"Sounds adventurous," Robin said, his gaze never leaving the paper.

Joanna poured herself a cup of coffee and carried it to her desk to drink black. The way she was feeling, she knew she'd need something strong to clear her head.

"I don't suppose you've been following what's happening at Spokane Aluminum?" Robin asked, refilling his own coffee cup.

It was a good thing Joanna had set her mug down when she did, otherwise it would have tumbled from her fingers. "Spokane Aluminum?" she echoed.

"Yes." Robin sat on the edge of her desk, allowing one leg to dangle. "There's another news item in the paper this morning on Tanner Lund. Six months ago, he bought out half the company from John Becky. I'm sure you've heard of John Becky?"

"Of…course."

"Apparently Lund came into this company and breathed new life into its sagging foreign sales. He took over management himself and has completely changed the company's direction…all for the better. I've heard nothing but good about this guy. Every time I turn around, I'm either reading how great he is, or hearing people talk about him. Take my word, Tanner Lund is a man who's going places."

Joanna couldn't agree more. And she knew for a fact where he was going Saturday night. He was taking her to dinner.

\* \* \*

"Mr. Lund's here," Kristen announced the following Saturday, opening Joanna's bedroom door. "And does he ever look handsome!"

A dinner date. A simple dinner date, and Joanna was more nervous than a college graduate applying for her first job. She smoothed her hand down her red-and-white flowered dress and held in her breath so long her lungs ached.

Kristen rolled her eyes. "You look fine, Mom."

"I do?"

"As nice as Mr. Lund."

For good measure, Joanna paused long enough to dab more cologne behind her ears, then she squared her shoulders and turned to face the long hallway that led to the living room. "Okay, I'm ready."

Kristen threw open the bedroom door as though she expected royalty to emerge. By the time Joanna had walked down the hallway to the living room where Tanner was waiting, her heart was pounding and her hands were shaking. Kristen was right. Tanner looked marvellous in a three-piece suit and silk tie. He smiled when she came into the room, and stood up, gazing at her with an expression of undisguised delight.

"Hi."

"Hi." Their eyes met, and everything else faded away. Just seeing him again made Joanna's pulse leap into overdrive. No week had ever dragged more.

"Sally's got the phone number of the restaurant, and her mother said it was fine if she stayed here late," Kristen said, standing between them and glancing from one adult to the other. "I don't have any plans myself, so you two feel free to stay out as long as you want."

"Sally?" Joanna forced herself to glance at the baby-sitter.

"Yes, Mrs. Parsons?"

"There's salad and leftover spaghetti in the refrigerator for dinner, and some microwave popcorn in the cupboard for later."

"Okay."

"I won't be too late."

"But, Mom," Kristen cut in, a slight whine in her voice, "I just got done telling you that it'd be fine if you stayed out till the wee hours of the morning."

"We'll be back before midnight," Joanna informed the babysitter, ignoring Kristen.

"Okay," the girl said, as Kristen sighed expressively. "Have a good time."

Tanner escorted Joanna out to the car, which was parked in front of the house, and opened the passenger door. He paused, his hand still resting on her shoulder. "I'd like to kiss you now, but we have an audience," he said, nodding toward the house.

Joanna chanced a look and discovered Kristen standing in the living-room window, holding aside the curtain and watching them intently. No doubt she was memorising everything they said and did to report back to Nicole.

"I couldn't believe it when she agreed to let Sally come over. She's of the opinion lately that she's old enough to stay by herself."

"Nicole claims the same thing, but she didn't raise any objections about having a babysitter, either."

"I guess we should count our blessings."

Tanner drove to an expensive downtown restaurant overlooking the Spokane River, in the heart of the city.

Joanna's mouth was dry and her palms sweaty when the valet opened her door and helped her out. She'd never eaten at such a luxurious place in her life. She'd heard that their prices were outrageous. The amount Tanner intended to spend on one meal would probably outfit Kristen for an entire school year. Joanna felt faint at the very idea.

"Chez Michel is an exceptionally nice restaurant, Tanner, if you get my drift," she muttered under her breath after he handed the car keys to the valet. As a newcomer to town, he might not have been aware of just how expensive this place actually was.

"Yes, that's why I chose it," he said nonchalantly. "I was quite pleased with the food and the service when I was here a few weeks ago." He glanced at Joanna and her discomfort must have shown. "Consider it a small token of my appreciation for your help with Nicole's birthday party," he added, offering her one of his bone-melting smiles.

Joanna would have been more than content to eat at Denny's, and that thought reminded her again of how different they were.

She wished now that she'd worn something a little more elegant. The waiters seemed to be better dressed than she was. For that matter, so were the menus.

They were escorted to a table with an unobstructed view of the river. The maître d' held out Joanna's chair and seated her with flair. The first thing she noticed was the setting of silverware, with its bewildering array of forks, knives and spoons. After the maître d' left, she leaned forward and whispered to Tanner, "I've never eaten at a place that uses three teaspoons."

"Oh, quit complaining."

"I'm not, but if I embarrass you and use the wrong fork, don't blame me."

Unconcerned, Tanner chuckled and reached for the shiny gold menu.

Apparently Chez Michel believed in leisurely dining, because nearly two hours had passed by the time they were served their after-dinner coffee. The entire meal was everything Joanna could have hoped for, and more. The food was exceptional, but Joanna considered Tanner's company the best part of the evening. She'd never felt this much at ease with a man before. He made her smile, but he challenged her ideas, too. They talked about the girls and about the demands of being a parent. They discussed Joanna's career goals and Tanner's plans for his company. They covered a lot of different subjects, but didn't focus their conversation on any one.

Now that the meal was over, Joanna was reluctant to see the evening end. She lifted the delicate china cup, admiring its pattern, and took a sip of fragrant coffee. She paused, her cup raised halfway to her mouth, when she noticed Tanner staring at her. "What's wrong?" she asked, fearing part of her dessert was on her nose or something equally disastrous.

"Nothing."

"Then why are you looking at me like that?"

Tanner relaxed, leaned back in his chair, and grinned. "I'm sorry. I was just thinking how lovely you are, and how pleased I am that we met. It seems nothing's been the same since. I never thought a woman could make me feel the way you do, Joanna."

She looked quickly down, feeling a sudden shyness—and a wonderful warmth. Her life had changed, too, and she wasn't sure she could ever go back to the way things had been before. She was dreaming again, feeling again, trusting again, and it felt so good. And so frightening.

"I'm pleased, too," was her only comment.

"You know what the girls are thinking, don't you?"

Joanna could well imagine. No doubt those two would have them engaged after one dinner date. "They're probably expecting us to announce our marriage plans tomorrow morning," Joanna said, trying to make a joke of it.

"To be honest, I find some aspects of married life appealing."

Joanna smiled and narrowed her eyes suspiciously. "Come on, Tanner, just how much wine have you had?"

"Obviously too much, now that I think about it," he said, grinning. Then his face sobered. "All kidding aside, I want you to know how much I enjoy your company. Every time I'm with you, I come away feeling good about life—you make me laugh again."

"I'd make anyone laugh," she said, "especially if I'm wearing a pair of roller skates." She didn't know where their conversation was leading, but the fact that Tanner spoke so openly and honestly about the promise of their relationship completely unnerved her. She felt exactly the same things, but didn't have the courage to voice them.

"I'm glad you agreed we should start seeing each other," Tanner continued.

"Me, too." But she fervently hoped her mother wouldn't hear about it, although Kristen had probably phoned her grandmother the minute Joanna was out the door. Lowering her gaze, Joanna discovered that a bread crumb on the linen tablecloth had become utterly absorbing. She carefully brushed it onto the floor, an inch at a time. "It's worked out fine...so far. Us dating, I mean." It was more than fine. And now he was telling her how she'd brightened his life, as though *he* was the lucky one. That someone like Tanner Lund would ever want to date her still astonished Joanna.

She gazed up at him, her heart shining through her eyes, telling him without words what she was feeling.

Tanner briefly shut his eyes. "Joanna, for heaven's sake, don't look at me like that."

"Like what?"

"Like...that."

"I think you should kiss me," Joanna announced, once again staring down at the tablecloth. The instant the words slipped out she longed to take them back. She couldn't believe she'd said something like that to him.

"I beg your pardon?"

"Never mind," she said quickly, grateful he hadn't heard her.

He had. "Kiss you? Now? Here?"

Joanna shook her head, forcing a smile. "Forget I said that. It just slipped out. Sometimes my mouth disconnects itself from my brain."

Tanner didn't remove his gaze from hers as he raised his hand. Their waiter appeared almost immediately, and still looking at Joanna, he muttered, "Check, please."

"Right away, sir."

They were out of the restaurant so fast Joanna's head was spinning. Once they were seated in the car, Tanner paused, frowning, his hands clenched on the steering wheel.

"What's the matter?" Joanna asked anxiously.

"We goofed. We should have shared a babysitter."

The thought had fleetingly entered her mind earlier, but she'd discounted the idea because she didn't want to encourage the girls' scheming.

"I can't take you back to my place because Nicole will be all over us with questions, and it'll probably be the same story at your house with Kristen."

"You're right." Besides, her daughter would be sorely disappointed if they showed up this early. It wasn't even close to midnight.

"Just where am I supposed to kiss you, Joanna Parsons?"

Oh Lord, he'd taken her seriously. "Tanner...it was a joke."

He ignored her comment. "I don't know of a single lookout point in the city."

"Tanner, please." Her voice rose in embarrassment, and she could feel herself blushing.

Tanner leaned over and brushed his lips against her cheek. "I've got an idea for something we can do, but don't laugh."

"An idea? What?"

"You'll see soon enough." He eased his car onto the street and drove quickly through the city to the freeway on-ramp and didn't exit until they were well into the suburbs.

"Tanner?" Joanna said, looking around her at the unfamiliar streets. "What's out here?" Almost as soon as she'd spoken a huge white screen appeared in the distance. "A drive-in?" she whispered in disbelief.

"Have you got any better ideas?"

"Not a one." Joanna chuckled; she couldn't help it.

He was taking her to a drive-in movie just so he could kiss her.

"I can't guarantee this movie. This is its opening weekend, and if I remember the ad correctly, they're showing something with lots of blood and gore."

"As long as it isn't *Teen Massacre*. Kristen would never forgive me if I saw it when she hadn't."

"If the truth be known, I don't plan to watch a whole lot of the movie." He darted an exaggerated leer in her direction and wiggled his eyebrows suggestively.

Joanna returned his look by demurely fluttering her lashes. "I don't know if my mother would approve of my going to a drive-in on a first date."

"With good reason," Tanner retorted. "Especially if she knew what I had in mind."

Although the weather had been mild and the sky was cloudless and clear, only a few cars were scattered across the wide lot.

Tanner parked as far away from the others as possible. He connected the speaker, but turned the volume so low it was almost inaudible. When he'd finished, he placed his arm around Joanna's shoulders, pulling her closer.

"Come here, woman."

Joanna leaned her head against his shoulder and pretended to be interested in the cartoon characters leaping across the large screen. Her stomach was playing jumping jacks with the dinner she'd just eaten.

"Joanna?" His voice was low and seductive.

She tilted her head to meet his gaze, and his eyes moved slowly over her upturned face, searing her with their intensity. The openness of his desire stole her breath away. Her heart was pounding, although he hadn't even kissed her yet. One hungry look from Tanner and she was melting at his feet.

Her first thought was to crack a joke. That had saved her in the past, but whatever she might have said or done was lost as Tanner lowered his mouth and tantalized the edges of her trembling lips, teasing her with soft, tempting nibbles, making her ache all the way to her toes for his kiss. Instinctively her fingers slid up his chest and around the back of his neck. Tanner created such an overwhelming need in her that she felt both humble and elated at the same time. When her hands tightened around his neck, his mouth hardened into firm possession.

Joanna thought she'd drown in the sensations that flooded her. She hadn't felt this kind of longing in years, and she trembled with the wonder of it. Tanner had awakened the deep womanly part of her that had lain dormant for so long. And suddenly she felt all that time without love come rushing up at her, overtaking her. Years of regret, years of doubt, years of rejection all pressed so heavily on her heart that she could barely breathe.

A sob was ripped from her throat, and the sound of it broke them apart. Tears she couldn't explain flooded her eyes and ran unheeded down her face.

"Joanna, what's wrong? Did I hurt you?"

She tried to break away, but Tanner wouldn't let her go. He brushed the hair from her face and tilted her head to lift her eyes to his, but she resisted.

He must have felt the wetness on her face, because he paused and murmured, "You're crying," in a tone that sounded as shocked as she felt. "Dear Lord, what did I do?"

Wildly she shook her head, unable to speak even if she'd been able to find the words to explain.

"Joanna, tell me, please."

"J-just hold me." Even saying that much required all her reserves of strength.

He did as she asked, wrapping his arms completely around her, kissing the crown of her head as she buried herself in his strong, solid warmth.

Still, the tears refused to stop, no matter how hard she tried to make them. They flooded her face and seemed to come from the deepest part of her.

"I can't believe I'm doing this," she said between sobs. "Oh, Tanner, I feel like such a fool."

"Go ahead and cry, Joanna. I understand."

"You do? Good. You can explain it to me."

She could feel his smile as he kissed the corner of her eye. She moaned a little and he lowered his lips to her cheek, then her chin, and when she couldn't bear it any longer, she turned her face, her mouth seeking his. Tanner didn't disappoint her, kissing her gently again and again until she was certain her heart would stop beating if he ever stopped holding her and kissing her.

"Good Lord, Joanna," he whispered after a while, gently extricating himself from her arms and leaning against the car seat, his eyes closed. His face was a picture of desire struggling for restraint. He drew in several deep breaths.

Joanna's tears had long since dried on her face and now her cheeks flamed with confusion and remorse.

A heavy silence fell between them. Joanna searched frantically for something witty to say to break the terrible tension.

"Joanna, listen—"

"No, let me speak first," she broke in, then hesitated. Now that she had his attention, she didn't know what to say. "I'm sorry, Tanner, really sorry. I don't know what came over me, but you weren't the one responsible for my tears. Well, no, you were, but not the way you think."

"Joanna, please," he said and his hands bracketed her face. "Don't be embarrassed by the tears. Believe me when I say I'm feeling the same things you are, only they come out in different ways."

Joanna stared up at him, not sure he could possibly understand.

"It's been so long for you—it has for me, too," Tanner went on. "I feel like a teenager again. And the drive-in has nothing to do with it."

Her lips trembled with the effort to smile. Tanner leaned his forehead against hers. "We need to take this slow. Very, very slow."

That was a fine thing for him to say, considering they'd been as hot as torches for each other a few minutes ago. If they continued at this rate, they'd end up in bed together by the first of the week.

"I've got a company party in a couple of weeks—I want you there with me. Will you do that?"

Joanna nodded.

Tanner drew her closer to his side and she tucked her head against his chest. His hand stroked her shoulder, as he kissed the top of her head.

"You're awfully quiet," he said after several minutes. "What are you thinking?"

Joanna sighed and snuggled closer, looping one arm around his middle. Her free hand was laced with his. "It just occurred to me that for the first time in my life I've met a real prince. Up until now, all I've done is make a few frogs happy."

# Chapter Eleven

Kneeling on the polished linoleum floor of the kitchen, Joanna held her breath and tentatively poked her head inside the foam-covered oven. Sharp, lemon-scented fumes made her grimace as she dragged the wet sponge along the sides, peeling away a layer of blackened crust. She'd felt unusually ambitious for a Saturday and had worked in the yard earlier, planning her garden. When she'd finished that, she'd decided to tackle the oven, not questioning where this burst of energy had come from. Spring was in the air, but instead of turning her fancy to thoughts of love, it filled her mind with zucchini seeds and rows of tomato seedlings.

"I'm leaving now, Mom," Kristen called from behind her.

Joanna jerked her head free, gulped some fresh air and twisted toward her daughter. "What time will you

be through at the library?" Kristen and Nicole were
working together on a school project, and although they
complained about having to do research, they'd come
to enjoy it. Their biggest surprise was discovering all
the cute junior-high boys who sometimes visited the library. In Kristen's words, it was an untapped gold mine.

"I don't know when we'll be through, but I'll call.
And remember, Nicole is coming over afterwards."

"I remember."

Kristen hesitated, then asked, "When are you going
out with Mr. Lund again?"

Joanna glanced over at the calendar. "Next weekend.
We're attending a dinner party his company's sponsoring."

"Oh."

Joanna rubbed her forearm across her cheek, and
glanced suspiciously at her daughter. "What does that
mean?"

"What?"

"That little 'oh.'"

Kristen shrugged. "Nothing… It's just that you're not
seeing him as often as Nicole and I think you should.
You like Mr. Lund, don't you?"

That was putting it mildly. "He's very nice," Joanna
said cautiously. If she admitted to anything beyond a casual attraction, Kristen would assume much more. Joanna
wanted her relationship with Tanner to progress slowly,
one careful step at a time, not in giant leaps—though
slow and careful didn't exactly describe what had happened so far!

"Nice?" Kristen exclaimed.

Her daughter's outburst caught Joanna by surprise.

"Is that all you can say about Mr. Lund?" Kristen
asked, hands on her hips. "I've given the matter serious

consideration and I think he's a whole lot more than just nice. Really, Mother."

Taking a deep breath, Joanna plunged her head back inside the oven, swiping her sponge furiously against the sides.

"Are you going to ignore me?" Kristen demanded.

Joanna emerged again, gasped and looked straight at her daughter. "Yes. Unless you want to volunteer to clean the oven yourself."

"I would, but I have to go to the library with Nicole."

Joanna noted the soft regret that filled her daughter's voice and gave her a derisive snort. The kid actually sounded sorry that she wouldn't be there to do her part. Kristen was a genius at getting out of work, and she always managed to give the impression of really wishing she could help her mother—if only she could fit it into her busy schedule.

A car horn beeped out front. "That's Mr. Lund," Kristen said, glancing toward the living room. "I'll give you a call when we're done."

"Okay, honey. Have a good time."

"I will."

With form an Olympic sprinter would envy, Kristen tore out of the kitchen. Two seconds later, the front door slammed. Joanna was only mildly disappointed that Tanner hadn't stopped in to chat. He'd phoned earlier and explained that after he dropped the girls off at the library, he was driving to the office for a couple of hours. An unexpected problem had arisen, and he needed to deal with it right away.

Actually Joanna had to admit she was more grateful than disappointed that Tanner hadn't stopped in. It didn't look as though she'd get a chance to see him before the company party. She needed this short separation to pull together her reserves. Following their dinner date and the drive-in movie afterward, Joanna felt dangerously close to falling in love with Tanner. Every time he came to mind, and that was practically every minute of every day, a rush of warmth and happiness followed. Without too much trouble, she could envision them finding a lifetime of happiness together. For the first time since her divorce she allowed herself the luxury of dreaming again, and although the prospect of remarriage excited and thrilled her, it also terrified her.

Fifteen minutes later, with perspiration beaded on her forehead and upper lip, Joanna heaved a sigh and sat back on her heels. The hair she'd so neatly tucked inside a scarf and tied at the back of her head, had fallen loose. She swiped a grimy hand at the auburn curls that hung limply over her eyes and ears. It was all worth it, though, since the gray-speckled sides of the oven, which had been encrusted with black grime, were now clearly visible and shining.

Joanna emptied the bucket of dirty water and hauled a fresh one back to wipe the oven one last time. She'd just knelt down when the doorbell chimed.

"Great," she muttered under her breath, casting a glance at herself. She looked like something that had crawled out of the bog in some horror movie. Pasting a smile on her face, she peeled off her rubber gloves and hurried to the door.

"Davey!" Finding her ex-husband standing on the porch was enough of a shock to knock the breath from Joanna's lungs.

"May I come in?"

"Of course." Flustered, she ran her hand through her

hair and stepped aside to allow him to pass. He looked good—really good—but then Davey had never lacked in the looks department. From the expensive cut of his three-piece suit, she could tell that his real-estate business must be doing well, and of course that was precisely the impression he wanted her to have. She was pleased for him; she'd never wished him ill. They'd gone their separate ways, and although both the marriage and the divorce had devastated Joanna, she shared a beautiful child with this man. If he had come by to tell her how successful he was, well, she'd just smile and let him.

"It's good to see you, Joanna."

"You, too. What brings you to town?" She struggled to keep her voice even and controlled, hoping to hide her discomfort at being caught unawares.

"I'm attending a conference downtown. I apologize for dropping in unexpectedly like this, but since I was going to be in Spokane, I thought I'd stop in and see how you and Kristen are doing."

"I wish you'd phoned first. Kristen's at the library." Joanna wasn't fooled—Davey hadn't come to see their daughter, although he meant Joanna to think so. It was all part of the game he played with her, wanting her to believe that their divorce had hurt him badly. Not calling to let her know he planned to visit was an attempt to catch her off guard and completely unprepared—which, of course, she was. Joanna knew Davey, knew him well. He'd often tried to manipulate her this way.

"I should have called, but I didn't know if I'd have the time, and I didn't want to disappoint you if I found I couldn't slip away."

Joanna didn't believe that for a minute. It wouldn't have taken him much time or trouble to phone before he left the hotel. But she didn't mention the fact, couldn't see that it would have done any good.

"Come in and have some coffee." She led him into the kitchen and poured him a mug, automatically adding the sugar and cream she knew he used. She handed it to him and was rewarded with a dazzling smile. When he wanted, Davey Parsons could be charming, attentive and generous. The confusing thing about her ex-husband was that he wasn't all bad. He'd gravely wounded her with his unfaithfulness, but in his own way he'd loved her and Kristen—as much as he could possibly love anybody beyond himself. It had taken Joanna a good many years to distance herself enough to appreciate his good points and to forgive him for the pain he'd caused her.

"You've got a nice place here," he commented, casually glancing around the kitchen. "How long have you lived here now?"

"Seven months."

"How's Kristen?"

Joanna was relieved that the conversation had moved to the only subject they still had in common—their daughter. She talked for fifteen minutes nonstop, telling him about the talent show and the other activities Kristen had been involved in since the last time she'd seen her father.

Davey listened and laughed, and then his gaze softened as he studied Joanna. "You're looking wonderful."

She grinned ruefully. "Sure I am," she scoffed. "I've just finished working in the yard and cleaning the oven."

"I wondered about the lemon perfume you were wearing."

They both laughed. Davey started to tease her about their early years together and some of the experimental meals she'd cooked and expected him to eat and praise. Joanna let him and even enjoyed his comments, for Davey could be warm and funny when he chose. Kristen had inherited her friendly, easygoing confidence from her father.

The doorbell chimed and still chuckling, Joanna stood up. "It's probably one of the neighborhood kids. I'll just be a minute." She never ceased to be astonished at how easy it was to be with Davey. He'd ripped her heart in two, lied to her repeatedly, cheated on her and still she couldn't be around him and not laugh. It always took him a few minutes to conquer her reserve, but he never failed. She was mature enough to recognise her ex-husband's faults, yet appreciate his redeeming qualities.

For the second time that day, Joanna was surprised by the man who stood on her front porch. "Tanner."

"Hi," he said with a sheepish grin. "The girls got off okay and I thought I'd stop in for a cup of coffee before heading to the office." His eyes smiled softly into hers. "I heard you laughing from out here. Do you have company? Should I come back later?"

"N-no, come in," she said, her pulse beating as hard and loud as jungle drums. Lowering her eyes, she automatically moved aside. He walked into the living room and paused, then raised his hand and gently touched her cheek in a gesture so loving that Joanna longed to fall into his arms. Now that he was here, she found herself craving some time alone with him.

Tanner's gaze reached out to her, but Joanna had trouble meeting it. A frown started to form, and his eyes clouded. "This is a bad time, isn't it?"

"No...not really." When she turned around, Davey

was standing in the kitchen doorway watching them. The smile she'd been wearing felt shaky as she stood between the two men and made the introductions. "Davey, this is Tanner Lund. Tanner, this is Davey—Kristen's father."

For a moment, the two men glared at each other like angry bears who had claimed territory and were prepared to do battle to protect what was theirs. When they stepped towards each other, Joanna held her breath for fear neither one would make the effort to be civil.

Stunned, she watched as they exchanged handshakes and enthusiastic greetings.

"Davey's in town for a real-estate conference and thought he'd stop in to see Kristen," Joanna explained, her words coming out in such a rush that they nearly stumbled over themselves.

"I came to see you, too, Joanna," Davey added in a low sultry voice that suggested he had more on his mind than a chat over a cup of coffee.

She flashed him a heated look before marching into the kitchen, closely followed by both men. She walked straight to the cupboard, bringing down another cup, then poured Tanner's coffee and delivered it to the table.

"Kristen and my daughter are at the library," Tanner announced in a perfectly friendly voice, but Joanna heard the undercurrents even if Davey didn't.

"Joanna told me," Davey returned.

The two men remained standing, smiling at each other. Tanner took a seat first, and Davey promptly did the same.

"What do you do?" her ex-husband asked.

"I own half of Spokane Aluminum."

It was apparent to Joanna that Davey hadn't even

bothered to listen to Tanner's reply because he immediately fired back in an aggressive tone, "I recently opened my own real-estate brokerage and have plans to expand within the next couple of years." He announced his success with a cocky slant to his mouth.

Watching the change in Davey's features as Tanner's identity began to sink in was so comical that Joanna nearly laughed out loud. Davey's mouth sagged open, and his eyes flew from Joanna to Tanner and then back to Joanna.

"Spokane Aluminum," Davey repeated slowly, his face unusually pale. "I seem to remember reading something about John Becky taking on a partner."

Joanna almost felt sorry for Davey. "Kristen and Tanner's daughter, Nicole, are best friends. They were in the Valentine's Day show together—the one I was telling you about…"

To his credit, Davey regrouped quickly. "She gets all that performing talent from you."

"Oh, hardly," Joanna countered, denying it with a vigorous shake of her head. Of the two of them, Davey was the entertainer—crowds had never intimidated him. He could walk into a room full of strangers, and anyone who didn't know better would end up thinking Davey Parsons was his best friend.

"With the girls being so close, it seemed only natural for Joanna and me to start dating," Tanner said, turning to smile warmly at Joanna.

"I see," Davey answered. He didn't appear to have recovered from Tanner's first announcement.

"I sincerely hope you do understand," Tanner returned, all pretence of friendliness dropped.

Joanna resisted rolling her eyes toward the ceiling.

Both of them were behaving like immature children, battling with looks and words as if she were a prize to be awarded the victor.

"I suppose I'd better think about heading out," Davey said after several awkward moments had passed. He stood up, noticeably eager to make his escape.

As a polite hostess, Joanna stood when Davey did. "I'll walk you to the door."

He sent Tanner a wary smile. "That's not necessary."

"Of course it is," Joanna countered.

To her dismay, Tanner followed them and stood conspicuously in the background while Davey made arrangements to phone Kristen later that evening. The whole time Davey was speaking, Joanna could feel Tanner's eyes burning into her back. She didn't know why he'd insisted on following her to the door. It was like saying he couldn't trust her not to fall into Davey's arms the minute he was out of sight, and that irritated her no end.

Once her ex-husband had left, she closed the door and whirled around to face Tanner. The questions were jammed in her mind. They'd only gone out on one date, for heaven's sake, and here he was, acting as though... as though they were engaged.

"I thought he broke your heart," Tanner said, in a cutting voice.

Joanna debated whether or not to answer him, then decided it would be best to clear the air. "He did."

"I heard you laughing when I rang the doorbell. Do you often have such a good time with men you're supposed to hate?"

"I don't hate Davey."

"Believe me, I can tell."

"Tanner, what's wrong with you?" That was a silly question, and she regretted asking it immediately. She already knew what was troubling Tanner. He was jealous. And angry. And hurt.

"Wrong with me?" He tossed the words back at her. "Nothing's wrong with me. I happen to stumble upon the woman I'm involved with cozying up to her ex-husband, and I don't mind telling you I'm upset. But nothing's wrong with me. Not one damn thing. If there's something wrong with anyone, it's you, lady."

Joanna held tightly onto her patience. "Before we start arguing, let's sit down and talk this out." She led him back into the kitchen, then took Davey's empty coffee mug and placed it in the sink, removing all evidence of his brief visit. She searched for a way to reassure Tanner that Davey meant nothing to her anymore. But she had to explain that she and her ex-husband weren't enemies, either; they couldn't be for Kristen's sake.

"First of all," she said, as evenly as her pounding heart would allow, "I could never hate Davey the way you seem to think I should. As far as I'm concerned, that would only be counterproductive. The people who would end up suffering are Kristen and me. Davey is incapable of being faithful to one woman, but he'll always be Kristen's father, and if for no other reason than that, I prefer to remain on friendly terms with him."

"But he cheated on you...used you."

"Yes." She couldn't deny it. "But, Tanner, I lived a lot of years with Davey. He's not all bad—no one is— and scattered between all the bad times were a few good ones. We're divorced now. What good would it do to harbor ill will toward him? None that I can see."

"He let it be known from the moment I walked into

this house that he could have you back any time he wanted."

Joanna wasn't blind; she'd recognized the looks Davey had given Tanner, and the insinuations. "He'd like to believe that. It helps him deal with his ego."

"And you let him?"

"Not the way you're implying."

Tanner mulled that over for a few moments. "How often does he casually drop in unannounced like this?"

She hesitated, wondering whether she should answer his question. His tone had softened, but he was obviously still angry. She could sympathize, but she didn't like having to defend herself or her attitude toward Davey. "I haven't seen him in over a year. This is the first time he's been to the house."

Tanner's hands gripped the coffee mug so tightly that Joanna was amazed it remained intact. "You still love him, don't you?"

The question hit her square between the eyes. Her mouth opened and closed several times as she struggled for the words to deny it. Then she realized she couldn't. Lying to Tanner about this would be simple enough and it would keep the peace, but it would wrong them both. "I suppose in a way I do," she began slowly. "He's the father of my child. He was my first love, Tanner. And the only lover I've ever had. Although I'd like to tell you I don't feel a thing for him, I can't do that and be completely honest. But please, try to understand—"

"You don't need to say anything more." He stood abruptly, his back stiff. "I appreciate the fact that you told me the truth. I won't waste any more of your time. I wish you and Kristen a good life." With that he stalked out of the room, headed for the door.

Joanna was shocked. "Tanner...you make it sound like I'll never see you again."

"I think that would be best for everyone concerned," he replied, without looking at her.

"But...that's silly. Nothing's changed." She snapped her mouth closed. If Tanner wanted to act so childishly and ruin everything, she wasn't about to argue with him. He was the one who insisted they had something special, something so good they shouldn't throw it away because of their fears. And now he was acting like this! Fine. If that was the way he wanted it. It was better to find out how unreasonable he could be before anything serious developed between them. Better to discover now how quick-tempered he could be, how hurtful.

"I have no intention of becoming involved with a woman who's still in love with her loser of an ex-husband," he announced, his hands clenched at his sides. His voice was calm, but she recognized the tension in it. And the resolve.

Unable to restrain her anger any longer, Joanna marched across the room and threw open the front door. "Smart move, Tanner," she said, her words coated with sarcasm. "You made a terrible mistake getting involved with a woman who refuses to hate." Now that she had a better look at him, she decided he wasn't a prince after all, only another frog.

Tanner didn't say a word as he walked past her, his strides filled with purpose. She closed the door and leaned against it, needing the support. Tears burned in her eyes and clogged her throat, but she held her head high and hurried back into the kitchen, determined not to give in to the powerful emotions that racked her, body and soul.

She finished cleaning up the kitchen, and took a long hot shower afterward. Then she sat quietly at the table, waiting for Kristen to phone so she could pick up the two girls. The call came a half hour later, but by that time she'd already reached for the cookies, bent on self-destruction.

On the way home from the library, Joanna stopped off at McDonald's and bought the girls cheeseburgers and chocolate milk shakes to take home for dinner. Her mind was filled with doubts. In retrospect, she wished she'd done a better job of explaining things to Tanner. The thought of never seeing him again was almost too painful to endure.

"Aren't you going to order anything, Mom?" Kristen asked, surprised.

"Not tonight." Somewhere deep inside, Joanna found the energy to smile.

She managed to maintain a lighthearted facade while Kristen and Nicole ate their dinner and chattered about the boys they'd seen at the library and how they were going to shock Mrs. Andrews with their well-researched report.

"Are you feeling okay?" Kristen asked, pausing in midsentence.

"Sure," Joanna lied, looking for something to occupy her hands. She settled for briskly wiping down the kitchen counters. Actually, she felt sick to her stomach, but she couldn't blame Tanner; she'd done that to herself with all those stupid cookies.

It was when she was putting the girls' empty McDonald's containers in the garbage that the silly tears threatened to spill over. She did her best to hide them and quickly carried out the trash. Nicole went to get her

MP3 player from Kristen's bedroom, but Kristen followed her mother outside.

"Mom, what's wrong?"

"Nothing, sweetheart."

"You have tears in your eyes."

"It's nothing."

"You never cry," Kristen insisted.

"Something must have got into my eye to make it tear like this," she said, shaking her head. The effort to smile was too much for her. She straightened and placed her hands on Kristen's shoulders, then took a deep breath. "I don't want you to be disappointed if I don't see Mr. Lund again."

"He did this?" Kristen demanded, in a high shocked voice.

"No," Joanna countered immediately. "I already told you, I got something in my eye."

Kristen studied her with a frown, and Joanna tried to meet her daughter's gaze. If she was fool enough to make herself vulnerable to a man again, then she deserved this pain. She'd known better than to get involved with Tanner, but her heart had refused to listen.

A couple of hours later, Tanner arrived to pick up Nicole. Joanna let Kristen answer the door and stayed in the kitchen, pretending to be occupied there.

When the door swung open, Joanna assumed it was her daughter and asked, "Did Nicole get off all right?"

"Not yet."

Joanna jerked away from the sink at the husky sound of Tanner's voice. "Where are the girls?"

"In Kristen's room. I want to talk to you."

"I can't see how that would do much good."

"I've reconsidered."

"Bravo for you. Unfortunately so have I. You're absolutely right about it being better all around if we don't see each other again."

Tanner dragged his fingers through his hair and stalked to the other side of the room. "Okay, I'll admit it. I was jealous as hell when I walked in and found you having coffee with Davey. I felt you were treating him like some conquering hero returned from the war."

"Oh, honestly, it wasn't anything like that."

"You were laughing and smiling."

"Grievous sins, I'm sure."

Tanner clamped down his jaw so hard that the sides of his face went white. "All I can do is apologise, Joanna. I've already made a fool of myself over one woman who loved someone else, and frankly that caused me enough grief. I'm not looking to repeat the mistake with you."

A strained silence fell between them.

"I thought I could walk away from you and not feel any regrets, but I was wrong," he continued a moment later. "I haven't stopped thinking about you all afternoon. Maybe I overreacted. Maybe I behaved like a jealous fool."

"Maybe?" Joanna challenged. "Maybe? You were unreasonable and hurtful and…and I ate a whole row of Oreo cookies over you."

"What?"

"You heard me. I stuffed down a dozen cookies and now I think I'm going to be sick and it was all because of you. I've come too far to be reduced to that. One argument with you and I was right back into the Oreos! If you think you're frightened—because of what happened with Carmen—it's nothing compared to the fears

I've been facing since the day we met. I can't deal with your insecurities, Tanner. I've got too damn many of my own."

"Joanna, I've already apologized. If you can honestly tell me there isn't any chance that you'll ever get back together with Davey, I swear to you I'll drop the subject and never bring it up again. But I need to know that much. I'm sorry, but I've got to hear you say it."

"I had a nice quiet life before you paraded into it," she went on, as though she hadn't heard him.

"Joanna, I asked you a question." His intense gaze cut straight through her.

"You must be nuts! I'd be certifiably insane to ever take Davey back. Our marriage—our entire relationship—was over the day I filed for divorce, and probably a lot earlier than that."

Tanner relaxed visibly. "I wouldn't blame you if you decided you never wanted to see me again, but I'm hoping you'll be able to forget what happened this afternoon so we can go back to being…friends again."

Joanna struggled against the strong pull of his magnetism for as long as she could, then nodded, agreeing to place this quarrel behind them.

Tanner walked toward her and she met him halfway, slipping easily into his embrace. She felt as if she belonged here, as if he were the man she would always be content with. He'd once told her he wouldn't ever hurt her the way her ex-husband had, but caring about him, risking a relationship with him, left her vulnerable all over again. She'd realised that this afternoon, learned again what it was to give a man the power to hurt her.

"I reduced you to gorging yourself with Oreos?" Tanner whispered the question into her hair.

She nodded wildly. "You fiend. I didn't mean to eat that many, but I sat at the table with the Oreos package and a glass of milk and the more I thought about what happened, the angrier I became, and the faster I shoved those cookies into my mouth."

"Could this mean you care?" His voice was still a whisper.

She nodded a second time. "I hate fighting with you. My stomach was in knots all afternoon."

"Good Lord, Joanna," he said, dropping several swift kisses on her face. "I can't believe what fools we are."

"We?" She tilted back her head and glared up at him, but her mild indignation drained away the moment their eyes met. Tanner was looking down at her with such tenderness, such concern, that every negative emotion she'd experienced earlier that afternoon vanished like rain falling into a clear blue lake.

He kissed her then, with a thoroughness that left her in no doubt about the strength of his feelings. Joanna rested against his warmth, holding on to him with everything that was in her. When he raised his head, she looked up at him through tear-filled eyes and blinked furiously in a futile effort to keep them at bay.

"I'm glad you came back," she said, when she could find her voice.

"I am, too." He kissed her once more, lightly this time, sampling her lips, kissing the tears from her face. "I wasn't worth a damn all afternoon." Once more he lowered his mouth to hers, creating a delicious sensation that electrified Joanna and sent chills racing down her spine.

Tanner's arms tightened as loud voices suddenly erupted from the direction of the living room.

"I never want to see you again," Joanna heard Kristen declare vehemently.

"You couldn't possibly want to see me any less than I want to see you," Nicole returned with equal volume and fury.

"What's that all about?" Tanner asked, his eyes searching Joanna's.

"I don't know, but I think we'd better find out."

Tanner led the way into the living room. They discovered Kristen and Nicole standing face to face, glaring at each other in undisguised antagonism.

"Kristen, stop that right now," Joanna demanded. "Nicole is a guest in our home and I won't have you talking to her in that tone of voice."

Tanner moved to his daughter's side. "And you're Kristen's guest. I expect you to be on your best behaviour whenever you're here."

Nicole crossed her arms over her chest and darted a venomous look in Kristen's direction. "I refuse to be friends with her ever again. And I don't think you should have anything more to do with Mrs. Parsons."

Joanna's eyes found Tanner's.

"I don't want my mother to have anything to do with Mr. Lund, either." Kristen spun around and glared at Tanner and Nicole.

"I think we'd best separate these two and find out what happened," Joanna suggested. She pointed toward Kristen's bedroom. "Come on, honey, let's talk."

Kristen averted her face. "I have nothing to say!" she declared melodramatically and stalked out of the room without a backward glance.

Joanna raised questioning eyes to Tanner, threw up her hands and followed her daughter.

## Chapter Twelve

"Kristen, what's wrong?" Joanna sat on the end of her daughter's bed and patiently waited for the eleven-year-old to repeat the list of atrocities committed by Nicole Lund.

"Nothing."

Joanna had seen her daughter wear this affronted look often enough to recognize it readily, and she felt a weary sigh work its way through her. Hell hath no fury like a sixth-grader done wrong by her closest friend.

"I don't ever want to see Nicole again."

"But, sweetheart, she's your best friend."

"*Was* my best friend," Kristen announced theatrically. She crossed her arms over her chest with all the pomp of a queen who'd made her statement and expected unquestioning acquiescence.

With mounting frustration, Joanna folded her hands

in her lap and waited, knowing better than to try to reason with Kristen when she was in this mood. Five minutes passed, but Kristen didn't utter another word. Joanna wasn't surprised.

"Does your argument have to do with something that happened at school?" she asked as nonchalantly as possible, examining the fingernails on her right hand.

Kristen shook her head. She pinched her lips as if to suggest that nothing Joanna could say would force the information out of her.

"Does it involve a boy?" Joanna persisted.

Kristen's gaze widened. "Of course not."

"What about another friend?"

"Nope."

At the rate they were going, Joanna would soon run out of questions. "Can't you just tell me what happened?"

Kristen cast her a look that seemed to question her mother's intelligence. "No!"

"Does that mean we're going to sit here all night while I try to guess?"

Kristen twisted her head and tilted it at a lofty angle, then pantomimed locking her lips.

"All right," Joanna said with an exaggerated sigh, "I'll simply have to ask Nicole, who will, no doubt, be more than ready to tell all. Her version should be highly interesting."

"Mr. Lund made you cry!" Kristen mumbled, her eyes lowered.

Joanna blinked back her astonishment. "You mean to say this whole thing has to do with Tanner and me?"

Kristen nodded once.

"But—"

"Nicole claims that whatever happened was obviously your fault, and as far as I'm concerned that did it. From here on out, Nicole is no longer my friend and I don't think you should have anything to do with... with that man, either."

"That man?"

Kristen sent her a sour look. "You know very well who I mean."

Joanna shifted farther onto the bed, brought up her knees and rested her chin on them. She paused to carefully measure her words. "What if I told you I was beginning to grow fond of 'that man'?"

"Mom, no!" Her daughter's eyes widened with horror, and she cast her mother a look of sheer panic. "That would be the worst possible thing to happen. You might marry him and then Nicole and I would end up being sisters!"

Joanna made no attempt to conceal her surprise. "But, Kristen, from the not-so-subtle hints you and Nicole have been giving me and Mr. Lund, I thought that was exactly what you both wanted. What you'd planned."

"That was before."

"Before what?"

"Before...tonight, when Nicole said those things she said. I can't forgive her, Mom, I just can't."

Joanna stayed in the room a few more silent minutes, then left. Tanner and Nicole were talking in the living room, and from the frustrated look he gave her, she knew he hadn't been any more successful with his daughter than Joanna had been with hers.

When he saw Joanna, Tanner got to his feet and nodded toward the kitchen, mutely suggesting they talk privately and compare stories.

"What did you find out?" she asked the minute they were alone.

Tanner shrugged, then gestured defeat with his hands. "I don't understand it. She keeps saying she never wants to see Kristen again."

"Kristen says the same thing. Adamantly. She seems to think she's defending my honour. It seems this all has to do with our misunderstanding earlier this afternoon."

"Nicole seems to think it started when you didn't order anything at McDonalds," Tanner said, his expression confused.

"What?" Joanna's question escaped on a short laugh.

"From what I can get out of Nicole, Kristen claims you didn't order a Big Mac, which is supposed to mean something. Then later, before I arrived, there was some mention of your emptying the garbage when it was only half-full?" He paused to wait for her to speak. When she simply nodded, he continued, "I understand that's unusual for you, as well?"

Once more Joanna nodded. She'd wanted to hide her tears from the girls, so taking out the garbage had been an excuse to escape for a couple of minutes while she composed herself.

Tanner wiped his hand across his brow in mock relief. "Whew! At least neither of them learned about the Oreos!"

Joanna ignored his joke and slumped against the kitchen counter with a long slow sigh of frustration. "Having the girls argue is a problem neither of us anticipated."

"Maybe I should talk to Kristen and you talk to Nicole?" Tanner suggested, all seriousness again.

Joanna shook her head. "Then we'd be guilty of interfering. We'd be doing the same thing they've done to us—and I don't think we'd be doing them any favors."

"What do you suggest then?" Tanner asked, looking more disgruntled by the minute.

Joanna shrugged. "I don't know."

"Come on, Joanna, we're intelligent adults. Surely we can come up with a way to handle a couple of pre-adolescent egos."

"Be my guest," Joanna said, and laughed aloud at the comical look that crossed Tanner's handsome face.

"Forget it."

Joanna brushed the hair away from her face. "I think our best bet is to let them work this matter out between themselves."

Tanner's forehead creased in concern, then he nodded, his look reluctant. "I hope this doesn't mean you and I can't be friends." His tender gaze held hers.

Joanna was forced to lower her eyes so he couldn't see just how important his friendship had become to her. "Of course we can."

"Good." He walked across the room and gently pulled her into his arms. He kissed her until she was weak and breathless. When he raised his head, he said in a husky murmur, "I'll take Nicole home now and do as you suggest. We'll give these two a week to settle their differences. After that, you and I are taking over."

"A week?" Joanna wasn't sure that would be long enough, considering Kristen's attitude.

"A week!" Tanner repeated emphatically, kissing her again.

By the time he'd finished, Joanna would have agreed to almost anything. "All right," she managed. "A week."

"How was school today?" Joanna asked Kristen on Monday evening while they sat at the dinner table. She'd waited as long as she could before asking. If either girl was inclined to make a move toward reconciliation, it would be now, she reasoned. They'd both had ample time to think about what had happened and to determine the value of their friendship.

Kristen shrugged. "School was fine, I guess."

Joanna took her time eating her salad, focusing her attention on it instead of her daughter. "How'd you do on the math paper I helped you with?"

Kristen rolled her eyes. "You showed me wrong."

"Wrong!"

"The answers were all right, but Mrs. Andrews told me they don't figure out equations that way anymore."

"Oh. Sorry about that."

"You weren't the only parent who messed up."

That was good to hear.

"A bunch of other kids did it wrong. Including Nicole."

Joanna slipped her hand around her water glass. Kristen sounded far too pleased that her ex-friend had messed up the assignment. That wasn't encouraging. "So you saw Nicole today?"

"I couldn't very well not see her. Her desk is across the aisle from mine. But if you're thinking what I think you're thinking, you can forget it. I don't need a friend like Nicole Lund."

Joanna didn't comment on that, although she practically had to bite her tongue. She wondered how Tanner was doing. Staying out of this argument between the two girls was far more difficult than she'd imagined. It was obvious to Joanna that Kristen was miserable without her best friend, but saying as much would hurt her case more than help it. Kristen needed to recognize the fact herself.

The phone rang while Joanna was finishing up the last of the dinner dishes. Kristen was in the bath, so Joanna grabbed the receiver, holding it between her hunched shoulder and her ear while she squirted detergent into the hot running water.

"Hello?"

"Joanna? Good Lord, you sounded just like Kristen there. I was prepared to have the phone slammed in my ear," Tanner said. "How's it going?"

Her heart swelled with emotion. She hadn't talked to him since Saturday, and it felt as though months had passed since she'd heard his voice. It wrapped itself around her now, warm and comforting. "Things aren't going too well. How are they at your end?"

"Not much better. Did you know Kristen had the nerve to eat lunch with Nora this afternoon? In case you weren't aware of this, Nora is Nicole's sworn enemy."

"Nora?" Joanna could hardly believe her ears. "Kristen doesn't even like the girl." If anything, this war between Kristen and Nicole was heating up.

"I hear you bungled the math assignment," Tanner said softly, amused.

"Apparently you did, too."

He chuckled. "Yeah, this new math is beyond me." He paused, and when he spoke, Joanna could hear the frustration in his voice. "I wish the girls would hurry and patch things up. Frankly, Joanna, I miss you like crazy."

"It's only been two days." She should talk—the last forty-eight hours had seemed like an eternity.

"It feels like two years."

"I know," she agreed softly, closing her eyes and savoring Tanner's words. "But we don't usually see each other during the week anyway." At least not during the past couple of weeks.

"I've been thinking things over and I may have come up with an idea that will put us all out of our misery."

"What?" By now, Joanna was game for anything.

"How about a movie?" he asked unexpectedly, his voice eager.

"But, Tanner—"

"Tomorrow night. You can bring Kristen and I'll bring Nicole, and we could accidentally-on-purpose meet at the theater. Naturally there'll be a bit of acting on our part and some huffing and puffing on theirs, but if things work out the way I think they will, we won't have to do a thing. Nature will take its course."

Joanna wasn't convinced this scheme of his would work. The whole thing could blow up in their faces, but the thought of being with Tanner was too enticing to refuse. "All right," she agreed. "As long as you buy the popcorn and promise to hold my hand."

"You've got yourself a deal."

On Tuesday evening, Kristen was unusually quiet over dinner. Joanna had fixed one of her daughter's favorite meals—macaroni-and-cheese casserole—but Kristen barely touched it.

"Do you feel like going to a movie?" Joanna asked,

her heart in her throat. Normally Kristen would leap at the idea, but this evening Joanna couldn't predict anything.

"It's a school night, and I don't think I'm in the mood to see a movie."

"But you said you didn't have any homework, and it sounds like a fun thing to do…and weren't you saying something about wanting to see Tom Cruise's latest film?" Kristen's eyes momentarily brightened, then faded. "And don't worry," Joanna added cheerfully, "you won't have to sit with me."

Kristen gave a huge sigh. "I don't have anyone else to sit with," she said, as though Joanna had suggested a trip to the dentist.

It wasn't until they were in the parking lot at the theater that Kristen spoke. "Nicole likes Tom Cruise, too."

Joanna made a noncommittal reply, wondering how easily the girls would see through her and Tanner's scheme.

"Mom," Kristen cried. "I see Nicole. She's with her dad. Oh, no, it looks like they're going to the same movie."

"Oh, no," Joanna echoed, her heart acting like a Ping-Pong ball in her chest. "Does this mean you want to skip the whole thing and go home?"

"Of course not," Kristen answered smugly. She practically bounded out of the car once Joanna turned off the engine, glancing anxiously at Joanna when she didn't walk across the parking lot fast enough to suit her.

They joined the line, about eight people behind Tanner and Nicole. Joanna was undecided about what to do next. She wasn't completely sure that Tanner had even seen her. If he had, he was playing his part perfectly, acting as though this whole thing had happened by coincidence.

Kristen couldn't seem to stand still. She peeked around the couple ahead of them several times, loudly humming the song of Heart's that she and Nicole had performed in the talent show.

Nicole whirled around, standing on her tiptoes and staring into the crowd behind her. She jerked on Tanner's sleeve and, when he bent down, whispered something in his ear. Then Tanner turned around, too, and pretended to be shocked when he saw Joanna and Kristen.

By the time they were inside the theater, Tanner and Nicole had disappeared. Kristen was craning her neck in every direction while Joanna stood at the refreshment counter.

"Do you want any popcorn?"

"No. Just some of those raisin things. Mom, you said I didn't have to sit with you. Did you really mean that?"

"Yes, honey, don't worry about it, I'll find a place by myself."

"You're sure?" Kristen looked only mildly concerned.

"No problem. You go sit by yourself."

"Okay." Kristen collected her candy and was gone before Joanna could say any more.

Since it was still several minutes before the movie was scheduled to start, the theater auditorium was well lit. Joanna found a seat toward the back and noted that Kristen was two rows from the front. Nicole sat in the row behind her.

"Is this seat taken?"

Joanna smiled up at Tanner as he claimed the seat

next to her, and had they been anyplace else she was sure he would have kissed her. He handed her a bag of popcorn and a cold drink.

"I sure hope this works," he muttered under his breath, "because if Nicole sees me sitting with you, I could be hung as a traitor." Mischief brightened his eyes. "But the risk is worth it. Did anyone ever tell you how kissable your mouth looks?"

"Tanner," she whispered frantically and pointed toward the girls. "Look."

Kristen sat twisted around and Nicole leaned forward. Kristen shook a handful of her chocolate-covered raisins into Nicole's outstretched hand. Nicole offered Kristen some popcorn. After several of these exchanges, both girls stood up, moved from their seats to a different row entirely, sitting next to each other.

"That looks promising," Joanna whispered.

"It certainly does," Tanner agreed, slipping his arm around her shoulder.

They both watched as Kristen and Nicole tilted their heads toward each other and smiled at the sound of their combined giggles drifting to the back of the theater.

# Chapter Thirteen

After their night at the movies, Joanna didn't give Tanner's invitation to the dinner party more than a passing thought until she read about the event on the society page of Wednesday's newspaper. The *Review* described the dinner, which was being sponsored by Spokane Aluminum, as the gala event of the year. Anyone who was anyone in the eastern half of Washington state would be attending. Until Joanna noticed the news article, she'd thought it was a small intimate party; that was the impression Tanner had given her.

From that moment on, Joanna started worrying, though she wasn't altogether sure why. As a loan officer, she'd attended her share of business-related social functions…but never anything of this scope. The problem, she decided, was one she'd been denying since the night of Nicole's slumber party. Tanner's social position and wealth far outdistanced her own. He was an important member of their community, and she was just a spoke in the wheel of everyday life.

Now, as she dressed for the event, her uneasiness grew, because she knew how important this evening was to Tanner—although he hadn't told her in so many words. The reception and dinner were all part of his becoming half owner of a major corporation and, according to the newspaper article, had been in the planning stages for several months after his arrival. All John Becky's way of introducing Tanner to the community leaders.

Within the first half hour of their arrival, Joanna recognized the mayor and a couple of members from the city council, plus several other people she didn't know, who nonetheless looked terribly important.

"Here," Tanner whispered, stepping to her side and handing her a glass of champagne.

Smiling up at him, she took the glass and held the dainty stem in a death grip, angry with herself for being so unnerved. It wasn't as though she'd never seen the mayor before—okay, only in pictures, but still… "I don't know if I dare have anything too potent," she admitted.

"Why not?"

"If you want the truth, I feel out of it at this affair. I'd prefer to fade into the background, mingle among the draperies, get acquainted with the wallpaper. That sort of thing."

Tanner's smile was encouraging. "No one would know it to look at you."

Joanna had trouble believing that. The smile she wore felt frozen on her lips, and her stomach protested the fact that she'd barely managed to eat all day. Tonight was important, and for Tanner's sake she'd do what she had to.

The man who owned the controlling interest in Columbia Basin Savings and Loan strolled past them and paused when he recognized her. Joanna nodded her recognition, and when he continued on she swallowed the entire glass of champagne in three giant gulps.

"I feel better," she announced.

"Good."

Tanner apparently hadn't noticed how quickly she'd downed the champagne, for which Joanna was grateful.

"Come over here. There are some people I want you to meet."

More people! Tanner had already introduced her to so many that the names were swimming around in her head like fish crowded in a small pond. She'd tried to keep them all straight, and it had been simple in the beginning when he'd started with his partner, John Becky, and John's wife, Jean, but from that point on her memory had deteriorated steadily.

Tanner pressed his hand to the middle of her spine and steered her across the room to where a small group had gathered.

Along the way, Joanna picked up another glass of champagne, just so she'd have something to do with her hands. The way she was feeling, she had no intention of drinking it.

The men and women paused in the middle of their conversation when Tanner approached. After a few words of greeting, introductions were made.

"Pleased to meet all of you," Joanna said, forcing some life into her fatigued smile. Everyone seemed to be looking at her, expecting something more. She nodded toward Tanner. "Our daughters are best friends."

The others smiled.

"I didn't know you had a daughter," a voluptuous blonde said, smiling sweetly up at Tanner.

"Nicole just turned twelve."

The blonde seemed fascinated with this information. "How very sweet. My niece is ten and I know she'd just love to meet Nicole. Perhaps we could get the two of them together. Soon."

"I'm sure Nicole would like that."

"It's a date then." She sidled as close to Tanner as she possibly could, practically draping her breast over his forearm.

Joanna narrowed her gaze and took a small sip of the champagne. The blonde, whose name was—she searched her mind—Blaise, couldn't have been any more obvious had she issued an invitation to her bed.

"Tanner, there's someone you must meet—that is, if I can drag you away from Joanna for just a little minute." The blonde cast a challenging look in Joanna's direction.

"Oh, sure." Joanna gestured with her hand as though to let Blaise know Tanner was free to do as he wished. She certainly didn't have any claims on him.

Tanner frowned. "Come with us," he suggested.

Joanna threw him what she hoped was a dazzling smile. "Go on. You'll only be gone a little minute," she said sweetly, purposely echoing Blaise's words.

The two left, Blaise clinging to Tanner's arm, and Joanna chatted with the others in the group for a few more minutes before fading into the background. Her stomach was twisted in knots. She didn't know why she'd sent Tanner off like that, when it so deeply upset her. Something in her refused to let him know that; it was difficult enough to admit even to herself.

Hoping she wasn't being obvious, her gaze followed Tanner and Blaise until she couldn't endure it any longer, and then she turned and made her way into the ladies' room. Joanna was grateful that the outer room was empty, and she slouched onto the sofa. Her heart was slamming painfully against her rib cage, and when she pressed her hands to her cheeks her face felt hot and feverish. Joanna would gladly have paid the entire three hundred and fifteen dollars in her savings account for a way to gracefully disappear.

It was then that she knew.

She was in love with Tanner Lund. Despite all the warnings she'd given herself. Despite the fact that they were worlds apart, financially and socially.

With the realisation that she loved Tanner came another. The night had only begun—they hadn't even eaten yet. The ordeal of a formal dinner still lay before her.

"Hello again," Jean Becky said, strolling into the ladies' room. She stopped for a moment, watching Joanna, then sat down beside her.

"Oh, hi." Joanna managed the semblance of a smile to greet the likeable older woman.

"I just saw Blaise Ferguson walk past clinging to Tanner. I hope you're not upset."

"Oh heavens, no," Joanna lied.

"Good. Blaise, er, has something of a reputation, and I didn't want you to worry. I'm sure Tanner's smart enough not to be taken in by someone that obvious."

"I'm sure he is, too."

"You're a sensible young woman," Jean said, looking pleased.

At the moment, Joanna didn't feel the least bit sensible. The one emotion she was experiencing was fear. She'd fallen in love again, and the first time had been so painful she had promised never to let it happen again. But it had. With Tanner Lund, yet. Why couldn't she have fallen for the mechanic who'd worked so hard repairing her car last winter, or someone at the office? Oh, no, she had to fall—and fall hard—for the most eligible man in town. The man every single woman in the party had her eye on this evening.

"It really has been a pleasure meeting you," Jean continued. "Tanner and Nicole talk about you and your daughter so often. We've been friends of Tanner's for several years now, and it gladdens our hearts to see him finally meet a good woman."

"Thank you." Joanna wasn't sure what to think about being classified as a "good woman." It made her wonder who Tanner had dated before he'd met her. She'd never asked him about his social life before he'd moved to Spokane—or even after. She wasn't sure she wanted to know. No doubt he'd made quite a splash when he came to town. Rich, handsome, available men were a rare commodity these days. It was a wonder he hadn't been snatched up long before now.

Five minutes later, Joanna had composed herself enough to rejoin the party. Tanner was at her side within a few seconds, noticeably irritable and short-tempered.

"I've been searching all over for you," he said, frowning heavily.

Joanna let that remark slide. "I thought you were otherwise occupied."

"Why'd you let that she-cat walk off with me like that?" His eyes were hot with fury. "Couldn't you tell I wanted out? Good Lord, woman, what do I have to do, flash flags?"

"No." A waiter walked past with a loaded tray, and Joanna deftly reached out and helped herself to another glass of champagne.

Just as smoothly, Tanner removed it from her fingers. "I think you've had enough."

Joanna took the glass back from him. She might not completely understand what was happening to her this evening, but she certainly didn't like his attitude. "Excuse me, Tanner, but I am perfectly capable of determining my own limit."

His frown darkened into a scowl. "It's taken me the last twenty minutes to extract myself from her claws. The least you could have done was stick around instead of doing a disappearing act."

"No way." Being married to Davey all those years had taught her more than one valuable lesson. If her ex-husband, Tanner, or any other man, for that matter, expected her to make a scene over another woman, it wouldn't work. Joanna was through with those kinds of destructive games.

"What do you mean by that?"

"I'm just not the jealous type. If you were to go home with Blaise, that'd be fine with me. In fact, you could leave with her right now. I'll grab a cab. I'm really not up to playing the role of a jealous girlfriend because another woman happens to show some interest in you. Nor am I willing to find a flimsy excuse to extract you from her clutches. You look more than capable of doing that yourself."

"You honestly want me to leave with Blaise?" His words were low and hard.

Joanna made a show of shrugging. "It's entirely up to you—you're free to do as you please. Actually you might be doing me a favor."

Joanna couldn't remember ever seeing a man more angry. His eyes seemed to spit fire at her. His jaws clamped together tightly, and he held himself with such an unnatural stiffness, it was surprising that something in his body didn't crack. She observed all this in some distant part of her mind, her concentration focused on preserving her facade of unconcern.

"I'm beginning to understand Davey," he said, his tone as cold as an arctic wind. "Has it ever occurred to you that your ex-husband turned to other women out of a desperate need to know you cared?"

Tanner's words hurt more than any physical blow could have. Joanna's breath caught in her throat, though she did her best to disguise the pain his remark had inflicted. When she was finally able to breathe, the words tumbled from her lips. "No. Funny, I never thought of that." She paused and searched the room. "Pick a woman then, any woman will do, and I'll slug it out with her."

"Joanna, stop it," Tanner hissed.

"You mean you don't want me to fight?"

He closed his eyes as if seeking patience. "No."

Dramatically, Joanna placed her hand over her heart. "Thank goodness. I don't know how I'd ever explain a black eye to Kristen."

Dinner was about to be served, and, tucking his hand under her elbow, Tanner led Joanna into the banquet room, which was quickly filling up.

"I'm sorry, I didn't mean that about Davey," Tanner whispered as they strolled toward the dining room. "I realize you're nervous, but no one would ever know it—except me. We'll discuss this Blaise thing later."

Joanna nodded, feeling subdued now, accepting his apology. She realized that she'd panicked earlier, and not because this was an important social event, either. She'd attended enough business dinners in her career to know she hadn't made a fool of herself. What disturbed her so much was the knowledge that she'd fallen in love with Tanner.

To add to Joanna's dismay, she discovered that she was expected to sit at the head table between Tanner and John Becky. She trembled at the thought, but she wasn't about to let anyone see her nervousness.

"Don't worry," Tanner said, stroking her hand after they were seated. "Everyone who's met you has been impressed."

His statement was meant to lend her courage; unfortunately it had the opposite effect. What had she said or done to impress anyone?

When the evening was finally over, Tanner appeared to be as eager to escape as she was. With a minimum of fuss, they made their farewells and were gone.

Once in the car, Tanner didn't speak. But when he parked in front of the house, he turned off the car engine and said quietly, "Invite me in for coffee."

It was on the tip of Joanna's tongue to tell him she had a headache, which was fast becoming the truth, but delaying the inevitable wouldn't help either of them.

"Okay," she mumbled.

The house was quiet, and Sally was asleep on the sofa. Joanna paid her and waited on the front porch while the teenager ran across the street to her own house. Gathering her courage, she walked into the kitchen. Tanner had put the water and ground coffee into the machine and taken two cups down from the cupboard.

"Okay," he said, turning around to face her, "I want to know what's wrong."

The bewilderment in his eyes made Joanna raise her chin an extra notch. Then she remembered Kristen doing the same thing when she'd questioned her about her argument with Nicole, and the recollection wasn't comforting.

Joanna was actually surprised Tanner had guessed anything was wrong. She thought she'd done a brilliant job of disguising her distress. She'd done her best to say and do all the right things. When Tanner had stood up, after the meal, to give his talk, she'd whispered encouragement and smiled at him. Throughout the rest of the evening, she'd chatted easily with both Tanner and John Becky.

Now she had to try to explain something she barely understood herself.

"I don't think I ever realized what an important man you are," she said, struggling to find her voice. "I've always seen you as Nicole's father, the man who was crazy enough to agree to a slumber party for his daughter's birthday. The man who called and disguised his voice so Kristen wouldn't recognise it. That's the man I know, not the one tonight who stood before a filled banquet room and promised growth and prosperity for our city. Not the man who charts the destiny of an entire community."

Tanner glared at her. "What has that got to do with anything?"

"You play in the big league. I'm in the minors."

Tanner's gaze clouded with confusion. "I'm talking about our relationship and you're discussing baseball!"

Pulling out a kitchen chair, Joanna sat in it and took a deep breath. The best place to start, she decided, was the beginning. "You have to understand that I didn't come away from my marriage without a few quirks."

Tanner started pacing, clearly not in the mood to sit still. "Quirks? You call what happened with Blaise a quirk? I call it loony. Some woman I don't know from Adam comes up to me—"

"Eve," Joanna inserted, and when he stared at her, uncomprehending, she elaborated. "Since Blaise Ferguson's a woman, you don't know her from Eve."

"Whatever!"

"Well, it does make a difference." The coffee had finished filtering into the pot, so Joanna got up and poured them each a cup. Holding hers in both hands, she leaned against the counter and took a tentative sip.

"Some woman I don't know from Eve," Tanner tried again, "comes up to me, and you act as if you can't wait to get me out of your hair."

"*You* acted as if you expected me to come to your rescue. Honestly, Tanner, you're a big boy. I assumed you could take care of yourself."

"You looked more than happy to see me go with her."

"That's not true. I was content where I was." Joanna knew they were sidestepping the real issue, but this other business seemed to concern Tanner more.

"You were content to go into hiding."

"If you're looking for someone to fly into a jealous

rage every time another woman winks at you, you'll need to look elsewhere."

Tanner did some more pacing, his steps growing longer and heavier with each circuit of the kitchen. "Explain what you meant when you said you didn't come away from your marriage without a few quirks."

"It's simply really," she said, making light of it. "Davey used to get a kick out of introducing me to his women friends. Everyone in the room knew what he was doing, except me. I was so stupid, so blind, that I just didn't know any better. Once the scales fell from my eyes, I was astonished at what a complete fool I'd been. But when I became wise to his ways, it was much worse. Every time he introduced me to a woman, I'd be filled with suspicion. Was Davey involved with her, or wasn't he? The only thing left for me to do was hold my head high and smile." Her voice was growing tighter with every word, cracking just as she finished.

Tanner walked toward her and reached out his hands as though to comfort her. "Joanna, listen—"

"No." She set her coffee aside and wrapped her arms around her middle. "I feel honored, Tanner, that you would ask me to attend this important dinner with you tonight. I think we both learned something valuable from the experience. At least, I know I did."

"Joanna—"

"No," she cut in again, "let me finish, please. Although it's difficult to say this, it needs to be said. We're not right for each other. We've been so caught up in everything we had in common and what good friends the girls are and how wonderful it felt to…be together, we didn't stop to notice that we live in different worlds." She paused and gathered her resolve before continuing. "Knowing you and becoming your friend has been wonderful, but anything beyond that just isn't going to work."

"The only thing I got carried away with was you, Joanna. The girls have nothing to do with it."

"I feel good that you would say that, I really do, but we both lost sight of the fact that neither one of us wants to become involved. That had never been our intention. Something happened, and I'm not sure when or why, but suddenly everything is so intense between us. It's got to stop before we end up really hurting each other."

Tanner seemed to mull over her words. "You're so frightened of giving another man the power to hurt you that you can't see anything else, can you?" His brooding, confused look was back. "I told you this once, but it didn't seem to sink into that head of yours—I'm never going to do the things Davey did. We're two entirely different men, and it's time you realized that."

"What you say may very well be true, Tanner, but I don't see what difference it's going to make. Because I have no intention of involving myself in another relationship."

"In case you hadn't noticed, Joanna, we're already involved."

"Roller-skating in the couples round doesn't qualify as being involved to me," she said, in a futile attempt at humor. It fell flat.

Tanner was the first to break the heavy silence that followed. "You've obviously got some thinking to do," he said wearily. "For that matter, so do I. Call me, Joanna, when you're in the mood to be reasonable."

# Chapter Fourteen

"Hi, Mom," Kristen said, slumping down on the sofa beside Joanna. "I hope you know I'm bored out of my mind," she said, and sighed deeply.

Joanna was busy counting the stitches on her knitting needle and didn't pause to answer until she'd finished. "What about your homework?"

"Cute, Mom, real cute. It's spring break—I don't have any homework."

"Right. Phone Nicole then. I bet she'll commiserate with you." And she might even give Kristen some information about Tanner. He'd walked out of her house, and although she'd thought her heart would break she'd let him go. Since then, she'd reconsidered. She was dying to hear something from Tanner. Anything. But she hadn't—not since the party more than a week earlier, and each passing day seemed like a lifetime.

"Calling Nicole is a nothing idea."

"I could suggest you clean your room."

"Funny, Mom, real funny."

"Gee, I'm funny and cute all in one evening. How'd I get so lucky?"

Not bothering to answer, Kristen reached for a magazine and idly thumbed through the pages, not finding a single picture or article worth more than a fleeting glance. She set it aside and reached for another. By the time she'd gone through the four magazines resting on top of the coffee table, Joanna was losing her patience.

"Call Nicole."

"I can't."

"Why not?"

"Because I can't."

That didn't make much sense to Joanna. And suggesting that Kristen phone Nicole was another sign of her willingness to settle this rift between her and Tanner. It had been so long since she'd last seen or heard from him. Ten interminable days, and with each one that passed she missed him more. She'd debated long and hard about calling him, wavering with indecision, battling with her pride. What she'd told him that night had been the truth—they did live in different worlds. But she'd overreacted at the dinner party, and now she felt guilty about how the evening had gone. When he'd left the house, Tanner had suggested she call him when she was ready to be reasonable. Well, she'd been ready the following morning, ready to acknowledge her fault. And her need. But pride held her back. And with each passing day, it became more difficult to swallow that pride.

"You know I can't call Nicole," Kristen whined.

"Why not? Did you have another argument?" Joanna

asked without looking at her daughter. Her mind was preoccupied with counting stitches. She always knitted when she was frustrated with herself; it was a form of self-punishment, she suspected wryly.

"We never fight. Not anymore. Nicole's in West Virginia."

Joanna paused and carefully set the knitting needles down on her lap. "Oh? What's she doing there?"

"I think she went to visit her mother."

"Her mother?" It took some effort to keep her heart from exploding in her throat. According to Tanner, Nicole hadn't seen or heard from Carmen in three years. His biggest worry, he'd told her, was that someday his ex-wife would develop an interest in their daughter and steal her away from him. "Nicole is with her mother?" Joanna repeated, to be certain she'd heard Kristen correctly.

"You knew that."

"No, I didn't."

"Yes, you did. I told you she was leaving last Sunday. Remember?"

Vaguely, Joanna recalled the conversation—she'd been peeling potatoes at the sink—but for the last week, every time Kristen mentioned either Tanner or Nicole, Joanna had made an effort to tune her daughter out. Now she was hungry for information, starving for every tidbit Kristen was willing to feed her.

The eleven-year-old straightened and stared at her mother. "Didn't Mr. Lund mention Nicole was leaving?"

"Er, no."

Kristen sighed and threw herself against the back of the sofa. "You haven't been seeing much of him lately, have you?"

"Er, no."

Kristen picked up Joanna's hand and patted it gently. "You two had a fight?"

"Not exactly."

Her daughter's hand continued its soothing action. "Okay, tell me all about it. Don't hold back a single thing—you need to talk this out. Bare your soul."

"Kristen!"

"Mom, you need this. Releasing your anger and frustration will help. You've got to work out all that inner agitation and responsive turbulence. It's disrupting your emotional poise. Seriously, Mom, have you ever considered Rolfing?"

"Emotional poise? Responsive turbulence? Where'd you hear about that? Where'd you hear about Rolfing?"

Kristen blinked and cocked her head to one side, doing her best to look concerned and sympathetic. "Oprah Winfrey."

"I see," Joanna muttered, and rolled her eyes.

"Are you or are you not going to tell me all about it?"

"No, I am not!"

Kristen released a deep sigh that expressed her keen disappointment. "I thought not. When it comes to Nicole's dad, you never want to talk about it. It's like a deep dark secret the two of you keep from Nicole and me. Well, that's all right—we're doing our best to understand. You don't want us to get our hopes up that you two might be interested in each other. I can accept that, although I consider it grossly unfair." She stood up and gazed at her mother with undisguised longing, then loudly slapped her hands against her sides. "I'm perfectly content to live the way we do...but it sure would be nice to have a baby sister to dress up. And you know how I've *always* wanted a brother."

"Kristen!"

"No, Mom." She held up her hand as though she were stopping a freight train. "Really, I do understand. You and I get along fine the way we are. I guess we don't need to complicate our lives with Nicole and her dad. That could even cause real problems."

For the first time, her daughter was making sense.

"Although heaven knows, I can't remember what it's like to be part of a *real* family."

"Kristen, that's enough," Joanna cried, shaking her head. Her daughter was invoking so much guilt that Joanna was beginning to hear violins in the background. "You and I *are* a real family."

"But, Mom, it could be so much better." Kristen sank down beside Joanna again and crossed her legs. Obviously her argument had long since been prepared, and without pausing to breathe between sentences, she proceeded to list the advantages of joining the two families.

"Kristen—"

Once more her daughter stopped her with an outstretched hand, as she started on her much shorter list of possible disadvantages. There was little Joanna could do to stem the rehearsed speech. Impatiently she waited for Kristen to finish.

"I don't want to talk about Tanner again," Joanna said in a no-nonsense tone of voice reserved for instances such as this. "Not a single word. Is that clearly understood?"

Kristen turned round sad eyes on her mother. The fun and laughter seemed to drain from her face as she glared back at Joanna. "Okay—if that's what you really want."

"It is, Kristen. Not a single word."

Banning his name from her daughter's lips and banning his name from her own mind were two entirely different things, Joanna decided an hour later. The fact that Nicole was visiting Carmen concerned her—not that she shared Tanner's worries. But knowing Tanner, he was probably beside himself worrying that Carmen would want their daughter to come and live with her.

It took another half hour for Joanna to build up enough courage to phone Tanner. He answered on the second ring.

"Hello, Tanner…it's Joanna." Even that was almost more than she could manage.

"Joanna." Just the way he said her name revealed his delight in hearing from her.

Joanna was grateful that he didn't immediately bring up the dinner party and the argument that had followed. "How have you been?"

"Good. How about you?"

"Just fine," she returned awkwardly. She leaned against the wall, crossing and uncrossing her ankles. "Listen, the reason I phoned is that Kristen told me Nicole was with her mother, and I thought you might be in need of a divorced-parent prep talk."

"What I really need is to see you. Lord, woman, it took you long enough. I thought you were going to make me wait forever. Ten days can be a very long time, Joanna. Ten whole days!"

"Tanner—"

"Can we meet someplace?"

"I'm not sure." Her mind struggled with a list of

excuses, but she couldn't deny how lonely and miserable she'd been, how badly she wanted to feel his arms around her. "I'd have to find someone to sit with Kristen, and that could be difficult at the last minute like this."

"I'll come to you then."

It was part question, part statement, and again, she hesitated. "All right," she finally whispered.

The line went oddly silent. When Tanner spoke again there was a wealth of emotion in his words, although his voice was quiet. "I'm glad you phoned, Joanna."

She closed her eyes, feeling weak and shaky. "I am, too," she said softly.

"I'll be there within half an hour."

"I'll have coffee ready."

When she replaced the receiver, her hand was trembling, and it was as though she were twenty-one again. Her heart was pounding out of control just from the sound of his voice, her head swimming with the knowledge that she'd be seeing him in a few minutes. How wrong she'd been to assume that if she put him out of her sight and mind she could keep him out of her heart, too. How foolish she'd been to deny her feelings. She loved this man, and it wouldn't matter if he owned the company or swept the floors.

Joanna barely had time to refresh her makeup and drag a brush through her hair. Kristen had been in her room for the past hour without a sound; Joanna sincerely hoped she was asleep.

She'd just poured water into the coffeemaker when the doorbell chimed.

The bedroom door flew open, and Kristen appeared in her pajamas, wide awake. "I'll get it," she yelled.

Joanna started to call after her, but it was too late. With a resigned sigh, she stood in the background and waited for her daughter to admit Tanner.

Kristen turned to face her mother, wearing a grin as wide as the Mississippi River. "It's that man whose name I'm not supposed to mention ever again."

"Yes, I know."

"You know?"

Joanna nodded.

"Good. Talk it out with him, Mom. Relieve yourself of all that inner stuff. Get rid of that turmoil before it eats you alive."

Joanna cast a weak smile in Tanner's direction, then turned her attention to Kristen. "Isn't it your bedtime, young lady?"

"No."

Joanna's eyes narrowed. "Yes, it is."

"But, Mom, it's spring break, so I can sleep in tomorrow—Oh, I get it, you want me out of here."

"In your room reading or listening to music should do nicely."

Kristen beamed her mother a broad smile. "'Night, Mom. 'Night… Nicole's dad."

"'Night."

With her arms swinging at her sides, Kristen strolled out of the living room. Tanner waited until they heard her bedroom door shut, then he started across the carpet toward Joanna. He stopped suddenly, frowning. "She wasn't supposed to say my name?"

Joanna gave a weak half shrug, her gaze holding his. No man had ever looked better. His eyes seemed to caress her with a tenderness and aching hunger that did crazy things to her equilibrium.

"It's so good to see you," she said, her voice unsteady. She took two steps towards him.

When Tanner reached for her, a heavy sigh broke from his lips and the tension left his muscles. "Dear Lord, woman, ten days you left me dangling." He said more, but his words were muffled in the curve of her neck as he crushed her against his chest.

Joanna soaked up his warmth, and when his lips found hers she surrendered with a soft sigh of joy. Being in Tanner's arms was like coming home after a long journey and discovering the comfort in all that's familiar. It was like walking in sunshine after a bad storm, like holding the first rose of summer in her hand.

Again and again his mouth sought hers in a series of passionate kisses, as though he couldn't get enough of the taste of her.

The creaky sound of a bedroom door opening caused Joanna to break away from him. "It's Kristen," she murmured, her voice little more than a whisper.

"I know, but I don't care." Tanner kept her close for a moment longer. "Okay," he breathed, and slowly stroked the top of her head with his chin. "We need to settle a few things. Let's talk."

Joanna led him into the kitchen, since they were afforded the most privacy there. She automatically took down two cups and poured them each some coffee. They sat at the small table, directly across from each other, but even that seemed much too far.

"First, tell me about Nicole," she said, her eyes meeting his. "Are you worried now that she's with Carmen?"

A sad smile touched the edges of Tanner's mouth. "Not particularly. Carmen, who prefers to be called Rama Sheba now, contacted my parents at the end of last week. According to my mother, the reason we haven't heard from her in the past three years is that Carmen's been on a long journey in India and Nepal. Apparently Carmen went halfway around the world searching for herself. I guess she found what she was looking for, because she's back in the United States and inquiring about Nicole."

"Oh, dear. Do you think she wants Nicole to come live with her?"

"Not a chance. Carmen, er, Rama Sheba, doesn't want a child complicating her life. She never did. Nicole wanted to see her mother and that's understandable, so I sent her back to West Virginia for a visit with my parents. While she's there, Carmen will spend an afternoon with her."

"What happened to... Rama Sheba and the baseball player?"

"Who knows? He may have joined her in her wanderings, for all I know. Or care. Carmen plays such a minor role in my life now that I haven't the energy to second-guess her. She's free to do as she likes, and I prefer it that way. If she wants to visit Nicole, fine. She can see her daughter—she has the right."

"Do you love her?" The question sounded abrupt and tactless, but Joanna needed to know.

"No," he said quickly, then grinned. "I suppose I feel much the same way about her as you do about Davey."

"Then you don't hate her?" she asked next, not looking at him.

"No."

Joanna ran a fingertip along the rim of her cup and smiled. "Good."

"Why's that good?"

She lifted her eyes to meet his and smiled a little shyly. "Because if you did have strong feelings for her it would suggest some unresolved emotion."

Tanner nodded. "As illogical as it sounds, I don't feel anything for Carmen. Not love, not hate—nothing. If something bad were to happen to her, I suppose I'd feel sad, but I don't harbor any resentments toward her."

"That's what I was trying to explain to you the afternoon you dropped by when Davey was here. Other people have a hard time believing this, especially my parents, but I honestly wish him success in life. I want him to be happy, although I doubt he ever will be." Davey wasn't a man who would ever be content. He was always looking for something more, something better.

Tanner nodded.

Once more, Joanna dropped her gaze to the steaming coffee. "Calling you and asking about Nicole was only an excuse, you know."

"Yes. I just wish you'd come up with it a few days earlier. As far as I'm concerned, waiting for you to come to your senses took nine days too long."

"I—"

"I know, I know," Tanner said before she could list her excuses. "Okay, let's talk."

Joanna managed a smile. "Where do we start?"

"How about with what happened the night of the party?"

Instantly Joanna's stomach knotted. "Yes, well, I guess I should be honest and let you know I was intimidated by how important you are. It shook me, Tanner, really shook me. I'm not used to seeing you as chairman of the board. And then later, when you strolled off with Blaise, those old wounds from my marriage with Davey started to bleed."

"I suppose I did all the wrong things. Maybe I should have insisted you come with me when Blaise dragged me away, but—"

"No, that wouldn't have worked, either."

"I should have guessed how you'd feel after being married to Davey."

"You had no way of knowing." Now came the hard part. "Tanner," she began, and was shocked at how thin and weak her voice sounded, "I was so consumed with jealousy that I just about went crazy when Blaise wrapped her arms around you. It frightened me to have to deal with those negative emotions again. I know I acted like an idiot, hiding like that, and I'd like to apologize."

"Joanna, it isn't necessary."

She shook her head. "I don't mean this as an excuse, but you need to understand why I was driven to behave the way I did. I'd thought I was beyond that—years beyond acting like a jealous fool. I promised myself I'd never allow a man to do it to me again." In her own way, Joanna was trying to tell him how much she loved him, but the words weren't coming out right.

He frowned at that. "Jealous? You were jealous? Good Lord, woman, you could have fooled me. You handed me over to Blaise without so much as a hint of regret. From the way you were behaving, I thought you *wanted* to be rid of me."

The tightness in Joanna's throat made talking difficult. "I already explained why I did that."

"I know. The way I acted when I saw your ex here was the other kind of jealous reaction—the raging-bull kind. I think I see now where *your* kind of reaction came from. I'm not sure which one is worse, but I think mine is." He smiled ruefully, and a silence fell between them.

"Could this mean you have some strong feelings for me, Joanna Parsons?"

A smile quirked at the corners of her mouth. "You're the only man I've ever eaten Oreos over."

The laughter in Tanner's eyes slowly faded. "We could have the start of something very important here, Joanna. What do you think?"

"I... I think you may be right."

"Good." Tanner looked exceedingly pleased with this turn of events. "That's exactly what I wanted to hear."

Joanna thought—no, hoped—that he intended to lean over and kiss her. Instead his brows drew together darkly over brooding blue eyes. "Okay, where do we go from here?"

"Go?" Joanna repeated, feeling uncomfortable all of a sudden. "Why do we have to go anywhere?"

Tanner looked surprised. "Joanna, for heaven's sake, when a man and a woman feel about each other the way we do, they generally make plans."

"What do you mean 'feel about each other the way we do'?"

Tanner's frown darkened even more. "You love me."

Only a few moments before, Joanna would have willingly admitted it, but silly as it sounded, she wanted to hear Tanner say the words first. "I... I..."

"If you have to think about it, then I'd say you obviously don't know."

"But I do know," she said, lifting her chin a notch higher. "I'm just not sure this is the time to do anything about it. You may think my success is insignificant compared to yours, but I've worked damn hard to get where I am. I've got the house I saved for years to buy, and my career is starting to swing along nicely, and Robin—he's my boss—let me know that I was up for promotion. My goal of becoming the first female senior loan officer at the branch is within sight."

"And you don't want to complicate your life right now with a husband and second family?"

"I didn't say that."

"It sure sounded like it to me."

Joanna swallowed. The last thing in the world she wanted to do was argue with Tanner. Craziest of all, she wasn't even sure what they were arguing about. They were in love with each other and both just too damn proud. "I don't think we're getting anywhere with this conversation."

Tanner braced his elbows on the table and folded his hands. "I'm beginning to agree with you. All week, I've been waiting for you to call me, convinced that once you did, everything between us would be settled. I wanted us to start building a life together, and all of a sudden you're Ms. Career Woman, and about as independent as they come."

"I haven't changed. You just didn't know me."

His lips tightened. "I guess you're right. I don't know you at all, do I?"

"Mom, Mom, come quick!"

Joanna's warm cozy dream was interrupted by Kristen's shrieks. She rolled over and glared at the digital readout on her clock radio. Five. In the morning. "Kristen?" She sat straight up in bed.

"Mom!"

The one word conveyed such panic that Joanna's heart rushed to her throat and she threw back her covers, running barefoot into the hallway. Almost immediately, her feet encountered ice-cold water.

"Something's wrong," Kristen cried, hopping up and down. "The water won't stop."

That was the understatement of the year. From the way the water was gushing out of the bathroom door and into the hallway, it looked as though a dam had burst.

"Grab some towels," Joanna cried, pointing toward the hallway linen closet. The hems of her long pajamas were already damp. She scooted around her daughter, who was standing in the doorway, still hopping up and down like a crazed kangaroo.

Further investigation showed that the water was escaping from the cabinet under the sink.

"Mom, Mom, here!" Dancing around, Kristen threw her a stack of towels that separated in midair and landed in every direction.

"Kristen!" Joanna snapped, squatting down in front of the sink. She opened the cabinet and was immediately hit by a wall of foaming bubbles. The force of the flowing water had knocked over her container of expensive bubble bath and spilled its contents. "You were in my bubble bath!" Joanna cried.

"I… How'd you know?"

"The cap's off, and now it's everywhere!"

"I just used a little bit."

Three bars of Ivory soap, still in their wrappers, floated past Joanna's feet. Heaven only knew what else had been stored under the sink or where it was headed now.

"I'm sorry about the bubble bath," Kristen said defensively. "I figured you'd get mad if you found out, but a kid needs to know what luxury feels like, too, you know."

"It's all right, we can't worry about that now." Joanna waved her hands back and forth trying to disperse the bubbles enough to assess the damage. It didn't take long to determine that a pipe had burst. With her forehead pressing against the edge of the sink, Joanna groped inside the cabinet for the knob to turn off the water supply. Once she found it, she twisted it furiously until the flowing water dwindled to a mere trickle.

"Kristen!" Joanna shouted, looking over her shoulder. Naturally, when she needed her, her daughter disappeared. "Get me some more towels. Hurry, honey!"

A couple of minutes later, Kristen reappeared, her arms loaded with every towel and washcloth in the house. "Yuck," she muttered, screwing her face into a mask of sheer disgust. "What a mess!"

"Did any water get into the living room?"

Kristen nodded furiously. "But only as far as the front door."

"Great." Joanna mumbled under her breath. Now she'd need to phone someone about coming in to dry out the carpet.

On her hands and knees, sopping up as much water as she could, Joanna was already soaked to the skin herself.

"You need help," her daughter announced.

The child was a master of observation. "Change out

of those wet things first, Kristen, before you catch your death of cold."

"What about you?"

"I'll dry off as soon as I get some of this water cleaned up."

"Mom—"

"Honey, just do as I ask. I'm not in any mood to argue with you."

Joanna couldn't remember ever seeing a bigger mess in her life. Her pajamas were soaked; bubbles were popping around her head—how on earth had they got into her hair? She sneezed violently, and reached for a tissue that quickly dissolved in her wet hands.

"Here, use this."

The male voice coming from behind her surprised Joanna so much that when she twisted around, she lost her footing and slid down into a puddle of the coldest water she'd ever felt.

"Tanner!" she cried, leaping to her feet. "What are you doing here?"

## Chapter Fifteen

Dumbfounded, Joanna stared at Tanner, her mouth hanging open and her eyes wide.

"I got this frantic phone call from Kristen."

"Kristen?"

"The one and only. She suggested I hurry over here before something drastic happened." Tanner took one step toward her and lovingly brushed a wet tendril away from her face. "How's it going, Tugboat Annie?"

"A pipe under the sink broke. I've got it under control now—I think." Her pajamas hung limply at her ankles, dripping water onto her bare feet. Her hair fell in wet spongy curls around her face, and Joanna had never felt more like bursting into tears in her life.

"Kristen shouldn't have phoned you," she said, once she found her voice.

"I'm glad she did. It's nice to know I can be useful

every now and again." Heedless of her wet state, he wrapped his arms around Joanna and brought her close, gently pressing her damp head to his chest.

A chill went through her and she shuddered. Tanner felt so warm and vital, so concerned and loving. She'd let him think she was this strong independent woman, and normally she was, but when it came to broken pipes and floods and things like that, she crumbled into bite-sized pieces. When it came to Tanner Lund, well...

"You're soaked to the skin," he whispered, close to her ear.

"I know."

"Go change. I'll take over here."

The tears started then, silly ones that sprang from somewhere deep inside her and refused to be stopped. "I can't get dry," she sobbed, wiping furiously at the moisture that rained down her face. "There aren't any dry towels left in this entire house."

Tanner jerked his water-blotched tan leather jacket off and placed it around her shoulders. "Honey, don't cry. Please. Everything's going to be all right. It's just a broken pipe, and I can have it fixed for you before noon—possibly sooner."

"I can't help it," she bellowed, and to her horror, hiccuped. She threw a hand over her mouth and leaned her forehead against his strong chest. "It's five o'clock in the morning, my expensive Giorgio bubble bath is ruined, and I'm so much in love I can't think straight."

Tanner's hands gripped her shoulders and eased her away so he could look her in the eye. "What did you just say?"

Joanna hung her head as low as it would go, bracing her weight against Tanner's arms. "My Giorgio bubble bath is ruined." The words wobbled out of her mouth like a rubber ball tumbling down stairs.

"Not that. I want to hear the other part, about being so much in love."

Joanna sniffled. "What about it?"

"What about it? Good Lord, woman, I was here not more than eight hours ago wearing my heart on my sleeve like a schoolboy. You were so casual about everything, I thought you were going to open a discussion on stock options."

"*You* were the one who was so calm and collected about everything, as if what happened between us didn't really matter to you." She rubbed her hand under her nose and sniffled loudly. "Then you made everything sound like a foregone conclusion and—"

"I was nervous. Now, shall we give it another try? I want to marry you, Joanna Parsons. I want you to share my life, maybe have my babies. I want to love you until we're both old and gray. I've even had fantasies about us traveling around the country in a mobile home to visit our grandchildren!"

"You want grandkids?" Timidly, she raised her eyes to his, almost afraid to believe what he was telling her.

"I'd prefer to take this one step at a time. The first thing I want to do is marry you. I couldn't have made that plainer than I did a few hours ago."

"But—"

"Stop right now, before we get sidetracked. First things first. Are you and Kristen going to marry me and Nicole?"

"I think we should," the eleven-year-old said excitedly from the hallway, looking smugly pleased with the way things were going. "I mean, it's been obvious to Nicole and me for ages that you two were meant to be together." Kristen sighed and slouched against the wall, crossing her arms over her chest with the sophistication that befitted someone of superior intelligence. "There's only one flaw in this plan."

"Flaw?" Joanna echoed.

"Yup," Kristen said, nodding with unquestionable confidence. "Nicole is going to be mad as hops when she finds out she missed this."

Tanner frowned, and then he chuckled. "Oh, boy. I think Kristen could be right. We're going to have to stage a second proposal."

Feeling slightly piqued, Joanna straightened. "Listen, you two, I never said I was going to marry anybody—yet."

"Of course you're going to marry Mr. Lund," Kristen inserted smoothly. "Honestly, Mom, now isn't the time to play hard to get."

"W-what?" Stunned, Joanna stood there staring at her daughter. Her gaze flew from Kristen to Tanner and then back to Kristen.

"She's right, you know," said Tanner.

"I can't believe I'm hearing this." Joanna was standing in a sea of wet towels, while her daughter and the man she loved discussed her fate as though she was to play only a minor role in it.

"We've got to think of a way to include Nicole," Tanner said thoughtfully.

"I am going to change my clothes," Joanna murmured, eager to escape.

"Good idea," Tanner answered, without looking at her.

Joanna stomped off to her bedroom and slammed the

door. She discarded her pajamas and, shivering, reached for a thick wool sweater and blue jeans.

Tanner and Kristen were still in the bathroom doorway, discussing details, when Joanna reappeared. She moved silently around them and into the kitchen, where she made a pot of coffee. Then she gathered up the wet towels, hauled them onto the back porch, threw them into the washer and started the machine. By the time she returned to the kitchen, Tanner had joined her there.

"Uh-oh. Trouble," he said, watching her abrupt angry movements. "Okay, tell me what's wrong now."

"I don't like the way you and my daughter are planning my life," she told him point-blank. "Honestly, Tanner, I haven't even agreed to marry you, and already you and Kristen have got the next ten years all figured out."

He stuck his hands in his pants pockets. "It's not that bad."

"Maybe not, but it's bad enough. I'm letting you know right now that I'm not about to let you stage a second proposal just so Nicole can hear it. To be honest, I'm not exactly thrilled about Kristen being part of this one. A marriage proposal is supposed to be private. And romantic, with flowers and music, not...not in front of a busted pipe with bath bubbles popping around my head and my family standing around applauding."

"Okay, what do you suggest?"

"I don't know yet."

Tanner looked disgruntled. "If you want the romance, Joanna, that's fine. I'd be more than happy to give it to you."

"Every woman wants romance."

Tanner walked toward her then and took her in his

arms, and until that moment Joanna had no idea how much she did, indeed, want it.

Her eyes were drawn to his. Everything about Tanner Lund fascinated her, and she raised her hand to lightly caress the proud strong line of his jaw. She really did love this man. His eyes, blue and intense, met hers, and a tiny shiver of awareness went through her. His arms circled her waist, and then he lifted her off the ground so that her gaze was level with his own.

Joanna gasped a little at the unexpectedness of his action. Smiling, she looped her arms around his neck.

Tanner kissed her then, with a hunger that left her weak and clinging in its aftermath.

"How's that?" he asked, his voice husky.

"Better. Much better."

"I thought so." Once more his warm mouth made contact with hers. Joanna was startled and thrilled at the intensity of his touch. He kissed her again and again, until she thought that if he released her, she'd fall to the floor and melt at his feet. Every part of her body was heated to fever pitch.

"Joanna—"

She planted warm moist kisses across his face, not satisfied, wanting him until her heart felt as if it might explode. Tanner had awoken the sensual part of her nature, buried all the years since her divorce, and now that it had been stirred back to life, she felt starved for a man's love—this man's love.

"Yes," she breathed into his mouth. "Yes, yes, yes."

"Yes what?" he asked in a breathless murmur.

Joanna paused and smiled gently. "Yes, I'll marry you. Right now. Okay? This minute. We can fly somewhere…find a church… Oh, Tanner," she pleaded, "I want you so much."

"Joanna, we can't." His words came out in a groan, forced from deep inside him.

She heard him, but it didn't seem to matter. She kissed him and he kissed her. Their kiss continued as he lowered her to the floor, her body sliding intimately down his.

Suddenly Joanna realized what she'd just said, what she'd suggested. "We mustn't. Kristen—"

Tanner shushed her with another kiss, then said, "I know, love. This isn't the time or place, but I sure wish…"

Joanna straightened, and broke away. Shakily, she said, "So do I…and, uh, I think we should wait a while for the wedding. At least until Nicole gets back."

"Right."

"How long will that be?"

"The end of the week."

Joanna nodded and closed her eyes. It sounded like an eternity.

"What about your job?"

"I don't want to work forever, and when we decide to start a family I'll probably quit. But I want that promotion first." Joanna wasn't sure exactly why that was so important to her, but it was. She'd worked years for this achievement, and she had no intention of walking away until she'd become the first female senior loan officer.

Tanner kissed her again. "If it makes you happy keep your job as long as you want."

At that moment, however, all Joanna could think about were babies, family vacations and homemade cookies.

\* \* \*

"That's her plane now," Tanner said to Kristen, pointing toward the Boeing jet that was approaching the long narrow landing strip at Spokane International.

"I get to tell her, okay?"

"I think Tanner should do it, sweetheart," Joanna suggested gently.

"But Nicole and I are best friends. You can't expect me to keep something like this from her, something we planned since that night we all went to the Pink Palace. If it weren't for us, you two wouldn't even know each other."

Kristen's eyes were round and pleading as she stared up at Tanner and Joanna.

"You two would have been cast adrift in a sea of loneliness if it hadn't been for me and Nicole," she added melodramatically.

"All right, all right," Tanner said with a sigh. "You can tell her."

Poised at the railing by the window of the terminal, Kristen eagerly studied each passenger who stepped inside. The minute Nicole appeared, Kristen flew into her friend's arms as though it had been years since they'd last seen each other instead of a week.

Joanna watched the unfolding scene with a quiet sense of happiness. Nicole let out a squeal of delight and gripped her friend around the shoulders, and the two jumped frantically up and down.

"From her reaction, I'd guess that she's happy about our decision," Tanner said to Joanna.

"Dad, Dad!" Nicole raced up to her father, and hugged him with all her might. "It's so good to be home. I missed you. I missed everyone," she said, looking at Joanna.

Tanner returned the hug. "It's good to have you home, cupcake."

"But everything exciting happened while I was away," she said, pouting a little. "Gee, if I'd known you were finally going to get rolling with Mrs. Parsons, I'd never have left."

Joanna smiled blandly at the group of people standing around them.

"Don't be mad," Kristen said. "It was a now-or-never situation, with Mom standing there in her pajamas and everything."

Now it was Tanner's turn to notice the interested group of onlookers.

"Yes, well, you needn't feel left out. I saved the best part for you," Tanner said, taking a beautiful solitaire diamond ring out of his pocket. "I wanted you to be here for this." He reached for Joanna's hand, looking into her eyes, as he slowly, reverently, slipped it onto her finger. "I love you, Joanna, and I'll be the happiest man alive if you marry me."

"I love you, Tanner," she said in a soft voice filled with joy.

"Does this mean we're going to be sisters from now on?" Kristen shrieked, clutching her best friend's hand.

"Yup," Nicole answered. "It's what we always wanted."

With their arms wrapped around one another's shoulders, the girls headed toward the baggage-claim area.

"Yours and mine," Joanna said, watching their two daughters.

Tanner slid his arm around her waist and smiled into her eyes.

\* \* \* \* \*

**Jill Kemerer** writes novels with love, humor and faith. Besides spoiling her mini dachshund and keeping up with her busy kids, Jill reads stacks of books, lives for her morning coffee and gushes over fluffy animals. She resides in Ohio with her husband and two children. Jill loves connecting with readers, so please visit her website, jillkemerer.com, or contact her at PO Box 2802, Whitehouse, OH 43571.

### Books by Jill Kemerer

#### Love Inspired

#### Wyoming Ranchers

*The Prodigal's Holiday Hope*
*A Cowboy to Rely On*
*Guarding His Secret*
*The Mistletoe Favor*
*Depending on the Cowboy*

#### Wyoming Sweethearts

*Her Cowboy Till Christmas*
*The Cowboy's Secret*
*The Cowboy's Christmas Blessings*
*Hers for the Summer*

Visit the Author Profile page
at LoveInspired.com for more titles.

# HERS FOR THE SUMMER

## Jill Kemerer

He brought me forth also into a large place:
he delivered me, because he delighted in me.
—*2 Samuel 22:20*

To my sister, Sarah. Writing this book brought back
so many good memories of growing up in the country,
riding bikes, playing with our dolls, arguing, giggling
and always having each other's backs. I love you!

# Chapter One

Maybe she wasn't meant to be a mommy. Maybe she was only meant to nurture other people's children.

Eden Page tucked her hands into the pockets of her winter coat as she strode toward Cattle Drive Coffee. The air was clear and cold, typical for Rendezvous, Wyoming, in mid-April. It had been another long, never-ending winter. Signs of spring were all around, though. Green shoots of flower bulbs poked out in front of the bank across the street, and a few of the trees had loosened their grips on the tight buds capping off their branches. For the first time since her sister died, Eden wondered if spring was on its way in her own life, too.

Mia had been gone for almost five years. Since then Eden had been drifting along, babysitting full-time for friends and waiting and hoping for Mr. Right to show up. Unfortunately, Mr. Wrong hadn't even knocked on her door at this point.

For as long as Eden could remember, she'd wanted to get married, have children and live in Rendezvous, preferably on a ranch. She didn't regret quitting college to be here for Mia's final months, and she was thankful she'd been able to babysit her nephew, Noah, until Mason Fanning, Mia's husband, got remarried last year. Eden still spent a lot of time with the five-year-old boy.

Rounding the corner, she picked up her pace. It was time to accept reality. While only twenty-six, she might never get married or have children. The guys around here weren't interested in her and never had been. If she didn't take charge of her life soon, another five years would pass by with little to show for them, either.

The faded maroon awning above the coffee shop entrance came into view. Maybe she could finish her degree in early childhood education and get a job teaching preschool. Or expand her babysitting services.

"Howdy, Eden." Mr. Jenkins, her favorite usher from church, tipped his cowboy hat to her as he walked his two black Labs. He got around well for a man his age. "Think it'll snow tonight?"

"I hope not. I'm ready for warmer weather." She gave him a smile and petted the dogs. Their tongues lolled as they lifted pet-me eyes to her. Chuckling, she scratched behind their ears.

"At least it's Friday, right?" His brown eyes twinkled. "You have big plans?"

She did not have big plans. She didn't have *any* plans.

"I'm keeping it low-key." She gave the dogs' ears a final scratch. "What about you?"

"There's a World War II documentary on I've been

looking forward to." He tugged on the leashes, and the dogs moved forward. "Well, I won't keep you. See you Sunday."

"Enjoy yourself." She opened the door to the coffee shop. Her night sounded even less exciting than Mr. Jenkins's. At least he had a documentary to look forward to. She had nothing. Normally, she offered to babysit Noah so Mason and Brittany could have some couple time, but the three of them had other plans this evening.

The coffee shop was almost empty, and why wouldn't it be? Friday nights were for hanging out with friends, ordering pizza or going to Roscoe's for burgers—not for heavily caffeinated beverages.

The warmth of the room and hardwood floors drew her forward, and she ordered her favorite latte. While the teenager behind the counter prepared the drink, Eden turned to stare out the front windows. A young couple laughed as they strolled past arm in arm. Across the street, Eden could just make out Stu Miller helping Gretchen Sable out of his truck. Stu and Gretchen were in their seventies, and they'd managed to find love. Why couldn't she?

She couldn't even get a date. It was like she was invisible to men. Was it too much to ask for a little romance?

"Here you go." The girl handed her the cup and began wiping down the counter like her life depended on it. The shop didn't officially close for another hour. She probably had plans, too.

Back outside, Eden braced herself against the chill. Her apartment wasn't far. Last year she'd moved out of her parents' house into the apartment above Brittany Fanning's dance studio. Eden was glad Mason had married Brittany, although it was strange to think of him married to anyone other than her sister.

What was she going to do about her future? She loved babysitting, but it didn't offer benefits like paid vacations or retirement plans, and taking care of her best friend Gabby's eighteen-month-old daughter, Phoebe, a few days a week wasn't exactly paying the bills. After selling the family ranch last year, Eden's parents had blessed her with a lump sum of money. She kept her expenses low, but it was a relief to have the financial cushion now that Gabby no longer needed her to babysit Phoebe full-time.

Pale pink and lavender streaked the sky as the sun slid down the horizon. She wrapped both hands around the takeout cup and sipped it as she turned onto Third Street. The coffee warmed her insides, kicking her pulse up a notch. She barely glanced at the bungalow converted into a dentist office or the parking lot with dead grass poking out of the cracked blacktop. Up ahead, the dance studio and her apartment beckoned.

Her phone dinged. She pulled it out of her pocket.

*Ryder.*

*Blech.*

Of all the people she did *not* want to deal with tonight, Ryder Fanning topped the list. It was inconceivable that Mason could have an identical twin so unlike him. Where Mason was quiet and thought things through, Ryder lacked patience and didn't consider how his words or actions affected the people around him.

The man annoyed her.

She shoved the phone back in her pocket and took a long drink of the coffee.

Her stride lengthened as she neared the dance studio. She cut through the side parking lot, headed to the rear and climbed the stairs leading to her apartment. When she reached the top of the landing, she paused. As she stared at the door, a terrible loneliness crept in.

Everyone she knew and loved was moving on. Her closest friends were either married or engaged. Even her parents had embarked on a new life, traveling around the country in their RV. She wasn't sure she could spend another night alone flipping through the channels.

For a moment she wished something—anything—would happen to relieve the monotony of her life.

Her phone dinged again, and she unlocked the door and went inside. Did she even want to know why Ryder was texting her? It wasn't only his lack of filter she resented.

He was the one who'd bought the family ranch.

After Dad told her in January that Ryder Fanning was buying the only home she'd ever known, she'd driven to her special place outside town and cried until her tears froze. It had put the first deep crack in her hopes for the future. The life she'd always imagined truly had no chance of reviving at this point.

She'd thought she'd get married and spend Christmases in the old farmhouse, baking with her children, hanging out with her parents. But all those hopes died when Ryder bought the ranch.

Next week he was moving to Rendezvous from Los Angeles. For the past two months he'd been having the house remodeled. Her house. Hopefully, she'd never have to go inside. It would break her heart. She'd made a million memories there with Mia. They'd shared secrets, held grudges, played games.

Eden sighed, juggling the coffee as she took off her

coat and kicked off her shoes. Her phone began to ring, and she glared at it until it stopped.

She had nothing to say to him.

When it started ringing again, she marched down the hall to the kitchen, gritting her teeth the entire way. Persistence was Ryder's middle name. He'd just keep bothering her until she answered. She might as well get it over with.

"What do you want?" she asked.

"Oh, hey, you answered." Ryder's low voice had the same effect on her as the warm latte. It heated her insides and jolted her pulse to life. Unlike with the latte, she didn't enjoy the sensation. "I've got something to ask you."

His phrasing implied a favor, and she didn't do favors for him. Eden adored Ryder's cute five-year-old identical twin girls, but she did not like their daddy. Not one bit.

"Eden?"

"I'm busy." A bold lie, even for her.

"I know. It's important, though, and I don't want to discuss it over the phone. I'm in Rendezvous."

"Sorry, I can't." *Won't* was more like it. And she wasn't sorry. Not at all.

"I'll only take a minute of your time."

A twinge of guilt hit her conscience, but she didn't respond.

"Will you give me one minute, Eden?"

A minute. Would she, the one who gladly gave hours and days and weeks to any of her friends at the drop of a hat, really deny Ryder sixty seconds?

It wouldn't kill her to hear what he had to say.

Then again, it might.

"Please?"

She'd never been able to turn down a heartfelt please. "Okay, but just for a minute. You can stop by my apartment." She looked around her place, grateful she was a neat freak.

"Good, because I'm right outside your door."

Of course he was.

Her heartbeat started doing the annoying hammering thing it tended to do in his vicinity. She was 99 percent sure it was her body's way of saying *don't even think about it.*

The man was good at getting his own way.

She, on the other hand, was used to letting other people have their way.

No wonder her danger signals were off the charts.

This was what she got for wishing something—anything—would happen instead of spending another Friday night flipping through the channels.

God surely had a sense of humor.

Eden padded to the door, girded her shoulders and took a deep breath. *Don't do anything stupid.* It was probably too late for that. Answering his call had been her first mistake. Opening this door was sure to be her next.

Ryder couldn't afford to make any more mistakes with his life. That was why he had to convince Eden to babysit the girls.

Starting over as a cattle rancher in the same town as his identical twin was the best decision he'd made in years. He'd have community, friends and the slower lifestyle he craved, not to mention he'd be able to raise Harper and Ivy out in the country far from Los Angeles.

It had been a dream come true to buy the large ranch from Eden's parents. His brother, Mason, was familiar with the property since he'd been married to Eden's sister before she died, and Ryder appreciated the fact Mason had urged him to purchase it. The renovations to the large farmhouse were almost complete. Ryder and his daughters were set to move to Rendezvous one week from tomorrow.

The life he wanted was within his grasp. And it was funny, but he hadn't even known he wanted it until recently.

He knocked on Eden's door. His nerves jittered as he tried to figure out how he could get her to agree to help him. He'd have to wing it. This conversation would be easier if she liked him. But she didn't. Not by a long shot.

He'd made a bad first, second, third and fourth impression on Eden. Had he ever made a good one?

Probably not, and it didn't matter. This was about his girls. They needed someone they could trust, who would love them and help them transition from a somewhat chaotic life in LA to a slower routine in Wyoming. And he needed to rest easy knowing Harper and Ivy were being well taken care of while he learned the ins and outs of raising cattle.

He knocked again.

His career as a CPA and financial planner for Hollywood bigwigs along with the divorce settlement from his ex-wife, actress Lily Haviland, had made him wealthy enough to buy the prime Wyoming property. And since he'd spent the first twelve years of his life on a sheep ranch, he wasn't a complete novice at ranching. But cattle? He didn't have much experience with those. Mason had been giving him tips every weekend that Ryder could make it back here, but he still had a lot to learn.

"Eden, it's me." He got the impression she was standing on the other side of the door. He could practically hear her breathing. Maybe that was wishful thinking. She was probably shimmying out a side window to escape.

The door opened, and he stared into the prettiest brown eyes he'd ever seen. A surge of warmth filled his gut. Every time he saw Eden, it was the same thing—he'd take one look at her, feel all warm and gooey inside and say something stupid. The woman had no idea how she affected him, and he wanted to keep it that way.

He wasn't getting entangled in a romance again. Look at how easily he'd been fooled by Lily. He'd believed every word that came out of his ex-wife's mouth, and they'd all turned out to be lies. The worst part about it was he didn't think Lily even intended to deceive him. It came as naturally to her as slipping into the roles she played on television and the big screen.

The pain of being discarded by her still cut deep.

"Thanks for letting me come up." His voice was scratchy, although he'd downed a bottle of water on the way over.

Eden wasn't quite five and a half feet tall, and her body was slender, graceful. Dark brown hair fell in a silky curtain over her shoulders. Her delicate eyebrows arched just so under a high forehead. She wore slim-fitting black pants and a burgundy sweater hinting at curves underneath. She didn't crack a smile, but then, she was serious by nature.

Maybe that was what he found attractive. Her reserved personality. He'd never seen her flirt with any guys. She was generous to a fault with everyone—well, everyone except him.

"Come in." She pivoted and walked down the hallway. After closing the door, he followed her. He'd never been inside her apartment before.

"Nice place." He shrugged his arms out of his jacket and slung it over a bar stool near the counter. "The outside doesn't do it justice."

"It's been remodeled. Brittany let me help pick out everything." Eden sat on a chair in the living area and tucked one leg under her body.

The apartment was full of Eden touches. Cubbies and shelves brimming with children's books and toys lined the back wall of the dining area, and a colorful rug housed a pretend kitchen, doll crib and other assorted play items. The living room was all adult. Framed photos of Eden's parents and friends were placed on bookshelves along with novels, candles and photographs of nature.

"Did you take those?" He pointed to a collage of photos depicting the same view of nearby Silver Rocks River in spring, summer, fall and winter.

"Yes." She hugged one knee to her chest.

"They're great. I like how you captured it in all four seasons." When she didn't reply, he gestured to the gray couch. "Mind if I sit down?"

"Go ahead." She licked her lips and stared as if she wasn't quite sure what to do with him.

"The move is all set for next Saturday." Was that a flicker of anger in her eyes? Why would she be mad? "What? What was that look for?"

"Nothing."

"I know I'm not your favorite person, but do you have a problem with me moving here?"

"No." No emotion came through. "I don't love the fact you bought my parents' ranch."

"Oh." It had been on the market for a year. Her father had seemed relieved to sell it to him. He hadn't realized Eden wasn't in favor of the sale. "Why not?"

He regretted asking as soon as the words were out of his mouth. He braced himself for the truth. She probably thought he wasn't qualified to raise cattle and was assuming he'd fail at it.

He couldn't fail at it. He needed this change—needed to belong here.

"It's my childhood home."

"And?" His muscles unlocked. At least she hadn't accused him of incompetence.

"And I didn't want them to sell it." Her voice trailed off at the end, and she directed her gaze to the wall.

"Did you not want them to sell it to me?" he asked. "Or did you not want them to sell it at all?"

"At all."

Okay, he could work with that. As long as it wasn't him personally she objected to.

"Why are you here, Ryder? I know it's not to ask my blessing about you moving to my ranch."

Her ranch. His lips twitched. There had been a time in his life when bluntness would have put him on the defensive, but after everything Lily had put him through, he found bluntness—Eden's especially—refreshing.

"I need you to babysit the girls through the summer. This fall they'll be in kindergarten all day, but in the meantime, they need someone like you to help them adjust to their new life here."

A wistful smile brightened her face for a moment, but it disappeared behind a frown. "Chandra Davis runs a good day care program in town. Talk to her."

"I already did, and she's booked. She can't take the girls."

"Then find someone else."

"I've tried." He kept his tone gentle as frustration started to build. "Martha McNally has agreed to come to the ranch early every day so I can do my morning chores. She'll get the girls dressed and fed, then drive them here, so you wouldn't have to do anything but open your door for them at eight in the morning."

"Maybe Martha would watch them all day." She wouldn't meet his eyes. Annoyance flared up, catching him off guard.

"Look, Eden, I know I'm not your favorite person. When we first met, you were right to call me out for arguing with Lily on the phone in front of the girls."

"Your relationship with your ex-wife is none of my business. If the girls hadn't been completely crushed at the time, I wouldn't have mentioned it at all. It was ages ago. I'm over it."

Then why did she avoid him whenever he was in town? It was on the tip of his tongue to ask her. However, that was not why he was here.

"Hey, I take full responsibility for putting my foot in my mouth a few times since then, too," he said. "I've tried to make things right with you, but I don't know how. And at this point, it really doesn't matter if you resent me or think I'm a class-A jerk. I just need my girls to be in good hands. You're the only one I trust them with."

Her stony expression softened a fraction.

"I'd need you to watch them Monday through Friday. Obviously, I'd make it worth your while financially."

"I'm sorry, but no." She stood and crossed over to the window, rubbing her forearms as if chilled.

"What can I say that will convince you to agree?" He forced himself to stay seated.

"Nothing."

He'd hoped Eden would see this for what it was—a business arrangement—and agree. Maybe her dislike of him was stronger than he'd thought.

Had he been mistaken about her? Was she the best person to take care of his twins? When it came to women, he didn't always see clearly.

Still…his gut was telling him the girls needed Eden. And he'd do anything for his daughters.

She wanted to say yes.

Eden gripped her biceps as she stared unfocused out the window. Ryder's twins, Harper and Ivy, had wriggled into her heart the moment she'd met them over a year ago. But she had to decline. She was supposed to be working on her long-term plans, not drifting into another babysitting job.

"I don't have any other options." Ryder's caramel-brown eyes pierced hers. Why was he so handsome? She'd never been attracted to Mason in all the years she'd known him, but she found his identical twin, Ryder, to be positively gorgeous. It was strange.

"Have you even asked Martha if she'd babysit them full-time?"

"I don't want her to." Ryder sat with his knees spread, elbows on his thighs. His hands were clasped and dangling between his knees.

The man looked so muscular and lanky and miserable sitting on her couch it was all she could do not to go over there and pet his head like she had Mr. Jenkins's dogs.

"Martha has a lot of experience." Eden could not cave. She had her own life to live and would not get caught up in his problems. She'd gotten caught up in everyone else's problems for five years, and look where it had gotten her. "She used to take care of her grandkids."

"Martha doesn't have the energy or desire to watch lively preschoolers all day." He blew out a frustrated breath. "Is this about me? You wouldn't have to spend time with me or anything."

"This isn't about you." She didn't hate the guy. That being said, he was correct. He'd put his foot in his mouth on more than one occasion, but he probably didn't even know why she'd been offended. Eden would never forget the look on the twins' faces when he'd taken a phone call from his ex-wife at Christmas Fest and argued with her in front of them. They'd been devastated. When Eden pointedly told him she'd watch the girls if he got another call, he'd rudely told her to mind her own business. Then a few days later, he'd pulled her aside and told her she couldn't possibly understand since she'd never been married.

That one had hurt.

And over the past year, he'd made comment after comment about how she had the right idea by staying single.

As if it was by choice.

Ryder Fanning should come with a warning: *Hazard—Do Not Touch*. He was not the guy for her, and if she ever forgot it, even for a moment, all she had to do was picture his former wife, Lily Haviland, the glowing, talented, beautiful actress and winner of a Golden Globe.

Even if Ryder was the greatest guy on earth—which he wasn't—he would never be into ordinary Eden Page after being married to spectacular Lily Haviland. What man would?

"What is this about, then?" Ryder watched her with a thoughtful expression.

What was it about?

Getting her life together. For five years she'd been babysitting for her loved ones. She'd been happy to be there for them when they'd needed her the most. They were her friends, her support group.

But Ryder? He wasn't one of her friends. And she didn't want him to be.

Starting here, starting now, she was saying no.

"Taking care of the twins doesn't fit in with my plans."

He raked his fingers through short dark blond hair and met her eyes. "It would only be for the summer."

Harper and Ivy with their adorable dark wavy hair and gigantic blue eyes came to mind. They were darling girls. She could do the summer, couldn't she?

*No.* She wasn't getting sucked into his problems.

"Look, Lily's been out of the country shooting a movie," Ryder said. "The girls have been struggling since I told them we were moving. Ivy asks me roughly eighteen times a day how Mommy will find her when we move to Rendezvous. And Harper gets real quiet when Lily is brought up. They need more care than the local day care center or Martha could give them."

Her heart ached for the poor girls. This wasn't just a move for them; it was a complete upheaval of their lives.

The day care would never do. And Martha was in her midsixties. It would be a lot for her to take care of the twins for hours every day. "My apartment isn't set up for multiple children."

"What are you talking about?" He stood and pointed to the dining area with all the toys. "You've got everything right there."

"But it would be cramped. I still babysit Phoebe a few times a week."

"They'll survive a few months of cramped. I'll pay you extra."

What else could she say? No argument came to mind.

"Well, I'd have to talk to Gabby," she said, caving. "She might not like the idea."

His face lit up. "Does this mean you'll do it?"

"I'll consider it. But if Gabby objects…"

"Thank you, Eden." He rose, crossed over and pulled her into a hug.

His arms were strong. In fact, the man was a wall of muscle. He smelled expensive, like department store cologne, and the overwhelming reality of him sent flutters to her stomach. She quickly stepped out of his embrace.

"Don't thank me yet. Gabby might say no." She doubted it, though. Gabby would probably rave about how Harper and Ivy would be like sisters to Phoebe.

"Why don't I get a pizza for us?" He grinned. "We can celebrate."

"Uh, no thanks. I have plans." The fib was necessary. Babysitting the girls was one thing. Pizza alone with him was another.

His grin faded away, but he cocked his chin to her. "Another time. Thanks, Eden. I'll see myself out."

After the door clicked shut behind him, she smashed a throw pillow into her chest. What was wrong with her? She'd done it again. Slid right into someone else's plans instead of concentrating on her own.

Was she being too hard on herself? She *did* want to babysit Harper and Ivy. They were going through a tough transition. It wasn't their fault she had issues with their father.

An uneasy feeling slithered down her spine. What if this wasn't about wanting to help the girls?

Ryder owned the ranch she grew up on.

He was single.

And alarmingly good-looking.

She'd have to be careful. Being around Ryder on a near-daily basis might revive her dream about getting married and raising a family on a ranch here in Rendezvous.

It had taken a long time to accept the dream wasn't going to happen.

The only one raising a family on the ranch would be Ryder, not her.

She'd try not to hold it against him.

# Chapter Two

"I'm not going to regret this, am I?" The following Saturday, Ryder and the twins were official residents of Rendezvous. The moving company had unloaded the truck earlier, and a group of friends were helping him unpack. Ryder had been riding a wave of adrenaline all day, but now reality was setting in. It wasn't the first time he'd second-guessed his decision, but standing in the newly renovated living room of the farmhouse reminded him how permanent this move was.

"You did the right thing." Mason clapped him on the shoulder. "You said it yourself, you wanted a fresh start. A back-to-nature lifestyle to raise the girls."

"I do." He rubbed his chin. "I'm worried about them adapting."

"They sound happy to me." Mason arched his eyebrows, pointing to the ceiling where little footsteps pounded up and down the hallway accompanied by squeals and shouts. Noah and the girls were up there along with Mason's friends Gabby and Dylan Kingsley, who'd recently married and were supposed to be helping the twins unpack their toys. Not much unpacking could be happening with all that noise. If Ryder had to guess, he'd say they were playing tag. Or wrestling. Maybe both.

He dropped onto the couch and sighed.

"What's wrong?" Mason asked.

"I think it all kind of hit me. The weekends I've spent with you have helped me get a feel for cattle, but there's so much I don't know."

"Have you talked to Chris?" Mason asked. "He's been doing a good job managing this place since Bill and Joanna started traveling last year. He'll fill you in on everything you need to know. And I'm always here. Call anytime. That's what brothers are for."

Chris Ashbury had been doing a good job from what Ryder could tell, and he was thankful the man had agreed to stay on now that he owned the place.

"Thanks, Mason." Two years ago, he hadn't even known his identical twin existed. Now he relied on him for emotional support. "Chris does seem to know what he's doing."

"He does. He grew up around here working for local ranchers. Moved away a while back to get married. It's a shame he got divorced, but I'm glad he's back and ranching again."

Ryder had sunk a lot of money into buying this place, and he wanted everything right. He'd updated the farmhouse. Convinced Chris to work for him. And he'd landed the best babysitter possible for the girls.

Eden had called earlier in the week and told him Gabby was okay with her babysitting all three children. So why was he having all these doubts?

"Has Eden been over yet?" Mason took in the room. "I can't get over the house. It's the same…but better."

"No, I invited her to come over tonight, but she's helping Nicole with the triplets." Ryder got up and opened a large box marked Living Room. Since he hadn't expected her to come over, it was stupid to be disappointed.

"Hey, Ryder," Brittany called from the kitchen. "Where do you want your pans?"

"Leave the man's pans alone," Mason yelled back. Brittany popped her head around the corner and stuck her tongue out at him, but the twinkle in her blue eyes teased.

"The cupboard next to the stove, please," Ryder said, then turned back to Mason. "I appreciate you guys helping me out."

"We're glad to. Noah has been racing around like he scarfed down a bag full of candy he's been so excited to have Harper and Ivy living here." Mason dug through a box and held up two remote controls. "Media cabinet?"

Ryder nodded.

Gabby, looking flushed, came down the staircase with a big grin. "Eden is going to flip when she sees this place, Ryder."

"Why?" He hoped that was a good thing.

"The changes." The petite, curvy brunette waved her arm. "It's the same layout but so much brighter. And am I mistaken or did you find more room in the kitchen? It feels bigger, and it wasn't exactly small before."

"The kitchen was closed off, so I had the contractor bump out a wall and add an island. It's a better use of the space."

"Well, it's amazing." Gabby backed up several steps to peek through the sunroom. "Oh, good! You left the sunroom the same. I can't tell you how many times I've had tea and cookies in there with Eden and her mother. In fact, Phoebe learned to crawl in there. It's always been my favorite spot in the house."

An uncomfortable feeling prickled the back of Ryder's neck. Everyone kept mentioning Eden. He hadn't thought about her when he was renovating. She'd grown up here. Lived in this house until last year. She didn't like that he'd bought *her* ranch. How would she react when she saw the place? Would she resent the changes he'd made?

That was assuming she'd ever come over to see it. At this point, he doubted Eden would step foot in here.

Harper, Ivy and Noah raced down the stairs louder than wild beasts. Dylan slowly followed with an amused grin on his face. "I promised them sodas."

"There's caffeine-free soda in the cooler on the porch." Ryder hitched his thumb toward the front door, even though the last thing those three needed was more sugar.

"Daddy, guess what?" Ivy stopped in front of him, looking up through impossibly large dark blue eyes.

"What?" He crouched to her level.

She wrapped her arms around his neck. "I'm sleeping in Auntie Eden's room!"

The girls had often heard Noah refer to her as Auntie Eden, and they must have decided to call her that, too. He'd have to run it by her on Monday.

"It's not fair." Harper stormed up behind Ivy and crossed her arms over her chest in a major pout.

"What's not fair?" He turned his attention to her.

"I want to sleep in Auntie Eden's room! Why does Ivy get to and not me?"

Before Ryder could react, Mason picked up Harper, settling her on his hip. "Because you got Mia's room."

"Who's Mia?" She gave him her full attention.

"Noah's mother. She's Eden's sister. I was married to her, but she died when Noah was a baby."

"Miss Brittany's my mommy now, aren't you?" Noah puffed out his chest as Brittany joined them.

"I sure am." Brittany ruffled Noah's hair. "But your mother was a wonderful person from what I hear." Brittany directed her attention to Harper, still in Mason's arms. "You're the oldest, right?"

"Yes, I am." Harper threw a triumphant look Ivy's way. Ivy gave her the stink eye.

"Well, Mia was Eden's older sister. So it makes sense you would have her room."

"I'm younger, just like Auntie Eden." Ivy seemed pretty pleased with herself.

"Don't brag, Ivy." Harper turned back to Brittany. "Was Mia pretty?"

"She was real pretty." Noah stepped forward proudly. "You saw her. There's a picture on the wall in my house with Daddy and me when I was a baby."

"That's your mommy. I forgot." Harper hugged Mason's neck. "Uncle Mason, you look like Daddy, but you smell different."

Mason chuckled as he set her down. "Is that bad?"

"No, you smell good. Like clouds and air."

Mason met Ryder's gaze, and they both shrugged.

Harper grabbed Noah's hand and they ran to the kitchen, announcing they were thirsty.

"Daddy?" Ivy had her worried face on again.

"What, pumpkin?"

"When is Mommy coming? Can she stay in my room?"

Ryder's heart sank. Ivy had been having a lot of separation anxiety in regard to Lily lately. *Lord, will You help me find the right words?* "She's shooting a movie in another country. Remember how I told you it's far away?"

"How come everyone else's mommies live with them and ours doesn't? It's not fair."

Ryder took Ivy by the hand and led her to the sunroom for privacy. He sat next to her on the small love seat.

"I know it's not fair, Ivy. But I can't do anything about it. We aren't married anymore, and Mommy will visit when she can. Until then, we'll enjoy our new house and our new friends, okay?"

A tear dropped to her cheek and slid down her face. Then another.

"Aw, Ivy, don't cry. Your mommy loves you."

"Then why isn't she here?" She hiccupped.

Not having an answer for her, he pulled her into a tight hug. "You'll always have me. That's one thing I can promise."

"Ivy, I got you a orange pop!" Noah yelled.

She wiped her face and let out a pitiful sigh, then left the room to claim her soda.

He pinched the bridge of his nose. Maybe this move was going to be more difficult than he'd imagined. He'd asked Lily several times to visit the girls as soon as possible, and she'd said she would. But he knew her. If she planned a visit, something would come up—an amazing opportunity or a meeting she just had to take—and she'd either cancel the trip or cut it short.

In time the girls would come to terms with their mother's ways. But they were too young to understand at this point.

They wanted to be with her.

And she didn't want to be with them.

He would never put anything—or anyone—above his girls. Their needs came first. Everything else was a distant second. He wished Lily would put the girls first for once, too. But he doubted she ever would. And he'd be the one left to deal with the emotional fallout. As usual.

Her first day with the Fanning twins. Eden checked the side window again on Monday morning. Mrs. McNally was set to arrive any minute, and Eden didn't want her to have to navigate the stairs to the apartment. A silver minivan turned into the parking lot. Eden threw on her coat and headed down to get the girls.

Had she done the right thing by agreeing to babysit them?

It was too late to back out now, and frankly, she didn't want to. She'd make this transition as smooth as possible for them. Get to know them better. Then she'd be able to plan a schedule to keep them active, learning and engaged.

The sky was overcast, and the temperature had dropped overnight. She shivered as she approached the minivan idling in the spot next to the SUV her mom and dad gave her when they started traveling.

"Hi, girls!" Eden slid open the door and waved to

them. They looked sleepy, but they both said hi. "Come on, let's get inside where it's warm."

After helping them out of the booster seats, she took their backpacks and thanked Martha. The girls waved as she drove away.

"This doesn't look like a house."

"It's not." Eden followed them up the stairs. "It's an apartment."

"Oh."

She opened the door and set their backpacks in the hall. "Go ahead and take off your shoes and coats. There are hooks in the closet for you."

The girls both had long brown hair with natural waves, big blue eyes and button noses. Eden sighed in relief when she saw that Ryder had pinned name tags on their sweaters. She thought she could tell them apart, but she wanted to be sure on the first day. Harper wore purple leggings with a green sweater featuring a purple puppy. Ivy wore pink leggings with a baby-blue sweater featuring a pink kitten.

Eden gave them a quick tour of her place before leading them to the play area. They instantly gravitated to the play kitchen and doll furniture. Ivy selected a doll, and Harper began baking a pretend cake.

"Do you like your new house?" Eden sat cross-legged on the rug. As much as she didn't like the thought of anyone else living in her old home, she wanted them to be happy there.

"Yes, it's big. Auntie Eden, I sleep in your room!" With shining eyes, Ivy brought the doll over and set it in her lap. Cradling the baby, Eden melted at Ivy's sweetness.

"And I sleep in Mia's." Harper looked up from the pretend stove. "That's Noah's mommy."

"His *real* mommy," Ivy said.

Eden stifled a chuckle. "Yes, I know. Mia was my sister. And I'm glad you like your rooms."

"Mommy's going to come visit us soon." Ivy took the doll back and attempted to wrap it in a quilted blanket before placing it in the crib.

"How wonderful." It would be good for the girls to see their mother. Eden could picture Lily Haviland—not that she'd ever met the woman. She'd watched every episode of *Courtroom Crimes* Lily had starred in, and she'd seen most of her movies, too. The actress seemed so warm and kind and vivacious and beautiful. Eden couldn't imagine what it would be like to actually meet her. "We'll have to plan something nice for your mommy. We could do some projects. Then you'd have something to give her."

Rendezvous would likely be seeing a lot of Lily Haviland now that Ryder had arrived. She'd have to ask him when Lily planned on coming. It must be difficult for her to be away from the girls so much.

"Yay!" Ivy threw her hands in the air. "I want to give something special to Mommy."

"Of course." Eden ticked through her mental list of projects the girls could do. "What do you enjoy? Drawing? Painting?"

"Yes!" they shouted in unison.

Eden laughed. "Harper, why don't you make us a big chocolate cake while Ivy feeds the baby her bottle, and I'll get my binder of ideas out."

"I can only make pretend cake." Harper had a worried look in her eye.

"I don't have a bottle!" Ivy's tone held an edge of panic.

"Pretend cake is extra yummy, Harper." Eden pointed to the purple basket in the cubbies. "Bottles, bibs, diapers and everything the baby needs is in there, Ivy."

Harper took out a plastic mixing bowl and pretended to pour flour in it, while Ivy lined up the baby supplies. Eden took the opportunity to go to her bedroom closet where she kept binders of project ideas, worksheets and games for children. She brought two thick binders back to the play area.

"You better cover that baby, Ivy." Harper reached for the manual mixer. "When I beat this cake, stuff is going to go flying."

"Wait!" Ivy found a scarf to put over the crib. "Okay, she's safe."

Harper made buzzing noises as she cranked the pretend mixer, and Ivy clapped her hands. "You're doing it, Harper! I can't wait to have a big piece."

"Well, it has to go in the oven first or it'll be all soupy." She made a big production out of pouring the imaginary batter into a pan. Then she opened the plastic oven door, shoved the pan inside, kicked it shut and wiped her hands dramatically. "Ivy, that kid stinks. You better change its dipey."

The girl held the doll up, bottom first, and took a sniff. "Hooey." Ivy waved her hand in front of her nose and grabbed one of the Velcro diapers from the cubby.

Eden enjoyed their interaction. They played instinctively. Every now and then they'd argue over something, but they quickly resolved it and returned to their make-believe.

What a precious gift to watch these children play.

Poor Lily. She was missing it all.

Had she fought Ryder about bringing the girls here? She probably saw the twins often in LA. Why would Ryder move them so far away?

It was none of her business.

To be fair, he did have full custody of them. And he'd mentioned Lily was on location somewhere. Eden had no idea what their arrangement was. He didn't talk about his ex-wife. Ever.

"It's done!" Harper, with her arms covered to her elbows in oven mitts, flourished the pan.

"It so chocolatey." Ivy pretended to smell it.

"Harper, why don't you serve each of us a slice? And Ivy, the teapot is behind you. Let's have a tea party." Eden steepled her fingers below her chin. The girls' mouths formed Os as they hurried to the cubbies for the play dishes.

As they oohed and aahed over the imaginary cake, Ivy poured them pretend tea from the plastic teapot and Eden asked them about their favorite toys, activities and movies. Harper claimed she loved chasing butterflies, playing the running game—Eden wasn't sure she wanted to know what that entailed—and riding Daddy like a pony. Ivy, on the other hand, loved coloring, playing with her stuffed animals, and dressing Daddy up fancy with makeup and a feather scarf.

Eden hadn't pictured Ryder as the type to let the girls put makeup on him or ride him like a pony, but then, she didn't know him well. She really didn't know him at all.

"We should have a tea party with Daddy tonight," Ivy said to Harper.

"I'll bake another cake." Harper stretched her arm as high as it would go. "This big."

Eden wished she could freeze this moment in time. Five-year-old children were a lot of fun.

"Did you know I have a friend who's a real baker here in Rendezvous?" Eden said.

"Really?" Harper lifted shining eyes to her.

"Maybe we can talk her into letting us stop by one day so she can show you how she bakes."

"Oh, yes, I want to go!" Harper said.

"Do you know what else?" Eden asked.

"What?" They watched her with rapt attention.

"She has three babies. Triplets."

"Like us." Ivy pointed to Harper.

Harper nodded. "Except one more."

"And they're real babies?" Ivy asked, looking skeptical.

"Yes, they're real babies."

"Can we hold them?"

"I don't know," Eden said. "We'd have to ask permission."

"I'm not touching a real dipey." Harper furrowed her eyebrows and shook her head.

Eden laughed. "Don't worry. She'll handle the diapers. Now, I understand you girls have been going to preschool…"

For the next couple of hours, Eden had them do activities to determine their learning levels and interests. They were up to speed on their letters, colors, shapes and numbers.

After lunch, they began to argue more often. They were probably tired. The three of them snuggled on the couch and watched a Disney movie.

Her thoughts went to the upcoming week. Once again, she couldn't help thinking her apartment, while spacious enough for a single woman, was awfully small to babysit three children in. And she didn't want them to be cooped up all the time when the weather got nice, either.

Her own childhood on the ranch had been wonderful. She and Mia would run around their big backyard, ride horses with their dad and help their mom bake and cook in the kitchen. The ranch had given her freedom, space, family and more.

She stole a peek at the girls on either side of her.

She wanted them to have a childhood like hers. Not stuck in an apartment while their mother was far away and their dad was working cattle.

It wasn't up to her, though.

There was nothing she could do about it, but it bothered her just the same.

"Daddy! Daddy!" The twins raced to Ryder after Eden let him into her apartment later that afternoon. They hung on his legs, both talking at once. Their happy faces pushed away the troubles of the day and took the edge off his doubts about making such a drastic life change.

"Easy does it. One at a time." He put his hands up in surrender, and they let go of his legs to hop up and down.

"We had a tea party, and I'm going to make you the biggest cake ever." Harper propped her little fists under her chin in excitement.

"I like cake." He was used to Harper being the first to jump in with whatever was on her mind. The kid tended to do everything heart first, head later. Her enthusiasm made life sweet, even if it did give him heart palpitations at times.

"I poured the tea." Ivy spun in a little circle. "And we watched a movie with kitties, and I want a fluffy white kitten so I can put a pink bow around her neck and she can sleep with me every night."

That was his Ivy. Always wanting a kitten. Now that they were living in the country, he could probably make it happen. The barn cats weren't tamed or he'd bring one of them inside for her.

"Sounds like you had a good day." He met Eden's eyes then, and his pulse roared to life. She was actually smiling. Man, she was pretty when she smiled.

"We made lots of pictures, Daddy." Harper took his hand and dragged him to the dining area. "See?"

He took in the table full of drawings and craft projects.

"We did our small letters, too." Ivy took his other hand and pointed to the stack of paper lined for handwriting.

"You were busy." Real busy. He couldn't believe they'd done so much in one day. They typically colored a picture or two with the nanny back in LA. That was it.

"You can take these with you, girls." Eden had paper clipped two piles, one for Ivy and one for Harper. "The other ones we'll bind into books for you to give to your mother when she comes to visit."

"Yay!" Ivy cheered. "I can't wait to show it to Mommy."

"Me, too!" Harper said.

Their mother? He wasn't sure why Eden was having them make books for her, but if it made the twins happy... "Well, girls, get your coats on while I talk to Eden a minute."

They raced to the closet at the end of the hall.

"I can't believe you did all this." Ryder looked at the table again. "You're really organized. I'm impressed."

"It's nothing." Her lips were still curved, making her look young, happy, serene. "I enjoyed it. Harper and Ivy are delightful. But I'd better warn you I don't know how much we'll be able to get done on their special books before Lily arrives. I'll do my best."

"What do you mean?" Was he missing something? She acted like Lily was coming in two days.

"I'll have the girls do some finger painting, collages, drawings, that sort of thing. We can include some of their letters and numbers, too, if you'd like."

"Lily isn't—" He realized the girls were standing behind him. He straightened his spine. "She'll love them."

"Great." Eden handed each girl her backpack. "Maybe we can talk later. I have a few questions, and I want you to have time to consider them before giving me your answers."

"Should I be concerned?" He guided the girls down the hallway.

"No, it's about field trips."

"Field trips? Oh. Okay." He opened the door. "Tell Miss Eden thank you."

"Thank you, Auntie Eden," they chimed, giving her a big hug. Then they held hands, went outside and made their way down the staircase, holding on to the rail and laughing all the way.

"Do you mind if they call you Auntie Eden?" He paused on the landing. "They picked it up from Noah."

"Not at all."

"I'll call you after supper. We can discuss the field trips and...whatever."

"Sounds good." She began to shut the door, and he had to force himself to move forward. It had been a long, hard day, and he wanted nothing more than to tell her about it. But they weren't friends, not really. And she was already doing him a big favor.

"Hey, Ryder," she said.

"Yeah?" He turned back, hope rumbling through his chest.

"Get some rest. Ranching this time of year, well, it's not easy with all the new calves."

"Thanks, Eden. I will." His spirits bounced back as he descended the steps. Maybe she didn't hate him. It was a start in the right direction at least. And working with those calves had been exhausting.

The girls stood next to his truck, and he opened the door and lifted each of them into it. Once they got settled in their booster seats, he checked to make sure they were buckled properly. Then he climbed into the driver's seat and fired the engine.

"Who wants burgers?" he asked.

"Me! Me!" they shouted.

Good, because he didn't have an ounce of energy left to cook.

Later that evening after the twins had conked out in their beds, Ryder sat on the couch in sweatpants and a long-sleeved T-shirt. It was the first moment he'd had to digest his day, and he'd rather forget it ever happened.

Right away he and Chris had fed and checked the cattle, then moved on to other chores. It seemed as if every five minutes ten new questions came to mind. They'd gone over the calendar so he'd know what to expect, and then Chris had excused himself to work on a busted piece of machinery. Ryder had left himself voice memo after voice memo of things to check into, and he still felt clueless even after studying the previous six months of books that Bill Page, Eden's father, had graciously left for him.

To say he was overwhelmed would be the understatement of the century.

He scrolled through his phone, noting the seventeen voice memos he'd left for himself, and decided they could wait. It was high time he called Eden. She answered on the third ring.

"I hope I'm not interrupting anything." He held his breath, anticipating a snippy reply.

"Nope." She sounded friendly. Huh. There was a first time for everything. "I'm so bored I'm watching a television special on what causes crop circles."

He chuckled. "Crop circles, huh? Any answers?"

"Besides teenage pranksters? No."

"Want me to let you go? I'd hate for you to miss anything."

Her laugh was a melody to his ears. "Watching this program is a new low for me. How are the girls? Did they seem okay tonight?"

Wait. Was he having an actual conversation with Eden? The woman who'd refused to give him the time of day since they'd met?

"They're great. They wouldn't stop talking all through supper. You must have tired them out, though, because neither one gave me any grief about bath time or going to bed."

"I'm glad. They're amazing little girls."

Hearing her praise his babies filled his chest with

pride. He loved those kids, but he worried he was failing them. The women in their lives hadn't been very reliable. Lily refused to share custody. She visited them when it suited her, which wasn't often. And every nanny Ryder hired had left for greener pastures within six months.

Eden continued. "I wondered if you'd be okay with me taking the girls to the library once or twice a week. I also thought they'd like to have a baking session with Nicole. It would give them a chance to see the triplets. This morning, Harper zoomed over to the play kitchen, and Ivy clearly loves babies. I think it would be fun for them both."

Gratitude flooded him. In one day, Eden had recognized Harper's and Ivy's different interests and wanted to make a special outing for them.

The woman was something.

All the ways Lily had misled him rushed back. She'd wanted kids right away, wanted to stay home with them, wanted to take a break from acting.

He'd thought Lily was something, too.

Until she'd proven him so spectacularly wrong.

"That would be great." He wasn't going to judge Eden based on Lily's behavior. "You have my permission to take them wherever you'd like. As long as it's local, I'm fine with it."

"Don't worry. I don't have any overnight stays planned at this point." There it was again—Eden teasing. He wouldn't have thought it possible a week ago. "On a serious note, though, I'll let you know ahead of time if we're planning something out of the ordinary."

"I appreciate it. But if it's a matter of going to the park or library or whatever, don't feel like you need my permission." He realized he hadn't discussed her expense account. He always gave the nanny a credit card to buy the girls' lunches or to go out and have some fun. "By the way, I have a credit card for you to use. For, you know, if you want to go out to lunch or grab some Dipping Dream ice cream."

"That isn't necessary, Ryder."

"It is." He wasn't going to have her pay for his children's fun. And he also needed to clear the air about Lily visiting. He wasn't sure why Eden assumed she was coming soon, but he figured the girls had said something. "Earlier you mentioned making books for Lily."

"Is that a problem?" Her tone shifted from friendly to ice-cold in an instant. He already missed the banter they'd been enjoying.

"No, not at all. It's thoughtful of you. But Lily isn't coming right away."

"When is she coming?"

He raked his hand through his hair. Lily was a touchy subject between him and Eden. He didn't want to make things awkward. He'd have to choose his words carefully.

"She's been on location in New Zealand. I'm not sure when shooting wraps up or when she'll be able to get away."

"Oh, I see."

From her quiet answer, he doubted she saw at all. But what was the point in setting her straight? He'd accepted that Lily Haviland's number-one priority in life was herself. She wasn't a bad person. She said the right things when she came around, but she'd let him and the girls down too many times to count.

He had no faith in his ex-wife at all. But it would do

the girls no good for him to bad-mouth their mother to Eden or anyone. It wouldn't do him any good, either. A lot of prayer had helped him get to this point, and he wasn't about to backslide now.

"When I have a firm date, I'll let you know," he said.

"Okay."

What could he say to get them back to a good place? "I guess this means it will give the girls more time to make the books."

"Yes." Her voice brightened. "I'll come up with some fun projects for them. Don't you worry."

Like he'd ever worry with her in charge of the girls. He'd seen her close relationship with Noah. And she always seemed to be babysitting for her friends whenever he came to town. She had a special touch when it came to children.

He'd been right to hire Eden. She was the dream babysitter every parent longed for. In her capable hands, his girls would be all right. He just had to be careful on a personal level. Eden didn't seem to like him much, anyhow. But if she changed her mind about him...he'd be tempted to explore the possibilities with her.

The truth was he didn't know Eden all that well.

And it was best if he kept it that way.

# Chapter Three

This arrangement wasn't working.

The following Saturday morning, Eden bit into a cinnamon roll as she strolled to the park. She'd stopped for coffee and picked up the pastry on her way to meet Ryder. The first day of May held the scent of possibility, or maybe it was the smell of the grass coming back to life after a snowy winter. Either way, the sun was shining.

The blue skies would help her deliver bad news. It would be cruel to hurt someone, even Ryder, on a gray day.

A white gazebo ahead encouraged her to *come on in*, but she decided to sit at a picnic table on the lawn to let the sun warm her face. The temperature was still cool enough to need her winter coat. At least she'd been able to leave her hat and gloves behind.

For the past three days she'd been trying to come up with a solution to her babysitting problem. Her apartment was too small for the children. And late in the afternoon, music from the dance studio below distracted the girls. Eden had learned to tune it out ages ago, but on the days Brittany held classes, the twins, already tired, struggled to pay attention and grew ornery.

If only Eden still lived on the ranch. It had been perfect for babysitting. The rambling farmhouse had a large family room in addition to the other common areas. Eden and Mia had played a million games in there, and more recently, Eden had spent many special days with Mia's son in there. She and Noah had read stories, played games and made too many crafts to count. When the weather was nice, they'd always go outside.

She couldn't imagine what the farmhouse looked like now. Her chest crumbled like an old sponge. She missed it. The day she'd said goodbye to it had been a low point for her. All the memories of Mia and her childhood were wrapped up in those walls. Were the pencil lines in the closet where Dad had measured them each year still there?

"Nice day, isn't it?"

She hadn't noticed Ryder striding up. His broad grin made her stomach drop like the first hill of a roller coaster. He wore loose-fitting jeans and a Henley under an unzipped jacket. A cowboy hat covered his hair.

"It is." Now that he was here, she had no idea what to say. She wanted to babysit the girls, but she didn't see how she could continue. Three small children bouncing off one another was stressful, and she couldn't continue to put them through an hour of music blaring at the precise time they were most tired.

"I take it you have something on your mind." He weaved his legs into the picnic table to sit opposite her.

Usually looking at his face turned her insides mushy, but the bags under his eyes and his drawn cheeks concerned her. He looked exhausted. And dejected. He was clearly making an effort to hide his mood behind a smile.

"Rough first week on the ranch?" she asked gently.

"Why?" His eyebrows drew together. "Did someone say something?"

"No, you look tired, that's all."

"Oh." He ran his hand down his cheek. "I guess I am."

"Not used to getting up at the crack of dawn to check cattle, are you?"

"It's getting easier." With that he yawned. "It is, really. Ignore that."

"What are you doing about night checks?" Funny, she hadn't considered how being a single dad on the ranch would affect calving. Her father had gone out at all hours of the night to check pregnant cows. His calving season began in March, was heaviest in April and finished in May. Cold weather and late storms always affected the herd. She hoped they wouldn't get more snow.

"I hired two people to take shifts in the night. Charlie agreed to stay on through June. Naomi might, too."

"Smart. That way you won't have to leave Harper and Ivy alone." She wondered if it bothered him to not be out there checking the cattle himself, though.

"Exactly. I'm thankful for the extra help. The cows…" His lips drew together in a tight line.

"What's wrong with them?" She ticked through the

various cattle issues her father had dealt with over the years. Malnutrition, freezing to death, losing newborn calves, predators...

"Everyone can see I'm new at this, including the cows." His jaw shifted, then he met her eyes and his expression softened. "Some of those new moms are ornery."

"Don't I know it." She stared off into the distance as the memories came back. "Dad used to come in cussin' up a storm when he had to deal with a protective mama cow."

His mouth curved upward but fell just as quickly.

She'd helped Dad with the cattle until she graduated high school. It wasn't her favorite thing in the world, but spending time with him and the ranch hands had taught her many tricks about raising cattle in the harsh Wyoming climate. She'd helped out in almost any situation whenever the need arose.

"I know raising cattle is new for you," she said, "but the rest of it isn't. You grew up in Montana, right? So you're used to the weather. And raising sheep means you had to deal with a lot of the same things we do. Keeping them safe, fed and alive are the top priorities. Don't worry. You'll get it."

He met her eyes then, and she took a sharp intake of breath at the gratitude radiating from them. He must have had a rough week if a few sentences of encouragement from her were helping him.

"You sure about that?" he asked. "I feel about as green as a new blade of grass, and everyone who works for me can see it, too."

"Oh, don't worry. They'll think you're an amateur for a while." She'd seen the way they teased each other.

Cowboys had to earn respect in these parts, even when they owned the ranch. "They'll respect you eventually. How bad is it?"

"I'll survive."

"By this time next year, you'll not only be the boss, but they'll look at you like one, too."

"Yeah, well, I hope by this time next year, I'll be worthy of their respect. I almost lost a calf yesterday, and I haven't stopped thinking about it. How can anyone look up to their boss if he can barely keep a fresh-born calf alive?"

"What happened?" Her forgotten coffee stood to the side, and she sipped it, still warm, as he shook his head.

"I drove the UTV to a group of cows with a bunch of calves born during the past two weeks. There in the middle of them was a mother and a fresh calf next to her. The baby was kneeling on his front legs and not getting up."

"She had the baby right in the middle of them?" Eden frowned. "Something must have been off."

"You think so?" He shrugged one shoulder. "Anyhow, I went up to it, and the mama took a step back—"

"Wait, she let you draw near without a fuss?"

"Yeah, she stayed close to the calf, but she let me check him out."

"Something really must have been off," she muttered. Pregnant cows usually separated from the other cattle to have their babies, and they typically pawed at the ground to protect the calf when someone came near.

"Well, I tagged him and tried to get him to stand, but he couldn't support himself. I didn't know what to do. I was going to leave him, figuring the mother would take charge, but I kept thinking something wasn't right. Last week I witnessed a dozen births, and none of them were like this. I hemmed and hawed for a good ten minutes and finally called Chris. He told me to take him to the calf warmer in the shop. After a couple of hours, Chris weighed him, got him on his feet, and I took him back to his mom. He was still pretty wobbly."

"Did he nurse?"

"Yeah. He's okay now. But I didn't even think of getting him to the warmer." He shook his head in disgust. "Chris told me he was quite a bit larger than most of our calves, and the mother probably struggled to give birth to him. The little guy might not have had the energy to stand."

For the past year, she'd believed Ryder thought only about himself, but this version of him wasn't lining up with the one in her head. This Ryder wasn't egotistical. He cared about the cattle, and he was humble enough to admit he needed help. "Well, now you know."

"True. But what else don't I know that could affect the herd? I'd hate to lose a calf due to my lack of knowledge."

"You have plenty of ranch hands and a brother a few miles down the road. You don't have to be an expert right now." She almost reached over to cover his hand but stopped herself. What would possess her to consider such a thing? She wasn't going to voluntarily touch him.

"Thanks, Eden. I needed the pep talk." His face had more color, and he didn't look as tired. "Now, what did you want to discuss?"

She mentally cringed. How could she kick a guy when he was down?

What was the alternative, though? For years she'd accommodated her friends when they needed her even when it wasn't ideal for her, and the accommodation needed to stop.

*I can't keep going along with other people's plans because it's good for them. It needs to be good for me, too.*

"My apartment is too small to watch the girls," she said. "This isn't working out."

As if he didn't have enough problems... Ryder slumped. Between the ranch hands exchanging raised eyebrows at his inexperience, his own high expectations of sliding into the role of cattle rancher, and the girls waffling between highs and lows, the one highlight of the move had been not worrying about the twins while Eden watched them. And now she wasn't going to?

She had to.

He couldn't let her quit.

"Okay, we'll come up with a solution." His mind raced in circles like a dog chasing its tail. "Space is the issue?"

She looked down at her coffee cup. "It's not the only one."

"Is it the girls? Are they acting up?" A fire roared in his core. They'd always been affectionate, happy children. Sure, Harper could be high energy, and Ivy sulked for reasons he'd never understand, but all in all, they were good kids. Weren't they?

"No, of course not, they're wonderful." She sounded so offended; the fire inside him immediately doused. "No, it truly is my space or lack of it. Kids their age need room to run and move. They're bouncing off the walls and off each other. My table is too small for their art projects, and the days Brittany has classes, the music comes straight up to my apartment. It bothers the twins, and I hate seeing them ornery because of it."

"So, watch them at my place." Problem solved. The tension gripping his neck relaxed.

Her face went completely blank. Grew a tad green. "I couldn't."

"Why not?"

"It's…" She appeared to be struggling for words. "I have Phoebe, too."

"So?" He didn't mind her babysitting Gabby's little girl at his house. "My ranch is closer to Dylan and Gabby's new home than your place anyhow. What's the problem?"

"It's not happening." The words came out rapid-fire.

"Why not?"

"It would be too weird."

Was she worried about being alone on the ranch with him? She had nothing to fear. He was so busy checking cattle, feeding them, coming up with spreadsheets to track their nutrition and trying to keep up with repairs that he could barely breathe.

"We wouldn't be alone." He held his palms out. "And even if we were, you wouldn't have to worry about me. I've got two priorities—the girls and my ranch. I'm never getting married again, either, so rest easy."

"That's not what I was talking about." Her expression had a horrified tinge to it. "I'm not interested in you like that. I mean, you're the identical twin of my brother-in-law. Do you really think I'd ever be attracted to someone who looks exactly like my dead sister's husband? Ew."

Put in those terms…

He stretched his neck from side to side. Eden had never found him attractive? He could see her point—

she'd been related to Mason before her sister died. And their friendship had continued for years. But he wasn't Mason, even if he was his double.

And Ryder was definitely attracted to Eden. Had been from the minute he'd met her.

It was just as well. Attraction could lead to more dangerous emotions—like love. And he wasn't doing *that* again.

She shivered, burrowing deeper into her jacket.

"Are you cold?" he asked. "We can take this to Riverview Lounge where it's warmer."

"I'm fine."

A long silence stretched. He kept turning over the fact she wasn't interested in him and didn't find him attractive because of Mason. The idea wouldn't have occurred to him in a million years. Strangely enough, it was like dangling forbidden fruit in front of him.

"What are you doing today?" He'd dropped Harper and Ivy off at Mason's to play with Noah this morning so he could meet Eden here. He figured once he was done, he'd take the girls on a ride around the ranch. Show them all the calves and cows. They'd love it. But with Eden giving him a hard time about babysitting… maybe it was time he brought her to the ranch. Let her see for herself it was the perfect solution to her space problem.

"I have plans." She sat primly with her hands in her lap.

"What kind of plans?"

"Plans that are none of your business."

Her closed-off tone matched her closed-off expression. He missed the ray of friendship she'd shown him mere moments ago.

"Why don't you like me, Eden?"

"I like you." It sounded weak.

"Never mind. You don't have to like me. I just—the girls need you. Come to the house. Look it over and tell me if it will work for babysitting."

"I can't."

"Can't or won't?"

"Both."

She was honest. He'd give her that.

"Why?"

"Because it's too hard." Only then did he notice how much emotion she seemed to be bottling in. "It was… home."

The word was infused with reverence, longing and loss. He knew she'd been living with her parents until last year. He'd assumed she'd moved into the apartment above Brittany's studio to get some independence. Now he wasn't so sure.

"I don't know what to say. Your parents were selling it. I feel like I should apologize, but I'm not sure what I'd be apologizing for."

She ducked her chin, avoiding his eyes.

"If you come over, you'll see it's got plenty of room for all three of the kids." Ryder couldn't afford to lose her—neither could the twins. "The big room in the back is practically empty. You can order any furniture and supplies you need. I'll pay for them."

"Noah and I spent a lot of time in the family room when I babysat him." Her thoughtful expression was like when the sun peeked through the clouds. Full of light.

"See? You already know what to do with it." He uncurled his legs from the bench, rounded the table and held out his hand. "The girls are at Mason's. Come on. I'll take you to the ranch. At least look it over before you say no to babysitting there."

Ignoring his hand, she stood. "I don't want to baby-sit at your house."

"It was your home. I get it. I can't change that."

"I'm not asking you to." Gone was her feisty tone, replaced by resignation.

"Then what's the problem?"

"It's complicated."

"I need you, Eden. Harper and Ivy need you. This move has been hard, and you're making it easy on them. And on me."

Eden rubbed her temples, then exhaled loudly. "Fine. You win. I'll babysit at your place. Starting Monday morning."

"This isn't about winning or losing. It's about solving a problem."

"Well, it feels like losing to me."

"I don't want you to feel that way. I mean, if there's any other thing you can think of—I want to work this out…" He didn't know what would make her happy.

"There isn't. You're right. It will be easier on everyone."

He could practically hear the words *except me* at the end.

"It might feel less win or lose if I give you the tour."

"No thanks." She stood.

"At least let me drop you off at your place." He hitched his chin toward his truck parked behind them.

"I'll walk."

As she turned to leave, he didn't feel like a winner, either. Maybe this was a lose-lose for both of them. The fact was he liked confiding in Eden. Had needed her encouragement about the ranch. And now a wall was up—a wall because of him.

He should be happy about it.

Eden was uncomplicated with everyone but him. He should let her build as many walls as she needed to keep an emotional distance between them.

*Yeah, right.*

The more walls she built, the more he'd want to tear them down. In fact, if he knew himself at all, he'd make sure every one of her walls were rubble before summer was over. And then where would he be?

He couldn't go through another heartbreak. Instead of worrying about her walls, he'd be smart to erect a few of his own.

# Chapter Four

The moment she'd been dreading had finally arrived. Eden trudged up the walkway to the front porch of her childhood home Monday morning and stopped before the porch steps. The weather had grown nasty overnight with freezing temperatures and gusty winds. The cold struck her cheeks, but she barely noticed. What if she went inside and the changes to her home were too much? What if she had an emotional meltdown in front of the twins?

The porch was full of shadows from the past. She could practically see her and Mia sitting side by side on the top step, each holding a doll and debating whether to take their babies on a picnic by the creek or leave them here and go pick wildflowers for their mother.

*Why did you have to die, Mia?* Her big sister had been her hero, her second mom, her best friend. And this house—like everything else around here—had moved on as if Mia never existed.

Eden forced her feet up the steps and, shivering, rang the doorbell. It would be just her and the twins today, since Gabby didn't need her to babysit Phoebe on Mondays. Martha was still driving here early to get the girls up and fed while Ryder tackled ranch chores. The front door opened, and instead of Martha, Ryder appeared. His hair was rumpled, and he wore a sweatshirt, jeans and bare feet. Seeing his toes felt oddly intimate.

"Hey," he said. His eyes brightened as his mouth curved into a self-deprecating smile.

"Hey."

He opened the door wide, and she went inside, trying to avoid brushing against him. In the foyer, she stooped to take off her boots, then slid off her coat. Ryder took it from her and hung it up in the hall closet.

"I thought you'd be out feeding cows or something." She clutched a tote full of supplies for the day.

"I wanted to be here to thank you and to give you the tour."

"You don't need to…"

"Yes, I do."

"I don't want—"

"You told me you didn't want your parents to sell this place." He made no effort to move from the foyer. "I know it's important to you, and I want you to feel comfortable here."

Everything he said was true, but he didn't get it. This was more than her childhood home. It held her memories of her sister, and she would never have the opportunity to make new ones.

"Auntie Eden!" Harper raced down the hall and

wrapped her arms around Eden's legs. Then she stared up at her through those big blue eyes. "You're here! I'm gonna show you my room!"

Mia's room. Eden's heart lurched, but she attempted to smile as she smoothed Harper's hair. "I would love that."

Ryder's cell phone rang. "Mind giving me a sec? It's Chris."

"Go ahead." Eden let Harper take her hand and was soon dragged to the staircase.

"I'm coming, too!" Ivy bounced down the hall to them as they reached the first step.

Eden glanced back at Ryder, who frowned as he talked to Chris. "No…yeah. Okay, I see your point. We'll keep an eye on her throughout the day…thanks for the heads-up."

"Everything okay?" she asked. The girls yanked on her arms to keep going upstairs.

"I think so. We still have some pregnant cows to check after last night's storm."

"Go ahead. We'll be fine." Eden held her breath, hoping he'd take the hint and leave them alone. She didn't want him around to witness her reaction. *Dear Lord, please help me hold it together in front of the girls.*

"If you're sure…" He hesitated, then nodded. "Text or call if you need anything."

"Come on, Auntie Eden!" The girls pulled her forward.

"Okay, okay, don't rip my arms off." She laughed, but dread bubbled in her gut.

At the top of the stairs, she paused. Everything had been freshly painted in pale gray with white trim. It seemed bigger than before. The girls began arguing over which room to show Eden first.

"Which room is closest?" It wasn't difficult to neutralize their tempers. Harper grudgingly admitted Ivy's was, so they went in there first.

As soon as Eden walked in, the dread vanished. The room was painted pale pink, and it had new carpet. Ivy's bed took up a big portion of the room, and a white desk and white dresser rounded out the furniture. Bookcases were lined with toys and books, and stuffed animals sat on the top. The room was precious.

"I love it, Ivy." And she did. Eden's memories of flopping onto her stomach on the floor, paging through a picture book and petting her beloved orange cat, Muffin, were still here despite the fresh paint and new furniture. "Do you?"

"Yes," Ivy said. "Daddy tucks me in every night and hugs Fluffybear extra tight."

"Who is Fluffybear?"

Harper raced to the bed and lugged a big floppy stuffed bear over. "He's right here. Ivy's not 'llowed to take him out."

"Harper! I wanted to show her."

"Sorry." Harper didn't sound sorry.

"Can I give him a hug?" Eden held her arms out, and Ivy took Fluffybear from Harper and pressed him into her arms. She could smell the faint scent of fabric softener and a whiff of Ryder's cologne as she lingered over it a second more than she should have. "Why don't you show me everything else?"

Ivy conducted the tour of the room, pointing out the special toys her mother had bought her and a framed picture of Lily crouching with her arms around the twins' shoulders. Her beauty stopped Eden cold. Ryder's ex-wife's skin was flawless, her eyes big and blue, her hair long and brown, the same as the twins'. Her groomed eyebrows, straight nose and full lips were perfection. She appeared kind, happy, outgoing.

"I want Mommy to stay in my room when she comes," Ivy said.

"That's not fair." Harper frowned.

Ivy got close to her sister and looked her in the eyes. "She can sleep with me one night and you the next."

Harper's face cleared. "Okay."

"Are you ready to show me your room?" Eden asked Harper.

They made their way down the hall to Harper's room. Mia's old room. Eden's heart pinched as strains of Mia's laughter echoed in her mind.

"C'mon." The girls ran ahead of her, and she took a moment to prepare herself. How many times had Mia slammed the door shut in her face when they were young and mad at each other? How many times had they played with their Barbies in there? Listened to music? Giggled about boys and friends? When Mia was a senior, she'd pulled Eden inside and shut the door. Her face had positively dazzled as she told her Ben Jones had asked her to prom. The high school quarterback! And so cute. They'd jumped up and down and discussed it all night.

That was what hurt the most about Mia being gone. She missed their bond. Missed the one person who knew all her secrets. She'd shared everything with Mia.

"Aren't you comin' in?" Harper's forehead wrinkled in concern.

"Of course I am." Eden forced a happy expression

on her face. It wasn't Harper's fault she was struggling today, and even if she had to fake it, she'd ooh and aah over her room.

Eden entered the butter-yellow room with the same furniture as Ivy's. Harper's was messier. Plastic horse figurines lay on their sides in front of the bookshelf, and three rumpled shirts had been tossed near the closet. A pile of books had toppled over by the bed.

"Why'd you look so sad?" Harper asked.

"Did I?" The girls were more perceptive than she realized. "You know this was my sister's room, right?"

"Uh-huh."

"I miss her. I have a lot of good memories with her in here."

Harper took Eden's hand and pressed it to her own cheek. "I'm sorry you miss her."

Ivy snuggled up against Eden's side. "I'm sorry, too, Auntie Eden."

Such sweet girls.

"I guess it would be strange if we didn't miss the people we love, wouldn't it?" She put her arms around them and hugged them both.

"I miss Mommy." Ivy sighed.

"Me, too." Harper's face couldn't droop any farther.

"Of course, you do. Just because she isn't here doesn't mean she doesn't love you." Eden had an idea. "Why don't I take pictures of you in your new rooms? We can add them to your special books for when she visits. Then when she misses you, all she has to do is open the books."

Both girls turned to each other and grinned. "Yes!"

For the next twenty minutes, Eden took pictures of the girls in every room of the house, except Ryder's bedroom. Finally, they ended up in the kitchen. As they wrapped up the tour, Eden marveled at the changes. The house was the same—but different. Brighter. More open. Still full of love.

"When it gets nice out, we can go on adventures around the ranch." Eden poured each girl a glass of milk. "I know all kinds of hidden places."

"You do?"

"I do. And pretty soon there will be wildflowers along the creek. You can pick them and make bouquets."

"I love flowers," Ivy said with a dreamy expression.

"I want to ride horseys." Harper had a milk mustache.

"What about you, Ivy?" Eden asked. "Do you want to ride a horse?"

"I don't know. They're big."

"I learned to ride when I was around your age." Eden had practically grown up riding. "I think you'll like it."

As the afternoon wore on, Eden felt more and more at home in her old house. And as she helped the girls glue cotton balls to construction-paper sheep, Eden couldn't help thinking she owed Ryder an apology. He'd bought the ranch and made the old farmhouse even better than it was before. Plus, because of him, the property was still being used to raise cattle. Her dad had worried that without the right buyer the ranch might cease to exist.

By coming here and seeing the house through Harper's and Ivy's eyes, Eden had finally gotten a sense of peace about letting go of the ranch. Her sister's memory wasn't being erased. Mia would always be with Eden. And the house would now hold Harper's and Ivy's memories in addition to hers and Mia's.

A tiny voice in her head whispered *Ryder is single. You could have it all—the house, the ranch, the family.*

No. She wasn't going down that road. She'd be nicer to Ryder and leave it at that. The stirrings and whispers inside her would disappear when summer ended. At least she hoped they would.

"Next week?" Ryder leaned back in the rickety office chair and glanced at the desk in the pole barn office while he talked to Lily on the phone. Since she rarely returned his calls and almost never picked up, he'd forced himself to take her call.

He still had to check a pregnant cow one more time before relieving Eden of her babysitting duties. The clock showed he was already late. All he wanted to do was find out how her first day of babysitting here had gone and make sure she was still willing to watch the girls here on the ranch. But no, he was going to be even later because he had to deal with Lily.

"I'm back in LA to promote my new movie, so I figured next week would be ideal to come see my sweethearts."

He clenched his jaw. *Don't be a jerk to her. You're better than that.* "They'll love seeing you. They've both been talking about you nonstop and can't wait to show you their new rooms."

There. He'd managed to keep his tone civil. Pleasant, even.

The long pause made him wonder if she'd heard him. Then her silky voice came through. "Perfect."

"When do you think you'll arrive? We have a guest room. You can stay here if you'd like."

"I'll have Mandy make the arrangements. Something in town will be fine." Her voice grew muffled as she called to her personal assistant, Mandy Drake, to check flights. Ryder had spent more time talking to Mandy over the past two years than to Lily herself.

"You know there aren't any direct flights here, right?" he asked. "You'll have to drive in from the nearest airport, and it's not close."

"I've been to remote places on location, Ryder. I can handle it." Her laugh was rich, and he tried to remember a time when he'd loved hearing it. He supposed it was before he realized it wasn't genuine. She used it as a prop.

"When you nail down the details, let me know." He tapped a pen against the desk and checked the clock again. "I'm not telling the girls unless you're one hundred percent sure you're coming."

"Why wouldn't I come?"

"I don't know. You tell me."

"I don't appreciate your tone. You act like I don't want to visit them. I'm the one making these plans, so I don't know why you're being like this."

He took a deep breath before answering. "I appreciate you making the effort. Like I said, call or text me the details after Mandy gets everything booked."

"Will do. Oh, my publicist did mention the possibility of a guest appearance while I'm in town, though. I'm sure nothing will come of it."

Ryder's blood pressure climbed. He wasn't going to say a thing. Not one thing. As soon as she'd uttered that nonchalant *oh*, he'd known the visit wasn't going to happen. If the sun stood still, maybe he'd get confirmation that Mandy had booked a flight and reserved a room here in Rendezvous. But until then, he wasn't mentioning it to the girls. Their hopes had been shattered too many times by Lily already.

"Gotta go," Lily said. "Give the girls hugs and kisses from me."

He didn't respond, and the line went dead.

Leaning way back in the chair with his hands behind his head, he tried to erase the conversation. But he couldn't, and the longer he sat there, the more his anger rose. What was the point in her calling him if she was only going to make empty promises?

Lurching to his feet, he grabbed his hat and shoved the cell phone into his pocket. Then he locked up and marched down the gravel lane to the house. In the mudroom, he pulled off his boots, hung up his coat and washed his hands. By the time he finished, his mood had improved enough to find Eden and the girls.

He made his way through the hallway leading to the kitchen.

And he stopped short. Behind the island, Eden was laughing. Both girls sat on stools, giggling as they had a sword fight with breadsticks. The aroma of garlic and spaghetti sauce filled the air. His stomach immediately began to growl.

"Well, this is more than I ever imagined coming home to." He kissed Ivy's cheek, then Harper's. Then he met Eden's eyes. "I'm real sorry I'm late. I can't believe you made dinner. You shouldn't have done that."

Her brown eyes shimmered. "I wanted to."

She wanted to? Had he entered another dimension? This was Eden, the woman who'd barely dragged herself inside his house this morning, right?

"I wanted to thank you." She tilted her head to the side.

Thank him? For what? His cell phone rang. It was Chris.

He held up a finger. He'd forgotten to check the pregnant cow. His lungs tightened. *Please, let everything be all right.*

"Hey, man, I've got bad news."

"Lay it on me." Ryder retraced his steps to the mudroom.

"The pregnant red tag sixty-two?" Chris coughed.

He felt sick to his stomach. "Yeah?"

"I found her just now. The calf didn't make it."

It was his fault. All his fault. He'd let Lily's call distract him, and he'd forgotten to check on the cow. Now the calf was dead.

"That's on me, Chris. I knew I needed to check her, and I got distracted. Forgot my final round." They discussed details a few minutes before hanging up. With his throat swollen with emotion, he returned to the kitchen.

"I'm sorry to do this, but can you give me half an hour? I... I've got to go." He didn't even wait to see Eden's reaction. He jogged away, shoved his feet back into the boots, grabbed his coat and headed out into the cold wind.

He had to do better. This ranch was depending on him. The cows, the calves, the employees. Even the girls.

He couldn't make another mistake like this.

He'd make it up to Eden somehow. But for now, he had a dead calf to deal with.

Thirty minutes later, after checking on the girls contentedly watching a cartoon in the living room, Eden put their plates in the dishwasher as she listened for Ryder. The side door had slammed moments ago, and the faucet was running in the mudroom. She hoped everything was all right. The way he'd sprinted out of there earlier had her concerned.

He entered the kitchen and didn't meet her eyes.

"Thanks for…everything. I can take it from here." His subdued tone set her back.

"What's wrong?" she asked.

"Nothing." But from the look on his face, something was wrong.

"You want to talk about it?"

"There's nothing to talk about."

Okay. So they were playing that game. All day she'd wanted to extend an olive branch to him about the great job he'd done remodeling the house and for taking over the ranch, but in this instant, her goodwill fled.

"Got it." She grabbed her bag and purse and headed to the front hall. "Goodbye, girls. I'll see you tomorrow."

The twins ran to her and hugged her.

"You promise you'll be back tomorrow?" Ivy clutched Eden's hand in her own. Worry darkened her eyes.

"Of course I will, silly. I have lots of fun things planned." Eden kissed the top of her head. Then she kissed the top of Harper's. "You two get some good sleep tonight, okay?"

They hugged her again and hurried back to the couch. Ryder stood a few feet away with his arms crossed over his chest and his shoulder leaning against the wall. She couldn't read his face at all.

"See you tomorrow," she said crisply and reached for the door handle.

"Eden, wait."

She turned.

"Thank you. For staying. For dinner." His demeanor made her think he wanted to say more, but he didn't.

"You're welcome." Oddly disappointed, she opened the door and left. The wind battered her coat against her, and she braced herself all the way to her vehicle. As she let the engine warm up, she looked back at the glowing windows of the farmhouse.

Welcoming. Warm. A haven.

Her haven.

If she needed reminding that it was no longer hers and wouldn't be again, Ryder's terseness accomplished it. His less attractive qualities had come out full force, reminding her why she hadn't liked being around him until recently. They'd been getting along better, but it had only distracted her from her goals.

As much as she enjoyed spending time with the girls, she had to keep in mind that the next few months were going to fly by. And when they were over, what was she going to do?

She'd put off long-term planning. But tonight was as good as any to start researching her options. If she didn't, her life would be in even worse shape come September, and then where would she be?

# Chapter Five

He wasn't the outsider looking in anymore.

Ryder had invited everyone over for pizza tonight. He stood with Mason, Dylan and local rancher Judd Wilson in his living room Friday evening. Eden, Gabby, Brittany and Nicole Taylor chatted and took care of Phoebe and the triplets in the family room. Harper, Ivy and Noah were upstairs singing at the tops of their lungs. Ryder hoped there would be many more gatherings with his new friends.

When he and Mason first met, he'd learned about Mason's support group with Gabby, Eden and Nicole. It had made him long to have a support group, too. People he could share his problems with and who would pray for him. Their group no longer formally met, but they were all still very close.

"The storm earlier this week did a number on a few

of my calves. I hope yours are all right." Judd gestured to Ryder and Mason. "I'm ready for the weather to get warm again."

Mason blew out a loud breath. "It was touch and go for two of my pregnant cows, but they all made it out alive, and for that I'm grateful."

"I lost another calf this week." Ryder had spent almost a decade confident in his abilities in the financial world. But ranching? Not so much. He doubted himself on a daily basis. "The first one was my fault. I should have checked on the mother, and I… I got distracted. The second one was stillborn."

"Don't beat yourself up." Judd's eyebrows drew together as he nodded. "It comes with the territory."

"Yeah, I had no experience when I moved here last summer," Dylan said. "If it wasn't for my boss, I wouldn't have any idea what to do with the cattle. Just keep praying."

"I'm trying." Ryder didn't need to hide his mistakes. These guys weren't judging him. And he did pray every night for the Lord's guidance with the ranch. "How's married life treating you, by the way, Dylan?"

"Good. Real good." Dylan grinned. "Gabby makes life special. And Phoebe gets cuter every day. She calls me *dada* now."

"I think I'm ready for another one." Mason puffed out his chest. "It's been too long since I've been called dada."

Ryder was surprised, but then again, he shouldn't be. It was natural for Mason to want more children now that he'd remarried.

"I don't blame you. I can't wait for Phoebe to have

a little sister or brother." Dylan then turned to Judd. "Have you and Nicole set a date?"

"We're working on it. Something simple. July, maybe," Judd said. "Her hands are pretty full at the moment."

They all turned to look through the archway at the women. Eden was playing patty-cake with Phoebe on her lap, and Brittany, Gabby and Nicole each held a triplet. Those babies looked good in their arms. For the first time, Ryder realized he might want another child, too.

*Another baby?* That wasn't going to happen.

Eden looked up just then and met his eyes. A flash of heat spread from his head to his toes. They'd been civil to each other all week. Hadn't spent much time together or anything, and he'd been careful to come home on time each day. The twins were happy. That was the important thing.

Staring into Eden's soulful brown eyes left a yearning inside, though, similar to the one he'd experienced seeing those triplets just now. She broke eye contact first and returned her attention to Phoebe. The chubby toddler with dark curls squealed in delight.

Eden would make a terrific mother.

He gulped.

Nope. Wasn't going there.

He had no doubt Eden would eventually marry and have children of her own. But he wouldn't be involved. Couldn't be. He'd already gotten burned once, and frankly, his girls continued to get the short end of the stick from their mother. He hadn't heard from Lily since their conversation on Monday. No flight plans or dates had been set for a visit.

He'd made the right decision to not tell the girls she

planned on coming. The woman changed her mind for the hollowest reasons without thinking how it would affect her daughters or him.

There had been a time when he'd thought Lily would be a terrific mother. She'd convinced him she wanted children and that her only dream was to be a stay-at-home mom. He'd told her if she wanted a career, it was fine with him. But she'd insisted she wanted to stay home. Then, after giving birth to the twins, Lily had gone behind his back and hired a nanny. She'd started auditioning again. He'd been the last to know.

She'd ignored the babies to focus on her career. She'd landed the lead in a highly anticipated movie. It had taken her away for months. She'd accepted roles on more projects until everything came to a head on the day of the twins' third birthday. He'd planned a big party for them, and that morning, Lily had pulled him aside and told him she wanted a divorce. She'd not only fallen in love with her director, but she was moving in with the guy.

She hadn't even stuck around for the girls' party.

His life had never been the same.

It had been a little over two years now, and he was still dealing with the fallout. He'd always be dealing with it. If he would have opened his eyes to acknowledge what was happening, he wouldn't have been so blindsided by Lily's betrayal.

"Ryder?" Mason asked.

He shook his thoughts back to now. "Yes?"

Laughing, Mason clapped his hand on his shoulder. "We boring you?"

"No, no. Sorry. What were you saying?"

"We're discussing moving the cattle to their summer pastures."

"Oh, right." Another thing he knew little about. "Tell me all your secrets."

"Secrets?" Mason chuckled. "There's not much to tell."

"I wait until the grass is coming in good," Judd said. "Toward the end of May is about right. Early June is fine, too."

They continued the discussion until the women came and joined them.

"It's about time I took these three home." Nicole held Amelia, the lone girl triplet, as she smiled at Judd.

"No problem." Judd nodded, taking the baby from her. Amelia yawned and wrapped her chubby arms around his neck.

"Yeah, we'd better take off, too," Dylan said to Gabby.

"I'd better get Noah." Mason moved toward the staircase, but Ryder stopped him.

"Noah can spend the night here if you want. We love having him around."

"I appreciate it, but not tonight. Brittany and I have a surprise planned for him tomorrow."

After the couples said their goodbyes, Ryder closed the door behind them and returned to the kitchen. Eden was transferring pizza slices from one box to another. He took the empty box from her hands.

"You didn't need to do that." He folded the box. He'd add it to his burn pile later. "I can clean up."

"It'll only take a minute." She blushed.

Everything about Eden was sincere. She did so many

behind-the-scenes chores without expecting recognition or thanks.

Eden Page was refreshing.

*Yeah, and you thought Lily was all that and a bag of chips way back when, too.*

But Eden was nothing like his ex, and the evening was ending too soon for his taste. "Do you have more than a minute?"

"Why?" she asked. "Is something wrong?"

"No." He shrugged. "We haven't had much time to talk, that's all."

"What do you want to talk about?" She faced him then, blinking in confusion.

"I don't know. This house. The town. Life in Wyoming." Anything she wanted. Anything at all. "Or are you in a hurry to go home?"

"I'm not in a hurry."

"Good. Let's go to the living room. Stay for a while."

She shouldn't be staying at all, let alone for a while. Eden opened her mouth to decline, but the vulnerability in Ryder's expression stopped her. To be honest, she didn't want the night to end yet, either.

"Daddy, can we watch *Cinderella*?" Ivy asked. Her face was flushed. Harper came up behind her, yawning widely.

"Not tonight. It's past your bedtime." Ryder shook his head. "Go upstairs and get your pj's on. I'll be up in a minute to tuck you in."

"But Daddy..." both girls wailed.

"No buts. It's late."

They wore matching pouty faces and stomped out of the room.

"You." He pointed both index fingers to Eden. "Stop cleaning. Go get comfortable on the couch. I'll be back in a minute."

She suppressed a smile and wiped down the countertops while he went upstairs. She could hear him teasing the girls and their subsequent giggles. Her heart squeezed at the precious sounds. When the kitchen was clean, she dimmed the lights and went to the living room. A large sectional faced the fireplace with a massive television to the right of it. She found a spot in the corner of the sectional and reached over for a soft throw before settling it across her lap.

Yesterday Ryder had mentioned having everyone over for pizza tonight and expressly told her he wanted her there. It had meant a lot to her. So after babysitting the girls all day, she'd stayed, and it had felt good. Honestly, entertaining her friends here had felt more than good—it had felt natural. Like she was cohosting the gathering.

She frowned. She wasn't cohosting it, though. This wasn't her house. Ryder and the twins weren't her family.

Good gravy, why was she being so hard on herself? She'd spent every night this week researching going back to college. She deserved a break. It was okay to enjoy tonight. It didn't mean anything.

"Sorry about that." Ryder strode into the room and took a seat on the sectional with her. He was far enough away to not be awkward but close enough for her to be aware of him. "I give it ten minutes before they're out cold."

"We had a busy day."

"I know." He shifted, relaxing into the corner so he could face her better. "I still can't get over how much you manage to pack into your time with them."

"I love it." She did. Babysitting the twins gave her the chance to do some of the projects she'd been saving. They tucked into each task with gusto. "I've always enjoyed organizing activities and spending time with kids."

"I can tell." His eyes darkened with appreciation. The hair on her arms rose. When he looked at her like that, it was hard to concentrate. "You're making this move so much easier than I anticipated. I've been so focused on the ranch and learning about the cattle it hasn't left me nearly enough time to do the things I want to for the girls."

"Like what?"

"I promised Ivy she could have a kitten, and Harper wants to learn how to ride horses. The weather hasn't been nice enough to fully explore the ranch. I know they're going to love it. And I want to take them fishing this summer." His voice trailed off at the end as if he was getting discouraged.

"You don't have to do everything at once." Eden hadn't realized he was putting so much pressure on himself.

"I worry I won't get around to it at all." He scratched his chin. "This has been harder than I thought."

"Which part?" Ranching? Taking the girls out of California? No longer living near their mother? Adjusting to life in the country?

"Balancing cattle ranching with raising the girls."

"Ah." She nodded. "It's not easy."

His face fell. "No, it's not."

Empathy poured in. All week she'd paid attention to his interaction with Harper and Ivy. Despite the bags under his eyes and the worry lines marking his forehead, he'd grin and hug them both, asking them to show him everything they'd worked on during the day. His patience with them and the way he put their needs first had gotten under Eden's skin.

He was nothing like the man she'd thought he was before moving here.

He was better. So much better.

"When the weather gets nice," she said, "you'll be able to show the girls all the best spots on the ranch. They will love it."

"Best spots, huh?" His mouth curved into a grin that reached his eyes. "I don't know where they are."

"Oh, you will." She wrapped her arms around a throw pillow.

"You know them better than I do. I'm still getting to know the land, and I haven't seen it thawed out."

"If you follow the creek, there's a great fishing spot close to where the forest starts. We used to picnic there and fish when we were younger. The wildflowers should be blooming soon. It will take your breath away." Good memories crowded her mind of her and Mia and her parents spending afternoons by the creek.

"Perfect," he said, nodding. "Follow the creek to the forest. What else have you got?"

She thought back on all her favorite things about the ranch. There were so many. "The girls will probably want to play in the stables. Dad kept the large stall in the corner empty for us. He even installed shelves. One summer it was a toy store. Then it was a library. Sometimes we made it into a hair salon. We had a lot of fun out there."

"Your dad sounds like a great guy."

"He is." She loved her parents. Missed them now that

they were traveling. They'd showered her with love as a child, and she was thankful for them every day. "Dad can come off kind of gruff, but he's a softy for kids. Oh, Mom and Mia and I used to garden, too. We canned a lot of vegetables."

"A garden." He bobbed his head side to side as if he'd never considered it. "The girls like flowers and digging and being outside. But I don't have a green thumb. I wouldn't know where to start."

"It's not overly complicated, but don't worry about it this year. You have enough to deal with." She didn't want to stare, but something in his eyes drew her in. "Ryder?"

"Yeah."

"I'm glad my parents sold the ranch to you." She meant it. He cared about it—had invested in the house, was invested in the cattle. He had a good heart. "The girls are going to be really happy here."

"Thanks, Eden. That means a lot to me."

"It's true." And it was.

"I'm not great at ranching. But I'll get there. At least, I keep telling myself I will." He ran his fingers through his hair. "I feel like my granddad's barking in my ear all day long. 'Do things right the first time. Your number-one priority is the livestock. If you lose even one sheep, you've failed.'"

"Really?" She scrunched her nose. The man sounded harsh. "Sheep die sometimes. Cattle, too. There's only so much you can control."

"I've lost two calves since taking this place over. I don't think Granddad would be too impressed."

Mason had told her that he and Ryder had been separated shortly after birth when their parents died in a car accident. Each was raised by a different set of grand-parents who kept the fact they were twins a secret. She regarded Ryder. "Did you have a happy childhood?"

"Happy?" He thought about it a minute. "No, I wouldn't describe it as happy. I was taken care of, and I learned a lot of life skills, so I'm not complaining. Granddad got cancer when I was young. We sold the ranch and moved to the city to be near the hospital. He died from cancer a year later. My grandmother kind of went through the motions after he died, and she passed away my senior year of high school."

"I'm sorry, Ryder." She reached over to touch his arm. His eyes met hers, and he covered her hand with his. Then his gaze flitted to her lips, and she wondered if he thought of kissing her.

But he glanced away, and she chided herself. Why would he want to kiss her? He wasn't into her like that. They were…friends. Starting to be, at least.

"What about you?" he asked. "I know you didn't want to babysit the girls here. Has it been hard? A lot of memories of your sister?"

"Actually, it's been easy. I thought it was going to be awful. The thing is, though, the memories are still here, and I'm more at peace with her death than I've ever been. I can't really explain it."

"You don't have to."

She thought back on the years since Mia had died. All the Tuesday-night meetings with Gabby and Mason had helped her through the grief of losing her sister. Then Nicole had joined their support group a year ago, and seeing what she'd been through had helped Eden understand that tough times happen to everyone.

Moving into the apartment, watching her parents

move on, being a bridesmaid in Brittany and Mason's wedding, and now coming here, to her old home, had given her the final push she needed to move on from her sister's death.

"I hope you don't mind me inviting all your friends here tonight." He looked sheepish.

"Why would I mind? It was fun. And they're your friends, too."

"I'm glad you had fun. I, well, I envied you and Mason, Gabby and Nicole—your support group. I could have used one after Lily left me."

Ryder never discussed Lily. Eden's pulse quickened as a million questions came to mind. Why did she leave? What happened? What was it like being married to a famous star? How often did she call the girls? When was she going to visit them?

"Most of us need a support group at some point in life." She swallowed all her questions. They weren't appropriate. "I'm blessed to be best friends with them."

His eyes had that intensity again, and she wanted to look away but couldn't.

"Eden, I have a very personal question to ask, and you don't have to answer it."

Her heartbeat started pounding. "Oh, yeah?" She tried to sound nonchalant.

"Why are you still single?"

Her stomach fell to the floor. How could she possibly answer that?

*I'm not pretty like Mia. I don't have the beauty, sparkling personality or talent of your ex-wife. I'm a homebody. Quiet. I have no idea how to flirt and don't want to, anyhow. Guys don't notice me. I don't really blame them.*

"Never mind. It was a stupid question," he muttered. "None of the guys around here deserve you, anyway."

*Wait, what?*

Did he think she'd actually turned down the single men in Rendezvous? Was he under the impression they'd asked her out and she'd said no? She almost laughed.

He tilted his head. "The weather is supposed to be nice tomorrow. Why don't you come over, and we'll take the girls on a tour of the ranch?"

She didn't know how to handle the feelings Ryder kept bringing up. It was fine to babysit the girls. And hanging out here when all her friends were around wasn't hurting anything. But spending additional time with Ryder?

"I don't know." She studied her hands, unwilling to commit.

"Do you have other plans?"

"No…"

"How will I know where to take the girls if you don't show me? I don't know how to find all these great spots you claim are on the ranch. Come over. We'll make a day of it."

The girls would love her favorite places on the ranch, and the weather *was* supposed to be warm and sunny for once. What would it hurt?

"Okay," she said. "I'll show you around."

"I'd like that." His slow grin made her gulp. "It will be an adventure."

An adventure. Yes, the ranch was an adventure. One she hoped would give Harper and Ivy years of fun. She'd show them her favorite hangouts, and later, when she wasn't part of their lives anymore, she'd rest easy knowing the ranch was being enjoyed the way it should be.

*Yeah, right.*

She was a hypocrite. Deep down, she wanted to spend more time getting to know Ryder. Spending it on the ranch was merely a bonus. She was playing with fire, and she knew it.

The next day, Ryder glanced over at Eden sitting in the passenger side of his truck. The girls were strapped into their booster seats in the back seat. The tires kicked up mud as they maneuvered the hills and crests of the land. Ryder had passed several places where evergreens flanked the overflowing creek. He hadn't been this way before and got excited thinking of all the acres he'd soon be able to explore.

Being out here on a sunny day made everything feel possible. Visions of fishing and riding horses and going to the twins' school events crowded his brain. They'd be happy here. He'd make sure of it.

Even Eden looked peaceful and content. She had that effect on him, too. Being around her made his problems disappear.

Rays of sun beamed on the land still recovering from winter. The grass was green and wildflowers had begun to unfurl. Maybe he'd be able to move the cattle to the summer pasture sooner rather than later.

"Once you get around the S in the creek up ahead, there will be a clearing." Eden pointed to the right. "You can stop there."

"I'm glad you know where we're going. I haven't ventured to this part of the ranch at all."

She turned to him with a smile, and he was pretty sure his heart stopped beating for a moment.

"You'll know every nook and cranny of this place soon enough."

"I hope so." He peeked at her again. "Thanks for showing us around."

"Thanks for inviting me." She returned her attention out the window.

The truck bounced over the uneven terrain, and Ryder focused on driving.

"There. See? Park up on that hill." Eden touched his arm, pointing with her other hand, and he practically jumped.

"Right." He sounded brusque.

After they parked, they all got out of the truck. Eden stretched her arms above her head. "Wow, it feels so good to be out here without wearing a coat."

Ivy and Harper held hands and ran in their new rain boots toward the creek.

"Stay away from the edge, girls," Eden called. "The water's high, and I don't want you falling in."

"Okay!" Ivy tugged Harper's hand and pointed to a clump of purple flowers growing near the trees. They bent over to inspect the blooms.

"This might be the prettiest spot in the entire state." Ryder strolled next to Eden.

"I agree." She smiled at him. "When Mia and I were young, we'd come out here in our bathing suits and lay out to get a suntan."

"Splash in the creek a little, too?"

"Yeah, a little." She laughed. "You have to be careful, though. The rocks can be sharp."

"Point taken."

"See the ridge beyond the creek?"

He squinted. "Yeah."

"If you sit up there and wait, you'll see pronghorns and mule deer and sometimes even wild horses in the distance."

"How patiently do you have to wait?" He wasn't one to sit still for long.

"It depends on the day. Bring a folding chair, a cooler and some binoculars. It's worth it."

"Maybe in ten years I'll have that kind of time." They ambled beside the creek until they reached a rocky area where the water hadn't spilled over. The girls were chasing a butterfly in the meadow.

"You need to make the time." Eden propped her foot on a boulder.

Easy for her to say. She wasn't in charge of a cattle ranch or the sole parent to twin five-year-old girls.

"Seriously, Ryder, I know what I'm talking about." Her eyebrows arched. "I'm assuming you moved here for a simpler life."

"Yeah."

"There's not much simple in this rugged land. You've got to enjoy what you can."

"Daddy, did you bring my butterfly net?" Harper ran up to him and halted, panting.

"I didn't."

"But Daddy, I *need* my net. We found a big butter-fly!"

"Sorry, pumpkin. We'll bring it next time."

"C'mon, Harper." Ivy trotted up and grabbed her arm. "Let's pick flowers for Mommy."

"They'll die before she gets here, Ivy."

"No, they won't. We'll put 'em in water."

The girls took off again, but Ryder's spirits sank. "Do they mention their mother a lot while you're watching them?"

"Not all the time, but, yes, they talk about her often." Eden tilted her head. "Why?"

"I'll have to call her again," he muttered under his breath.

"I'm sure it's a big adjustment for them to not see her as often as they used to."

Not see her as often? He cocked an eyebrow. "What are you talking about?"

"Lily. Their mother." She opened her hands as if it was the most obvious thing in the world.

"What about her?"

"They miss seeing her. I'm sure this is hard on them. Being so far away from her."

"Right." He backed up, squaring his shoulders. "Lily didn't see them all that often in Los Angeles. They don't spend much time with her."

Eden frowned. "Why not?"

*Because she's too busy being important.* He swallowed the words. He didn't want to criticize his ex. He wouldn't. He'd learned his lesson. But he wasn't going to pretend she was something she wasn't, either. "I don't know. She didn't want to share custody, and the visitation schedules I suggest never seem to work out."

"Oh." Eden stared at the grass near her feet. "Well, the girls miss her and love her. I'm sure she'll come soon."

Eden said it like it was a good thing. He was trying to do everything in his power to help them get over the fact their mother was never around. Even when Lily did visit, she found a way to mess things up, because after she left, it took two days for him to pick up the pieces. The girls would be on cloud nine while they had her, and as soon as she left, they missed her and knew it might be months before they saw her again.

It devastated them.

And seeing them devastated always hurt him.

"Whether she comes or not doesn't change anything." He clenched his jaw. "A few days. A week. It's never enough. Our marriage—" He shook his head. "I won't make that mistake again."

"The custody arrangement?" She looked confused.

"No, marriage in general. It's not worth it."

Eden seemed to be chewing on his statement. He shouldn't have said so much.

"Daddy?" Ivy yelled. "What's this hole?"

"That hole looks like it's for a prairie dog." Eden stopped near the girls.

"A prairie dog?" Ivy shook her head. "Do they bark?"

"Kind of. They yip and make chirpy sounds." Eden chuckled. "They're not dogs at all. They're small and cute. We'll have to look up some pictures of them this week."

The girls inspected the hole for another minute, then raced off when they spotted another cluster of flowers.

"Have you given more thought to getting Ivy a kitten?" Eden asked.

Another thing he'd put on the back burner. "Not really."

"Mrs. Ball's long-haired white cat had kittens. You know Ivy has her heart set on a fluffy white cat. Want me to tell her to save one for you?"

"When would I pick it up?" He'd need to prepare. Cat litter. Food. What else did cats need?

"Oh, in a few weeks, I imagine. What about Harper?"

"What about her?"

"Do you think she'd want a kitten?"

"I don't know. Let's ask her. Hey, Harper." Up ahead, Harper turned back to him, her eyes wide and expectant. "If Ivy gets a kitten, do you want one, too?"

"I want a pony," Harper shouted.

Eden chortled. "Well, I can't help you with that."

Ivy raced to him with Harper on her heels. "Am I getting a kitty today, Daddy?"

"Not today, Ivy." He shook his head. "And Harper, no ponies. We have good horses already. I'm teaching both of you girls how to ride."

"I'm too scared, Daddy." Ivy held on to his leg, looking up at him. He ruffled her curls.

"That's exactly why I want you to learn. So you won't be scared. If you know what you're doing, horseback riding isn't scary."

"Your daddy's right, Ivy." Eden bent to her level. "It's fun when you know how."

"Are you sure, Auntie Eden?" Ivy disentangled herself from Ryder's legs to wrap her arms around Eden's neck.

"Yes."

"Okay." Turning back to Ryder, Ivy clasped her hands in front of her chest. "Can we get the kitty tomorrow?"

"No, ma'am. But we might get one in a few weeks."

"A few weeks," Ivy said breathlessly. "Did you hear that, Harper? I'm getting a kitty!"

"I still want a pony." Harper kicked at the grass. "Not a dumb old horse."

Ryder exchanged an amused glance with Eden. He'd

never taught anyone how to ride horses before, and he didn't want the girls getting hurt.

"How would you feel about helping Ivy learn how to ride?" he asked Eden.

"I'm glad to be here for moral support, but if you want the girls to learn properly, talk to your brother. Mason had Noah riding pretty much from the time he could walk. You should ask him."

"Thanks, I will."

Sometimes Eden seemed too good to be true.

He'd thought Lily was everything he ever wanted, and she turned out to be a mirage. But Eden was different...

He wasn't going to throw caution to the wind now. Too much was on the line with this move. Too much could go wrong if he let his heart get too close.

# *Chapter Six*

Two weeks later Eden stood on the corner of Third and Centennial as she waited for the Memorial Day parade to start. Brittany, Mason and Noah waved as they approached. Ever since she'd started babysitting at Ryder's place, life had been great. There was plenty of room for structured play, doing crafts and running around outside. Most evenings Eden enlisted the twins to help put together a meal. They loved tearing lettuce for a salad or putting biscuits on a plate. Ryder always invited her to stay. She usually did.

Not that she was eating supper to be near Ryder or anything. It was just lonely eating by herself in her apartment.

"Thanks for saving us a spot." Mason gave Eden a side hug, and Noah attached himself to her legs.

"Hey there, Noah-bear." Eden bent to kiss his forehead. "Are you ready for the parade?"

"I'm ready for candy." Noah wore an unzipped jacket, jeans and cowboy boots. As usual, he was bursting with energy.

Eden exchanged an amused glance with Brittany.

"He's been wound up for hours. I'm not sure candy is a good idea." Brittany pointed to her half-zip lavender pullover, identical to Eden's. "Hey, we match."

"Sissy's Bargain Clothes?" Eden asked.

"Thirty percent off." Brittany raised her palm for a high five, and Eden slapped it. "I almost bought one for Nan, too."

"How is your grandma?"

"Slowly declining, but that's to be expected. She's still getting around okay."

"I see Ryder." Mason was craning his neck around the Johnson family, who'd squeezed in next to them. He held up his arm, and Ryder waved.

Eden hadn't realized she was holding her breath until Brittany nudged her. "Any progress on your plans?"

Plans? What plans? Seeing Ryder holding the twins' hands had erased her thought process.

"About finishing your degree." Brittany scooted closer as a couple strode by.

Oh, right. *Those* plans. Duh.

"Yeah, I'm considering it. But I don't know if early childhood education makes sense anymore. I love kids, but teaching preschool wouldn't be full-time, and I need benefits."

Brittany nodded, her blond ponytail bobbing. "I hear you. Given my job history, I'll be the first to admit they're important. Have you ever thought about teaching elementary school?"

"Not really." Eden had always been drawn to babies and toddlers, but she was enjoying Noah and the twins, too. Maybe she should consider going that route. "I'm not against it. I don't know what opportunities I'd have here in Rendezvous. The last time a teacher retired was three years ago."

"Look into it. It can't hurt." Brittany's upbeat personality always made Eden feel better.

"Thanks. I will." Whatever she did, it would be here in Rendezvous. Being an active part of Noah's life wasn't something she'd willingly turn her back on. Speaking of… Brittany and Mason had a date tonight, and Eden was looking forward to babysitting for them. "What time are you bringing Noah over?"

"Would six thirty work?"

"Perfect."

"Hey, sorry we're late." Ryder somehow created a spot next to Eden, although Bertha Johnson had staked her ground there earlier. His proximity made Eden's nerves twitch. He set the twins on the ground, then he leaned in and said, "Thanks for saving us a spot."

His warm breath near her ear was a shock. She hadn't saved him a spot—he'd shoved his way in. And she liked it. She turned her attention to the girls. "Are you excited about the parade?"

"Yes!"

"Come on, the front's where the candy's at!" Noah waved them to the curb where he stood with Mason. They wriggled through until they stood on the front lines.

"Are we all set for tomorrow?" Ryder asked Eden.

"Yes," Eden said. "Mrs. Ball has the white kitten reserved and ready for Ivy."

"Good. Last night we bought a kitty-litter box and a collar, food and a scratching post. I have no idea what else we'll need."

"It sounds like you've got the big stuff. You'll be fine. What have you done about Harper's wish?"

"Nothing." His mouth broke into a cheeky grin. "But I'm on top of it." He tapped his brother's shoulder. "Hey, Mason."

"Yeah?"

"Since the weather's nice, I'm thinking it's time to get the girls on horseback."

"Yes." Mason pumped both fists. "You are talking my language. Do you have time to buy some gear after the parade?"

"If you have time to help me."

"I've got time." Mason grinned. "Brittany? You okay with that?"

She scoffed, waving. "Go ahead. I need to stop in at the studio anyhow. Oh, there's Gabby and Dylan." Brittany beckoned them over.

"Hey, guys," Gabby said. Dylan carried Phoebe and found a spot near Mason. "I was really hoping to not have to wear a jacket today. When is it going to warm up?"

"July?" Eden teased.

"Probably." Gabby rolled her eyes, then hugged Eden and Brittany.

Nicole and Judd pushed two strollers their way. The boys were in a double umbrella stroller, and Amelia was in a single. Eden had to admit this setup appeared much more manageable than the triple stroller Nicole used to bring to church every week.

"You made it," Eden said to Nicole, then bent to greet the babies. "I hear you got into your mama's cupcake liners a few days ago, Amelia Bedelia."

"I've got to hear this," Gabby said.

"Ugh. It was the worst." Nicole bent to straighten Henry's hat. "A shipment of supplies came in, and I foolishly left the box on the floor. I turn my back for a minute, and there's Amelia tossing pink cupcake liners in the air like they're confetti."

They all laughed.

"How are you little cuties doing?" Eden covered her eyes with her hands, then played peekaboo with the boys. Eli and Henry kicked their tiny feet and grinned at her. A familiar ache made her straighten. She loved children so much. Holding a baby was one of the greatest things in life. She'd always thought she'd hold her own someday.

She snuck a peek at Ryder, patiently listening to Harper. He didn't want marriage. And, yeah, she got along well with him, but how much of it was due to the fact she was babysitting the girls? Ninety percent? Ninety-five percent? When summer was over, he wouldn't need her anymore, and she'd be invisible Eden Page again.

Alone.

Wondering what was wrong with her.

She took in her friends, chatting, holding babies, faces glowing, and she had the sensation of being left behind. Not by them. By her circumstances.

They'd all found love. They all had families.

Was this what the rest of her life would be like? She'd be the single friend. The one secretly envying them their spouses and children. *Lord, I don't want to envy my friends. Keep me from going down that road.*

The parade kicked off with a short speech by the grand marshal followed by members of the National Guard. As high school girls dressed in fancy Western outfits and carrying flags rode horseback, Harper whirled and yelled to Ryder that she wanted a horsey and sparkly shirt, too. Eden couldn't hear his reply. She wanted to scoop the girl up and tell her of course she'd have a horse and she would buy her the sparkliest shirt in the store.

Her lungs tightened. She backed up a few steps to get some air. What was her problem?

*I love these girls.* She glanced at Ivy, clutching a handful of suckers and Tootsie Rolls, and Harper, bouncing around with the biggest smile. One summer with them would never be enough.

Gripping her hands together, she squeezed her eyes shut. *God, help me. I can't start wanting it again. I can't slip into the fantasy of wanting a husband and family, and I especially can't delude myself about Ryder, the girls and the ranch. I'll lose what little peace I've found.*

She'd spent the past year putting the husband, the family and the ranch off-limits. She didn't know if she could do it again. She might not have the self-control to try.

Throwing herself into finishing her degree might be the only way she could halt her growing attachment to Ryder and the girls. She'd be wise to move forward with it.

He was getting too close to Eden. The next morning in church, Ryder handed packets of fruit snacks to the girls as they waited for the service to begin. Harper sat to his right. Ivy to his left. They each had a small notebook, a sheet of stickers and a few crayons to keep them occupied.

Ivy kept poking her head around to look at the entrance. The twins had been tired this morning when he'd gotten them up. After the parade yesterday, Eden had slipped away without giving him a chance to say goodbye. He and Mason had taken the kids shopping at the Western store for riding gear, and he'd found himself wishing Eden had joined them.

"Auntie Eden's here!" Ivy whispered loudly. Kneeling on the pew, facing the entrance, she waved Eden over. As soon as Eden neared, Ivy hopped down and reached for her hand. "Sit with us."

Ryder didn't bother reprimanding her. He'd have a talk with her later about not messing around in the pew. At the moment, all he could do was fight awareness. Eden wore a short-sleeved white shirt with a flowy coral-colored skirt and strappy sandals. Her hair spilled over her shoulders, and he caught the scent of her perfume. Clean and floral. All Eden.

She glanced at him and smiled. His mouth went dry. He'd been enjoying their time together every evening. When he came in from the ranch each weekday, he wanted to pinch himself. Eden was usually directing the girls how to set the table, where a hearty meal would be waiting.

How did she do it? How in the world did she spend so much time preparing activities for the girls, playing with them, reading to them, helping them make their books for Lily and, on top of it all, cooking supper?

He'd already slipped a bonus for her into each week's

check. She'd called him out on it, of course, but he told her she earned it.

She earned every penny and more.

The opening hymn filled the air, and he scanned the bulletin to follow along. Ivy had settled on Eden's lap, and from the corner of his eye he could see Eden's fingers stroking her hair. She was so good to his girls.

Why hadn't she gotten married? A beautiful woman like her—one who loved kids, was dependable and genuine, and could cook better than most people he knew—should have gotten snatched up long ago by a local cowboy.

There he went again. Making assumptions. Maybe Eden had something against marriage. Or the right guy hadn't come along yet. He'd made assumptions with Lily, too, and look where it had gotten him.

Ryder turned his attention back to the hymn and sang along. Several minutes later, Harper yawned loudly and climbed onto his lap. He peeked at Eden. She stared straight ahead as the pastor gave the sermon. Then she kissed the top of Ivy's head and held her closer.

His heart contracted. His little girls hadn't had much maternal affection in their lives.

*Stop thinking about Eden. Get your mind on the sermon.*

He tried. He really did. But beyond noting the theme of God knows our needs better than we do, he didn't get much out of it. If he wasn't thinking about Eden, he was thinking about the ranch. They'd started prepping the summer pasture this week. He was getting the hang of cattle. Of course, every day or two a new problem arose that he had no idea how to deal with. Thankfully, Chris had a good head on his shoulders. And if Chris didn't know what to do, Ryder called Mason.

The congregation got to their feet, and Ryder easily hefted Harper up as he stood. Eden shifted. Ivy had fallen asleep, too, so she picked her up, and it was as if he was momentarily outside his own body. With Eden standing next to him, each holding a twin in their arms, the image appeared so right he could barely breathe.

They looked like a family. A real family. A mom, dad and their two girls.

"Let us bow our heads and pray," the pastor said.

Ryder ignored the pastor's prayer for one of his own. *God, I need some help here. I knew I was playing with fire asking Eden to babysit the girls. It doesn't help that I'm friends with all of her friends. Spending all this time together is making me feel things I don't want to feel. Will You give me strength? Help me avoid temptation?*

When the service ended, the girls rubbed their sleepy cyes. As ushcrs directed people out of their pews, Ivy's face lit up and she gasped. "It's kitty time, isn't it, Daddy?"

He'd almost forgotten. They were picking up the kitten right after church.

"You're coming with us, right, Auntie Eden?" Ivy's big eyes grew worried.

"Yes, I am. I can't wait to see your kitten." Eden tapped the tip of Ivy's nose. "I'm going to go to my apartment and change first, though. Okay?"

"Okay."

Another afternoon with Eden. His pulse sped up at the thought. But fear was mixed with anticipation. Nothing involving his heart was ever simple. Not even picking up a kitten.

\* \* \*

An hour later, Ivy cradled the wiggly kitten in her arms back at the ranch. Eden had met Ryder and the girls at Mrs. Ball's house, and when Ivy spotted the white kitten reserved for her, she'd burst into happy tears, thanking her daddy over and over. Even Harper, who hadn't been enthused about getting a cat, had oohed and aahed over the remaining kittens. She'd fallen hard for a striped gray one, and in the end, Ryder had brought it home, too. Eden was helping the girls with the felines while Ryder went upstairs to change out of his church clothes.

"What are you going to name yours, Ivy? Mine looks like Scruffy or Silver or Wonderkitty. She's so soft. Maybe I should name her Dandelion, like the fluff we blow and make a wish on." Harper didn't seem to mind that her kitten had climbed onto her shoulder and was batting at her hair with one paw.

"I want a pretty name. She's like a princess. Meow. Meow." Ivy's kitten tried valiantly to escape her grip, but Ivy wasn't letting go. "Stop squirming."

In jeans and a T-shirt, Ryder jogged down the staircase. "Why don't you let the kittens explore for a while. They won't want to be held every minute."

"Good idea. Let's keep them in one spot for now." Eden pointed to the sunroom. "I'll watch them for you while you change into play clothes."

"Do I have to change?" Ivy whined, kissing her kitten's head again and again. "My kitty will miss me."

"Yes." Ryder was firm. "Cats do not want to be held all the time."

*Or at all.* Eden kept her thoughts to herself. Some cats loved being held. Others hated it.

"Goodbye, kitty. I'll be right back. I'm not leaving you. Promise." Ivy took hers to the sunroom and set it on the love seat. Harper did the same, then skipped out the door behind her sister.

Eden started to shut the French door, but Ryder blocked it with his foot.

"You trying to get rid of me or something?" His eyes gleamed in amusement as he slipped into the room, closing the door behind him. "Thanks for setting us up with the kittens. They are a hit."

"You're welcome. I'm glad you got Harper one, too. It's easier to deal with young littermates than introducing another cat later on." Eden thought back to when Mia had found a cat on the side of the road and brought it home. Their older cat, Brownie, had not been happy. There had been a few days of hissing before the two could tolerate being in the same room.

Eden scooped up the striped kitten and sat on the love seat with it. It immediately began to purr. The little rumbles cheered her heart. "This one is so cute. I'm tempted to go back and get the last kitten for myself."

"Why don't you?" He plunked his body down on an oversized chair. Ivy's kitten crawled between his chair and the wall.

"I don't know. Where would I put the litter? I don't even know what my plans are after the summer. It wouldn't be fair to the poor little thing." The kitten launched itself off her lap onto the floor and chased its sister.

Ryder scooched forward. "What do you mean? What's happening after the summer? You're not moving, are you?"

"No, definitely not. I would never leave Noah. I

promised Mia I'd always be part of his life. I want to be here to spend time with him and watch his sports and school plays. I love him so much."

He nodded, his face clearing. "Then what's the deal with this fall?"

"I'm at a crossroads." Somehow over the past month, she'd gotten comfortable being with him. She wanted to open up to him. "When I found out Mia had cancer, it was the first semester of my junior year of college. I finished the term and moved back home. Noah was only six months old when my sister died, and Mason couldn't take care of the baby and the ranch, so I became Noah's full-time babysitter. It saved me."

"Saved you?" He eased back, crossing one leg and resting his ankle on his knee. "What do you mean?"

"Losing my sister so young was something I never could have imagined. It was unbelievable. Indescribable. I had a hard time accepting it. Taking care of her baby gave me a purpose. I'm very thankful for that time."

"Didn't you want to go back to college?"

"No."

Harper's kitten saw a leaf blowing outside and jumped onto the other chair in front of the window. Its little tail swished back and forth quickly.

"You babysat him until Mason and Brittany got married, right?"

"Yeah. And by then I was babysitting Phoebe, too." She picked a piece of lint off the cushion next to her. "But a lot has changed in five years. Everyone's moving on, and I need to, too. I'm thinking of finishing my degree online. I originally went to school for early childhood education, but I'm looking at other majors. I need benefits."

"What are you going to do instead?"

"I don't know. Maybe I'll be an elementary school teacher."

"You'd be terrific at it."

"You think?" His compliment planted seeds of hope in her heart.

"Look at how great you are with the girls. The activities you plan, the books you read to them, the projects you've been preparing for their mother. I can't thank you enough."

"Have you heard from Lily? Does she plan on visiting soon?" Eden was surprised their mother hadn't come out yet. The girls were so enthusiastic whenever they added pages to their books.

"I don't know."

"I'm having a hard time putting them off." Eden didn't want to make him feel bad, but it was true. "They talk about her a lot."

"I know." He tapped his thumb against his leg. "It would make it easier on all of us if she would visit."

Eden was taken aback. She'd assumed he didn't want Lily to visit, especially after his cryptic words about marriage being a mistake. She'd been pounding it in her head every time the urge hit to think of him as more than a friend.

"Maybe you could ask her," she said softly.

"I have." His eyes were bleak. He shifted his jaw. "I'll keep trying."

He had asked her. Why had she assumed he hadn't?

"I never imagined an entire month would go by without her seeing them," Eden said almost to herself.

"It's been longer than a month." He lifted one shoulder in a careless shrug, but Eden wasn't fooled. It bothered him. "She was on location for their birthday, so I guess it would have been around Christmas since they last saw her."

"Is that normal?" It couldn't be right. Surely Lily spent more time with them than that. There had to be an explanation. "Was she shooting a movie or series or something?"

"She's not always great about following through with plans. She'll tell them she's coming to see them, and at the last minute, she'll back out, or worse, not show up at all."

Eden tried to wrap her head around this new information.

"Before you defend her—" he raised his hands "—I'm not trying to bad-mouth her. She's not an awful person. Trust me, I want the girls to have a mother. I do what I can, but…"

Eden wasn't sure what to think. Maybe Lily was really busy or felt uncomfortable with Ryder or something.

"I've told her over and over she can take them for a weekend or go to Disneyland with them, whatever." Ryder turned his attention out the window. "For a while, I worried she was trying to avoid me and that's why she wasn't showing up. But she wasn't around much even when we were married."

Well, there went that theory.

"Where's my kitty?" Ivy opened the door and ran inside with her arms wide-open, fingers curling in and out. Harper wasn't far behind. The white kitten poked its head out from under Ryder's chair. "Daddy! You're not s'posed to let her get dirty!"

His expression softened. Harper bounced over to the striped cat rolling on the area rug. "My kitty can do whatever she wants. If she feels like jumping in a mud puddle, I'm gonna let her."

"She better not get *my* kitten all muddy." Ivy got down on her knees and dragged the white kitten out from under the chair. Carefully holding her the way Mrs. Ball demonstrated, Ivy proceeded to scold the cat. "You're not a dust mop. Now go lick your fur and get clean." The kitten wiggled to be set down, and Ivy lost her grip. It pounced on Harper's, and they rolled around, playing.

"Can we call Mommy?" Ivy set her hands on Ryder's knees and gazed at him. "I want her to help me name my kitty."

Eden held her breath as she watched Ryder for his reaction. Would he approve?

"I'll call her now." His tender smile for Ivy sent a wave of warmth through Eden's core.

He hadn't shot down his daughter's desire to talk to her mommy.

An uncomfortable feeling tugged at her conscience. Why did she keep assuming the worst about him? And why did she keep giving his ex-wife the benefit of the doubt?

Eden had never even met her.

Maybe it was time to face facts. Shortly after meeting Ryder, Eden had taken sides—Lily's—without ever having met her.

And now that she knew Ryder, she could admit he wasn't an inconsiderate jerk who kept his daughters from their mother. He was a hardworking man doing the best he could to make a nice life for them.

The bricks she kept trying to pile up against him were toppling down one by one. She wasn't sure how to keep propping them up anymore.

All she knew was if she didn't, she'd be in trouble. Because the man in front of her wasn't the ogre she needed him to be.

# Chapter Seven

"That's going to be a problem."

Wednesday afternoon, Ryder looked ahead to where Chris pointed. They were checking the fence surrounding the first section of summer pasture in preparation for moving the herd. Strands of barbed wire had gone slack near the bottom of one of the fence posts. Ryder dismounted. After hammering it to secure it, he turned back to inspect the wire. Looked good.

"Good eye, Chris." Ryder got back in the saddle, and they continued on. They still had miles of fence to inspect. They couldn't have asked for a better day to do it. The first week of June had brought mild temperatures, a breeze and sunshine. He wished every day could be this pleasant.

"I've had a lot of practice." A thin man in his late thirties with a scruffy brown beard, Chris had a body as tough as beef jerky. He seemed tense. Normally, he chatted about the ranch, cattle, his son or the upcoming rodeo season. Today he'd been quiet.

"Something on your mind?" Ryder pulled up alongside him.

"Just making sure we have this pasture locked down. The cows have a knack for finding the weakness in a fence and waving all their girlfriends through."

Ryder had seen it firsthand himself. "You're not wrong."

"They must be related to my ex," Chris muttered.

"She giving you problems?" Every once in a while, Chris would comment on how unreasonable his ex-wife was about their custody arrangement, but most days the man didn't say much on the topic.

"When doesn't she? She knows my weaknesses and uses them against me, too, just like the cows." Chris continued to scan the fence as they rode through thick green grass. "I was supposed to take Trevor to the rodeo Friday night, but now she's claiming they have some family event to attend. This is the fifth time this year she's done this. If it's not a cousin's birthday, it's a surprise party for her parents' wedding anniversary. I get every other weekend with Trevor, starting Friday afternoon, and I'm mighty tired of giving up my days for her family."

Ryder could see his point. "Can you switch dates with her?"

"I have. Half the time, she finds an excuse to keep him on the days we switched, too. I'm tired of it. I've told Trevor time and again we would be going to the rodeos all summer long. They're on Friday nights. If she takes my Fridays, I can't keep my word to my son."

Chris shook his head. "Women aren't worth it. They trick you into thinking they're sweet and nice, and then—bam! They mess you up."

Uneasiness stirred in Ryder's gut. What Chris was describing had been his own experience, too. Lily had been sweet and nice when they'd met. He hadn't been able to believe his good fortune when the amazing, gorgeous, and very famous actress noticed him. They'd had a whirlwind romance, and he'd been smitten.

"I'm not giving in this time," Chris said. "She'll throw a hissy fit, but I don't care. Smartest thing I ever did was go through the courts to nail down a custody arrangement. I'm picking up my son this Friday no matter what she says. She'll hear from my lawyer if she gets in my way."

"How does your son feel about it?" Ryder thought of Ivy and Harper and the hope shining on their sweet faces every time they thought their mother would call or visit. How many times had their hopes been crushed? Too many to count. Just look at Sunday when he'd left message after message for Lily to call the girls. They'd been so excited to tell her about their kittens. He'd yet to hear back from her.

"I don't know." Chris glanced his way and blew out a frustrated breath. "Stuck in the middle, I suppose."

Ryder could relate. He often felt stuck in the middle between Lily and the girls. It made him feel helpless.

He couldn't force Lily to care about their daughters' feelings.

He couldn't force her to show up.

"Working here has been a lifesaver." Chris's hazel eyes sharpened as he stared at Ryder. "Rendezvous is close enough for me to be around my son, but far enough away to not be under her family's judgmental eye. I had to get out of that town."

"You've been a lifesaver for me, too." They continued to ride along the fence. "Mason gave me a crash course in ranching on the weekends I could get here, but riding out with you every day is what's really gotten me up to speed."

"You took to it quickly," Chris said. "Do me a favor, boss. If I ever start talking about dating again, give me a swift boot in the backside, okay?"

Ryder laughed. "Will do." He almost asked Chris to do the same for him, but Eden's face came to mind. *Sweet and nice.* Unlike Lily, Eden *was* sweet and nice. But like Lily, she had goals and dreams that didn't involve him, like getting her degree. She'd already set aside her college plans once. He didn't want her to set them aside again.

He saw how she was with the girls—devoted, loving, selfless. Having her around made life so much easier for him. But it didn't mean he could pursue anything with her.

When was the last time life had been this smooth?

*When Lily was pregnant with the twins...*

They'd hired a decorator to help design the babies' rooms, taken child-birthing classes, gone out to restaurants, laughed a lot and picked out names. Lily had wrapped up the final season of *Courtroom Crimes* before they got married and was on a hiatus. They'd decided to start our family right away. That year—the marriage, the pregnancy—had a surreal quality to it. Everything had been like a dream come true.

Then the twins came. Two beautiful, squawking, healthy girls. Ryder had never felt so much sheer love in his life. Within days, Lily scrapped the idea of being a homemaker, and she hired a nanny. He understood. Two babies were a lot.

But then things changed, and he'd been trying to keep his head above water ever since.

"Looks like we've got another section down." Chris slowed where wire dangled between posts. "It's a good thing we're checking this before we move the herd in. Nothing worse than having to track down cattle when we could be getting other work done. This will prevent a lot of problems later on."

Truer words had not been spoken. Remembering how Lily played him for a fool, how she'd lied to him and acted like the twins were disposable would prevent a lot of problems for Ryder, too.

He didn't think he was capable of trusting a woman again the way he'd trusted Lily. He was not getting sucked into a relationship where the woman he loved claimed to want one thing but really wanted something else entirely. Something that didn't involve him.

Repairing this fence would keep the cattle in. Repairing the fence around his heart would keep complicated feelings out.

"I want twisty ice cream with sprinkles!" Harper held on to the edge of the counter at Dipping Dream's take-out window.

"I want chocolate with sprinkles," Ivy said.

Eden hiked Phoebe higher on her hip. They'd just loaded up on books from the library and had walked the two blocks to the ice-cream stand. Harper had skipped the entire way here, while Ivy held Eden's hand and walked beside her.

Sunday afternoon, she'd made a to-do list involving ordering her transcripts, setting up a phone call with an adviser and printing out the current requirements to get certified as a teacher in Wyoming. Then, yesterday, while the girls watched a video, she'd called the local elementary principal. Eden had been pleasantly surprised to find out she could do her student teaching there when the time came, and later she could substitute teach as a gateway to full-time employment.

Phoebe reached a chubby hand toward Harper's hair. "Oh, no, you don't." Eden stopped her from grabbing a fistful of waves. "I'm getting you ice cream, too, Phoebe-kins."

"Cwee," Phoebe said, her eyes lighting up.

"Yep."

"What can I get for you?" the teen behind the window asked.

Eden sensed Phoebe getting ready to go for Harper's hair again, so she shifted out of reach. "We'll take one twisty cone with sprinkles, one chocolate cone with sprinkles, one vanilla cup and a hot fudge sundae."

"Coming right up." He disappeared from view.

Eden scanned the area for places to sit. A picnic table nearby was free. "Why don't you girls sit at that table while I wait for the ice cream?"

She watched as they raced over and sat opposite each other. Shifting shadows from the tree nearby partially shaded it. An employee held two cones with sprinkles out the window. Now what? She had only one hand free.

"I'll be right back for the other one." Eden carefully took the twisty cone to the table, where, to her surprise, Misty Sandpiper was taking a seat.

Harper sat on her knees, leaning in to hear Misty

better, and Ivy's gaze was glued her face. Eden wasn't exactly friends with Misty. She didn't dislike her or anything, but they ran in different circles.

Misty was outgoing and popular and always had a boyfriend. In other words, the exact opposite of Eden.

"Want me to hold Phoebe for you?" Misty always looked put together and pretty in a natural way with her long light brown hair and carefully applied makeup. She was wearing denim shorts with a low-cut hot-pink T-shirt.

"Thank you, that would be great." Eden handed Phoebe to her and hurried back to get the rest of the ice cream. It took two trips, but finally, she was able to sit next to Harper. Then she realized she'd stuck Misty with the baby. "Oh, what am I thinking? Here, I'll take Phoebe."

"I don't mind feeding her." She made cute faces at Phoebe, who extended both hands toward the cup of vanilla with her mouth wide-open.

"Are you sure?" When Misty nodded, Eden rummaged through the diaper bag. "I'll get her bib. She can be messy."

She handed it to Misty, who snapped it over Phoebe's T-shirt. The sprinkles were already starting to fall off the sides where the ice cream dripped from the twins' cones.

"Girls," Eden said, "lick those drips before they fall onto your hands. Here are some napkins." She pushed a few napkins to them.

"What brings you out today?" Eden asked, keeping an eye on each of her charges. Harper had licked one side of her cone, but sprinkles freely dripped onto the back of her hand. Ivy was valiantly circling hers, but it was dripping nonetheless. And Phoebe was smiling and clapping every time Misty gave her another bite from her cup of vanilla ice cream.

"I have the day off," Misty said. "I'd just finished my shake when I saw these two sit down."

"We got kitties," Harper said. An ice-cream mustache crested her lip. "Mine is silver and has stripes like a tiger."

"What did you name him?" Misty directed her attention to Harper. Phoebe tried to grab the spoon and held her mouth open for another bite. Misty fed her a spoonful of vanilla.

"She's a girl. Her name's Dandy. It's short for Dandelion, cuz she's so fluffy. Do you ride ponies? I started to learn. My uncle Mason's teaching me. Daddy's helping Ivy cuz she's scared." Harper took another long lick.

"Am not!" Ivy furrowed her eyebrows. "I rode Nugget. Daddy told me I did good."

"Well, Uncle Mason says I'm real good at it. Patches can tell."

"Stop bragging, Harper."

This type of back-and-forth happened several times a day, so Eden quickly changed topics. "Why don't you tell Misty what you named your kitten, Ivy?"

"Princess Cutie." Ivy took another lick from her cone. "She's white and fluffy and she purrs all the time. I just call her Cutie. It's easier that way. And she sure is cute."

Harper jumped in. "I have a sparkly shirt to wear when I ride Patches. Do you have sparkly shirts when you ride a horse? Mine's purple and white. I like the baby-blue one I saw in the store, too. Have you seen it?" Harper's ice cream was beginning to melt down the back of her hand. "Auntie Eden, it's a river!"

Eden sopped up the mess with the napkins she had on hand.

"Cwee, cwee!" Phoebe yelled, slapping her palms on the picnic table.

Misty's eyes had the overwhelmed expression Eden often felt when dealing with three young girls. She reached over for the baby. "Let me take her."

Misty transferred her to Eden and pushed the ice-cream cup her way, then turned to Harper once more. "I used to have a lot of sparkly outfits. In fact, I competed in rodeos."

"Rodeos," Harper said reverently. "I want to ride in one."

"Not me." Ivy licked the drips around her cone.

"That's cuz you're scared."

"Am not!"

"Girls." Eden tried to keep her voice even. "Let's be nice."

"I was scared of riding when I was younger," Misty said. "My mama got so mad at me. She said no self-respecting Wyoming girl didn't know how to ride a horse."

"What did you do?" Ivy watched Misty above her cone.

"First, I cried a little. I thought she was so mean. Then I toughened up. My daddy took me out and told me he'd be right there next to me and not to worry. So I didn't."

"My daddy told me the same." Ivy nodded.

"You've got a good daddy." Misty smiled. "He won't

let you fall. I wouldn't mind coming out to help if you want."

Great. Now Misty would be at the ranch, and Ryder would be dazzled by her bubbly personality and pretty face. Eden spooned the last bite of ice cream into Phoebe's mouth. "I need to clean her up."

"I'll stay here with the girls."

"You don't mind?"

"Not at all."

"Thanks."

Eden grabbed the diaper bag and took Phoebe to the public restroom at the side of the ice-cream stand. The mirror showed white smears on the shoulder of her shirt where Phoebe had placed her sticky hands. Eden's hair was frizzing near her face, and strands of hair had escaped her ponytail. Needless to say, the swipe of tinted lip gloss she'd applied this morning had worn off hours ago.

Misty always looked impossibly fresh and nice. No wonder she always had a date while Eden sat home. And Eden couldn't even hate the girl. She'd been really nice and helpful today.

She wet a paper towel and washed Phoebe's hands and face with it as the child did everything in her power to avoid getting wiped. In the end, Phoebe let out a few high-pitched shrieks before Eden was confident she'd eliminated all the stickiness.

Back outside, her stomach dropped at the sight of Ivy and Harper hanging on Misty's words and laughing at something she said. Eden had been around Rendezvous enough to see the writing on the wall. She'd had Ryder to herself since he'd moved to town, but that would be changing.

She didn't want Ryder to fall for pretty, flirty Misty Sandpiper. She wanted him to fall for her.

And that wasn't going to happen.

Friday afternoon, Ryder took a seat in the ranch office and glanced at the whiteboard listing all the projects he needed to get done this summer. The day was warm and sunny. He and Chris had started moving the cattle to their new pasture. Everything was going well for the moment. The kittens had distracted Ivy from her constant questions about when her mother was coming, and Harper hadn't stopped begging to ride Patches again. Both girls were getting another horseback-riding lesson tomorrow when Mason was free to help him.

His cell phone rang, and he glanced at it. Lily's name appeared. A copper taste coated his tongue.

"What's up?" He kept his tone friendly, crisp.

"Hi, Ryder." Her silky voice slid through the line. "How are the girls?"

"They're fantastic." His grip on the phone tightened. It was on the tip of his tongue to tell her she'd know how they were if she'd ever get around to seeing them.

"Good. I have a break in my schedule. I'm making arrangements to visit."

He'd believe it when she appeared on his doorstep. Not one second sooner.

"Good." He drummed his fingertips on the desk. "My offer still stands if you want to stay here at the ranch."

"I've actually had Mandy rent a cabin for me."

A cabin implied rustic. What she really meant was she'd rented a luxury log home. But what did he care? Cabin, mansion—at least she was coming.

Maybe.

"When do you arrive?"

"Next Friday. I plan on staying a week."

That gave him a week to get ready. No problem. "They will be very happy. They want to see you. By the way, I bought them kittens. Maybe you could Face-Time the girls later so they can show them to you. And you can let them know you're coming."

"Yes, absolutely," she said brightly. "Oh, gotta run. I'll have Mandy send you the information." And she hung up.

He stared at the phone in his hand and shook his head. Would she keep her word? And if she did come, would she spend an entire week with the girls?

He wasn't counting on it. Couldn't count on her. Maybe he could ask Eden to be on call that week. Leaning back, he sighed.

Harper's and Ivy's faces came to mind with all their innocent questions about their mother coming to see them.

Lily had better not let them down this time.

At least if she didn't show up, Eden would be around to help him pick up the pieces.

But what would he do when summer ended? He'd be on his own again, doing his best to raise the twins by himself. They needed their mother, too, and he couldn't force her to be involved in their lives.

He wouldn't think about it now. He had a ranch to run.

"No, Dandy, don't hide under there." Harper crouched down on all fours and peeked under the couch. Then she scrambled to her feet. "Auntie Eden, Dandy doesn't like me!"

Eden calmly went over to where Harper stood. "What's the problem?"

"She's under the couch, and I told her not to. Bad kitty!" Harper stamped her little bare foot on the hardwood floor and pouted.

"Cutie is being bad, too." Ivy carried the wiggly kitten over from where she'd plucked her off the curtains. "Her claw scratched me, and Daddy said she can't climb the curtains."

"Why don't you both leave the kittens alone for a while, and we'll have some cookies outside. Your daddy will be home soon."

Late afternoon could be cagey with the twins, even on a beautiful, sunny summer Friday. At least Phoebe had been happy all day. Gabby had picked her up an hour ago, leaving Eden alone with the twins.

"Okay." Ivy set the kitten on the couch, but it promptly leaped off and raced to the curtains. "Auntie Eden! She's doing it again!"

"Let's put the kitties in a time-out in the sunroom." Eden reached under the couch and moved her arm until she got a grip on Dandy. Then, holding the kitten, she hustled over to the curtains and plucked Cutie off. After depositing the furballs in the sunroom and shutting the door, she headed back down the hall, where she could hear the girls bickering in the family room.

"No, I get to tell Mommy about the kitties first." Ivy jabbed her thumb into her chest.

"Fine. We never talk to her anyhow." Harper sounded mad. "Who cares?"

"Don't say that about Mommy." Ivy's voice went up an octave. "She's busy. Daddy said so."

"Phoebe's mommy isn't too busy for her," Harper said.

"Maybe Mommy doesn't know where Wyoming is. I told Daddy she couldn't find us."

"She can use her phone like Daddy does when he gets lost." Harper's face fell. "She doesn't love us."

"She loves us." Ivy didn't sound so sure.

Eden's heart fell to the floor. She'd better go in there before the girls argued themselves into a puddle of hurt they couldn't get out of.

"Don't cry," Harper said. Eden paused at the end of the hall and watched them. Harper wrapped her arms around Ivy. "You're right. She loves us. She does."

Eden didn't know what to do. What could she say? She didn't know how to handle this situation. Retracing her steps to the kitchen, she selected a package of cookies. They probably weren't the healthy solution, but the girls needed a distraction at the moment.

"Ready, girls?" She pasted on a bright smile. "We'll have a snack outside. Grab a blanket."

Eden slid open the patio door and followed them to the grass where they spread out the blanket. She knelt on it and took out the cookies. The girls joined her. After a few minutes of munching, they all sprawled out and played several rounds of I spy.

"I spy with my little eye..." Harper chanted. "Daddy!"

"Hey there, Harper." Ryder stopped at the edge of the blanket. "Ivy. Eden."

"We didn't hear you coming." Her breath caught at

how rugged he looked in his T-shirt and jeans. His face had a carefree expression she wasn't used to seeing.

"This looks fun. Is there room for me?" He crouched with his elbows on his knees.

"Yes, Daddy, right here." Ivy patted the spot between her and Eden. He raised his eyebrows and squeezed into the spot.

Eden should have moved aside. She still could. But she didn't want to.

Ryder was all cowboy. Sitting next to him was sweeter than the chocolate sandwich cookies she'd just devoured.

"You know what day it is?" he asked the girls.

"Friday!" They hopped to their feet. "Pizza day!"

"Yep. Why don't you go inside and get washed up? I'll be in there in a minute."

"Okay!" They ran inside, leaving Eden all too aware she was alone with their very handsome daddy.

"Want to join us? Roscoe's makes a mean meat-lover's." His eyes gleamed with appreciation and more.

Did she want to join them? Of course she did. She loved being with the girls, enjoyed eating supper with the three of them.

But caution held her back. Maybe it was seeing Misty the other day or the fact she'd spoken with an academic adviser and was 99 percent sure she was enrolling in online classes this fall. Regardless, she needed to face facts.

She'd been getting too wrapped up in this family.

"No, I can't. I have plans." She *did* have plans, too. Mason had asked her to babysit Noah tonight.

"Oh." His face fell. "Too bad. While I've got you here, I figure I'd better mention Lily called earlier. As of right now she plans on flying in next Friday and spending a week with the girls."

Eden tried to keep her face from crumbling. Wasn't this what she wanted? Why did it feel like the beginning of the end? "That's great. The girls really miss her. It will do them a world of good to see their mom."

"Yeah, well…" He shrugged. "She's not always reliable."

"You mentioned that." Eden treaded carefully. "They were upset earlier. They argued about her. Spending time with their mom will help."

"She said she'll FaceTime them tonight." He cocked his head as if he didn't believe it. "She told me the same thing last week, and it never happened."

"I'm sure her job has a lot of pressures." Even so, Eden couldn't imagine not talking to Harper and Ivy if they were hers.

"It does." He turned to stare at her. "I hope she keeps her word. Can you still be available to babysit in case she changes her mind about coming? I'll pay you no matter what. In fact, I might need you to be on call."

"Of course." She wanted to be there for Ivy and Harper. And Ryder. "It's not a problem."

"Thank you." Appreciation and more shimmered through his eyes. "About the girls being upset…maybe I should talk to them."

"Please don't. They didn't know I heard them."

"I have a feeling I don't know half of what they're going through. I wish…" He shook his head. "Never mind. Some mistakes can't be undone."

She frowned. "What do you mean?"

"I wish I could have done it all differently. I want better for them. Their mother has incredible gifts. She can be the life of the party, the most understanding friend."

Eden's heart bottomed out with each word.

"But it's temporary. It doesn't last. If she had any idea how much the twins look up to her and want her to be in their lives, she'd…" Once more he shook his head.

The girls came back out as his ringtone sounded. "Speaking of Lily. I have a FaceTime coming in. Do you mind?" He stared at Eden.

"Not at all." She stood. "I'll show myself out."

"Mommy!" Ivy screeched as Ryder answered the call.

As Eden walked toward the house, she heard Lily's soothing, upbeat voice and the girls tripping over each other's words in an effort to speak. She trudged inside, packed her supplies, straightened the art projects and let herself out the front door.

She was only the babysitter. Ryder had been clear he considered marriage a mistake. And he was right that if Lily had any idea how much the twins looked up to her, she'd make more effort with them.

Sometimes the hardest things to do were the right ones. If Lily was coming next week, Eden would do her best to show the woman what amazing little girls she had. And in the meantime, she needed to limit her own time with their daddy.

She was in no shape to fall for Ryder Fanning, and if she didn't keep reminding herself, she'd tumble over the cliff and never recover.

# Chapter Eight

"Surprise!" Eden's mom and dad stood in the doorway of her apartment the next morning. She'd just showered and brewed a pot of coffee. Her parents hadn't planned on coming back to town until next month, so this was a happy development. Dad looked like he'd put on ten pounds since leaving the ranch, and Mom was as beautiful as ever with her gray eyes and shoulder-length dark brown hair.

"When did you get here?" After ushering them inside, Eden hugged them both. "Why didn't you call?"

"We wanted to see the look on your face when we arrived." Her dad winked at her. "How are you doing, kid?"

"I'm good, Dad." She pointed them to the living room and detoured into the kitchen. "Coffee's ready if you want some."

"I'll take a cup," her mother called. "Cream and sugar, please."

"Black for me." Dad followed her to the kitchen and reached into an upper cabinet for a mug. He selected a big one with a sketch of a bull. "Ah, you still have my favorite."

"It reminds me of you." Eden laughed. She prepared a mug of coffee for her mom as Dad poured his own. "How was Tennessee?"

Together, they headed to the living room.

"The Smoky Mountains were something. But it's good to be back where you can see miles of land without so much civilization getting in the way."

"We've met so many people." Mom accepted the mug from Eden with a smile. Eden sat on one of the chairs adjacent to the couch. "I never imagined how different each state could be."

"Different in some ways, but the same in others." Dad took a seat opposite Eden. "There's a McDonald's everywhere you turn. Same stores, same highways. And a lot of traffic." He pretended to shudder.

"Sounds like you're missing Wyoming, Dad." Eden studied him. Aside from his not-too-serious aversion to civilization, he looked more carefree than he had in years. Retirement seemed to be suiting him.

"Yeah, I guess I am." His wistful expression ended with a slight shrug. "Don't get me wrong. I'm enjoying seeing new places."

"I know." She was glad her parents were doing something that made them happy. Still, it came as no shock to her that her dad might be missing home. "Do you want to stay here while you're in town? I can get the air mattress out."

"Oh, no." Mom waved her off. "We're set up at Rendezvous Pines campground. The spacious campsites are a welcome change from some of the tiny lots where we've parked."

"How's Ryder doing with the ranch?" Dad's knee bounced as he watched her.

"Fine, I guess."

"The herd? He's doing okay with the cattle?"

"Yep. Same as I told you last week." She regularly talked to her parents, and her dad always asked about the ranch. "I think they moved cattle this week."

"Good. Good." Dad took a drink of his coffee. "Did he check all the fence? Get the calves branded?"

"Yes, he did." Over supper each night, Ryder would tell her the checklist of what he'd accomplished and always end it with a frown that he wished he could have gotten more done. Why was he so hard on himself?

"And the water?" Dad asked.

"I'm sure he's set up the water, too. You do know I don't ride out there with him, right?" she teased. "I take care of the girls."

"Aw, I know." His cheeks grew pink as he chuckled. "I've been thinking about the place a lot lately."

"I get it. You miss it."

His cell phone rang. "It's Mason. I'm going to take this. I'll go outside." He pointed to the hall and answered the phone. "Howdy…"

As his voice faded and the click of the door produced silence, Mom turned to her. "So tell me what's going on with you. Harper and Ivy are so darling, and it sounds like you've been seeing a lot of their daddy."

Her mom had a sparkle in her eye along with a little too much hope. But it was true. She'd been getting to know Ryder better. After supper while they cleaned up, she'd been telling him about her childhood, stories of her and Mia and their games and fights. How they'd bake Christmas cookies for days on end with their mom. How she'd loved growing up in Rendezvous, where everyone knew everyone else. She'd even told him about a few of the elderly shut-ins from church she visited because they'd been so kind to her when she was a girl.

He, in turn, had told her about his college days, working in an upscale office and how he loved California weather but couldn't stand the traffic.

She could no longer pretend she wasn't getting close to Ryder.

"The girls are amazing." She'd skip her mom's statement about seeing a lot of their daddy. "You know the brag books I've been having them make to give to their mother? They're almost done. It's been fun coming up with new projects to put in them. Last week we hiked around the ranch and picked wildflowers. Then we pressed them and glued them to paper. I laminated the papers to add to the books."

"You always were creative like that." Mom held the cup near her lips as happiness lit her eyes.

"Well, I learned from you." A burst of nostalgia made her heart tender. She'd been missing her mom and hadn't realized it. They'd spent so much time together these past years.

Mom leaned forward. "So…when do you get to meet Lily?"

"I don't know. She might be arriving next week. Ryder isn't sure."

"We've watched all her shows."

"Yeah, but remember, I'm just the babysitter. There

might not be any reason for me to be there, so I don't know that I'd meet her."

"Well, maybe Ryder could get an autograph…"

"No." Before getting to know him better, Eden would have jumped at the chance of getting Lily Haviland's autograph. But it no longer held any allure for her. The stars in her eyes when it came to the actress had been erased. "Lily is a sore subject with him."

Mom tapped her chin. "Yes, I imagine it would be hard to divorce someone famous."

"It's probably hard to divorce anyone."

"True." She took another sip of her coffee. "But now that I think of it, it has to be difficult when your ex-wife is a beloved actress and on the cover of magazines whenever a new movie comes out."

"Being constantly reminded of your ex when getting groceries or flipping through channels can't be a good feeling."

"Do you think it's one of the reasons he moved to Wyoming?" Mom asked.

"What do you mean?" She hadn't thought about it.

"Well, there are fewer chances of bumping into reminders of Lily out here."

This wasn't helping. She liked to think of Ryder and the girls embarking on a new life here, not escaping from the old one.

What would happen when the old collided with the new?

What if Ryder fell for Lily all over again when she was here? And the woman would have to be blind not to see how wonderful the girls were and want to be with them. What if Lily and Ryder got back together?

Her time with the girls would come to an end.

A swoosh of sadness hollowed her out. It wasn't just the thought of missing the girls. She'd miss Ryder, too.

*Stop thinking about him. He's never been yours.*

"He likes being closer to Mason. Maybe he just needed a change." Eden was more than ready to move on to a different subject. "And speaking of changes, I've officially decided to finish my degree. I'm switching my major to education so I can teach elementary school."

"That's great news." Mom cheered up. "I've been praying for God to lead you on the right path. What made you finally decide?"

"Everyone's moving on, and it's time for me to, as well."

"I understand."

"No matter what, though, I plan on staying here." Eden's mind hadn't changed on that, at least.

"Are you sure? Maybe a change of scenery would do you good."

"I'm glad you and Dad are traveling and enjoying yourselves, but I can't imagine leaving my friends, and I'd miss Noah too much."

"We miss him, too." Mom nodded. The sound of the door opening and male voices had them craning their necks to see who'd arrived.

"Look who I found outside." Dad appeared in the living room with Ryder next to him.

She locked gazes with him and a tingling sensation shivered down her spine. He held up a black cardigan. "You forgot your sweater, and since I was stopping at the grocery store, I figured I'd drop it off."

"You didn't have to do that." Eden was ridiculously pleased he had, though.

"Hi, Joanna." Ryder crossed over and bent to give

her a hug. "You look great. How's touring the country been going?"

"We love it." She patted the spot next to her on the couch. "Sit down. We need to catch up."

"Oh, no, I can't. I need to pick up the girls from Mason's." He looked like he wanted to, though. "But hey, why don't you all stop by the ranch later? Mason and Brittany are bringing Noah over. Mason's been helping me teach the girls how to ride horses. We're grilling burgers, too. I'd love to have you join us."

Eden opened her mouth to decline, but her dad clapped Ryder on the back and said, "Sounds great. What time should we come over?"

Wait—what was happening? Why were her parents agreeing to hang out at Ryder's all afternoon?

"Mason's coming over at noon." Ryder's gaze slid to Eden again, and her cheeks grew warm.

"We'll bring a side dish." Mom got the faraway look in her eye that happened whenever she heard there was a potluck. Eden figured they'd be putting together a dish of potato salad within the hour.

"You don't have to bring anything." Ryder shook his head.

"We want to." Mom scoffed as if he'd grown a horn. "It's so nice of you to invite us."

"Well, I'd better get back. See you in a few hours." Ryder cast one final glance at Eden, and she watched him until he turned to leave. Her dad escorted him down the hall, peppering him with questions about the ranch the entire way.

"How many potatoes do you have on hand, Eden?"

She tucked her lips under to keep from laughing. Potato salad. Coming right up.

\* \* \*

Thank the good Lord for family. Ryder helped Ivy fasten her safety helmet, while Mason checked Harper's. It was a few minutes before noon. The horses were saddled and ready for the girls. What a perfect day. Blue skies. Nice breeze. The sun heated his bare arms, and every now and then he'd check over his shoulder to see if Eden and her parents had arrived. He wouldn't mind picking Bill's brain about the ranch, and he always felt accepted by Joanna.

But what if Bill was like Granddad, though? Impossible to please. Would the man think Ryder wasn't doing a good job?

"It's too tight, Daddy." Ivy looked nervous. "Can I play with Cutie instead?"

"I thought you liked riding Nugget last week." He hoisted her into his arms so their faces were level. She curled her body into his chest.

"I did, but..."

"Hey there, Skeeter." Eden's father marched over to Harper with a big grin. Ryder must have missed their truck pull up. He instantly searched for Eden. Didn't see her. Had she stayed home? He hoped not.

"I'm Harper. Not Skeeter." She wore her most serious face.

Bill tweaked a lock of hair poking out from under her helmet. "Harper, you say? I thought you were Skeeter. Next you'll be telling me that girl in your daddy's arms isn't Catfish."

Harper broke into a loud giggle. "No, silly, that's Ivy."

"Ivy?" Bill scratched his chin. "I don't think so. Looks like Catfish to me."

"Grandpa!" Noah raced to Bill, and Bill caught him up in his arms.

"Spurs!" Bill kissed Noah's cheek. "You're a sight for sore eyes."

Ivy wriggled for Ryder to set her down, and he obliged. She ran to Harper and they looked up at Bill. "That's not Spurs. That's Noah."

Noah hugged Bill's neck, and the man let out a throaty laugh. Joanna came up next to Bill and held out her arms to the twins.

"Look at you two. You've gotten so tall and pretty." Joanna pointed to Ivy. "Let me guess. You're Ivy, right?" Ivy nodded. Joanna turned to Harper. "And Harper. I'd know you any day."

The girls exchanged pleased glances. Ryder had to give it to Eden's mom—she could tell the girls apart better than most people, and she'd been around them on only a handful of occasions.

"And how is my Noah?" Joanna asked. Bill set Noah down.

"I'm great! Daddy's teaching Harper and Ivy how to ride horses, and I'm helping." He lifted his chin proudly. "They're my cousins."

"I know, isn't it wonderful?"

"Did you bring the camper? Does it still have a special bed for me? Did you buy popsicles?" Noah asked. "I want to go in it."

"My, my." Joanna laughed. "You have a lot of questions. The RV is at the campground. Grandpa drove his truck."

Noah's face fell, then he asked, "Where's Auntie Eden?"

"She's putting the potato salad in the fridge. She'll be right out."

Joanna hugged Ryder. "We're thankful you're taking such good care of the place." She patted his cheek, and the maternal gesture filled a longing he'd pushed away years ago.

Most of the time, he didn't think about the fact he was an orphan. His grandparents had raised him after his parents died in a car accident when he was a week old. But having Joanna here treating him almost like he was part of the family touched him. Mason was his only family, and since Lily was estranged from her parents, the twins had no grandparents in their lives.

For the first time, Ryder grasped how much his girls were missing. And it made him sad.

"Good to see you, son." Bill pulled Mason into a half embrace, clapping him on the back. "Need some help?"

Mason grinned. "Yeah, we're getting these two up to speed riding horses. They're Wyoming girls now."

"We'd better giddyup and get 'em riding, then." Bill winked at Ivy.

"My kitty needs me." Ivy's pitiful eyes made Ryder almost cave and tell her she could skip the lessons today. He didn't want to push her too hard. He knew riding the horse intimidated her.

"A kitty, you say?" Bill stood before her. "I'm scared of cats."

"Scared?" Her expression broke into astonishment. "Of a kitty? Mine is real nice, Grandpa Bill. She's white and fluffy and purrs and loves to sit on your chest when you're trying to sleep. You'd like her."

Bill shook his head. "She sounds nice, Catfish, but kittens have claws. She'll scratch me."

"She's scratched me." Ivy twisted her lips. "But it didn't hurt too bad."

"You're braver than me," Bill said. "Now, see, riding a horse doesn't scare me. I've ridden them since I was knee-high. But petting a kitten?" He had a grim look on his face.

"Grandpa Bill, you don't need to be scared." Ivy took his hand in hers. "I'll hold Cutie and you can pet her."

"You'd do that for me?" He seemed to think it over. "Okay. But I'd feel better if I could spend some time out here with the horses first. They help me feel calm, you know what I mean? Why don't you get on your horse and I'll lead it for a while? It'll help my nerves."

Ivy gave Nugget a skeptical glance. Then she pulled back her little shoulders. "If I get on the horse, do you promise to pet Cutie?"

Lines deepened in his forehead as he nodded. "I promise."

Bill took Ivy's hand, let her into the corral and explained to her how to mount the horse. Mason was already leading Harper around the corral. Ryder leaned against the fence and watched in awe as Ivy listened to the man and followed his instructions. Bill was a gem.

"They look like naturals."

Ryder almost jumped. He hadn't noticed Eden approach. With a quick scan, he noticed Joanna and Brittany deep in conversation walking toward the patio. Which left him and Eden alone.

"Your dad just pulled off something I never thought I'd see." He nodded to where Bill continued to talk to Ivy up on Nugget as they made their way around. Ivy giggled loudly. "She's not afraid up there."

The back of Eden's hair lifted in the slight breeze,

and her profile was serene. "He's great with kids. He taught me how to ride, and trust me, I was a reluctant rider."

"Did you learn here?" He shifted to face her.

"Yes. Right here in this corral, to be exact. I don't remember much. I know Dad had taken me riding with him since I was old enough to walk, but he must have decided it was time for me to ride solo when I was four or five. I was scared and stubborn."

"You?" He laughed. "I can't picture you scared or stubborn."

"Oh, I can be both." She smiled. "What about you? When did you learn to ride?"

"I'm not sure." Vague recollections of his gruff grandfather came to mind, riding in silence over the hills and plains of the sheep farm in Montana where he grew up. "I feel like I've always been riding."

"Like Noah," Eden said, pointing to the boy.

Mason had brought over Noah's horse in a trailer, and the kid was a natural, the expression on his face pure joy.

"What was the name of your first horse?" he asked.

"Dixie." She grinned. "Yours?"

"Coal. Needless to say, he was pure black. A beautiful horse." His granddad might have been a man of few words and high standards, but he'd made sure Ryder had the best horse he could afford.

As the kids rode, he and Eden shared tales of growing up in the country. An hour passed by and the lessons were finished. Ryder reluctantly peeled himself away from Eden to help Mason and Bill unsaddle the horses.

"Noah! Harper! Ivy!" Joanna called. "We're making cupcakes. Why don't you come help us?"

"Yay!" The trio raced to the patio.

"I'm going to help them." Eden hitched her thumb to the house.

He wanted her to stay. Had enjoyed her easy presence next to him. Liked sharing childhood memories. But Mason and Bill approached, and she was already walking away.

"I've missed this place." Bill looked around. His straw cowboy hat tipped to the sky.

"We can ride around, check it out if you'd like." It would give Ryder the chance to ask him more about the ranch.

"Don't have to ask me twice." Bill grinned. He cocked his head toward Mason. "You up for it?"

"On a day like this?" Mason spread his arms wide. "What are we waiting for?"

In no time at all, the three of them were riding horseback out to where the cattle grazed. Bill pointed out landmarks, like the gully where he'd found a calf half-eaten by coyotes years ago and the plain where the pronghorn liked to cross. Ryder enjoyed listening to him and Mason talk about the land.

Soon they were checking cows. Bill grew quiet. Just barked out observations, like "Keep an eye on the seventy-seven tag. Phlegmy eyes."

Ryder approached a calf he'd been keeping tabs on. Was it his imagination or was it losing weight?

"He's got an abscess," Bill said. "We'll need to lance it."

"Where?" Ryder strained to see any lumps, but the calf hid behind his mother. "Is that why he's losing weight?"

"Under here." Bill raised his chin and pointed to the

side of his neck. "From my experience, yes. Probably hurts him to nurse. You rope the head. I'll get the heels. When I've got him, you'll have to keep the rope tight so I can lance it. We'll get him some penicillin and he should be good to go."

Ryder followed Bill's instructions. Soon he was gripping the rope as Bill lanced the abscess quickly before giving the calf medicine. In no time flat, the calf was back on its feet, trotting over to his mama.

"Wow. I'm impressed. If that was a sporting event, you two would win." Mason pretended to applaud them.

"Pshaw, that's nothing." Bill looked especially pleased with himself. "It's nice to know I still got it, though."

"You've still got it, all right." The three of them continued to check more cows until Mason's cell phone rang. He answered it, and after a few *yes*es and *sure*s, he hung up.

"Time to head back. The kids want Grandpa to have cupcakes with them."

Bill let out a guffaw. "The only thing better than riding out across this land is having cupcakes with those kiddos. I made Ivy a promise to pet her kitten, too. Let's go."

As they rode back to the stables, Ryder's heart was full. The Lord's blessings were overflowing. He'd enjoy them while they lasted.

What a terrific afternoon. Eden wiped the crumbs off Ryder's countertop while her parents talked to Mason and Brittany in the hall. Ryder was in the sunroom with the kids and the kittens, and she pretended—just for a moment—this was her house again. As soon as the thought occurred, she pictured Ryder coming into the kitchen and wrapping his arms around her from behind. Resting his chin on her shoulder, and her laughing, turning her face just so...

"Change of plans." Mom breezed into the kitchen. "Your dad and I are taking the kids to Mason and Brittany's for a while. We'll be back around six to help cook the burgers. Love you!" And she trotted away before Eden could respond.

Tossing the washcloth into the sink, Eden pursued her to the front porch while the others headed to their vehicles. "Wait, I'll come with you."

Mom smiled. "You stay here with Ryder. Take a break."

"I don't need a break."

"Yes, you do." Mom walked ahead with a backward wave.

"What just happened?" Ryder came up and stood next to Eden as doors slammed shut and engines roared to life.

"I have no idea."

"One minute everyone's having a good time, stuffing their faces full of cupcakes..." He frowned. "It's like they wanted to get away from us."

"Do I smell?" She turned her head and sniffed. "I'm wearing body spray."

"You smell great." He stepped closer to her. "And I don't think it was something I said."

"No, they weren't offended. They're...happy."

He blew out a breath. "Well, I guess it's their loss."

"Yeah." Now what was she supposed to do? Her parents were gone. Her nephew had left. The twins weren't around, either. There was no reason to stay. "I guess I should get out of your hair."

"No way. And leave me all alone? Then I'll really feel like a leper."

"What are we going to do?" She wrung her hands.

He considered for a moment before snapping his fingers. "What do you say we get out of here for a while?"

"Where will we go?"

"Anywhere. I'm new to the area. Show me something I haven't seen before."

She thought about it. "You've been to all the stores in town. And the park. Nothing new there."

"True."

A vision of her special place outside town crowded her mind. No, she couldn't take him there. It was special for a reason. Private. But the longer the silence stretched, the more she realized she wanted him to see it.

"I know where we'll go." Nervousness tightened her chest, but she tried to tamp it down. "Do you want to drive?"

"Sure. Do we need anything?"

"A blanket and some snacks wouldn't hurt."

"Coming right up." He wiggled his eyebrows, and she shook her head, trying not to laugh.

What would he think of it? It was just a flat top of a hill with a spectacular view. Maybe Ryder wouldn't appreciate it.

She hoped he would.

She washed her hands and did a once-over of the kitchen to make sure everything had been put away.

"All set." Ryder held a small cooler in one hand, and a plaid blanket was tucked under his arm. He spun his keys on his index finger. "Where are we going, Captain?"

"Captain?" She gestured for them to go outside. "I'm not taking you on a boat ride."

"And here I was hoping…"

As Ryder helped her into the passenger side of his truck, she tried not to notice his strong hand at her elbow. He jogged around to the driver's side. Soon they were driving along back roads. Neither spoke much. They didn't need to. It was a beautiful, peaceful day. If she could bottle it, she would.

She gave him directions, and miles later, they'd parked on a grass lane and began hiking.

"What are those white flowers?" Ryder asked as they climbed the hill.

"Cushion phlox. Pretty, aren't they?" She breathed in the fresh air and took in the wildflowers dotting the prairie grass. "You'll see clusters of them all summer long. The taller bluish-purple flowers are lupine."

"I know lupine. If our sheep ate too much of them, they got sick."

"Really? Tell me about raising sheep." Eden kept a moderate pace. They'd almost reached the top of the hill. "How in the world did you go from sheep ranching in Montana to financial planner in LA?"

His eyes crinkled as he smiled. "It's different from raising cattle, that's for sure."

"Raising sheep or living in LA?"

"Both." The land leveled off, and Ryder stopped in his tracks. He looked over the valley and the acres before them. Mountains in the distance broke up the blue sky. "Wow. What is this?"

"My special place." The words were out before she

could analyze if it was wise to reveal that part of herself. "If it wasn't owned by the federal government, I would buy it. I love this land. Don't worry, we're not trespassing. The Bureau of Land Management allows public access."

"It is special." He pointed to the left. "Look, pronghorn. They're running."

The sight of them leaping and bounding over the ground always sent a thrill through Eden, and today was no exception. "Breathtaking."

"It is." His voice grew husky, and she glanced at him. He was looking at her with a serious expression, and it sent heat to her cheeks.

"Here, I'll spread out the blanket." She reached for it as he handed it to her. Their fingers touched, spiraling her nerves to high alert. Maybe she should have opted for camping chairs instead. She shook out the blanket and let it float over the grass. Ryder stretched the corners, and they both sat down.

"Why is this your special spot?" he asked, leaning back on his elbows with his legs stretched out before him. He wore jeans, a T-shirt, cowboy boots and a straw hat.

He was all lean muscles.

"You first. I asked about raising sheep." She wasn't sure she could put into words what this spot meant to her.

"By the time my parents died and my grandparents took me in as a baby, Granddad's sheep ranch was already declining. I helped him out at a young age. I remember him taking me out to the sheep wagons in the summer to check on the herders and bring them supplies. I can still see those trailers in the middle of nowhere. Loneliest things I could imagine."

Eden could picture it. "Did you ever stay in one?"

"Me? No." He shook his head. "I stayed on the main ranch. In the winter, I'd help out in the lambing shed. I learned a lot about life there. My favorite job was hand-feeding the orphans."

An image appeared in her mind of Ryder as a boy holding a lamb on his lap and feeding it a bottle.

"How did you end up in California?" She wanted to learn more about him. Get a complete picture of the man next to her.

"After Grandma died, there was no reason for me to stay in Montana. I got a scholarship to Cal State, interned for a financial-planning firm catering to Hollywood stars, and they hired me right out of school."

The last part sounded like a fairy tale—glamorous, adventurous. Eden couldn't imagine taking off to California at such a young age.

"Was it hard for you?" she asked. "Losing your grandparents, setting out on your own. I mean, California is a long way from Montana."

He considered it for a few moments. "Yes, but I didn't know any better. And I knew God would guide me. One thing I'm thankful for? My grandparents took me to church. I don't know that I'd have my faith if it wasn't for them."

"My parents laid the foundation for my faith, too," Eden said. "After Mia died, we grew closer, got through it together. When life gets me down, Mom tells me to pray. When life looks up, Mom tells me to pray. She gets on my nerves sometimes, if I'm being honest." She chuckled.

"Your mom's a wise woman." He shifted to his side, facing her. "So, your turn… This spot?"

This spot. The place she always ran to when life was too much.

"I come here when I can't take it anymore." She didn't look at him.

"Take what?" he asked quietly.

"Life." She turned to him then. "I was away at college when I found out Mia was diagnosed with cancer. I came home for Christmas break, and I remember trudging up this hill in a foot of snow and sinking to my knees and begging God to save her. A couple of months after she died, Gabby and I decided to celebrate Mia's life by camping up here. It was summer, and the black sky, the millions of stars overhead and the peace of this place helped heal my heart. I come here whenever life gets to be too much."

"I can see why."

"I came here when I found out my parents wanted to sell the ranch."

"Ah…" His expression was sympathetic as he pushed up to a seated position. "You probably came here when you found out I was buying it, too."

"I did."

"You didn't like me."

"I didn't know you."

"Do you know me now?"

"Yes. I think so, at least." She licked her lips, nervous all of a sudden. Undercurrents swam beneath their conversation.

"Did you leave anyone special behind at college?" His caramel eyes captured her, and she inhaled sharply.

Someone special? Yeah, right. She'd never had a real

boyfriend. It wasn't that she'd lacked for dates in high school to school dances and such. And a few guys had asked her out in college. She'd even said yes to them. But no one had captured her interest. Not the way she'd hoped.

"No."

"Why aren't you seeing anyone?" He sounded curious, not judgmental. "I don't get it."

It was on the tip of her tongue to snap that it certainly wasn't by choice, but maybe that wasn't true. She'd been blaming the men in town for not being interested in her. The truth was she wasn't interested in them, either.

With a slight shrug, she gazed out over the prairie. "They aren't into me, and I'm not into them."

He shifted slightly closer. "High standards?"

"Them?" Her head told her to lean away and create some distance between them. But her body remained frozen in place. "Or me?"

"You." His glance fell to her mouth, and she shivered.

"No, not high standards. More like unrealistic expectations."

His mouth curved into a smile, and her pulse pounded like the pronghorn herd over the prairie they'd watched earlier.

"You're not the only one, Eden." The sound of her name on his lips flashed goose bumps over her skin. "I'm the king of unrealistic expectations."

"I'm sorry, Ryder. I guess real life caught up with both of us."

His eyes darkened and his cheek muscle flexed. "I wonder…"

What? What did he wonder? She got the impression

he wanted to kiss her. She shouldn't be having these feelings, but she wanted him to kiss her. Desperately.

He squinted as if he'd had a thought he didn't want. Then he shook his head and eased back. "No."

Disappointment hit her hard.

It was better this way. She was under no illusions. She wasn't his type.

Even so, it sure felt like another unrealistic expectation had just popped.

# Chapter Nine

These feelings for Eden were another unrealistic expectation waiting to destroy him.

Tuesday morning Ryder and Chris rode behind several cows and their young calves, encouraging them to join the rest of the herd. It was a cool, windy day, and he wore a black sweatshirt to protect himself from the chill. He wished he had something he could put on to protect his heart from these inconvenient feelings he had for Eden.

"Looks like we missed a few." Chris nodded to another small bunch of cows and their calves hiding behind a hill near a stretch of cottonwoods.

Ryder followed him to the group, and together they pushed them along with the rest of the stragglers. As his horse trotted, he kept an eye on the cattle and let his mind wander.

He'd enjoyed having Eden's parents over on Saturday. They'd treated Harper and Ivy like they were family. They'd treated him like he was, too. And ever since, he'd been thinking he liked the idea of being part of a bigger family. He liked the thought of the girls having grandparents.

But that desire took a distant second to what he'd felt when Eden had taken him to that beautiful piece of land. He could see why she was drawn to the place, and he'd been honored when she'd opened up her private thoughts to him. Her claim about having unrealistic expectations had struck him to the core.

He'd been let down by unrealistic expectations his entire life.

And for whatever reason, acknowledging it there— on the hill overlooking the prairie full of grass and wildflowers—had sent his attraction to Eden to a whole new level.

He'd almost kissed her.

The only thing that had stopped him was remembering the twins' third birthday when Lily had told him she was leaving him. He'd been blindsided. Looking back, he wasn't sure why. They'd had problems for years. The relationship had been all but over a few months after the twins were born.

But still…hearing Lily tell him she was leaving him, watching the movers come and pack her things, knowing she would be living with another man from that moment forward… It had taken an emotional toll.

He couldn't afford another crippling emotional event at this point in his life. The twins needed him to be strong. They needed their daddy. They certainly didn't have a mother to rely on.

"If we push 'em to the gate, we can do a quick check on the forty-five tag." Chris looked bright-eyed today. "Is something wrong?"

"No, I'm fine." He had to get his mind back on the cattle where it belonged. "I'll open the gate."

When they'd gotten the cattle through, they checked on the calf and headed back.

"Is it okay for me to kick off a little early on Friday?" Chris asked.

"Sure. You have plans with Trevor, right?" Ryder asked as they loped across the land. Yesterday, Chris had asked for the weekend off. Ryder had no problem giving it to him. He could handle this place without Chris for a few days. He still had part-time ranch hands to help out, and if he got desperate, he could always call Mason.

"Yep. We're driving to Dubois for the rodeo. He's been texting me his picks for bareback bronc riding." Chris laughed, and Ryder was struck at how much younger he appeared. Chris often seemed to have the world on his shoulders. "That kid. He's already competing in breakaway roping, bareback steer riding and even bull riding. He hopes to join the high school team when he's older."

"My nephew's been mutton busting." Ryder couldn't imagine the twins competing in a rodeo at their age, although Harper would probably be a natural fit. "Did you teach him how to ride?"

"Of course. I had him mutton busting and barrel racing by the time he was in first grade. Kid loves the rodeo."

"Is your ex giving you any more trouble?"

"When doesn't she?" He wiped his forehead and

shook his head. "I'm sure I'll get a text Friday morning about a distant cousin's birthday party or whatnot. I'm not bending this time."

The barns came into view. Lily was supposed to be arriving on Friday. Mandy had emailed him the flight time and the address of the luxury log cabin Lily would be staying in. He still didn't think she'd actually show up.

Maybe he, like Chris, was bending too much when it came to her. Everything was on Lily's terms. What was the alternative, though? He didn't know, and he didn't want to find out.

"There. You're all set." Eden tied an apron with images of kittens chasing balls of yarn around Ivy's waist Tuesday afternoon. She'd already tied Harper's pony-themed apron. Eden and her mom had sewed the aprons on Sunday after church. Mom had come up with the idea and, frankly, done most of the work. Spending the day with her mother had lifted Eden's spirits, not to mention it had helped take her mind off the near kiss with Ryder.

She was falling too hard, too fast. It was better to put the brakes on now, rather than be demolished later. At least she'd had the gumption to not eat supper with him and the girls last night. She didn't plan on eating with them anymore moving forward.

"What are we making today?" Harper asked. The girls waited in eager anticipation in Nicole Taylor's small kitchen. Eden had babysat Phoebe all morning, and Gabby had picked her up right after lunch. It was just Eden and the twins baking this afternoon.

Nicole was a pretty blonde with green eyes and a

kind way about her. She wore a cute pink apron that said Bakers Gotta Bake on it.

"I heard you two like chocolate." Nicole watched them carefully. They yelled "Yes!" and clapped. She grinned. "We're making a triple-layer chocolate cake."

Ivy turned and took Harper's hands in hers. They jumped in excitement.

"Are the babies gonna help?" Harper grew serious.

"No, they're still too little."

"Can I hold one after we make the cake?" Ivy asked.

"I don't see why not." Nicole's smile lit her eyes. "They seem to like you."

The triplets were all bouncing in ExerSaucers in the dining area. Eden took a seat near them while Nicole instructed the girls.

"Okay, Ivy, why don't you pour the sugar into the mixer. And Harper, unwrap this stick of butter…"

Henry, the baby with the darkest hair, thumped the meat of his palms on the tray and yelled when a rubber squeeze toy shaped like a penguin went flying. Eden picked it up and gave it back to him. His gummy grin dripped with drool. He was the cutest thing she'd seen all day. And that was saying something considering she was surrounded by cute.

Eli was parked next to Henry, and his little tongue stuck out as he concentrated on trying to move a squeaky tiger down a curved, plastic-coated wire. Amelia was bouncing and chirping and smiling away.

Eden really wanted a baby. As much as she tried to push the urge away, it was still there. It had been there for years.

*Don't go there. Think about something else—think*

*about something you can actually have. Like a teaching career.*

While a part of her was excited at the thought of getting her degree, another part ached at what felt like goodbye. Making the final decision to go back to school felt like she was locking the door to her other dreams—the ones of becoming a wife and mother. Her logic might not make sense, but she couldn't shake the feeling, just the same.

"Our mommy's coming on Friday," Ivy said to Nicole.

"She is? That's wonderful!" Nicole's enthusiasm must have pleased Ivy because she beamed.

"She's not staying at our house, though." Harper was more matter-of-fact.

"That's okay." Nicole handed Harper a whisk and gestured for her to whisk the dry ingredients they'd added to a separate bowl. "The important thing is you get to spend time with her."

"I want to show her how I can ride a horse." Harper whisked a little too hard and some flour went flying. "Sorry! I didn't mean it."

"It's fine, Harper." Nicole chuckled. "I do it all the time. Baking is messy."

Eden's heart swelled in appreciation for her friend. The woman was one of a kind. She'd lost her husband when she was only a few months pregnant, then she'd moved back to Rendezvous and had the triplets. Last Christmas, she'd fallen in love with Judd Wilson, the cowboy who owned the ranch her cabin sat on. Nicole and Judd were engaged but hadn't set the date yet. And even with her hands so full, Nicole had still carved out time to make two little girls very happy today.

Amelia started cooing, "Ooh, ooh, ooh," and Eden laughed.

"After the cake is all done, we're going to put it in a pretty pink box to take home." Nicole turned the mixer on low.

"You mean we get to keep it?" Harper asked.

"Yes."

"Daddy likes chocolate." Ivy nodded.

Harper peered into the mixer. "Can we lick the bowl?"

"We'd better not." As Nicole gave them tips about not eating batter with raw eggs, Eden's mind drifted back to Saturday.

Taking Ryder to her special place had been a mistake. Spending the afternoon alone with him had deepened her connection to him, and her feelings had already been inching too close to begin with. Later that night, after the cookout, when she was alone in her apartment, it had hit her that Ryder didn't have family. Not the way she did.

He had no parents. His grandparents were gone. Besides Mason, Ryder didn't have extended family to depend on when life got rough.

Eden had always been close to her mother and father. She still was.

Maybe she'd overreacted when her parents sold the ranch. After all, a house was just a bunch of walls if her loved ones weren't there with her.

For the next few minutes the mixer whirred loudly, then Nicole turned it off and instructed the girls how to pour the batter into three round pans. Soon, the cakes were in the oven and the timer was set.

"Can I hold a baby now?" Ivy steepled her hands with the tips of her fingers below her chin.

"After we wash our hands. Eden, would you mind taking Eli out and setting him in the living room? There's a quilt on the floor." Nicole guided the girls down the hall to wash their hands in the bathroom. "I'll be right there."

Eden lifted Eli out and cuddled him to her chest. He stared at her with a serious expression, and she kissed his forehead. "You are way too cute, little guy."

She brought him over to the quilt and talked to him for a while before setting him down, and before she knew it, Nicole had carried over Amelia and Henry.

"Sit on the couch, Ivy, and I'll hand her to you." Once Ivy was settled, Nicole placed Amelia in her open arms.

"She's heavy." Ivy smiled down at the child and kissed the top of her head. "She's prettier than my baby. I wish I could take her home."

Nicole laughed. "That's nice of you to say. Maybe when you're older, you'll babysit her. You never know."

"I'd like that." Ivy hugged the child. "Would you like me to babysit you, Amelia?"

"Harper, would you like to hold Henry?"

"No thanks." Harper got down on the quilt and spread out on her tummy. She propped her elbows on the floor and rested her chin on her palms, with her feet in the air. "Can this one crawl?"

"He can."

"Why isn't he?" Harper asked.

"He's playing."

"Arc you gonna let him eat that puppy?" She seemed concerned he was chewing on the ear of the stuffed animal.

"Yes."

"Can I set her on the quilt?" Ivy asked. "I want to play down there, too."

Nicole took Amelia from her and set her on the quilt with the boys. The twins played with the triplets while Eden and Nicole watched them and chitchatted.

"I've decided to take online classes this fall." Eden figured it was time to start getting her friends used to the idea. She'd already told Gabby last night.

"You are?" Nicole curled her knees to the side where she sat opposite Eden on the couch. "What kind of classes?"

"I'm going to finish my degree." Saying the words out loud bolstered her courage. "I'm switching majors. I want to be a teacher."

"You'll be fantastic! Remind me what your original major was."

"Early education. Preschool, mainly."

"Ah." Nicole's smile encouraged her. "What changed your mind?"

"It's time." And those two words spread peace to the nooks and crannies clinging to her old dreams. "Mason's moved on. Gabby's moved on. You've moved on. It's time for me to move on, too."

"Have you moved on where it counts?" Nicole pointed to her chest. "In here?"

"Yes." It was true. She'd moved on from Mia's death.

"That's all that matters. Tell me everything."

Eden kept an eye on the girls, who were happily giving the triplets toys, as she filled Nicole in on what steps she needed to take to get her degree.

"I'm really impressed," Nicole said. "But I hope you aren't planning on moving away."

"Oh, no. This is my home."

"Good." Nicole cast a sly glance at the twins, then raised innocent eyebrows. "Rendezvous has a lot to offer."

Heat rushed to Eden's cheeks. "All I'm asking for is a full-time job. Preferably teaching younger grades."

"Nothing else?" Nicole gave a quick jerk of her head toward the girls.

"No." But it was a lie. Eden wanted it all, including Ryder and the girls.

One of the triplets let out a cry, and Nicole excused herself.

An uncomfortable thought weighed on her chest. If Ryder didn't have the twins, would she still be drawn to him?

She tried to picture him without the girls and couldn't. They were a package deal.

Why was she thinking about it anyhow?

Ryder *did* have the girls.

And he had a beautiful, glamorous ex-wife along with a firm resolution he was never getting married again.

So regardless if she was falling for him and wanted to be part of the girls' lives, it wasn't going to happen. She had no say in it.

The inevitability of it all crashed down on her. Their time together would end in a few short months. She would not be a permanent part of their lives.

Always the babysitter. Never the bride.

Ryder stood in front of Eden's door at eight o'clock that night. The girls were watching an animated film with Noah at Mason's house. All day he'd been looking forward to having supper with Eden and then talking to her in private. But Eden had left as soon as he'd finished his ranch chores. He really needed to speak to her alone. There was still a good chance Lily would cancel her visit, but if she didn't, Ryder needed backup with the girls on Saturday and Sunday morning.

He knocked twice.

She opened the door, and her eyes grew round. "What are you doing here?"

Not the most welcoming words, but he'd take them. "Can we talk?"

Her eyelashes fluttered, but she moved aside to let him in. She'd changed into leggings and a long exercise shirt. Her slim gracefulness captivated him as he followed her to the living room.

"Is something going on? Is it the girls?" Eden sat down, concern radiating from her brown eyes.

"No, nothing's wrong." He took a seat on the couch. "It's about Lily's visit."

"Oh, right. I actually meant to speak to you about it earlier, and it slipped my mind. Don't worry—I know it's important for the girls to spend some good quality time with their mom. I'll stay away."

"I would never ask you to stay away. In fact, I'm asking the opposite. I was hoping you could help me out this weekend."

"Help you? How?"

"Chris has the weekend off, and one of my ranch hands might not be able to help me out, which means I need to do the things he normally does on Saturday and Sunday morning. So regardless if Lily comes—"

"If she comes? Did she say she might not?"

"No." He kept his voice even. "But a last-minute cancellation is always possible. And either way, she might not get to the ranch early enough for me to leave the girls to check on the cattle."

Understanding washed away the worries on Eden's face. "Oh, I understand now. Yes, I can come early both days. I'll stay with them while you deal with the ranch. Then, when Lily arrives, I'll get out of everyone's hair."

Get out of their hair? What was she talking about? He immediately glanced at her silky hair and wanted to run his fingers through it.

"You're not in anyone's hair. You wouldn't be in the way. You're an important part of our lives."

She looked stricken. What had he said now? It had been a good long while since he'd put his foot in his mouth with her. He didn't even know how he'd offended her this time, but it was obvious by her pale face that he had.

"Look, Eden," he said, moving his neck back and forth to work out the kinks. "Lily might seem like this special movie star, but she's just a person the same as you and me. When I met her, I was starstruck, so I get it. And the fact she even gave me the time of day blew my mind back then. Lily has a way about her—she has charisma. She can be nice, generous. She pulls you into her orbit." He still remembered that light, anything-is-possible feeling he'd gotten when they'd first met.

"She's always been one of my favorite actresses." Eden averted her eyes.

"Most people put Lily on a pedestal. Maybe we all expect her to be as amazing as the characters she plays on television and in movies. I don't know."

A sense of heaviness weighed on his shoulders. He'd been over every nuance in their relationship a hundred times or more. At first he'd blamed himself. Then he'd blamed her.

But the truth was they both were to blame.

"Have you ever been in love?" he asked quietly.

Eden froze. Blinked. Didn't answer.

Of course she'd been in love. That was why she wasn't married—she'd loved and lost, too. Jealousy built inside him, spinning like a tornado at the thought of anyone letting her down.

She stood and crossed to the window, looking out onto the neighboring yard with her arms over her chest. Ryder padded over to stand behind her. He set his hands on her shoulders. Her head jerked to look back at him, but she didn't step away from his touch.

"Whoever he is—was—he doesn't deserve you." His voice was low, husky.

Lily had been smoke and mirrors.

Eden was genuine. The real deal.

She turned then. Slowly. Deliberately. But she didn't create distance between them. They were only inches from each other, and she looked up at him through those piercing, soulful eyes.

His heart slammed into his ribs. He caressed her upper arms as he drew her closer. He couldn't look away from her lips.

Her hands crept up and slipped around his neck. Uncertainty and fascination warred in her eyes. He couldn't take the suspense a minute longer. Dropping his hands to her waist, he lowered his mouth to hers.

She was delicate but strong, soft but firm. Impressions raced through his mind—of his lonely childhood, the sheep trailers in the middle of nowhere, the hollowness he'd felt after Grandma died, the kick in the gut when Lily left him—and all of them spun together and burst into tiny pieces as the kiss promised he never needed to be alone again.

Eden was who he'd been waiting for his entire life.

And he hadn't known it until now.

He kissed her deeply, reveling in the curve of her body near his. Finally, he broke away from the kiss. The revelations he'd just learned still thrummed in his head.

He'd promised himself he wasn't falling in love again. No marriage for him. He wasn't putting himself through the pain of trusting someone and getting cheated on and discarded ever again.

But Eden made him want to.

Even if he lost it all.

# Chapter Ten

"Dandy jumped on my flowerpot!" Tears swam in Ivy's eyes.

Eden scooped up the rambunctious kitten and set it on the floor of the family room, where she'd arranged a long folding table. A lime-green felt mouse caught her eye, and she tossed it across the room, where the kitten sprinted after it. The girls were painting flowerpots for their mother, and tomorrow they'd fill them with potting soil and plant gerbera daisies to give to Lily. Well, they would be if Eden could concentrate.

Her head was filled with memories of last night's kiss.

"There. Dandy's gone." Eden scrunched her nose to smile at Ivy.

When Ryder had assumed she'd been in love and claimed the man didn't deserve her, she'd almost laughed—she'd never been in love. But this morning, after a sleepless night, she'd realized she was wrong.

She was in love.

And the revelation colored everything, because nothing could come of it. Especially after hearing him talk about Lily's good traits. Sure, he'd accepted their marriage was over. But what woman could ever live up to his ex-wife? Not her.

"Everything's dirty!" Ivy had been emotionally fragile yesterday, and today everything was setting her off. Eden could only assume Lily's impending visit was the cause.

"Dandy didn't mean it, Ivy." Harper slid out of the chair and hugged her sister.

"I know." Ivy sniffed, wiping under her eyes. "But I want the flowers to be perfect for Mommy."

"They don't have to be perfect, Ivy." Eden walked around the table and kneeled between the twins. She put her arms around each of their shoulders. "Your mom is going to love them because you gave them to her."

"It's ugly now." Ivy's voice broke as she pointed to the colorfully painted clay pot with drips of paint smeared down the side.

Eden reached for a roll of paper towels, tore one off and carefully wiped the smears. "There. All better."

Ivy inspected it and let out a shaky breath.

"You know you don't have to be perfect for your mommy to love you, right?" Eden asked.

Ivy averted her eyes, but Harper glued her attention to Eden.

"What's the book the pastor reads from every Sunday in church?" Eden asked as she went back to her seat across the table from them.

"The Bible." Harper propped her elbows on the table. Ivy climbed into her chair and slumped.

"Right. And the Bible is God's word. He tells us we can't be perfect, because we all sin. But—" Eden held up her index finger "—since Jesus died for us, we don't have to be perfect. He was perfect for us. He takes away all our sins."

"But that's Jesus." Ivy met her eyes then. "Not Mommy."

"That's true, but I happen to know you have a daddy and mommy who love you very much, and they don't expect you to be perfect, either." As she said it, doubts tiptoed through her mind. Ivy was extremely hard on herself. Had Lily made her feel that way? Or was it a natural reaction to missing her mother?

*God, please give me the right words for these children.*

"I wish Mommy lived here," Ivy said almost under her breath.

"She's not going to live here, Ivy, even if your pot's perfect." Harper's voice rose sternly.

*Ah...* A wave of understanding came over Eden. Ivy blamed herself for Lily being gone.

"Girls, let's take a break from painting. Go wash your hands, and when you come back, we're going to sit together and talk."

Neither looked happy about it, but they slunk away to the bathroom anyway. Eden wasn't great at pep talks, but the twins clearly needed one. She could hear them talking from the other room.

"If she likes it here, she'll stay..." Ivy's voice rose.

"She won't."

"She might."

"Mommy never stays."

"This time she will. She'll see Daddy. He's the most handsomest daddy there is, and she'll hug him and he'll say he's sorry, and she'll stay forever."

"She's not gonna." Harper's voice was sharp.

Oh, no. Ivy wanted her parents to get back together. Of course.

The girls wanted their mother here for good. And from everything Ryder had told her, it wasn't going to happen.

An icky sensation climbed her throat. How could she be in love with Ryder when the twins needed Lily?

*Oh, Lord, I've been wrong. I haven't been thinking about these precious girls. I've been thinking about myself. I don't know how to reassure them, but they're hurting so badly. Please give me the words to help them. Let me put their needs first.*

She took a deep breath and straightened her shoulders. They were in the bathroom scowling at each other, and she herded them back into the family room. The three of them sat on a big comfy chair. Harper laid her head against Eden's upper arm, but Ivy held herself stiffly.

"Girls, I know you're hurting. This isn't easy. Living without your mother isn't easy."

Ivy gazed up at her through watery eyes.

"But I don't want you to doubt her love for you. And I don't want you to doubt your daddy's love, either. They both love you. And you'll always be a family, even if it doesn't look the way you'd hoped."

Ivy seemed skeptical, and Harper burrowed against her arm.

"I wish families always stayed together." Eden was

extra thankful for her parents at this moment. "But sometimes they don't, and there's nothing you can do about it."

"But…" Ivy's mouth twisted. "I want Mommy to live here."

"I know, sweetheart." Eden smoothed her hair.

"She's so pretty. Prettier than Cinderella." Ivy looked perplexed. "When Daddy sees her, he'll kiss her and they'll live here together happily ever after." She peered over to Harper. "Won't they, Harper?"

"That's a cartoon." Harper shook her head. "Mommy isn't going to stay here no matter how pretty she is."

"But Daddy can tell her…"

This wasn't going well. And thinking about Ryder seeing his beautiful ex and falling in love with her all over again wasn't helping Eden, either. Because it very well could happen.

"Ivy, you know Mommy has a boyfriend." Harper glared at her sister.

"He's old and ugly!" The girl was on the verge of losing it.

Frankly, Eden was on the verge, too, if this conversation continued much longer.

"It doesn't matter what anyone looks like," Eden said. "What counts is in here." She pointed to her heart. "God looks at the heart, not at your outward appearance. What kind of person you are is what makes you attractive."

"What do you mean?" Harper twirled a section of Eden's hair around her finger.

"Well, what do you love and admire about Ivy?" Eden asked.

"She gives me her best stickers when I'm sad. She lets me sleep with Fluffybear if I have a bad dream."

Eden kissed the top of her head. "And Ivy, what do you love and admire about Harper?"

"She's brave. She doesn't squish the bugs she finds— she makes houses for them—and she jumps off the picnic table even though it's really high. And she always knows when I'm sad. She hugs me."

Okay, it was her turn to get teary eyed. She willed her emotions back in place. "The things you described have nothing to do with your pretty blue eyes or your cute noses, do they?" Eden looked at Ivy, then Harper.

"No." Harper shook her head.

"That's what I mean. Your beauty comes from who you are, not what you look like. And both of you are very beautiful on the inside."

Harper hugged her neck and whispered softly in her ear, "I love you, Auntie Eden."

Sweeter words had never been spoken. She kissed Harper's cheek. "I love you, too." Then she kissed Ivy's cheek. "And I love you."

They hugged her tightly.

"Okay, we'd better get these pots painted. We still have a lot of surprises to prepare for your mommy."

As Eden watched the girls skip over to the table with renewed enthusiasm, her mood plummeted. They hadn't recovered from the divorce, didn't understand why Lily wasn't around, and wanted their parents back together. They needed a delicate touch right now.

It would be cruel to pursue a relationship with Ryder if it meant hurting the twins. She'd keep her feelings hidden, and maybe someday, her love would fade.

"The coast is clear. What's going on?" Ryder checked one more time to verify the girls were far enough away in the backyard so that he and Eden could talk openly. The four of them had eaten turkey sandwiches and pasta salad outside before the girls ran off to chase butterflies. He was glad Eden had stayed for supper. It had been a while since she'd stayed to eat with them. He watched her expectantly. She'd claimed they needed to talk.

He could guess why.

The kiss. The over-the-top, incredible kiss that had left him shaken and confused and more scared of his feelings than ever.

He loved her.

And he couldn't do a thing about it.

What was she going to say? That it was inappropriate for him to have kissed her? He never should have crossed that boundary? She didn't like him that way?

He could handle the first options, but the last one would hurt. It hadn't been that long ago since she told him she wasn't attracted to him because he looked exactly like Mason.

His neck tensed as he waited for her to reject him. Again.

"The girls were wound up today." Her words were so quiet he almost asked her to repeat them. He hadn't been expecting a conversation about the twins.

"I think they—Ivy in particular—are hoping you and Lily will get back together."

Him and Lily? Back together?

The thought was ludicrous and he would have laughed, but Eden's serious expression killed his humor.

"Why would they think that? I don't talk about her. She barely calls or visits." He rubbed his chin. Had Lily said something to make them believe they'd get back together? When could the subject have even come up? He'd been there for every short call, and he hadn't caught a hint of it.

"I think it's a normal reaction of kids whose parents have divorced. Plus, I could be wrong, but it seems as if Ivy is putting a lot of pressure on herself right now."

"What kind of pressure?" His gaze traveled to where the girls crouched over something in the grass. Then they were up and running once more.

"It's almost as if she thinks she has to be perfect— that everything has to be perfect—when Lily comes. I wonder if she blames herself in some way for her mother not being around."

"Why would she think that?" His spine grew rigid. "The problems were between Lily and me. Not the girls."

"It doesn't have to make sense to be true," Eden said softly.

He couldn't argue with that. "I'll talk to them."

"What will you say?" Her eyes held no judgment.

"I don't know. I'll figure something out." He rubbed the back of his neck. How was he supposed to handle this? He didn't know where to start.

Eden seemed withdrawn. Subdued. He knew he was to blame.

"Look, about last night…"

Her wan smile hit him in the chest. "Let's not talk about it. We both know nothing can come of it."

Logic told him she was correct. In fact, he'd told her as much more than once. Told himself the same, too. But hearing it on her lips only made him want to dig in and prove her wrong.

"I care about you." He reached over and covered her hand with his.

"I know." She slipped her hand free. "I also know you have good reasons why you're against a serious relationship. You haven't been shy about them, and I appreciate that you opened up about your marriage. But I think you're right. The twins have different emotional needs at this time."

He should be relieved, but he wasn't. Was this about marriage? The twins? Or her own lack of feelings for him?

"Do me a favor and be extra patient with Ivy." Eden stared at him then. He felt like he was swirling into the depths of her inner world.

She had a heart bigger than the sun.

"I guarantee they're picking flowers for their mother." A smile teased her lips. "You have the most precious, thoughtful daughters."

The truth hit him harder than the stray bull that plowed through the fence last week—Eden would always put the girls' needs above her own, and the fact it was a sacrifice wouldn't even occur to her because she wanted them to be happy.

His throat tightened. He'd never known anyone like Eden. Her love for the twins humbled him, and dejection settled between his shoulders. Eden was a temporary blessing.

He wished things were different. Wished he and the girls could have her forever.

"Do you mind if my mom comes over tomorrow?" Eden asked.

He pulled himself together quickly. "That's fine."

"She enjoys Harper and Ivy. I think she needs a break from all the one-on-one with my dad."

"If she's coming, tell Bill he's welcome to ride out

with me if he'd like." Checking the cattle and tooling around the ranch with Eden's dad would take his mind off his problems.

"Daddy, Daddy!" Harper's cheeks were pink and her eyes sparkled as she ran to him with her palms cupped together. Ivy followed behind with a bouquet of wild-flowers clenched in her hand.

"What?" He forced himself to grin.

"I found a caterpillar!"

Ivy poked Harper's hands. "Show him."

She cautiously opened her hands, and a fuzzy pale yellow caterpillar inched up her fingers. She giggled. "It tickles."

Ivy tentatively petted it. "It's soft. Not as soft as Cutie, though."

"Can I keep it?" Her eyes shined and her toothy smile pleaded.

"I don't think so." Ryder tried to let her down gently. "Kittens eat caterpillars."

Her face fell, but she nodded. "I don't want him to get eaten."

"You can play with him for a while outside, though, okay?"

"Okay." She wrangled it back onto her palm and cupped her other hand over it again. "Come on, Ivy! Let's make a house out of sticks for him."

Ivy thrust the flowers to Eden. "These are for you, Auntie Eden."

Ryder noted the slight dampness in Eden's eyes and her generous hug for Ivy.

"Thank you," Eden said. "They're beautiful. You're so thoughtful."

Ivy beamed. Then she pivoted and ran to catch up to Harper.

"I guess I was wrong." Eden bent her head to sniff the blue, yellow and white blooms. "They weren't picking them for their mommy."

Eden was more of a mommy to the girls than Lily had ever been.

And it wasn't fair of him to want her to play the part without offering her all she deserved.

Maybe she was right. Nothing could come of their kiss. Even if it had rocked his world and tempted him to offer her everything.

Eden needed to talk to Gabby. Now.

She waited on the porch of the house Dylan and Gabby had moved into after recently getting married. It was a large home with several acres of land and a river snaking around the back of the property.

"Eden? What are you doing here?" Gabby held Phoebe on her hip as she let Eden inside. Phoebe instantly squirmed with both arms held out to Eden. "Looks like someone misses you."

Eden laughed and took Phoebe. "How's my Phoebe-kins? You get to spend the morning with me and the girls tomorrow."

The child wriggled to be let down. Eden held her hand as they went into the living room. Phoebe instantly toddled over to the colorful plastic blocks on the floor, while Gabby took a seat on the tan sectional. Gabby's dark hair was pulled back into a ponytail, and she wore black leggings with a blousy red T-shirt.

Eden collapsed on the other end of the sectional.

"What. Is. Going. On?" Gabby asked. "Something's wrong."

"Nothing's wrong." Eden shook her head. "I'm just confused. I need help sorting out my thoughts."

Her friend brightened. "Tell me everything."

Oh, boy. She probably should have thought this through before showing up. But she and Gabby had shared a lot these past years.

"Ryder's ex-wife is coming to town on Friday."

"Lily Haviland? Here?" She let out a small squeal. "Just think. We might get to see her. Remember when we went to see *The Wrong Kind of Right*? She was amazing in it. I wish they made more rom-coms like that."

Eden was taken aback. She thought of Lily less as a movie star and more as Ryder's ex-wife at this point. Not long ago, her own reaction would have been similar to Gabby's. So much had changed since Ryder moved here.

"She *was* great in that movie." Eden tried to figure out where to start. "This isn't about Lily, though."

"Oh?" Gabby tilted her head. "What is it about?"

*Ryder kissed me. And I love him. But we can't be together. He doesn't want to get married. Ever. And even if he did, it wouldn't be fair to the twins. They want their mom and dad together, and can you blame them?*

"It's kind of hard…" Eden smoothed the edge of her shirt. "It's going to sound dumb."

"Seriously?" Gabby gave her the deadpan stare. "If it's bothering you, it's not dumb."

"I care about the girls. They're so full of life." She wasn't sure how to put in words what she was feeling.

"They are adorable. Phoebe loves them, too. They're like her big sisters."

She thought back to when she'd first asked Gabby if it would be okay for her to babysit all three girls. Her friend had agreed instantly, claiming they'd be like siblings for Phoebe. Gabby had such a big heart.

"They're wound up about Lily coming. Super excited, but nervous, too."

"Oh, poor things. I'm sure it must be hard on them not having her around."

"Yeah, it is. Ivy wants them to get back together."

"Understandable."

"Ryder claims it will never happen."

"Again, understandable."

"He also claims he'll never get remarried."

"I wouldn't be too sure about that." Gabby's self-satisfied grin made Eden's arm hair stand on end. She ran her palms over her arms to ease the sensation.

"I want him to be happy. I want the girls to be happy." Her neck felt warm. "I'm confused."

"Are you attracted to him?" Gabby leaned in. "I know you weren't before…"

"Yes." She stared at the ceiling. "I'm attracted to him. I've always been attracted to him. I just didn't like him before."

"Oh." The word lilted upward in hope.

"No. It's wrong. I can't do that to the girls."

"The girls?" Gabby pulled a face. "What about Ryder? What about you?"

Her heart throbbed at the thought of him. His honesty. His work ethic. His patience. His generosity.

"Eden, maybe this is your chance. How many times over the years did you say you wanted to get married and have a family and live on a ranch and have Christmases in your childhood home? Ryder could offer you all of those things."

Yes, he could. Her lungs squeezed more than she thought possible.

Gabby continued. "But it wouldn't be fair to him if you wanted him only for what he could give you."

She agreed.

"Take away the ranch—your family's ranch—and the twins. Put Ryder all by himself with none of the extras. Would you be interested in him?" Gabby's gaze seared her.

Would she still love Ryder without the girls or the ranch?

*Yes. A thousand times over.*

But could he ever love her? Enough to rethink his marriage stance?

She didn't know.

And until she did, she had to put these feelings into cold storage. Because her love for Ryder was real, but her love for the girls was, too. And regardless of what was growing between her and Ryder, she couldn't act on it. The twins needed their real mommy now.

## Chapter Eleven

"You're a fast learner, Ivy." Thursday afternoon, Eden's mom planted a kiss on the girl's head, then held out the tissue-paper flower they'd made. "Now you can have bouquets of flowers anytime you want."

"I'm going to make another one." Ivy raced over to the plastic bag Mom had brought full of assorted colors of tissue paper and other craft items.

Eden locked eyes with her mom, and they both chuckled. Her parents had shown up bright and early at Ryder's, and while Dad was spending the day trotting around the ranch with him, Mom was hanging out with Eden and the twins. Phoebe had been here earlier. Gabby picked her up after lunch and stayed for about an hour before taking off.

Right now Eden could use Mom's moral support. She had a bad feeling that after Lily arrived tomorrow, everything would be different. Between her and Ryder, at least.

One more day... She could enjoy life the way it was for one more day.

Harper carried Dandy over to Mom. "She wants to sit on your lap."

"My lap's plenty big enough for both of you." Mom's lips twitched in amusement.

Harper didn't need to be told twice. She climbed up and rested the back of her head against Mom's chest, trying to hold the squirming kitten.

"It's okay if Dandy wants to get down," Mom said. "You and I can still snuggle."

Harper released the kitten, and Dandy made a clean getaway. The fact the girls liked her mother made Eden happy not just for their sakes, but for Mom's, too. She was a wonderful grandma. She'd spent countless hours with Noah over the years. They had a special bond.

"I'm so happy I could come spend the day with you two." Mom stroked Harper's hair. "Grandpa Bill doesn't always want to do crafts and have tea parties."

Ivy came up to Eden with pink tissue paper in one hand and purple in the other. "What color should I make?"

"How about both?"

"At the same time?" The possibility made her mouth form an O.

"Yes. If we alternate the colors before folding, the flower will have pink *and* purple petals." Eden patted the chair next to her, and they spread out the first layer of pink tissue paper, then topped it with purple and continued alternating until finishing. Ivy folded it the way Eden's mom showed her earlier. "Why don't you make a few more to give to your mother tomorrow?"

"She'll like that." Ivy's blue eyes glimmered like sunshine on a lake. "Grandma Page, our mommy is coming tomorrow."

"Yes, you've mentioned it a time or two." Mom smiled at her. "I think it's wonderful you're taking the time to make special things for her."

Harper twisted her neck to stare up at Mom. "I'm going to show her how I can ride a pony."

"Patches isn't a pony," Ivy muttered.

Harper glared at her sister until she returned her attention to making the flowers. "Daddy said I can wear my new shiny shirt. It's purple and white. It's fancy."

"We made lots of presents for her." Ivy abandoned the tissue paper and raced to the books Eden had finished last night. The girls had helped select the pictures, projects and worksheets to put in each binder. They'd each made a collage of their names on craft paper, and Eden had inserted them into the clear protectors of the binder covers.

"Want to see?" Harper climbed off Mom's lap. "Come on."

The flowerpots and other gifts were in the sunroom with the door closed so the kittens wouldn't destroy them.

"These are works of art." Mom inspected each project lined up on the coffee table and asked questions as she did. The twins were happy to answer her. Sunlight filled the room, and Eden had flashbacks of her and Mia lounging in there, reading or giggling about something from school. This room would always hold good memories.

"Daddy said she'll have to leave the flowerpots here, but we can ship everything else to her if it won't fit on the plane." Harper had one hand on her hip and gestured to the projects with her other hand.

"Mommy will find a way to take the flowerpots home." Ivy stood with her feet together and chin high.

Eden exchanged a glance with Mom. She should have thought that particular gift through better. She'd forgotten about the plane.

"I'm sure she'll want to take them with her," Mom said. "But the airline might not let her."

"We can wrap them in plastic bags, right Harper?" Ivy sounded confident.

Harper shrugged.

"She'll take them," the girl declared again.

"Your mother will have to leave them here, Ivy," Eden said gently. "But you can tell her you'll think about her every time you look at the flowers."

Ivy's cheeks grew splotchy and her eyes filled with tears, but she held herself together.

"Oh, would you look at that?" Eden pretended to check her phone. "Almost four o'clock. It's about time for your favorite cartoon. Why don't you two wash your hands and get comfy on the couch? Mom and I will make you a snack."

"Okay!" They raced out of the room.

"Ivy's a little wound up, huh?" Mom asked.

"Yeah. I've talked to her and tried to be as tender as I can, but I have a bad feeling she's going to be disappointed with this visit. Her expectations are so high."

"Poor thing."

"Harper's on edge, too. She's more realistic, but… both girls could use a long stretch of time with their mother. I'm glad Lily is coming." She was glad for the girls' sake, but for her own? She wouldn't think about it.

"I am, too." Mom led the way out of the room, and Eden closed the doors. "They're both so sweet—I want them to be happy."

"Same here. I'm doing my best." Eden frowned. "I love them. It's going to be hard when summer ends."

"It's not as if you won't ever see them again." They crossed the hall and headed to the kitchen.

"I know, but it won't be the same." Eden knew that firsthand. She'd babysat for Noah until he was almost four years old, and she still spent time with him, but it wasn't as intimate as when they'd spent every day together.

"You'll have other things to focus on. Have you registered for your classes yet?"

"I started to, but one of the classes is full." Eden rummaged through the pantry for juice boxes and pretzels. "I need to talk to an adviser about either getting on a waitlist or switching classes."

"Are you excited?" Mom opened the fridge and found a bag of clementines. She peeled two of them while Eden filled two small bowls with pretzels.

"I will be." She was trying to help the twins prepare for this visit first. "Other things have been distracting me, but I'm sure I'll get more excited as fall approaches."

Mom cast her a sly glance. "I like the things that have been distracting you."

Her and her big mouth.

"Ryder is a wonderful man," Mom said. "Babysitting the girls here has been good for you."

Her mom knew her too well.

"I agree." Eden gave her mom a pointed stare. "But that's all it is. Babysitting."

"I can't help but see God's hand in this. Your dad and I wrestled with selling this place, and when we found out Ryder wanted it, we knew it was an answer to our prayer. It's practically in our family, since Mason is his brother. And buying the RV helped get the restlessness out of your father. He still gets antsy, though. It was nice of Ryder to invite him over today. Your dad misses ranching."

"I'm sure Ryder appreciates Dad helping out."

"Your dad appreciates being included. God knew Ryder and the girls needed you, too."

As much as she'd like to think God had a master plan for her involving Ryder and the girls, her gut told her otherwise.

"Don't get your hopes up, Mom."

"What do you mean?"

Eden took a few steps backward to check on the girls. They'd turned on the television and were sitting together on the couch. "I mean, I can see where you're going with this. It's not going to happen. Ryder went through a lot with his divorce and doesn't want a commitment again. And the girls have a lot of unresolved issues concerning their mother."

Mom frowned. "I didn't realize." Then she brightened. "God can heal any wound. Anything is possible."

Anything *was* possible, but probable? Not likely.

The doorbell rang. Eden almost jumped. "I'll be right back."

She loped to the hall and opened the front door.

Lily Haviland stood in front of her.

Long waves of silky dark brown hair cascaded over

her shoulders. She wore a stylish red blouse, pencil-thin dark jeans that ended at her ankle and red high heels. Her makeup accentuated her piercing blue eyes, the same shade as the twins'.

"Oh, hi," Eden stammered. "We weren't expecting you until tomorrow. Come in."

"I had a break in my schedule and figured I'd get a jump start."

Only then did Eden realize Lily wasn't alone. A full-figured woman in her early thirties stood behind her. Eden ushered them inside and introduced herself.

"Nanny Eden." Lily smiled, revealing perfect white teeth. "The girls have been raving about you." She turned to the other woman. "This is my assistant, Mandy Drake."

Mandy wore black pants and a white shirt and carried a large black tote. Earbuds were in her ears, and she was furiously typing something into her phone. Then she finished and offered her hand. Eden shook it, unsure of what to make of Mandy's no-nonsense persona.

"This is my mom, Joanna Page." Eden flourished her hand toward her mother.

"Oh, my, it's nice to meet you." Mom wiped her hands on a kitchen towel as she stepped forward. "We loved *Courtroom Crimes*. We watched every episode, didn't we, Eden?"

Eden nodded, suddenly embarrassed. The fact she was standing in front of one of her favorite movie stars and babysitting the woman's children hit her in an odd way. She didn't feel in awe of Lily anymore. No, it was more of a feeling of insignificance, like who was she to harbor dreams of forever with this woman's ex-husband and daughters? What a joke.

"Where's Ryder?" Lily asked.

Before Eden could answer, the twins ran into the kitchen. "Mommy, Mommy!" They attached themselves like barnacles around her legs, and she laughed. "There you are. My sweethearts."

"You came! Did you miss us?" Ivy hopped up and down, her face flushed with joy.

"Of course, I missed you!" She hugged them one by one. "That's why I'm here."

"We made you presents!" Ivy dragged her by the hand in the direction of the sunroom. Harper took Lily's other hand.

Even Lily's laugh seemed to be brighter than the average person's. "You did? Aw, thank you."

As the three of them left the kitchen, Mandy looked torn on if she should follow her boss or stay put.

"Would you like to sit down?" Eden belatedly remembered her manners. "We were just getting ready to have a snack. I'll put on a pot of coffee. Mom, where are the muffins you brought?"

"I'd love a muffin and coffee, thanks." Mandy visibly relaxed, setting the tote bag in the hallway before taking a seat on a stool at the island. "I didn't realize the drive from the airport would take so long."

"The mountains and two-lane roads add on extra time." Mom lifted the lid off a plastic container filled with blueberry muffins. "Here, take one. Or two. We're not shy here."

Mandy selected one as Eden filled the coffeepot. The twins' chipper voices could be heard, along with Lily's voice, from the other room. As Mom made small talk with Mandy, the coffee maker rumbled softly.

Harper yelled something. Then Ivy shouted back.

And Eden wondered if she should check on them to intervene.

"Go get your nanny," Lily said loudly. Dead silence weighed oppressively in the air.

Eden excused herself. "I'll see how they're doing."

She went to the sunroom, where Lily spotted her right away. "You did all these crafts with the girls?"

"Yes. They're for you." Eden peeked at Ivy, who seemed subdued, and then Harper, who scooted closer to Ivy and took her hand in hers. "The girls wanted to make you presents. They are so thoughtful."

The sight of those two darling children holding hands, supporting each other, tore at her heart. Eden would do anything to make this visit go well for them, and they both looked like they were struggling at the moment.

"Ivy took extra care with the necklace. She dyed the noodles hot pink and picked the best noodles for it. She thought you'd like pink the best." Eden smiled at Ivy. "And Harper spent hours making the mosaic butterfly out of gem stickers. She's drawn to nature. They're very talented."

"I see that," Lily said softly.

Eden hoped so. *God, please let Lily see how much her daughters need her.*

"Oh, girls, why don't you go get your books?" Eden asked brightly. "You can show them to your mom."

"You can show them to me later," Lily said to the twins. "I need to talk to your father first." She addressed Eden. "When do you expect him back?"

"Um, it depends. Between five and six, I guess."

Lily swiped her phone and typed into it. When she finished, she smiled broadly. "There. He's on his way."

\* \* \*

Ryder about dropped his phone when he read Lily's text. She was here? Now? So much for arriving tomorrow evening. He clenched his jaw and turned to Bill. They'd finished taking care of the horses and were reviewing Ryder's to-do list in his ranch office.

"Looks like I've got to wrap this up. Lily's here."

"Oh?" Bill took off his cowboy hat and wiped his forehead, then put it back on. "I thought she was coming tomorrow."

"So did I." He wasn't prepared to deal with her yet. His muscles tensed as he realized his ex-wife was at the house now saying who knew what to Eden and her mom.

His stomach clenched. Lily had a knack for being nice to people and playing the perfect mommy role. But she could keep it up for only a limited period before she cracked. He didn't want the girls to be on the brunt end of her dismissal—not on day one, at least.

"I really appreciate you spending the day with me, Bill." Ryder led the way outside where the sunshine made the grass a little greener and the sky a little bluer. "I wish you were around more often. I could use a master rancher like you teaching me."

Bill guffawed. "Master? I don't know about that. Just years and years of experience. The place grows on you, and it takes time. But if we lived around here, I'd take you up on it. I miss riding out and checking cattle. I even miss checking fence, and I never thought I'd say those words."

"Anytime you're in town, come over. You're always welcome. In fact, you're more than welcome."

"I appreciate it, Ryder." His voice was gravelly. "You're doing a good job here."

"That's kind of you to say." The praise lifted his spirits, but he was well aware of all the ways he didn't measure up.

"I wasn't saying it just to say it." Bill gave him a shrewd sideways glance. "You've got good instincts, and the improvements you're considering will bring in extra revenue in the long run. Ranching isn't only about knowing cattle—it's a business, son, and you've got the head for it."

A sudden rush of emotion hit him, but he'd tuck the words aside to enjoy later. The side door to the house was a few feet away, and he had his ex-wife to contend with.

He opened the door for Bill, and they took turns washing up before entering the kitchen.

Ryder took in the scene like a snapshot. Lily sat on a stool at the island with Ivy and Harper on either side, their stools as close to hers as they could possibly get them. Mandy was making small talk with Eden as Eden poured coffee. Joanna was watching Lily and the girls with a puzzled expression on her face.

Lily's phone rang, and she stood and raised her finger to the girls, her face aglow. "Sam? Yes..." She left the room, her heels clicking across the hardwood floor.

The twins noticed him then. "Daddy! Mommy came early and she loves her presents..."

"What a good surprise, huh?" He kept his tone upbeat for their sake. Personally, he wished she had arrived when she'd said she would.

"We'll get out of here." Joanna crossed over and gave Ryder a hug. "I'm sure you want some family time."

Eden startled. "Oh, yes, I'm leaving, too. It was nice to meet you, Mandy."

"Yes, nice to meet you. Delicious muffins, Joanna." Mandy hitched her thumb toward where Lily had disappeared. "I'll just get some air…"

Normally, Ryder would ask them all to stay, but this visit would be best done alone. The girls deserved uninterrupted time with their mother.

He followed them all to the door and held it open for them to leave. The twins stood in front of him, waving and saying their goodbyes. He sensed Lily come up behind him, and she called out goodbye, too. He tried to meet Eden's eyes, but her glance back lasted only a split second.

A large black SUV with tinted windows was parked outside. Lily's security detail, most likely.

With the Pages gone, he closed the door and straightened his spine. "Hello, Lily."

"Ryder." She tilted her head as her features transformed to her wide-eyed, I-have-bad-news-but-am-totally-not-to-blame expression. He'd seen it many times. His temples started to throb. She smiled. "You look good."

"You, too." He willed himself not to clench his jaw. "A little surprised to see you. Thought you were arriving tomorrow night."

"There was an unexpected break in my schedule."

The twins were watching them in silence.

"Where's Mandy?" he asked.

"She needed to make some calls. She's hanging out with Andre." Lily pointed to the door. He figured Andre was in the SUV.

"She's welcome to stay inside."

"That's okay."

"Well, why don't we go to the living room." He extended his arm. The girls skipped ahead and sat on the couch, patting it for Lily to sit with them, which she did. He eased his aching joints into the chair across from them. "We're glad you could come."

A calculated look flitted through her eyes. If he didn't know her better, he'd convince himself he was imagining it. But he did know her.

It was another sign that unpleasant news was pending.

He wanted to sigh and run his fingers through his hair, but he needed to keep up a strong front for the girls. Whatever bad news Lily was about to share would be best heard alone.

"Harper, Ivy, can you give your mother and me a few minutes to talk? Why don't you play with the kittens in one of your rooms for a little bit?"

"But Daddy…" Ivy whined.

"I know," he said. "You'll see lots of Mommy, don't worry. Just for a bit, okay?"

"Yes, Daddy." They slid off the couch and meekly trudged upstairs.

"What's going on?" he asked when the coast was clear.

"What do you mean?" She crossed one leg over the other. The red stilettos reminded him of sharp, bloody weapons.

Usually this would be the time he goaded her into an argument about arriving early without warning him, but he could tell something was off. And a sense of calm permeated his body as he studied the stunning woman he'd once loved.

He didn't feel an ounce of anything for her anymore. Not anger. Not love. Not guilt.

The silence stretched until her chin rose. "I do have some news, actually."

"Oh?" He prepared himself for the announcement of a three-movie deal with extensive worldwide travel. Or she'd landed a series and would be working sixteen-hour days all summer. Maybe she was moving to France. Who knew? He was used to it, and for the first time it evoked no reaction from him.

"Sam and I..." She averted her eyes, her thumb and index finger rubbing together in a nervous tic. "This isn't... I don't know why this is so hard..."

Uncertainty pooled in his gut. Who was Sam?

"We're getting married."

A strange sensation spread through his body. She was getting married. To Sam. But he didn't know a Sam. She'd moved in with Derrick when she left him.

"Who's Sam?" He was surprised his voice sounded so normal.

"Sam Pendleton. The producer of *Shimmy Lies*." She made it sound as if everyone knew Sam Pendleton. Everyone in Hollywood probably did. He'd stopped caring about that scene long ago.

So she was getting married. He supposed he should be upset, but he wasn't. He didn't know what he felt. Maybe nothing at all.

"Okay." He leaned back in his chair.

Two tiny wrinkles appeared above the bridge of her nose. "That's all you're going to say? Okay?"

"Congratulations?" What did she want from him?

Her tongue worked over her teeth under her tightly closed lips. "We haven't set a date yet, and naturally, we'll be keeping it a tight secret for security reasons. The twins will be flower girls."

The twins. His heart dropped. While the idea of her getting remarried didn't bother him, it would definitely bother the girls.

"After you tell them—" she'd adopted her sweet, innocent persona, the one he'd fallen in love with way back when "—I'll send my stylist out here with dress samples and to have them fitted."

Now he understood the previous glint in her eye. It wasn't because she'd worried about his reaction to her news.

She didn't want to tell the girls she was getting remarried.

She wanted him to do it.

She expected him to do her dirty work.

"The stylist is fine with me." He shrugged, keeping his cool. "But you have to tell the girls yourself. They need to hear it from you."

"Me?" She stood, fanning herself, and began to pace. "But Ryder, you're with them all the time. They'll take it better from you."

"Lily, they've been bouncing off the walls all week they've been so excited to see you. I can't be everything for them."

"Everything?" She gave him a look that said *get real*. "Don't be dramatic. You're out all day living out some cowboy fantasy. Nanny Eden is spending all the time with them."

"It's not Nanny Eden," he said through clenched teeth. "It's Auntie Eden, and she isn't the nanny. She's a good friend of mine who is doing me—doing us—a favor."

"Well, if she's such a good friend, maybe the girls would take the news better from her."

His jaw dropped. Had she really just suggested that Eden tell the girls about her upcoming nuptials?

*Selfish. She's unbelievably selfish. What did I ever see in her?*

The familiar anger and resentment started building steam within him. He curled his fingers into his palms. *Let it go. Don't get worked up. She's not worth it.*

He took a deep breath. "Lily, they need to hear it from you."

"Why? What's the big deal?" She tossed her hair. The motion was all bravado. Her eyes revealed her fear. "They'll adore Sam. He has three kids, too."

Three kids? Ugh. The girls would have stepsiblings. And who knew how they were being raised. Would Lily start wanting to have regular visitations? Would she expect the girls to be best friends with their new stepbrothers and stepsisters?

"His kids are older, of course." Lily flicked her fingernails. "His youngest is in college."

He wasn't entirely sure why he was so relieved to hear it.

"This all happened quickly. Sam wanted to put a ring on it." She pointed to the gigantic engagement ring Ryder hadn't noticed until now. Then she sat again, letting her forehead drop into her hands. "Of course I had to say yes, but I didn't realize how hard all this would be."

Of course she had to say yes? What an odd phrase. And that was when it hit him. She was already looking for a way out of the engagement. Just like she'd gotten out of their marriage and how she continually shirked her duty to the girls.

He saw her clearly, maybe for the first time.

Lily hadn't left him because of something he did or who he was.

She'd left him because she couldn't handle commitment.

Pity for her swept through him. To the outside world, Lily had it all. But he knew the truth—she rejected what really mattered. She was missing out on the most important things in life.

He went over and sat beside her.

"You don't have to marry him, Lily, but I don't think this is about him."

"You don't?" She glanced up at him.

"Do you love him?"

"Yes, I do."

"Then give him a chance. Be honest with him. Don't walk away from him the way you did me."

As his words sank in, her face fell.

"If you need moral support telling Harper and Ivy about getting remarried, I'll be right there with you. Do you want to tell them now? Or do you want to wait until next week before you leave?"

"About that…" She had the grace to flush.

He didn't even get irritated. He knew her well enough to know she'd never planned on staying an entire week. It had sounded good. Something a caring mother would do. And for Lily, words were more important than actions.

"I'm heading out tomorrow night." She flashed him a quick look. "I have rehearsals…"

Instead of railing at her or giving her the silent treatment or even pleading with her to change her mind, he simply nodded. "Then I guess we'd better make the most of your visit. I'll get the girls. You might as well tell them now."

He stood and turned in the direction of the stairs. Tonight was going to be rough on the twins. But his heart grew lighter with each step.

He finally had peace about his marriage and divorce.

Lily couldn't handle being perceived as anything but America's sweetheart. Telling him one thing and doing another was her way of convincing herself good intentions were enough.

He'd married her thinking he didn't deserve her. But now he understood the truth—she didn't deserve him.

Ryder paused in the doorway of Ivy's room, where the girls sat on the floor whispering.

"Why don't you two come downstairs?" He smiled at them. "Your mother has something to tell you."

Gone was their joyful exuberance. Gone was their excitement about seeing their mother. They both stood. Ivy reached for his left hand, and Harper reached for his right. Together, they walked down to the living room.

*Please, Lord God, help me comfort them when Lily breaks it to them.*

He wished Eden was here. She'd know how to soothe them. She'd know what to say.

*God, I need her. I need Eden. Not just for the summer. Not just for the girls.*

When Lily's visit was over, he was going to figure out how to tell Eden the truth.

He needed her. Forever.

## Chapter Twelve

"I was surprised at how often Lily checked her phone," Eden's mother said as she poked her fork into the mound of mashed potatoes and gravy on her plate. Dad sat next to her, attacking his order of meat loaf with gusto. Eden and her parents had driven to Riverview Lounge after leaving Ryder's place.

"I'm sure she's busy." Eden hadn't really noticed. She'd been lost in her own little world—a world that had seemed to shrink the instant Lily appeared in her fabulous red shoes, stylish outfit and perfect hair.

The fantasy was officially over.

"I didn't like how she referred to you as the nanny, and she wasn't there five minutes before she took a phone call. Didn't she notice how excited the girls were to see her?" Mom patted her lips with her napkin and shook her head. "All that work you put into those gifts and books—and she said the right things, but it was like her heart wasn't in it."

"It's okay, Mom. She'll be here for a week. It's not fair to judge her for being distracted for ten minutes." All Eden could picture was the four of them—Ryder with Lily next to him and the twins in front of them—waving and calling goodbye from the front porch.

The perfect family.

Eden lost what little appetite she had.

"Ryder's doing a good job with the ranch." Dad paused to take a sip of iced tea. "He told me I can stop by anytime."

"That's nice of him. He's so thoughtful." Mom patted Dad's arm.

"I don't think he was just saying it, either." Dad looked serious.

"I'm sure he wasn't." Eden found it easy to reassure her father. "You could teach him a thing or two about raising cattle in Rendezvous."

His face brightened. "I wouldn't mind." He shot a quick glance at her mom. "When we're in town, of course."

"If Ryder doesn't mind you riding out with him now and again, we might have to park here more often." Mom gave him an understanding smile. "I know you miss it."

Warning flags started popping up in Eden's mind.

She wasn't the only one losing her heart to Ryder and the girls. Her parents were, too.

How had she missed it? Her mom treated Harper and Ivy like they were her own granddaughters. And in Mom's eyes, the sun rose and set on their daddy. And what about Dad? He acted like he'd been thrown a lifeline because Ryder wanted him to hang out at the ranch.

Eden should have seen it coming. All three of them craved a familiar life with their ranch at the heart of it. But they weren't being fair to Ryder.

"I'm sorry to do this, but I've got to go." She covered her half-eaten bowl of minestrone with a napkin, grabbed her purse and scooted out of the booth.

"You sick? I'll drive you home." Dad sprang to his feet.

"No, no. You two stay here. I'll walk. It's not far." She dragged her finger across her eyebrow. "I just need to think. I'll see you tomorrow."

Her parents exchanged glances, but they let her walk away.

She weaved through the busy restaurant until she made it outside. A picture-perfect summer evening greeted her as she turned left and headed to her apartment.

The warm air couldn't penetrate the chill over her heart. She'd been an idiot, letting herself fall in love with Ryder. The girls, well, she'd loved them from the day she'd met them. That couldn't have been prevented. But Ryder? She could have—should have—done a lot of things differently.

He had enough problems. He didn't want the complications love brought, and Eden finally understood why. Lily wasn't just a movie star or his ex-wife. She was the mother of his children. He would be dealing with her the rest of his life.

Eden tried to swallow the lump forming in her throat. The memory of his arms around her roared back. His lips on hers had been the best thing she'd ever experienced. He'd made her feel safe, cherished, desirable. She'd never felt that way before.

Her phone chirped. A text came through from Ryder. You don't have to come over tomorrow. I'll see you on Monday.

The words hit her like a punch in the stomach. Just as she'd thought. He'd taken one look at Lily and forgotten Eden existed. She was just the babysitter. Nothing more.

She was used to it.

She might as well accept it and move on. Everyone else seemed to be good at going forward. Everyone except her.

"Come give Mommy a hug goodbye." Lily was likely to topple over as she crouched in the foyer in a pair of pink stilettos Friday afternoon with her arms spread wide. Ryder wanted to roll his eyes.

Harper hugged her willingly. Ivy hung back, a stony expression on her face.

"Now, Ivy, I'm not going to see you for a long time." Lily pretended to pout, but Ivy didn't budge. Lily straightened and tapped her chin. "If I don't get a hug, you might not be a flower girl."

Ryder let his head fall back in exasperation as he gazed at the ceiling and ground his teeth together. Why was she so clueless when it came to her own children? Hadn't Ivy's tears last night when Lily broke her news about getting married clued her in that the girls could not care less about being in her wedding?

"I don't want to be a flower girl!" Ivy shouted, turning and racing upstairs. Harper quickly followed.

Lily gaped at him. "And how am I supposed to respond to that?"

She acted like Ivy was to blame. Ryder narrowed his eyes. "You can't expect them to be overjoyed at your news."

"Why not? Not every little girl gets to wear a custom-designed dress to her mother's wedding. It will be an exclusive event. They should be happy."

"They're five. They don't even understand that you're a movie star."

"Great." Lily pulled her sunglasses out of her oversize purse and set them on her head. "I don't have time for this."

"Maybe you should make the time."

"Look, I'm not going to be held hostage by those two."

"They're your daughters, not dolls to dress up. They have feelings, Lily."

"I know that, Ryder," she said with an abundance of sarcasm. "What about my feelings? Shouldn't they be glad I'm getting married?"

*Don't react. Do not react.*

"I've got to go." She flourished her hand to the door. "Tell them bye for me."

"Will you wait five minutes?" he asked. She was really going to leave without attempting to soothe their feelings? The woman had hit a new low in his book. "Go up and talk to them. For crying out loud, this isn't the time to leave."

"Fine." Her tone could have sliced through metal. She click-clacked down the hall and went upstairs. He followed at a distance and waited in the doorway while she went into Ivy's room.

"Why don't you want to be a flower girl?" Lily asked brusquely. "Don't you want a pretty dress?"

Ryder peeked through the doorway. Ivy had her back to Lily.

"It's not the dress," Harper said. She snuck a glance at Ivy, still ignoring her mother.

"What is it, then?"

"Harper," Ivy warned.

Harper's glance darted back and forth to Ivy and Lily.

"You can tell me." Lily nodded encouragingly.

"You tell her, Ivy." Harper closed the distance to her twin and took her hand in hers. "Go ahead."

"I don't want you to marry him." Ivy faced Lily then, with tear marks racing down her cheeks. "Why aren't you marrying Daddy?"

"You haven't even met Sam. And as for Daddy, no." Lily let out a strangled laugh. "We're not getting married again."

"But why not?" Ivy inched closer to her. "Daddy's so handsome."

"Well, of course he is," Lily said. "But I love someone else now."

"What if we moved back to California?" Ivy tipped her head slightly to look up at Lily. "Then you'd see Daddy lots, and we'd all be together. We could live in the same house."

Ryder held his breath. *Come on, Lily, tell her the truth. Don't tell her what she wants to hear because it will be easier for you.*

"I'd love it if you moved back to California."

He closed his eyes, dread lashing at him like a winter storm.

"But we're not all going to live together again. I'm marrying Sam."

The relief was so sudden he propped his hand against the doorjamb to keep his balance.

"I don't want you to marry Sam!" Ivy stamped her foot. "I want you to marry Daddy!"

"That's enough, Ivy. I'm marrying Sam, and I don't need your permission." Lily straightened. "Now I have to go. It's your last chance for a hug."

Ivy turned her back to her once more.

"Okay. It's your choice. Bye."

Lily breezed past Ryder, down the hall to the stairs. He debated following her. He could hear her heels clicking as Ivy ran out of the room, yelling, "Mommy!"

She sobbed all the way down the stairs, hysterically yelling for her mother. Ryder and Harper followed close behind. He hated seeing her so upset. Wished this all could have worked out differently. How? He had no clue. He just hated that the divorce had caused so much pain. Still caused so much pain.

At the bottom of the staircase, he stopped short. Lily held Ivy in her arms as Ivy sobbed.

"I'll always love you, you know. It's just... Daddy and I aren't getting back together. Ever." Lily met his eyes, and he nodded in thanks. Then she set Ivy back on her feet. "Now be good, okay?"

Ivy sniffled and nodded.

Lily waved to them and walked out the door. As the screen door shut, Ivy pressed her little hands against it and watched her go.

"Come on." Ryder reached out to touch her shoulder, and she launched herself into his arms. He picked her up and held her tightly. "It'll be okay."

Ivy started crying again, and Harper glued herself

to his side. He held her hand, leading her to the living room, where they all smooshed together on the couch.

"I'm sorry." He looked down at Harper and at Ivy. "I know you're both disappointed. This wasn't how you wanted the visit to go. You were hoping to have Mommy all week, and instead you found out some tough news, and your time was cut short."

"Mommy never stays more than a day." Harper sounded matter-of-fact, but her lower lip wobbled.

"At least you had her for a little while." He pulled her closer. "And I don't blame either of you for wanting us to get back together. That's normal."

Ivy lifted waterlogged eyes to him and wiped the back of her hand under her nose.

"You can talk to me about anything, okay?" he said. "I'm always here for you. I'm always going to be here for you."

Harper hugged his arm and kissed his biceps. "I love you, Daddy."

"I love you, too."

Ivy looked crushed. He kissed the top of her head. "I'm sorry, Ivy. I know you're really disappointed."

She seemed at a loss for words. He had a feeling this was one of those events where only time would heal her. He couldn't rush it.

He thought about his own wounds and how time had healed them.

Ever since meeting Eden, he'd been trying to convince himself he couldn't have a future with her—or with any woman. He'd been wrong.

Eden had opened his eyes to what real love, a lasting partnership, could be.

And he wanted it. The connection, the commitment, the peace deep down that he could always count on her.

But did she feel the same?

Saturday morning Eden printed out the courses she'd signed up for. Too bad she felt zero enthusiasm about them. She wanted more than a career. She wanted Ryder. The girls. The ranch.

As usual, she wanted it all.

She'd slept poorly with bad dreams. Every one of them involved her being paralyzed or not being able to speak while trying to warn someone of danger.

Mom and Dad had stopped by yesterday and called earlier this morning to check on her, and she'd assured them she was fine and shooed them out of the apartment. Thankfully, they were spending a few days at the hot springs a county over with friends.

A knock on the door lured her to the hall. Eden opened the door. Ryder, freshly showered from the looks of it, stood before her with brooding eyes. Her mouth went dry.

"What are you doing here?" she asked. "I thought you didn't need me this weekend."

"The ranch hands agreed to handle the chores so I could be with the girls." He sighed. "Lily left last night." He didn't seem upset about it.

"Already? Are the girls okay? Ivy?" She hated to think of poor Ivy distraught. Harper, too, but Ivy had built up this visit so much in her mind.

"She was upset, but they're both coming around. Can I come in?" He shifted his weight from one foot to the other.

"I don't think that's a good idea."

"Why not?"

*Because all I want to do is wrap my arms around you. But you don't want a relationship. And I'm not the one for you even if you did.*

"Please?" He looked so sincere that she caved, held the door open and moved aside to let him in.

They went to the living room. She sat on the couch and waited for him to settle in a chair.

"Lily's getting married."

Married? She sucked in a breath. Ivy would be crushed. Harper, too. Her already low spirits plummeted. "Oh, no."

"She told me as soon as you all left the other night. The twins were pretty upset, but Ivy took it the worst."

"I'm sorry, Ryder."

"Don't be. It was inevitable. And it has nothing to do with you…"

He was right. It didn't have anything to do with her. But she wanted it to—she wanted so badly to be part of their lives. Not as the babysitter, and not as a bystander.

"I think Ivy's starting to accept it," he said.

"And Harper?"

"Has a more realistic view of her mother than Ivy does."

Eden silently agreed.

"I'm glad she came," Ryder said. "And I'm glad she's getting married, and I'm glad she left early."

Eden frowned. What was he getting at?

"I finally realized something, Eden." He stared at her then, and his gaze was hot, intense. "I'm ready to move on, too."

She wasn't sure what to say. It seemed sudden.

"You and I have grown close—don't try to deny it.

I admire your devotion to the girls. I like being with you. I trust you. I want to explore this—" he pointed his fingers to her, then back to himself "—whatever this is between us."

Her mind went haywire. He didn't mean it. Couldn't mean it.

This was too easy.

And too convenient.

Lily had barely left.

He was hurting. Not thinking straight. Shocked by his ex's news.

"I think you're confused." She tried to be gentle. "Lily is getting married, and it brought up a lot of emotions for you, I get it. But you don't want this. You don't want me."

"You're wrong." His jaw clenched.

"Ryder, you've been clear that you aren't getting married again. Now your ex-wife comes to town—your glamorous, movie star of an ex-wife—tells you she's getting married, and all of a sudden you want to *explore* whatever is between us? I don't buy it."

"There's nothing to buy, Eden. What about our kiss?"

"It was a kiss." She shot to her feet and turned away. A great kiss. An unbelievable kiss. "Give this a few days, and you'll see I'm right. This is a reaction to Lily's announcement, nothing more."

Ryder gaped at her. Her cheeks were drawn. Her eyes sincere. Did she really think he'd come here as some sort of rebound move?

"It's not a reaction, Eden. I care about you. I have feelings for you."

She shook her head.

"Look me in the eye and tell me you don't have feelings for me, too." He stood and in two strides was in front of her. She looked up at him, and her beautiful brown eyes swam with uncertainty. He waited to hear her say it. But she didn't.

He deserved this, he supposed. He'd barged his way into her life over and over since meeting her. Coming here had been dumb. He shouldn't have pressured her. Something—someone—had ruined love for her.

"Spending time with you... I know you feel it, too." Ryder kept his tone low. "Why won't you tell me the truth? Did someone break your heart? Is that why you won't take a chance on me?"

Her eyes darted back and forth like a caged animal. She looked positively queasy. But then she tilted her chin up a fraction and met his eyes.

"You want the truth?" The words were sharp.

He braced himself, not sure he wanted it anymore.

"The past five years broke my heart."

"Is this about your sister?"

"Partially." She shook her head. "Look, I do have feelings for you. I think you're an amazing father. You care about the ranch. You work hard to protect the cattle. Dad was right to sell it to you. You're fun to be with. Adventurous. I like that you ask for my opinion and actually listen to me."

His mind scrambled to capture each word and lock it inside so he could remember it all later.

"But I also think you're reacting to Lily's visit and her getting engaged. I mean, be real, Ryder. You can't possibly want to date me."

"Why not?" What was she seeing that he wasn't?

"I'm not your type." She widened her eyes to emphasize her point.

"Says who?"

"Says the entire free world." She pointed to the hall. "It's best if we pretend this conversation never happened. You'll wake up tomorrow or next week and be relieved I saw the truth. We never have to talk about it again."

Was he imagining the tremble in her lips? The pain in her eyes?

What did she see when she looked at him? A desperate single dad, hungry for love, glomming on to the babysitter of his kids out of some weird reaction to his famous ex-wife's announcement she was getting remarried?

Maybe she was right.

The image embarrassed him.

"If that's what you want." He held his breath, willing her to change her mind.

"It's for the best."

And with that, an iron door slammed over his heart. Ironic.

He'd been so adamant about not wanting to get involved again, and the one woman he'd fallen for had taken him at his word.

Ryder cast one more look at her, then stalked down the hall and out the door.

Rejection was one thing he'd learned early on in life. No one ever wanted him for keeps.

# Chapter Thirteen

Eden pressed her forehead against the door and slowly turned the dead bolt to lock it. He could give her everything she wanted.

*Stop imagining it could have been different.*

Too many hopes had gone up in flames over the years.

She'd done the right thing. Ryder would wake up in a few days, and he'd be grateful she'd been the voice of reason. And she'd continue to babysit the girls, albeit with a lump in her throat. She'd avoid him. Bury herself in college plans and helping out her friends—anything to ease the pain of loving Ryder Fanning and knowing he'd never be hers.

He was an honorable man. She'd been honest with him—to a point. She hadn't told him she loved him. She hadn't told him how much he meant to her or how close the girls were to her heart. She would never let him know how tempting he and everything he could offer her were.

Ryder was the one man who could fulfill her dreams.

A husband. Children. Right here in Rendezvous. Living on the ranch, the only home she'd ever known.

She hadn't told him any of those things because it would have trapped him.

It wasn't fair to prey on his confusion right now. Not to him, and not to her, either. Because she didn't want a husband or kids or the ranch if it meant not having his complete devotion.

Without true love, she'd never be happy. The dream would merely be a mirage.

Eden padded to her bedroom and sprawled out on her bed. It had been foolish to fall in love with him and to get so close to the girls.

Another disappointing end in a long string of private heartbreaks.

She'd tossed aside her college plans to come home and be with Mia.

She'd begged the Lord to let Mia live, yet she'd died.

She'd been like a mother to Noah after Mia's death, then Mason had remarried and her services were no longer needed.

She'd spent the bulk of her days caring for baby Phoebe when Gabby had been thrust into motherhood unexpectedly. Then Gabby got married, and those precious days with Phoebe had dwindled to a few hours a week.

It didn't take a genius to see the writing on the wall in her current situation. She'd been given the summer with the girls. After that, the arrangement would be over. And no matter what Ryder said, it would take only a week, tops, for him to realize he wasn't really interested in her.

But…

What if she was wrong?

What if Ryder did have feelings for her and she'd just kicked him out?

Sheer panic shot through her brain.

No, it wasn't possible.

There wasn't a guy in this county who'd shown an ounce of interest in her in years—years! Ryder Fanning—the gorgeous, intelligent man who wasn't afraid to take risks or ask for help—surely hadn't seen something in her no one else had.

She'd babysit the girls and stay away from him as much as possible.

Tears spilled down her cheeks, because just once in her life she wanted to be wrong. She wanted him to love her. Forever.

"You look like ten miles of dirt road."

Ryder arched his eyebrows at Mason as he stood on his porch. He'd headed directly here after leaving Eden's. He could hear the girls' voices mingling with Noah's from somewhere in the house.

"Want to talk about it?" Mason asked.

He'd planned on picking up the twins, driving back to the ranch and wallowing in rejection all day, but looking at his brother, he realized he *did* want to talk about it.

"Not in there."

"Let's take a walk." Mason gestured toward the outbuildings down the lane.

It was a beautiful day. An eagle flew overhead. Sunshine poured out of the blue skies. But the scene could have been in black and gray for all he cared. Life stank.

They'd made it halfway to the first barn before Ryder could figure out where to start with his messed-up life.

"Did someone break Eden's heart?" The words were out before he could think them through.

Mason squinted, giving him a confused glance. "I don't know, why?"

"Just wondering."

"I mean…" Mason rubbed his chin, looking straight ahead. "I can't think of anyone offhand." He exhaled and shook his head. "I tell you what, I can't even think of the last guy she dated."

A ray of hope lit his heart.

"I'm sure she must have dated in college, but unless she kept it a secret, she hasn't gone out with anyone around here that I can remember, and she's been back for over five years."

"Really?" Ryder frowned. "Are the guys around here stupid or something?"

Mason guffawed. "You have a point. Eden's pretty special."

He wouldn't argue with that.

"The thing about Eden, though… She's quiet. Serious." Mason kept an easy pace. "In some ways, she's easy to overlook. I guess you could say she's in the shadows."

In the shadows? Why? Ever since he'd met her, he'd gravitated to her. Every barbecue, every get-together— all he'd been able to see was Eden.

"I don't get it. Why isn't she married? She's…" Beautiful, real, trustworthy. "She's amazing with kids."

"I know. She was basically Noah's surrogate mom

for the first three years of his life. I don't know what I would have done without her."

"And you never considered…" Ryder felt funny bringing this up. "That is…you were never attracted to her?"

Mason pulled a face. "No. I mean, I appreciate her friendship and could see how great she was with Noah, but I wasn't in a mental place to have those kinds of thoughts. And I never got that vibe from her, either."

Eden's declaration about not being attracted to someone who looked like her brother-in-law echoed back. But the weeks had changed her. She hadn't been disgusted by his kiss. Not at all. Warmth pooled all the way to his toes just thinking about it.

"Why all these questions about Eden?" Mason asked. "I thought you were upset about Lily getting remarried."

Why did everyone assume Lily's plans meant anything to him?

"I'm not upset about it." He honestly wasn't. "It's taken some time, but I understand our divorce wasn't really about me. Maybe our marriage wasn't, either. I've made peace with it. I feel bad for the girls. Ivy, especially, has put her mom on a pedestal higher than the Empire State Building."

"For what it's worth, she's been okay today." Mason glanced at him. "She spent some time talking with Brittany while Noah and Harper played tag, but they asked her to play pirates with them, and she ran off with a big smile on her face."

"Good." They reached a split-rail fence. Ryder propped his boot on the bottom rail and looked out over the beautiful land. "I think I'm in love with Eden."

"What?" Mason turned to face him. Ryder just nodded.

"I know. I wasn't prepared for it, either, but I am. I might have started falling for her that day at Christmas Fest. Do you remember? You and I had met, what, a few weeks prior?"

"Yeah, I remember. That was the day Brittany told me it was okay to remember the good times I had with Mia. We were all ice-skating."

"And Lily called while Eden and I were skating with the girls. Eden tore into me after she heard us arguing over the phone in front of the twins."

"Eden always puts kids first." Mason shrugged.

"I think it's one of the reasons I love her. Lily has never put them first. Not one day in her life."

Mason let out a humph. "I love you, Ryder. You know that, right?"

His throat tightened as he nodded.

"But Eden deserves more. If you think you love her only because she'll be a good mom to the twins, well, that's kind of selfish."

Selfish? How could Mason even suggest it?

"Take the twins out of the equation." Mason opened his hands. "Would you still love her?"

"Are you kidding me?" His blood started simmering. "For you to suggest I have feelings for her because I'm looking for a mom for my girls is insulting. And coming from you, it's pretty rich."

Mason looked taken aback. "What do you mean coming from me?"

"Yeah, you." Ryder pointed to him. "Eden practically raised Noah, and then you got married, and it was, 'Oh, by the way, we don't need your services anymore.' Gabby, too. I mean, I get it—they're your kids, not hers.

But she put her life on hold to raise your son and Phoebe when you guys needed her. And where did it get her?"

Mason's jaw dropped.

"Eden's more than a babysitter." The fire in Ryder's blood boiled. "She's beautiful. And smart. And she knows the ranch inside and out. She's patient. She sees when I need cheering up and always has the right thing to say. She's got more energy than anyone I know. Do you have any idea how much time she spends planning projects and activities for the girls? I've gone through a dozen nannies—none of them did a fraction of what she does. So, no, I'm not in love with her because I want a mom for the girls, but I do admire how great she is with them."

Mason opened his mouth to speak, but Ryder wasn't finished.

"She deserves more. From all of us. How many nights does Eden babysit Noah even now? I doubt she accepts any pay, either."

Mason clamped his mouth shut.

"So don't ever stand there and give me a lecture about loving her." Ryder jabbed his finger into Mason's chest. "Look in the mirror, bro."

He should have controlled his temper. He inhaled deeply and waited for Mason to start yelling. This was his brother, the man who'd generously taught him the basics of ranching, who'd invited him into his home countless times since they met. He shouldn't have accused him of all those things.

"You're not wrong." Mason hung his head.

*Wait...what?*

"I never even thought about it, but you're right. I've taken her for granted. Did she say something?"

"No, man. It wouldn't even occur to her." His shoulders slumped. "She loves Noah. Wants to spend time with him. You know how she is."

"Yes, I do." Mason was subdued. "And you're right. She deserves more from me. More from all of us."

"I'm sorry." Ryder felt lower than a grass snake. "I shouldn't have said all that. Honestly, I've never even thought any of it until just now."

"Because you love her. And things get clear when you realize something like that."

"I guess they do."

They turned to stare over the fence at the meadow once more.

It didn't matter if he loved her. Didn't matter if he wanted the world to appreciate her the way he did. She wasn't willing to take him seriously, and he had no one to blame but himself.

Two hours later, Eden trudged up the hill, indifferent to the beauty of her special place. It wasn't that she didn't notice how the sun brought out the luster of the grass and wildflowers. She was aware of the prairie dogs chasing each other in the distance and the hawk perched on top of a dead tree trunk as it watched for its next meal. Life continued around her, but hers had hit the pause button.

When she reached the flat area, she spread out a quilt and sat cross-legged.

She couldn't shake the feeling she'd made a huge mistake. That she was in the wrong. That she'd miscalculated, violated something precious by sending Ryder on his way.

Sighing, she eased back. The image of Ryder with

Lily and the twins waving from their doorway wouldn't let her go. Lily's elegant beauty, her glowing presence had been a shock. She was even more beautiful in person than on-screen. And she hadn't been a diva. Who cared if she'd called Eden the nanny? Technically she was the nanny. Sure, Lily had checked her phone a lot, but she'd been warm to the girls.

Eden hoped Ivy was okay. She wanted to text Ryder and check, but…she couldn't. Ivy had pinned so many hopes on the visit, and finding out her mother was marrying someone else must have been a blow.

She wanted to tuck each girl against her sides, put her arms around them and tell them not to worry, they were loved, that she would always be there for them.

But was it true?

Soon they'd be in school full-time, and she wouldn't see them as much. She would no longer be an important part of their lives, just like she was less and less important to Noah and, to some extent, Phoebe.

It was the way it should be. She wasn't their mother. She'd been blessed to help each one of those children during a critical time in their lives.

Ryder would move on. His heart seemed to be in a better place already. He'd date again. Maybe get married. Misty Sandpiper was more his type. Pretty, put together, bubbly, outgoing. The girls liked her.

A puffy cloud passed overhead, dimming the sunlight. She felt tired. She couldn't remember the last time she felt this weary. Closing her eyes, snippets of memories filled her mind.

Coming here to pray for Mia. Camping with Gabby. Feeling lost and alone when her parents told her they were selling the ranch. Utter dejection when they sold it to Ryder.

She flung her forearm over her eyes. Why was she doing this to herself? What did she think was going to happen? Everything was just going to work out? That she'd get the guy, the twins and the family ranch? Life didn't work that way. Not for her. Life worked out for other women. The pretty, outgoing ones.

Eden sat up. She could hear her voice telling the girls, *Your beauty comes from who you are, not what you look like.*

When had she decided she was unattractive and defective?

She wasn't either. Sure, she was quiet, but that didn't make her ugly or incapable of being loved.

*God, what is wrong with me? I've convinced myself that Ryder couldn't possibly love me, not after having been married to Lily. But why do I believe that?*

A memory came back—one she'd forgotten—from long ago. It must have been early fall, Eden's freshman or sophomore year of high school. Mia had gotten a twinkle in her eye, grabbed Eden by the hand and said, "Come on, let's get out of here."

Mia had driven them to this very spot, where they'd joked around and talked about the future. It all came back to Eden as if it had happened yesterday.

*"I'm not going to college."* Mia had been firm. *"I'm staying right here in Rendezvous. I mean, look at this."* She'd expanded both arms out to the view before them. *"Why would anyone leave?"*

"What will you do?" Eden asked.

*"Get married. Have a few kids."*

*Mia had a natural beauty and easy presence, and Eden didn't doubt it for a minute.*

*"I can't wait to see who you marry."* Smiling, Mia nudged her.

*"Me?"*

*"Yes, you."* She laughed. *"Who else would I be talking about? Whoever he is, he'll have to be pretty amazing to deserve you. Hey, do you think our husbands will be friends? Maybe we'll go on vacations together. Our kids will run around..."*

The memory faded, and Eden was left with a sense of wonder.

Mia had firmly believed Eden would get married someday. There hadn't been a hint of hesitation. Mia had always thought the best of her.

And Eden had stopped believing in herself after Mia died.

What would her sister tell her in this situation? *Ryder's a great guy. I'll have to talk with him, of course, to make sure he understands how blessed he is to have you...but isn't it crazy? We'll be married to brothers!*

Something tickled Eden's hand, and she looked down at where an ant crawled over it. She shook the insect off.

*I wish you were here, Mia. You'd tell me Lily doesn't hold a candle to me. You'd be wrong, of course, but you always gave me confidence. I lost it when you died. But I'm getting it back.*

Eden tucked her knees to her chest and wrapped her arms around them as she took in the surrounding area. The beauty seeped into her bones, leaving her relaxed.

One of her favorite Bible passages came to mind, and she spoke it out loud. "He brought me forth also into a large place; He delivered me, because He delighted in me."

*Lord, thank You for bringing me here, for letting me remember that day with Mia.*

Maybe God always had more in mind for her.

Eden was ready to claim all His blessings. Starting now.

"Can we see Auntie Eden, Daddy?" Ivy asked from the back seat of his truck as they drove home from Mason's an hour later.

"Yeah, let's go see Auntie Eden!" Harper yelled.

"Uh, not right now, girls." He wanted nothing more than to drive to town and invade her apartment with the twins, but he didn't have that right.

Mason's comment about Eden being in the shadows kept jabbing his conscience.

She *was* in the shadows. She was humble. Kind. Loyal. Committed. Would do anything for her friends.

Everything he'd ever wanted in a woman.

"I miss her, Daddy. I *need* one of Auntie Eden's hugs," Ivy pleaded.

He knew the feeling. He needed her, too.

For so long he'd told himself—and everyone who'd listen—he was never falling in love again. Marriage wasn't for him. He'd thought he wasn't good at it, that he couldn't trust a woman to not break his heart.

But he'd been wrong. And he might not be able to prevent his heart from being broken, but he could tell Eden the truth—he loved her and wanted to make her happy.

What would make her happy?

He tapped the steering wheel with his thumbs. She

never expected appreciation. She acted like being in the shadows was fine.

Well, it wasn't fine. He wanted her to know down to the last detail how much he appreciated her. He wanted to shout to the entire town that this woman was a priceless jewel.

Maybe he had something to offer that no one else had.

Pure love for her.

Devotion.

Commitment.

*Lord, I need that woman. My girls do, too. How can I show her? How can I get through to her?*

And it hit him.

"I've got an idea, girls." He glanced at them through the rearview mirror. "Why don't we throw a surprise party for Auntie Eden?"

They exchanged excited looks and squealed. "Yes!"

"I'll have to make some calls. I don't know if she's busy."

"I love parties!" Ivy clapped her hands.

"We need cake!" Harper kicked the seat in front of her.

He pulled into his drive, mentally listing everyone he needed to contact. Hopefully they'd be free. He'd ask Gabby to get Eden to his house. Nicole might be willing to contribute dessert. Mason could help grill burgers...

Ryder didn't have much time. He didn't want to wait a day, a week or a month. He was doing this now.

His lips curved into a grin.

And it just might work.

# *Chapter Fourteen*

It was after six when Eden gave herself a final look-over in the mirror. She'd curled her hair, carefully applied her makeup and found a pretty short-sleeved blouse to wear with her favorite dark jeans. After driving home from her special place earlier, she'd stretched out on her bed and fallen into a deep sleep. When she'd woken, she'd been confused, then realized it was still Saturday, and she did indeed still need to take charge of her life.

She was going over to Ryder's.

Speaking of… She went into the kitchen where she'd left her phone earlier. She wanted to make sure he'd be home before driving there. She had so much to say.

Her phone showed three missed calls and two texts from Gabby. Hopefully, there wasn't an emergency. Her heartbeat thudded as she checked them.

Are you busy tonight? I need to talk.

Then Call or text me when you get this.

Weird. Gabby wasn't one to be dramatic. Something serious must have happened.

Eden called her. Gabby answered after the first ring. "Where have you been?"

"Napping. Why?" She closed her eyes tightly, silently praying that nothing bad had happened.

"Oh, good. I, uh, needed to talk to you. Are you busy tonight?"

"Kind of…" She should confide in Gabby, but she didn't know what to say.

"Can you cancel your plans?" Gabby sounded worked up.

"What's going on, Gabby? You're scaring me."

"I am? I'm sorry. I didn't mean to. I just need some advice."

"Okay."

"I'll pick you up. We can go out to dinner. It will give me an excuse to wear something besides yoga pants. I'll be there in five."

The line went dead. What had just happened? How had she gone from worrying about an emergency to going out to dinner with Gabby? In thirty seconds, no less?

She sighed. Her plans to talk to Ryder could wait until dinner was over. Maybe it would be better that way. If she got to his place later, the girls might be asleep, and she'd be able to talk to him privately.

Five minutes later, Gabby arrived looking bouncy and cheerful. This all felt very strange.

"Ooh, I love that shirt. You look really pretty, Eden."

"Thanks, so do you."

They walked to Gabby's car and got inside. As she drove, Gabby kept up a steady stream of commentary about the cute bathing suit she'd found online for Phoebe and the new bedspread she'd bought.

Gabby took a right at the stop sign, and Eden turned to her. "Hey, you went the wrong way."

"No, I didn't. We have to make a side trip first. Sorry." She shrugged, then launched into how she and Dylan had decided it was time to try for a baby.

"A baby? Really?" Eden perked up. "I hope you get pregnant right away. Just think, Phoebe will have a little brother or sister."

"I know, right?" Gabby's cheeks were flushed as she smiled. "Will you pray for us?"

"Always."

As they chatted about babies, Eden's nerves got jittery. Maybe after she talked to Ryder, he would still want to date her. Maybe he'd even fall in love with her at some point. And what if they got married? One day it would be her turn to tell Gabby they were trying to have a baby.

Her palms grew clammy. So much depended on tonight's conversation. Maybe she should ask Gabby to turn around. Or confide in her about her feelings for Ryder. Ask her to take a rain check on dinner?

The countryside grew familiar. Why were they pulling in to the ranch?

"Um, Gabby?"

"Yes?" Her innocent expression didn't fool Eden.

"Why are we at Ryder's?"

She drove up the driveway and parked. Then she opened her door and waved for her to follow. "Come on."

"I'll wait out here." Eden stayed in the passenger seat.

"Look, I didn't want to say anything, but Mason called me earlier and said the twins were upset this morning when he and Brittany watched them. I'm dropping off a little care package for them. But I think a word and a hug from you would make a world of difference to them right now."

If the girls were struggling...

She'd do her best to help them cope. Eden unbuckled the seat belt and got out of the car. They walked to the front porch and knocked. The door opened, and they entered the house.

Something wasn't right. Where was Ryder? Who had opened the door? Why was it so quiet?

Gabby dragged her into the kitchen.

"Surprise!"

All of her friends were in there.

Had she forgotten a birthday or something?

Ryder strode forward and took Eden's hand. His eyes gleamed with affection for her. She couldn't look away and didn't want to. "Eden, welcome to your party."

"My party?" She loved the feel of her hand in his. Her heartbeat sped up. But she shook her head, even more confused than before. "What are you talking about?"

"It's our official Eden Page Appreciation Extravaganza."

Ivy, Harper and Noah raced over to her. "We're throwing you a party, Auntie Eden!"

Tears stung the backs of her eyes. "Why?"

Mason stepped forward. "Because you've done so much for us."

"You rescued us." Gabby slung her arm over Eden's shoulders and side-hugged her.

"You were there when we needed you the most." Nicole, holding Henry, stepped closer. Judd held Amelia, and Eden noticed Brittany carrying Eli.

Her knees wobbled. She couldn't take it all in. This party was for her?

"Come on." Ryder stayed close to her. "Let's take this to the family room." He leaned in and whispered, "You look beautiful."

Then he kept her hand in his as they all made their way to the back of the house. Everyone took seats, except the twins and Noah, who were playing in the corner with a cluster of balloons. The room had been decorated with crepe paper, balloons and a homemade sign that read We Love You, Eden.

She had to wipe away tears at the sight. She had no idea what this was all about, but she wanted to remember every second of it.

Ryder helped her sit on the couch, then moved to the center of the room, facing her. Everyone turned their attention to him.

"Eden, you've selflessly devoted yourself to each one of us, and we all want to pay you back in some small way." He gestured to Mason. "Do you want to begin?"

Mason grinned and stood. He gave Ryder a half embrace and took his spot.

"Eden, you were like a mother to Noah after Mia died. I don't know how you did it, considering you were grieving, too, but you're the main reason I was able to hang on that first year. I can never thank you enough or repay you for giving Noah such a firm foundation of love."

Noah ran up to her, and she hauled him onto her lap. He kissed her cheek and hugged her. "I love you!"

"I love you, too," Eden said, and then he hopped off her lap and ran back to the girls.

Gabby had switched spots with Mason. "Eden, you're my best friend. I don't know what I would have done without you after my sister died. Here I was, suddenly a single mom with no clue how to raise a baby or deal with my grief. But you stepped in and babysat Phoebe. You're the one who told me so many times that I was a great mom and that Allison would be proud. I love you, girl."

Nicole handed Henry to Mason and switched spots with Gabby.

"Last Christmas Eve, I was at one of the lowest points in my life." Nicole's lips trembled. "And you showed up on my doorstep because I hadn't answered your texts and you didn't want me to spend Christmas Eve alone. I will *never* forget your kindness. You have no idea how much I needed you that night."

The lump forming in Eden's throat had grown to the size of a walnut. No matter how many times she swallowed, it wouldn't go away.

Ryder took Nicole's spot as she sat back down.

"I met you two Christmases ago, shortly after meeting my brother." Ryder nodded to Mason. "Eden, you weren't afraid to tell me the truth when you saw me behaving badly. Even then you had the twins' best interests in mind. I didn't like it—wasn't used to being called out. But it made a big impression on me."

She wasn't sure where he was going with this, but he looked so sincere and she couldn't look away.

"I was drawn to you. Am drawn to you. When I decided to move here, I knew one thing—you're the only one I was comfortable with watching my girls."

Ivy and Harper shouted, "We love you, Auntie Eden!"

She clapped her hand over her heart.

"You put your life on hold for us. You came here, to your childhood home, even though you had a lot of misgivings about it, and took care of not only Harper and Ivy but me, too. I am honored to call you my friend. I hope you know what a special person you are."

He crossed over to her then and held out his hand. She let him help her stand. He pulled her into his arms and hugged her. Then he whispered, "I have more to say to you, too, but not in front of the girls."

Everyone surrounded her, hugging her and telling her how much she meant to them.

"It's my turn." Eden waved them all to sit. "I don't know what to say. This is more than I deserve. Mason, thank you for the privilege of taking care of Noah when he was a baby. It saved me from my grief over Mia."

He looked emotional himself as he nodded to her.

"Gabby, you *are* a terrific mother," Eden said. "You're my best friend. I would never have forgiven you if you wouldn't have let me babysit Phoebe. I love her. And I love you."

Gabby wiped under her eyes.

"Nicole," Eden said. "You're my hero. You took a desperate situation—losing your husband while pregnant with triplets—and chose to embrace your future. I know you and Judd are going to be very happy together."

Nicole smiled up at Judd, who'd placed his hand on her shoulder.

"And Ryder," Eden said. She couldn't tell him everything in front of the girls. It wouldn't be fair to them, but she owed him thanks, too. "I'm glad you moved here. You've given me the courage to want more from life."

Everyone stared at her, waiting in breathless anticipation. But she wanted to do this right. In private. Ivy and Harper had dealt with too many emotional ups and downs this week already.

"Thank you all." Eden's lips wobbled. "I don't know what I ever did to deserve such good friends."

"Let's get the cookout going," Mason hollered. As if on cue, everyone dispersed outside. Everyone except Ryder and the twins.

Ivy hugged her first. "I missed you."

"I missed you, too." Eden smoothed her hair away from her forehead. "And you, too, Harper."

Harper wrapped her arms around both her and Ivy.

"I'm sorry your mom couldn't stay longer." She kissed both their cheeks. They nodded, their faces falling. "But I'm glad I got to meet her. She's very nice."

They glanced at each other and smiled. "She is nice."

"And I could tell she loved the gifts you made her."

"She took our books home with her." Harper's eyes shone.

"Mommy's getting married." Ivy's cheeks drooped.

"That's what I heard."

"We're flower girls." Harper shrugged.

"We get fancy dresses." Ivy didn't sound excited.

"Well, you'll be the prettiest girls there." Eden held the twins close. When she let them go, they smiled at her. "I love you both."

"Come on, Harper! Ivy!" Noah bellowed. "I'm gonna pop this balloon!"

The girls ran off.

And only Ryder remained.

Her heart was bursting with love for this man. She just prayed she had the right words to let him know exactly how important he was to her.

The twins ran outside and shut the sliding door so hard it bounced open an inch, but Ryder didn't care. He took Eden's hand in his and kissed the back of it.

"I can't believe you put all this together." She shook her head. "I was getting ready to text you to see if I could come over when Gabby called."

"You were going to come over?" Hope began to grow inside him.

Her eyes were shy as she nodded. "Yeah."

All he wanted to do was kiss her. Tell her how much she meant to him.

Tell her he loved her.

Her eyelashes dipped. "I wasn't entirely truthful with you this morning."

"Oh?" An uneasy pit formed in his stomach.

"I thought I was, but…" She met his eyes. "I *do* want to explore whatever this is between us. I felt inferior to Lily. It's not just her, though. You asked me if someone had broken my heart. The answer is no. I've never given it to anyone to break. Until now."

Was he hearing her correctly?

"I'm in love with you. I love you, Ryder. I didn't want to be, but I couldn't stop it." She stared at him through those rich brown eyes, and he was helpless to look away. "I've been attracted to you since we met. I lied that day when I said I wasn't. You're gorgeous. Smart. You get things done. You don't let anything get in your way. You love your daughters—I know you'd make any sacrifice for them."

A thousand things popped up to say to her, but none of them came out.

"As for exploring our feelings," she said, "I have to warn you, I'm kind of past the exploring phase. My heart is already yours."

He held his breath.

"But I think you should know..." She glanced down at her hands for a moment. "All I ever wanted was to get married, have a family and live on a ranch. Because of that, I don't want you to ever think I'm telling you I love you because of what you can offer me. I love you because you're a good man, a good father, a good friend."

He wrapped his hands around her back and hauled her to him. He could feel her heart beating against his chest. His was beating double-time.

"I love you, Eden." He stared down into her incredible eyes. "I love you. It feels so good to say it out loud. You're the most beautiful woman I've ever seen. And your heart—it's so big. I don't know how you do it. You give and give. I want to give *you* everything. I want to be worthy of you."

"You? Worthy of me?" She scrunched her nose and laughed. "You've got it all wrong."

"No, I don't." He wanted her to know he was dead serious. "I don't think there's a man on earth worthy of you. All the guys around here have thumbtacks for brains, and I'm glad. Because you're mine."

He leaned in and pressed his lips to hers. And she softened into his embrace. This woman. He'd never get his fill of her.

When he ended the kiss, she smiled. He tenderly brushed her lips with his thumb.

"Oh, my," she said.

His thoughts exactly.

"I think every day should be Eden Appreciation Day." He kept his hands on her waist, enjoying having her in his arms.

"My head would get too big."

"If it meant getting to hold you and kiss you, I wouldn't care."

"What will we tell the girls?"

"The truth," he said. "They can handle it."

"Are you sure? They've been through a lot."

"Yeah. But they deserve nothing less than the truth."

"I think you're right."

"Of course, I'm right." He grinned. "If, by chance, I'm wrong, I can always buy Harper a pony and promise Ivy a bunny."

"You're terrible." She chuckled, swatting at his chest.

"And you're wonderful. I'm your biggest fan, and I'll never stop letting everyone know how blessed I am to have you."

"You're the blessing, Ryder."

"I guess God blessed us both."

# Epilogue

She was going to be their mommy! Eden hugged Ivy, then Harper. How blessed she was to nurture these children.

The twins were dressed in identical white dresses with tiaras in their curled hair, and each of them carried a small basket with rose petals. Organ music spilled from the church to where they stood near the entrance to the sanctuary.

"Are you ready, girls?" Eden fluffed the material of her wedding gown and tried to rein in her nerves.

"Yes!" they said in unison.

"You look bee-yoo-tiful." Ivy had stars in her eyes.

"You look like Cinderella." Harper nudged Noah, in his tuxedo. "Doesn't she look like Cinderella?"

"You do, Auntie Eden. You're even prettier than Cinderella." He clutched a white satin pillow with the wedding rings on top. "I'd marry you if Uncle Ryder didn't."

"Thank you, Noah-bear." Her heart was overflowing with love. "All three of you are making our day very special."

"It's time." One of the church ladies pointed to the children. Noah pulled back his shoulders and walked between the girls as they tossed rose petals down the aisle of the church. Eden spotted Gabby, her matron of honor, at the front standing next to Nicole and Brittany in their pretty coral dresses. Dylan and Judd were across the aisle with Mason, who was Ryder's best man.

Eden hadn't seen Ryder yet, and she edged closer to her dad. Her knees felt wobbly, and her heart was ready to beat out of her chest. She'd already cried twice that morning, and the self-manicure incident had thrown her into a panic. Maybe if she kept her hands tucked under the bouquet, no one would notice the clumps of glitter in the polish.

"You ready, honey?" Dad took her hand and rested it on his arm. "You look beautiful. I couldn't be happier for you. You've got a good man, there."

"Thanks, Dad." A memory of Mia and Dad at this very spot years ago brought a sense of calm to her nerves.

Life was full of ups and downs, and she was ready for them. She'd started her online classes a few weeks ago, and now she'd have a partner to weather whatever came her way.

They waited another moment and then headed down the aisle.

And there was Ryder.

She locked eyes with him and held her breath. He

looked like a model in his tux, but it was the intensity in his eyes that sent a thrill down her spine. Like in a dream, she was vaguely aware of Dad leaving her with Ryder, and she barely heard the pastor's words as he conducted the service.

Before she knew it, she and Ryder had exchanged vows and the ring was on her finger. Then the announcement came—they were man and wife. It was really true!

They made their way to the back of the church and out onto the lawn where the guests would greet them. The late-September sun made everything shiny and special.

"Mrs. Fanning." Ryder swept her into his arms and twirled her around. "You look—wow—you take my breath away."

She smiled, reaching up to give him a light kiss. "You look handsome, more than handsome."

"But you…wow, you are magnificent." He kissed her with passion. His kiss promised everything she'd ever wanted, and she sank into his embrace.

A round of applause interrupted them, and she looked up at him, her face on fire as he ended the kiss, keeping his arm around her waist.

All their family and friends surrounded them, offering well wishes and congratulations. Eden took it all in and said a silent prayer of thanks. Nicole and Judd were holding hands—they'd gotten married a month ago in a small ceremony. Gabby had the slightest baby bump under her gown as she gestured for Dylan to hand her Phoebe. Mason and Brittany had announced last night at the rehearsal dinner they were expecting a baby, too. And Ryder had whispered that he wanted a baby ASAP.

At which she told him he needed to make an honest woman of her first. He'd responded with "Twenty-four hours."

The next hour was a blur of hugs and well wishes and pictures.

"Well, my lovely bride," he said as the bridal party dispersed. "How are you holding up?"

"Fabulous."

"Mama!" Ivy and Harper ran to her and threw their arms around her waist.

Eden was shocked. Ryder merely smiled and tilted his head. "I told them they could call you whatever they wanted."

"Are you sure you want to call me that?" She hugged the girls. "You don't have to, you know."

"We want to." Harper slung her arm over Ivy's shoulders. "Right, Ivy?"

"Right." She nodded, her eyes twinkling. "Mommy's far away, but Mama lives with us."

Eden's heart spilled over. She pulled them close to her. "I love you so much. I'm honored."

"We love you, too."

"You're everything I've ever wanted, Eden." He tucked her arm in his. "I plan on showing you my appreciation every day."

"Every day, huh?" She pressed her palm against his chest and stared up at him.

"Yes." His eyes smoldered. "What do you want? Name it. It's yours."

"You've already given me everything, Ryder. All I want is you."

\* \* \* \* \*

# HARLEQUIN
## PLUS

Try the best multimedia subscription service for romance readers like you!

---

## Read, Watch and Play.

Experience the easiest way to get the romance content you crave.

Start your **FREE TRIAL** at
[www.harlequinplus.com/freetrial](www.harlequinplus.com/freetrial).